Praise for the nove

"One of the premier authors o
Gena Showalter delivers an u
—Kresley Cole, #1 N

"I love this world and these alpha males—this is Gena Showalter at her best!"
—J.R. Ward, #1 *New York Times* bestselling author, on *Shadow and Ice*

"Gena Showalter never fails to dazzle."
—Jeaniene Frost, *New York Times* bestselling author

"Showalter...rocks me every time!"
—Sylvia Day, #1 *New York Times* bestselling author

"Showalter writes fun, sexy characters you fall in love with!"
—Lori Foster, *New York Times* bestselling author

"Showalter makes romance sizzle on every page!"
—Jill Shalvis, *New York Times* bestselling author

"A fascinating premise, a sexy hero and non-stop action,
The Darkest Night is Showalter at her finest."
—Karen Marie Moning, *New York Times* bestselling author

"Sexy paranormal romance at its hottest! The Gods of War series is my new obsession."
—Christine Feehan, #1 *New York Times* bestselling author, on *Shadow and Ice*

Also available by Gena Showalter

From HQN

The Warlord
The Darkest King
Frost and Flame
Shadow and Ice
The Darkest Warrior
Can't Let Go
Can't Hardly Breathe
The Darkest Promise
The Darkest Torment
The Harder You Fall
The Hotter You Burn
The Closer You Come
All for You (anthology
    featuring "The One You Want")
The Darkest Touch
Burning Dawn
After Dark (duology featuring
    "The Darkest Angel")
The Darkest Craving
Beauty Awakened
After Moonrise (duology
    with P.C. Cast)
Wicked Nights
The Darkest Seduction
The Darkest Surrender
The Darkest Secret
The Darkest Lie
The Darkest Passion
Into the Dark
The Darkest Whisper
The Darkest Pleasure

The Darkest Kiss
The Darkest Night
The Vampire's Bride
The Nymph King
Jewel of Atlantis
Heart of the Dragon
Twice as Hot
Playing with Fire
Catch a Mate
Animal Instincts
Prince of Forever
Prince of Stone

**From Harlequin
Nonfiction**

Dating the Undead
    (with Jill Monroe)

From Inkyard Press

The Glass Queen
The Evil Queen
Everlife
Lifeblood
Firstlife
A Mad Zombie Party
The Queen of Zombie Hearts
Through the Zombie Glass
Alice in Zombieland
Twisted
Unraveled
Intertwined

GENA SHOWALTER

HEARTLESS

HQN

ISBN-13: 978-1-335-91377-7

Heartless

Copyright © 2021 by Gena Showalter

This edition published by arrangement with Harlequin Books S.A.

For questions and comments about the quality of this book, please contact us at CustomerService@Harlequin.com.

HQN
22 Adelaide St. West, 40th Floor
Toronto, Ontario M5H 4E3, Canada
www.Harlequin.com

Printed in Lithuania

Recycling programs for this product may not exist in your area.

MIX
Paper from responsible sources
FSC® C021394

To the women who cheered me on when I said,
"So I have this idea." A thousand thank-yous
to Jill Monroe, Mandy M. Roth and Naomi Lane.
You have helped me in more ways than I can express.
I love and adore you all.

HEARTLESS

PROLOGUE

Twelve-year-old Kaysar de Aoibheall wiped blood and other things from the metal claws secured to his hand. His third kill in eight months. He choked down his shock and abhorrence and raced around a line of trees to collect his baby sister.

When the troll had first lunged from the shadows, eager to snack on the five-year-old little girl, Kaysar had pushed her into a thicket and driven the seven-foot monster back with his most powerful ability—a voice of compulsion. But as frightened as he'd been, his ability had...twisted, and a brutal fight had broken out. A match he'd barely won.

Littered with gashes, he looked a terrible fright, but Viori hardly noticed. She stared off into the distance, her expression as blank as ever.

"All is well," he told her, displaying a brittle smile as he helped her to her feet. She held fast to her doll, Drendall. "Come, love. Let us hurry from here." Trolls ran in packs. Where you found one, you would find others.

Heart thumping, he squired Viori forward, away from the carnage. Which way, which way? The blood-map he'd drawn on his arm had gotten smeared during battle, and he cursed inwardly. Guess he'd have to improvise.

Kaysar decided to follow a winding path provided by a babbling brook, and quickened his step. Nature sweetened his panting breaths, an overwarm wind twirling fallen leaves from here to there. He maintained a tight clasp on Viori's hand, lest she and the doll blow away, too.

Despite the morning hour, thick shadows crept and slithered on the other side of the water, carnivorous foliage beckoning unwitting prey. On their side, at least, sunshine bathed the land in golden light. Problem was, pixies buzzed about. Known thieves.

Another threat. Kaysar could afford to lose nothing. Everything he owned, he required for Viori's survival.

"Why don't I sing to you, hmm?" he asked, feigning nonchalance.

Minutes ticked by in silence. His sister hadn't spoken a word since their parents had died.

At first, Kaysar hadn't fretted about her lack of communication. He'd been flooded with new responsibilities, too busy to deal with his own grief, much less another's. Now he thought of little else.

"I'll sing anything you wish," he said, trying again. "Something about a princess and her prince, perhaps?" Once her favorite subject. "Or, what if I sing to Drendall? Would she like a song all her own, do you think?"

Viori continued to stare straight ahead, offering no response.

A sigh of dejection seeped from him. *I'm failing her.*

Kaysar knew guilt imprisoned her tongue. He also knew why. Eight months ago, a plague had swept through their village, infecting their mother and father. Since their livelihood had depended on their parents' ability to work the fields, harvesting pixiepetals, Viori had opted to use her glamara. An innate supernatural ability. The strongest a fae possessed.

Like Kaysar, she wielded a voice steeped in compulsion. When she issued a command, listeners obeyed. Fighting did no good. Except, her glamara had not yet been honed. What she hadn't comprehended back then? Emotion affected tone. Always. Bad things happened when the wrong sentiments layered her words.

Fearful, upset and desperate, Viori had ordered their parents to feel better. And the pair had indeed felt better—when they'd died.

The siblings had been on their own ever since. Viori had ceased speaking altogether.

Tears of regret stung Kaysar's eyes. The day after he'd burned his parents' bodies, according to fae custom, a tax collector had arrived to settle outstanding debts by seizing the farm. Later that day, a neighbor had invited both Kaysar and Viori to stay with him...if they found a way to "repay such incredible generosity." He'd declined. Another couple had approached him, hoping to adopt Viori, and only Viori. He'd declined their offer, as well, unable to soothe his fears about the girl's safety and unwilling to disregard his parents' final wish. *Stay together, no matter what.*

Kaysar might not have a permanent shelter or funds, but he offered what the others couldn't. Unconditional love. His sister was his only remaining family, and he would protect her with his life. Could anyone else say the same?

"Forget the song. Why don't I tell you about the village we're visiting?" He tended to pick settlements a good distance from the Summer Court. Their kingdom's bustling capitol. Rumors suggested orphans were often snatched off the streets, never to be seen or heard from again.

As silence stretched, a sense of urgency strengthened inside him. "Tell me how I can help you," he pleaded.

Again, she said nothing.

How could he diminish his sister's anguish and guilt? How did he convince her of the truth? He didn't blame her for what happened. He, too, had made life-and-death mistakes with his glamara.

Should he rethink his decisions? Would the traumatized girl do better with the couple? They came with a permanent home. Stability. Three meals a day, prepared with home-grown food rather than morsels stolen from any available source. If left behind for any reason, Viori wouldn't need to hide. There'd be no danger of a troll attack. Or worse. Worry about the weather? Never again. Opportunities for friendships would abound. Pretty dresses would replace the rags her brother filched from clotheslines.

And when the new family discovered the extent of her glamara? Few fae brandished one like it. While their mother's humming had entranced those around her, and their father's every word had inspired unnatural excitement and anticipation, neither parent had ever compelled others to submit to their will.

What if the family used Viori for their own advance, treating her as an object?

He inhaled sharply, different muscles knotting. No, his sister wouldn't be better off without him. He did everything in his power to keep her safe, and he understood her struggles in ways others could not. By any means necessary, he fed her a fulfilling meal each day, acquired plenty of fresh water, and secured the warmest shelters. Who could say the same?

Often he stole what they needed. As a last resort, he used his glamara. When that happened, he and Viori packed up and moved on the very next day, just in case someone realized the truth. People feared what they couldn't control and attacked what they feared.

Another group of pixies flew past, twittering with excitement, leaving a trail of glittery dust in their wake.

Where were they headed with such haste? Was something going on?

Kaysar helped Viori over a fallen log and drew to a stop. "One second, love." He studied what remained of the map. The only landmark up ahead seemed to be a small clearing.

Did people congregate there? They must. Where people flocked, provisions brimmed. Food. Clothing. Weapons.

Either the pixies stole everything, or Kaysar did.

His next inhalation proved as piercing as a blade. If he got caught, Viori would be alone in the forest rather than a village, where she might search out a kind soul for help.

To go forward or switch direction?

Wait. The tips of his pointed ears twitched. Voices. He dropped to a crouch, pulling Viori down, as well.

He focused on the noise, his ears twitching faster. Oh, yes. Voices. Two of them. Three? All male. Fae. Authoritative. Angry.

Emotions were high, adding to the level of danger. He and Viori could source provisions elsewhere. Yes. The better choice. He straightened halfway, pulling his sister to her feet, and eased forward.

Only two steps into their retreat, her stomach rumbled. In the quiet, that rumble struck him as obscenely loud.

Shame scalded him, and he slowed. When it came to Viori's well-being, he had no fears, no lines and no friends. Only foes with temporary possession of his things.

To feed his hungry sister, the risk was worthy of the reward.

I'll do it. A twig snapped as he ushered Viori closer to the brook. Clear water rushed along crushed gemstones, lapping white foam over the shore. Where to stash the little girl?

A quick scan revealed two options. Clusters of toxic

poisonvine or massive tree trunks with thick buttress roots that played host to legions of fireants.

The poisonvine it is.

Kaysar urged Viori across the distance, trembling as the air sweetened. Poisonvine stunned a fae upon contact. Few ever approached it.

He encouraged her to hunker between the stalks and settled the doll on her lap. As long as Viori kept still, she wouldn't brush against the foliage. "You know I'll always protect you, yes? Stay here, and remain unmoving," he whispered, placing their satchel at her feet. The cloth carried their few but precious belongings.

His sister offered no reaction, too lost in her head to notice what transpired around her.

"I'll find out what's going on," he told her anyway. "While I'm gone, I want you to remember how much I love you. All right? I'll return shortly." He might be injured and bloody again, but he would return.

She peered beyond him, silent.

Chest clenching, he cupped her cheeks and kissed her forehead, then kissed Drendall's forehead and darted off before he changed his mind. His vision blurred for a moment.

Don't look back. Focus.

Kaysar waded through the cool brook and came out the other side, his feet and calves soaked. As he snuck through spindly trees cloaked in shadows, he trailed water behind him. Gnarled branches scraped his cheeks, stinging, but he refused to slow.

The scent of flowers faded, overpowered by a stench of rot. He held his breath and trod over a red-and-yellow mushroom growing from a jagged stone.

A male bellowed a terrible insult seconds before a woman's cry of pain echoed.

Kaysar quickened his pace, freed the bow anchored to his shoulder and nocked an arrow. Closing in... He wove through a maze of jagged branches and brittle leaves, where hundreds of pixies gathered, enthralled. Closer...

Near the last tangle of trees, he caught sight of three males and a lone female. He stilled to take stock. Small girl, big brutes. They must be soldiers. Rich—royal? Two were older. The third was young, perhaps sixteen or seventeen.

At this vantage point, Kaysar observed everyone in profile. The girl remained on her knees, while the males stood. A bright red bun drooped at her nape. She looked older than the teen but younger than the others. Her dress, though plain, appeared well-made, a low neckline displaying the diamond-studded collar around her throat.

"Please," she cried, pressing her hands together, forming a steeple. "Don't do this."

The youngest male sneered, and the older two scoffed. Were they brothers? Both had white hair, the sides braided and pinned back. They were tall and muscular, sporting finely knit sweaters, leather pants and combat boots. Short swords topped with icebone hilts extended over each man's broad shoulders. Icebone. A crystal found only in the Winterlands.

Kaysar's brow furrowed with confusion. Why were Winter Court royal guards so far from home?

He took aim, keeping the biggest man in his sights. Though he knew a handful of arrows couldn't fell fae warriors as strong as these, he also knew a few well-placed missiles could slow them down, buying him time to escape.

"Did you hope to win my kingdom through my son, girl?" the tallest male demanded, crackling with fury.

His kingdom? King Hador Frostline was said to be tall

and bulging with muscle, with a mop of white curls. Reports suggested Prince Lark, his younger brother, resembled him.

Fear chilled Kaysar's blood. What had he stumbled upon?

The king patted the teenager's shoulder. *He must be Prince Jareth Frostline, the son.* "Do you have anything to say to this female?"

"Why would I?" he replied, seeming offended by the prospect. "She's nothing to me."

Anger heated Kaysar's chest. What if this trio ever treated Viori this way?

The girl crumpled, her shoulders rolling in. As she dropped her head into her upraised hands, quiet sobs shook her slender frame.

Prince Lark made a noise of disgust.

"I'll be good." She reached out to ward him off or cling, Kaysar wasn't sure. "I can…I can leave the Winter Court. Yes. I'll leave and never return. Please. Let me leave."

The onlookers laughed with each other.

"Take care of her, brother." The king nudged Prince Lark. "You need the practice."

"My ability is almost as stalwart as yours," Prince Lark protested.

"Almost. But you lack control. So go ahead." He waved to the girl as if she were a thing of little importance. "Practice."

Kaysar realized he had a choice. Save the girl and his conscience, perhaps condemning himself and Viori in the process, or walk away and condemn the girl and his conscience.

Could he save her? One boy against three fae royals? And if he failed? What of Viori?

The need for debate ended there. He lowered his bow. For Viori's continued well-being, he must do nothing.

His stomach turned as Prince Lark cupped the girl's face and her eyes widened with terror. Choking sounds left her as black lines appeared in her skin. She struggled against him, doing her best to sever their connection, but the prince held on and on and on.

The lines spread through her eyes. Down her neck, disappearing under her clothes.

Kaysar watched, his insides on fire.

She struggled less and less.

He curled his hands into fists.

The girl went limp, and Kaysar stopped breathing entirely.

With a simple twist of his wrists, Prince Lark casually ripped off her head. He laughed as blood spurted. Laughed as her body hit the ground, the diamond-studded collar tumbling a few feet away. The king and his son cheered.

Bile rose, singeing Kaysar's throat. Prince Lark lifted the head as if it were a war prize. No, a child's toy. He kicked it a good distance away, then flittered. An ability to teleport from one location to another. An ability Kaysar had yet to develop.

The other two royals followed the prince within seconds.

A hoarse bellow exploded from Kaysar then, the pixies taking flight. He sucked in a mouthful of air and fought to center his thoughts. Forget the atrocity he'd witnessed. Emotions could be dealt with later. With the right buyer, that diamond collar could provide a month's worth of meals for his sister.

Kaysar performed a visual sweep. About twenty feet of wildflowers separated him and the collar, with no obvious rocks or stumps littering the path. Ignoring his trembling, he hooked the bow over his shoulder, and drew in a deep breath.

Go! He sprinted out of the tangle of branches. Halfway there...

Bending down and reaching out...

A hard arm coiled around his throat, yanking him against a harder body. Though he struggled, his captor twisted his arm behind his back, trapping him further.

"I thought I smelled someone in the shadows." A husky chuckle fanned hot breath over his forehead. "So who do we have here, hmm?" Prince Lark smacked his lips against Kaysar's cheek. "A naughty thief planning to steal Winter Court property?"

When the king and his son reappeared a few feet away, panic surged.

The king frowned. "We can't have a witness spilling our secrets."

"A shame to waste such a pretty face." Prince Lark rubbed against Kaysar. "Give him to me. I'll ensure he stays quiet."

No, no, no. Left with no other recourse, Kaysar concentrated on his glamara. When his throat heated, he spoke. "You will release me." *Calm, steady.* "You will walk away and forget me."

The king paled, and the princes tensed. But none of the trio obeyed him. They exchanged glances instead.

"Did I detect a thread of compulsion?" King Hador raised his brows, as if impressed.

"I think you did." Prince Lark expelled a breath, then ran the lobe of Kaysar's ear between his teeth. "Don't you know? To command a royal fae, your glamara must be stronger than his, no matter what ability you wield."

Icy cold invaded Kaysar's limbs.

"Let me kill him instead." An evil grin lifted the corners of Prince Jareth's mouth. "Like Uncle, I need practice."

Smiling with a sick kind of glee, the king unsheathed a dagger. "Sorry, my boy, but I owe your uncle a treat. I'll take no chances, however."

Horror threatened to drown Kaysar. He erupted into motion, bucking, straining. The bigger male had no difficulty gripping his chin, prying open his mouth and aligning a blade against the side of his tongue. Once again, the princes laughed and laughed and laughed.

The king began to saw, *removing* his tongue. Searing pain, utter agony. Black spots flashed before Kaysar's eyes. Blood clogged his airways. *So dizzy.* When his knees buckled, the prince let him go. He crashed into the ground, black dots weaving through his vision.

He tried to crawl away. *Must return... Viori.* But darkness swallowed him.

One year later

A *CLINK-CLANK* OF METAL. A high-pitched groan as unoiled hinges ground together. Then, a continuous thud of footsteps as Kaysar's tormentor ascended an eternity-long but too short staircase.

A ragged inhalation stabbed his nostrils and cut his lungs. Heart banging like a hammer, he slinked back and pressed against the wall, where shadows engulfed him. Bare flesh met frigid stone, and he hissed, his chain rattling ever so slightly, adding a new note to the ominous melody.

Lark was back.

The prince could have flittered, appearing directly in the room, but he preferred to draw out his approach and build anticipation.

Kaysar darted his gaze, focusing on inane details. The sun had begun to fall. Muted beams of light streamed through the only window, illuminating the highest room in the highest tower of the Winterlands Palace, the crown jewel of the Winter Court. Here, Kaysar had some of the comforts he'd longed to give Viori. A built-in bed with a goose-down mattress. A freestanding tub and access to fresh water, a true luxury. But oh, how he despised this place.

He'd suffered every moment of his capture. Prince Lark and King Hador had abused him however they'd pleased, whenever they'd pleased, keeping Kaysar confined with the diamond-studded collar he'd once hoped to sell. A length of chain stretched between the collar and the wall, the links impenetrable. The royals fed him only enough to exist.

In the beginning, he'd felt like a trapped animal. He'd fought his circumstances with the full force of his might. When all the rage, hatred, guilt and shame had finally reached a tragic crescendo, his mind had…broken. In the aftermath, he'd discovered only the hatred remained.

Every minute of every day he seethed with the desire—the consuming *need*—to slaughter his enemies. The screams he would elicit. Oh, the screams. Then, his hunt for his beloved Viori could begin.

His chest constricted. Was she all right? Had someone found and helped her? Had someone harmed her? In his worst nightmares, he imagined her dying of thirst days after he'd abandoned her in those vines.

A tear escaped, sliding down his cheek.

Thump-thump. Kaysar stiffened as the prince's footsteps drew closer. Today, he launched his escape. If he failed…

He couldn't fail.

He wiped his damp brow with the back of his hand

and hummed a soft melody. Vibrations raced along his tongue—a tongue now in the process of regrowing. Lark had no idea. But he would.

Kaysar smiled as he imagined blood pouring from the prince's every orifice.

Another *clink-clank* of metal. Another serenade of hinges followed as the door swung open...and Lark appeared, consuming the space. Pale curls disheveled, pointy ears on display. Blue eyes glassy. He wore a wrinkled white tunic and leathers, a pair of daggers sheathed at his waist. The scent of sour wine and sweat tainted the air.

"I don't think you're going to like what I've planned today," the prince said with a grin.

Hate him. Hate them all. Lark and Hador had taken so much from Kaysar. His sister. His freedom. His honor. His sanity. Even his future.

They take no more.

Laughing, always laughing, the prince stalked forward, removing and dropping his shirt along the way.

The hatred collected in Kaysar's throat, singeing him. He shouted, "Stop."

Lark...obeyed. The prince's brow furrowed with confusion. He resisted the immobility—but he didn't take another step.

Then. That moment. Kaysar tasted victory and only craved more.

"How?" Lark demanded, throwing the question at him.

How had Kaysar, who'd yet to freeze into his immortality, regrown a portion of his tongue? "I've been humming a healing song to myself." He hadn't used his voice in so long. The simple joy of it! "Now," he said, rubbing his hands together, "I make you *hurt*."

The prince recommenced his struggles, fighting with

terrible ferocity. Too late. Kaysar locked his gaze with Lark's, opened his mouth and screamed. Such a lovely sound. Beautiful and horrifying. Haunting and maddening. He'd screamed before, but never like this. Louder and louder, the cadence echoing. The tower shook, the air crackling with more power than he'd known he possessed.

Blood poured from Lark's ears, a glorious sight to behold. Kaysar's thoughts fragmented and crystalized. *Kill Lark. Escape. Kill everyone else. Find Viori.*

Oh, the fun he'd have on his way out of the Winter Court.

Lark collapsed, writhing in agony. When he failed to gain relief, he blindly patted his waist until he clutched a dagger.

Kaysar's scream broke as the prince stabbed himself in his ears.

Heaving his breaths, Kaysar prowled closer. Crimson poured from the prince's every orifice, exactly as he'd imagined. His smile returned. What a marvelous beginning.

"Help." Pale and shaking, the prince reached for him, reminding Kaysar of the servant girl who'd once reached for Lark. "H-help me."

His pain and helplessness acted as a balm to Kaysar's battered soul. "Yes, let me help you," he whispered, dropping to his knees.

Relief emanated from Lark as Kaysar gently wiped blood from his pale eyes. Then the prince caught Kaysar's gaze, and the relief morphed into fear.

Delicious.

As the male shook his head in negation, Kaysar claimed the dagger—and struck. Again and again and again. Every blow deluged him with joy, even the barest hint of satisfaction. Like the Frostlines, he laughed and laughed and laughed. Only when Lark's head detached from his body did Kaysar's laughter stop.

He frowned. The prince was dead, his life extinguished. But...Kaysar wasn't finished killing him. He *needed* to kill Lark again. A mere handful of stabbings wasn't nearly enough.

Nothing will ever be enough.

Dripping crimson and panting, Kaysar used the dagger to unhinge the collar. When the metal hit the floor, he remained in place. He was free. He should be overflowing with triumph. Instead, he wallowed in fury as the prince's corpse taunted him. No life meant no misery.

Instead of suffering for eternity, one of Kaysar's tormentors rested. How was this fair? Lark had tortured Kaysar for a year, only to die in a moment? Unacceptable.

Kaysar would leave the kingdom without making another kill, he decided. He would return to deal with King Hador and Prince Jareth only after he'd built his strength. Soon the entire Frostline family would experience the horrors they had liked to visit upon him. Kill them too soon? No.

It was a mistake Kaysar refused to make again.

CHAPTER ONE

Astaria, the Fae Realm
Midnight Court

"HOW DARE HE!" Kaysar the Unhinged One, King of the Midnight Court, banged his fist on the arm of his throne, an elaborate seat made from stalks of poisonvine. Bloodred flowers with sharp, jagged petals bloomed along the upper arch, perfuming the air with a sweet, intoxicating fragrance. "Something must be done."

Prince Jareth of the Winterlands had lied to him. Kaysar despised liars. He despised the prince for a thousand other reasons, of course, but the lies... In his estimation, there was no worse crime.

He goes too far.

Another shout brewed. If you couldn't own your evil, mayhap you shouldn't commit the act.

With one metal-tipped hand, he braced to rise, ready to strike at Jareth this very moment. With the other metal-tipped hand, he gripped the poisonvine to keep himself seated. "Tell me again, word for word, changing nothing," he commanded his seer. "Fill my ears with his crime once more."

"Word for word?" Her tone said what she didn't. *Must I?*

"You must." Though she had mentioned her name once or three dozen times, he knew her only as Eye, a beauty he'd saved from goblins however long ago. Years? Eons? Time had lost all meaning to Kaysar, one day the same as any other. He awoke, thought of ways to punish his foes, and then punished his foes. His methods might vary, but his goal remained unchanged.

"Very well." Evincing dread, Eye repeated, "I'm so sorry to tell you this, majesty, and please don't shout, but Prince Jareth approaches your—" She cringed. "Border."

"How dare he," Kaysar exploded again.

His companion flinched. "Perhaps you should study your map," she suggested as a mother to an upset child. "You wish to study your map, yes?"

His map. He tensed before he softened, melting into his throne. "Yes, I wish to study my map." He plucked his fingers free of the poisonvine and traced his claws along his forearm, the way he used to do as a boy. He welcomed the sting, the drip of blood.

Over the centuries, he'd memorized the layout of Astaria and each of the five fae courts, yet the art of creating a map still calmed him. His sole remaining link to his sister. If he'd ever really had a sister? Sometimes he wondered if he'd imagined her. A figment of his imagination to keep him sane during the worst year of his existence. But deep down, he knew the truth.

He etched crimson lines into his skin, applying more pressure, cutting deeper and using torn flaps as markers. The latest stings barely registered as tension seeped from him.

"Majesty?"

The softly spoken question snagged his attention, and he snapped up his head. He narrowed his eyes and focused on the woman standing before him. Surrounded by onyx walls and torchlight, Eye wore an ivory gown, appearing as ethereal as a dream. A glorious mane of dark hair framed a delicate face, her skin a shade lighter than her rich brown eyes.

Pushing the words through clenched teeth, he told her, "What is my one and only rule for you, Eye?"

She grimaced before admitting, "I'm not to interrupt you. But if I must, there are only two instances I'm never to do so, even if I'm dying."

"That's right." Eye had more privileges with Kaysar than anyone else in existence, but there were lines even she must not cross. "Name those instances."

"When you're studying your maps that aren't maps." She shifted from foot to foot. "And every moment in between."

Maps that aren't— He flicked his tongue over an incisor. Was it his fault that others couldn't read his works of art?

As a boy, he'd had no spare money for ink and paper, so he'd adapted. As often as he and Viori had dashed from village to village to avoid being punished for simply surviving, he'd *needed* a map. The Forest of Many Names was an infamous labyrinth known for gobbling up visitors and spitting out their bones. Eventually.

His greatest fear was finding *Viori's* bones in the wooded terrain.

His lungs squeezed, his breath thinning. "Your insolence this day is concerning, Eye. But I'm a merciful king. Upon occasion. Too merciful, perhaps. I'll give you one chance to save yourself from reprisal. Show me what Prince Jareth is doing right this second."

The seer had the ability to meld her mind with another's and reveal whatever images she observed in a vision—the past, present or future. It was a painful process for her. He didn't care.

As she'd done thousands of times, she projected a picture into his mind. An image of Jareth Frostline, Crown Prince of the Winter Court, traveling through the Forest of Many Names with his bride. Princess Lulundria, the darling of the Summer Court.

"Show me the end result of our coming skirmish." And there would be a skirmish.

Jareth *craved* a fight. Why else would the prince near Kaysar's borders?

Did the husband hope to impress the new wife with his bravery, mayhap?

He will face only humiliation.

After Kaysar's escape from captivity, he'd hunted for Viori ceaselessly, but she'd vanished without a trace. He gripped his throne, his claws digging deep. Even Eye had failed to catch a glimpse of her.

The Frostlines had taken everything Kaysar had ever loved. For centuries, he'd nursed his hatred like a fine wine. Now, he lived to ensure the royal family suffered and suffered and suffered and suffered and suffered. Exactly as he'd planned. Until Hador and Jareth experienced the same devastation they'd caused an innocent boy and his sister, Kaysar had no intention of ending his personal war. Which meant the war would *never* end.

His suffering endured throughout the ages. Theirs would, too.

"To show you the end, I must watch the beginning." Eye's distaste for the sight of blood was her biggest fault. Along with dozens of others. "Why should I bother? We both know you'll win."

"You bother because I command it." Kaysar smiled at her. An expression many had deemed "the most terrifying sight in all the land."

Did he know he'd win? Yes. But he still enjoyed a peek at the end result.

In battle, he had no equal. Not because he was born with a natural or even unnatural talent for killing. In his formative years, he'd worked as a farmer, like his parents. No, he succeeded because he let nothing dissuade him from a goal.

It helped that he'd trained under the harshest conditions. That he'd spent centuries battling trolls, goblins and ogres. The worst of the worst.

Perhaps he was a monster himself, eh? But at least he wasn't a liar.

After he'd taken control of the Nightlands—a former prison territory inhabited only by the dregs of society—he'd created a new court, Midnight, with no one able to stop him. To the fae, might equaled right, every kingdom ruled by the one with the strength to hold the crown.

Over the years, the Midnight Court had become the wealthiest kingdom with resources the others lacked. Even better, the Nightlands were infinitely more dangerous. Well, except for the Dusklands.

Just for fun, he'd also conquered the barren wasteland teeming with monsters. He hadn't yet set up another court to rule—but he would. When he tired of hurting the Frostlines.

He and his army would have no trouble accomplishing whatever he decided, his soldiers motivated to succeed. In battle, the men he'd trained had no equal either. Without hesitation, they savagely killed anyone who served the Frostlines. But. As ordered, they always spared the Frostlines themselves. To this day, Kaysar lamented ending Prince Lark's life so soon.

You couldn't torture a dead man. Kaysar had tried.

His only solace came from making the rest of the family wish they were dead.

"You will show me the end and anything else I should

see." He leaned back and tapped a claw against the arm of the throne. Poisonvine venom leaked from the punctures.

Contact with the smallest drop paralyzed most fae for minutes and weakened them for weeks. With prolonged exposure, Kaysar had developed an immunity—and a bone-deep adoration.

"There is *always* more you should see," Eye muttered, "but you only ever acknowledge what you wish to acknowledge."

"And I'm right to do so. Now show me what I demand and nothing more."

Eye shook her head, disappointed in him, then projected another image into his mind. In a flash, he saw a bloody Jareth on his knees, his head bowed as he sobbed.

Prince Jareth, dejected enough to squeeze out a few tears? Kaysar *must* witness this.

The royal seer anchored her hands on her hips. "Why don't you kill King Hador and Prince Jareth and be done with your hatred once and for all?"

Foolish girl. "You don't part with the things you love. You hold them close and never let go." His hatred was his oldest and dearest friend. His closest family. If he lost it the way he'd lost Viori, he'd have *nothing*.

Eye gave him a pitying look, then motioned to the tattoo on his bicep. A snake curled into a figure eight, eating its own tail, with a sword running through its center. His kingdom's symbol, meaning "eternal war." "Why does your desire for vengeance matter more than my dream of peace? I tire of war, King Kaysar. *All* of your people tire of war. Do you even care?"

"What a ridiculous question. Of course I don't care. My people have shelter, food and protection, a slight to them a slight to me. I demand *only* what I'm owed in return."

"You believe you're owed blind obedience."

"No. I believe I'm owed obedience *and* truth." If anyone lied to him, they immediately lost the privilege of breathing.

She tossed her hands up. "You make it impossible for your people to find happiness."

Wrong. "Happiness is the only thing I've left up to them. If they go without, they can only blame themselves." He tilted his head, intensifying his study of the oracle. "Have you decided my terms are unacceptable, Eye? If so, you are more than welcome to leave my lands. I'll even allow you to do so with your head attached."

To reach another kingdom, she must travel through the Forest of Many Names. A jot difficult to do, considering Kaysar had relocated centaurs, ogres and trolls into the wilds however long ago. For anyone not bearing his protection— his seal or the Frostline name—moving from kingdom to kingdom came with a high likelihood of failure.

"I have no desire to leave you," she said, then heaved a familiar sigh. "Don't you crave love, accolades, and re- spect?"

"No," he replied, and he meant it. Highborn and low- born alike often accused him of being cruel and heartless, obsessed and maddened. Why change? He liked himself this way.

Her shoulders sagged, as if she'd failed him. "If you don't let go of your vengeance, you won't grab hold of your future and your mate, the only person able to give you what you so desperately crave. And it isn't vengeance, I promise you."

What he so desperately craved. To return to the forest as a twelve-year-old boy, with his sister's hand clasped in his. "I have no mate, I want no mate, and I crave only vengeance." His single form of satisfaction. Why require a specific bedmate? A lover was a lover, one the same as another; they simply wore different faces. The least important feature.

In desperation, Eye burst out, "You *could* have a woman. You could have more than loneliness and pain."

Lonely? Him? "I'm beginning to question your sanity, Eye."

"If you continue on this path, you will condemn yourself to an eternity of misery," she stated, sympathy in her dark gaze. "You will lose everything that matters to you."

"I have *already* lost everything that matters," he grated. "Now I merely repay."

"But—"

"Enough of this." Temper verging on dangerous, he leaped to his feet. "The Frostlines planted seeds of hate in the rich soil of my heart. For twelve months, the king and his brother watered those seeds, ensuring they sprouted and grew roots. Yet here you stand, daring to complain to the tree for producing its harvest? How dare *you*? The Frostlines will eat the fruit of their labors, that I swear to you."

"Kaysar—"

"You'd best mind your tongue, Eye, before I add it to my collection." Yes, he displayed severed tongues in jars, on special shelves in his bedroom. He displayed other organs, too. What made a better trophy than a literal piece of his foes?

"Very well. Go." She made a shooing motion. "Start the beginning of the end."

Before he did something he might possibly consider regretting at some later date, Kaysar flittered to the Forest of Many Names, appearing in a location he recognized from Eye's vision.

He turned his focus to his mission—hurting Prince Jareth in the worst way imaginable. Let the fun begin.

CHAPTER TWO

ARMED WITH CLAWS, short swords and daggers, Kaysar
stalked Prince Jareth, his new bride and the royal Winter
guard without detection, a skill he'd honed to perfection.
As expected, he went unnoticed, observing his foes unim-
peded as the twenty-two-member party trotted through the
forest on horseback.

The prince and princess rode together, constantly touching. It wasn't long before the lusty pair called a halt to the
procession, ordering the guards to patrol as they bathed.

The guards were nervous about an ambush and clearly
eager to return home. Kaysar tsk-tsked. *Such selfish little
royals.* Their actions put other lives in terrible danger.

Alternately slinking and flittering, Kaysar moved from
one spot to another, checking the perimeter. Ogres and
trolls had already gathered. Pixies, too, voyeurs as much
as thieves.

Fifteen guards positioned themselves around a small
grotto, ten to thirty feet away, a hand resting on a sword
hilt. They remained stationary, their gazes darting as they
searched for predators. The remaining five guards marched
in a circle outside the others.

What to do, what to do? At certain points in the past,
Kaysar could have taken Hador's or Jareth's head the way
he'd taken Lark's. He'd always refrained. What was his
purpose, if not the misery of the Frostlines?

A plan quickly formed, and he grinned. Today, he took Princess Lulundria.

As quietly and swiftly as possible, he moved through the unit. First, he slit the throats of the males on patrol, easing their bodies to the ground with no one the wiser. Excitement building, he worked his way through the rest, getting creative. A cruel twist of his wrist here. A triple jab there. Each of the twenty died with a muted groan of shock. He only wished there'd been more guards.

He so enjoyed his work.

Kaysar wiped his bloody hands on the last victim and flittered closer to the water, where he sat. The couple swam in the grotto that teemed with lush green leaves and purple flowers. A lovers' paradise. Moss-covered stones surrounded the pool, shimmers of pollen dancing on a gentle breeze. Incredible scents saturated the air: the sweetness of the blooms, the crispness of the sun, the freshness of the water.

"How much do you want me, husband?" Lulundria asked with a low tone, walking backward and tracing her fingers between her breasts.

She was certainly Jareth's type: tall, slender, and as delicate as a cameo with her waterfall of pink curls, emerald eyes, and pale, sparkling skin. If Kaysar remembered correctly, her glamara involved plants, allowing her to cultivate an entire garden in minutes. Her people adored her gentle nature and kind heart. Something Kaysar might have developed himself, if not for the Frostlines.

"Well?" She eased onto the shore. "Have I stolen your thoughts?"

Jareth waded closer, into the shallow end, and offered her a heated grin. Lids heavy, he gripped the base of his shaft and stroked up, saying, "I want you this much."

Princess Lulundria gave a throaty laugh, and Kaysar scowled. "If you get any bigger, my darling, you won't be able to fit inside me."

What right did Jareth have to enjoy a woman like this, after what he'd done to the servant girl?

Did the princess know her marriage to Prince Jareth placed her dead center in the Unhinged One's crosshairs?

If she didn't, she would.

"Oh, I'll fit, all right." When Jareth joined her on the shore, she molded her soft curves to his tattooed body. The towheaded warrior, and the pink-haired beauty. He wrapped his arms around her and nipped her bottom lip. "I'll work it in nice and slow."

And I'll surprise you as soon as you reach the point of no return.

The besotted couple kissed. They stretched out on their pile of clothes, Jareth's weapons beside them. Hands wandered, and moans rang out.

Kaysar had never enjoyed kissing or touching. He did it only when necessary, using the pleasure he doled as a weapon. He seduced married women from their husbands and learned secrets he couldn't ferret out in other ways. He'd never understood the pleasure his conquests derived from his ministrations.

He raked his claws over his forearm, patiently waiting for the perfect moment to strike. Though he wished to study his latest map, he didn't. He wouldn't allow himself to lose track of his surroundings. There were decisions to make.

What should he do with Princess Lulundria once he had her ensconced in his palace? So many options appealed.

He could kill her, of course, causing Jareth untold grief. But grief tended to dull far too quickly. He could even seduce her and steal her affections from the prince, initiating centuries of humiliation and fury. That one never got old.

Emotion wasn't something Kaysar compelled, however. Could he win a devoted princess from her adoring husband with his charm alone? The challenge intrigued him.

Who was he kidding? Challenge? He snorted. Yes, he could win her. He could win any woman of his choosing. None had the strength to resist his handsome face and powerful physique.

It was ironic, really. He inspired great lust in others, yet he himself had never experienced genuine passion. The torture he'd endured with Lark and Hador had caused a permanent disconnection between his mind and body. Few sensations registered as anything more than pressure, heat or cold. He'd never felt close to a lover, not the way others seemed to do. A fact he celebrated.

To Kaysar, sex would forever be a tool. He'd never wanted someone for reasons outside of vengeance, and he never would. Who could he trust?

As Jareth positioned his wife on her hands and knees, an idea budded. Something truly vile. Something Kaysar had never done before. What if he…impregnated her?

It was a disgusting idea, worse than the abduction and seduction…and absolutely perfect. In the fae realm, a husband suffered great dishonor if ever he disinherited his wife's child, no matter the reason for it.

To keep Kaysar's child off the throne, Jareth would be forced to expose the black heart he so expertly hid from the rest of the world. Something he wouldn't do, preventing Hador's descendant from ever inheriting the crown.

Was any revenge sweeter?

The plan was set then. As soon as Lulundria conceived,

Kaysar would return her to her husband and enjoy the fallout.

Eager to begin, he flittered to a stand, rolled his shoulders and prepared his claws. Then, he flittered directly behind the thrusting male, fisted his hair with one hand, yanking his head up, and tearing out half his throat with the other hand. Enough to cause agonizing pain, but not enough to kill. He jumped back as the prince clutched at his throat.

No doubt Jareth would recover in seconds and use his glamara. Like one of his Frostline ancestors, he wielded an ability to summon ice and spew shards from his fingertips.

"Jareth?" The princess glanced over her shoulder, probably wondering why her husband no longer thrust into her. Spotting Kaysar several feet behind the male, she screamed and scrambled to don a tunic.

The choking, bleeding prince fell forward. Kaysar flittered in front of the couple and grinned.

"Congratulations, Jareth. By some miracle, you didn't tear your bride with your massive size. How thrilled you must both be." He clapped. "Between the two of us," he added with a low tone, as if he shared a secret, "I'm not sure I'll be able to say the same. I'm *actually* size gargantuan. Shhh. Don't tell. I want to surprise her."

"You don't touch her." Spittle sprayed from the prince's mouth as he regained his voice and lumbered to his feet. "You don't even get to look at her."

The princess rushed behind her wild-eyed husband. Nearly fully recovered, Jareth waved in Kaysar's direction, flinging small slivers of ice.

Kaysar flittered in and out, the missiles embedding in the tree behind him. Grin widening, he faced off with the prince. "Go ahead. Call your royal guard. Demand help… my darling."

Realizing he'd been observed from the beginning, Jareth charged within striking distance. Kaysar could have moved, avoiding the fist thrown his way, but he gladly absorbed the blow—while disemboweling his opponent. Ah, an old favorite.

The prince stumbled backward, and another scream burst from the princess.

"Go," Jareth commanded, his voice little more than a rasp as he shoved her toward the trees.

The foolish royal hesitated, as if she actually thought to aid her husband, allowing Kaysar to flitter and catch her wrist in a vise-grip. She tried to flitter, as well, but his resistance proved greater. In a battle of wills, he won, every time.

Jareth drew back his elbow to hurl more ice, and an idea took root. Why not make the prince hurt his wife in the worst way?

Just as the prince slashed his hand, unleashing another volley of shards, Kaysar flittered and thrust the princess forward, making it appear as if she lunged on her own. The ice sank into her torso, and she lurched.

Jareth barked a hoarse denial as Lulundria tottered, bumping into Kaysar. Too weak to absorb impact, her knees buckled. He held her up, enjoying her discomfort as sublimely as Jareth was regretting it.

While it wasn't the best start to her seduction, Kaysar wasn't worried. He'd overcome far worse. "Did we learn our lesson today, prince? Protecting others before we protect ourselves never ends well for anyone."

Jareth didn't seem to hear him. Shell-shocked, he dropped to his haunches. His head bowed and a sob escaped him, Eye's vision coming to life. "My ice is poison

to Summerlanders. To royals more than any others. She…
she's going to… You've killed her. You've killed my Lulu."

"Don't listen to him, my sweet." With the prince im-
mobilized by devastation, Kaysar eased the princess upon
a bed of wildflowers and grinned. "I'll patch you right up
after I install you inside your new home." Truth. He owned
a sliver of elderseed. Perhaps the last in existence. The
mystical seed had many uses, and healing the unhealable
was one of them.

"No," Jareth bellowed, diving on him. "I won't let you
have her body."

They rolled over the ground, grappling for dominance.
Seizing her opportunity, the princess scrambled to her feet
and tripped into a run. He let her go. For now.

On their feet again. Huffing his breath, Jareth swung
at Kaysar again and again. "She did nothing to you. She
never hurt you. Never hurt anyone."

"She aligned herself with your family." He blocked
and clawed, laughing as he tore through muscle. "That's
enough."

Jareth slowed with every injury, but he never stopped
swinging. "What do you want from me? What will end
your sick obsession? Tell me, and I'll do it."

Certainly. "I want everything and nothing, always and
never, but only if you don't want to give them to me." He
stalked a circle around his prey. "Why are you so worried, prince? I meant what I said. I'll patch up your wife,
and she'll be as good as new. I'll even return her to you.
Eventually."

Blue eyes blazing, Jareth attacked with mounting vigor.
Kaysar avoided the next punches before going in for the kill.
Well, not the kill, but close. He opened his mouth and sang.

In seconds, the prince lost all color. He pressed his hands

over his ears, but it did him no good. Blood poured from his nose, and he toppled, soon writhing in agony. Kaysar only quieted when Jareth lay unconscious.

He waited, expecting a surge of satisfaction. A flicker of triumph. Something. He'd won another round, as predicted. But...

Over too soon!

No matter. He had another shot at it. Soon he'd have the princess in his bed. But first he must catch her.

Brimming with anticipation, he scanned the trees. There. She had slowed her pace. Blood soaked her tunic.

As he stalked her, twigs snapped under his boots. She cast a frantic glance over her shoulder. Crying out, she swung her arms at a faster clip.

"I can help you, princess," he called. Truth. Always. Kaysar never lied.

Too easily did he remember watching the Frostline king and princes through his window in the tower. How he'd fumed as the trio had played to the crowds, smiling and waving, accepting the praises and cheers as if they owned hearts of gold.

Another frantic glance over her shoulder. Lulundria tripped over a log and careened, landing in a mud puddle. Though weaker than before, she trudged to her feet. She—what was *this*? Thorny green vines flowed from her hands, slithering over the dirt and unfurling like snakes. Growing. The stalks stretched before her and seeped mist. A good distance away, the end of both the right and left vine switched direction, rising toward the sky and twining together, forming an arch.

Her ability surpassed a plant-based glamara. She'd opened a portal to the mortal world, something only a doormaker could do.

Realization stripped him of calm. If she made it through that doorway, Jareth's ice would kill her, as feared, and Kaysar would lose an invaluable opportunity.

He flittered directly behind her and reached out... Argh! She slipped from his hold. The vines remained attached to her, curling from her wrists to her fingertips, pulling her closer and closer to the door.

"I only wish to aid you, princess." He flittered again, but she contorted, avoiding his clasp.

If he appeared in front of the portal, she might barrel into him, knocking him into the mortal world along with her. Or without her. Leave the Frostlines without a guaranteed means to return to Astaria? Never. But he *needed* to put his own child on the Winter Court throne. His vengeance demanded it. So Kaysar used the only option available to him. Compulsion.

As Princess Lulundria zipped through the portal, he readied his glamara and called, "Return to me, princess. Return to me by any means necessary."

A moment later, she vanished in the mist. As the vines withered to ash and twirled away on the wind, Kaysar stopped and cursed. Doormakers required weeks to recharge after opening a portal. Was his glamara strong enough to recharge her now? Today?

An hour ticked by, frustration gnawing at his temper.

She *must* return. She must, she must, she must. The desire to obey him probably consumed her by now, aiding her survival. So where was she? How long must he wait?

CHAPTER THREE

The Mortal Realm
Oklahoma City, Oklahoma

Present Day

"I HOPE YOU like the taste of your balls, Nick, because I'm about to shove them down your throat." Chantel "Cookie" Bardot tapped her fingers over the game controller at lightning speed, guiding her female Mad Hatter to beat the fire out of a Prince Charming wannabe.

Would she receive a dozen emails in the next two minutes, asking her to act more professionally, but also less professionally, and oh, yes, could she keep doing exactly what she was doing and also change everything? Don't get her started on the texts.

Nick—screen name Nicobra—fought back with merciless precision, a well-placed kick sending her across the battlefield. On impact, her magic hat tumbled across the forested terrain. One of four power bars vanished.

He purred through her headset, "How about you choke on my balls *first*, Cookie."

Oh, no he didn't. "I tried, remember? But yours are the size of Tic Tacs." *Careful.* There were lines. What she dished, he had a right to serve back to her. Plus, he wasn't worth the hassle she'd face with her sponsors.

Though Cookie hated Nick, she loved her job. *I mean, come on!* Companies paid her to stream video games and be on camera. As a secret side hustle, she accepted jobs as a digital hit woman, charging other gamers to annihilate their competitors within the game world.

Once, Nick had tried to hire her to take out *herself*, never knowing who seethed behind the screen.

Who *wouldn't* love her job? What's more, she needed it. Born with a severely damaged heart, she'd undergone various surgeries, countless medical tests, numerous trials and a plethora of experimental drugs in her twenty-six years; the bills had stacked.

"Did you know you're the worst girlfriend I've ever dated?" Nick asked, unwilling to let the trash talk end. "You beat the cheater and the thief. Congrats."

Ouch. For those watching her face rather than the game, Cookie let a sugary sweet smile bloom, as if Nick had just issued a sweet compliment. Never let an opponent see you rattled.

Your hot spots became an eternal target and offered endless ammunition. Nick proved this theory every time they interacted. During their yearlong relationship, he'd discovered her deepest vulnerability—rejection. Now he liked to poke and prod until she snapped.

Game face on. "Is someone feeling defensive about his size?" She tsk-tsked. "Don't worry, baby boy. Size doesn't really matter. Since the beginning of time, women have lied about preferring a man with girth. The smaller the better, we say."

Nick missed a series of punches, allowing Cookie to reclaim her hat. Had his confidence gotten the stinky boot? Too bad, so sad.

On the right side of her screen, comment bubbles blew

up. Key words jumped out, the messages behind them clear. Drags on Cookie…drags on women in general…drags on men…a death threat…a threat of rape…support…another death threat…a death threat against anyone who supported her.

Whatever. She activated the "elderseed," charging her hat to full capacity in seconds and head-butting the prince, cracking his skull. Yes! Cookie *lived* for blood and gore. On a screen, of course, only a screen. Although, yes, okay, sometimes she envied her avatar. Every so often, she even wondered if she herself were maybe kinda sorta…murder curious. But only every so often.

Oh, she would never kill anyone in real life. She wasn't a psychopath or anything like that. Mostly, she enjoyed force-feeding bad guys a heaping helping of justice. On screen and off. And yeah, she'd always been this way.

After her parents' acrimonious divorce, she'd stayed with her mother most of the year and her father on holidays. As the two created new families, she'd lost herself in Court TV and video games.

At eighteen, she'd packed up, moving from Dallas, Texas, to Oklahoma City, Oklahoma, to work for the company who'd created a multilevel game called *The Fog A.E. The Forest of Good and Evil*.

Each level offered a different experience. As a whole, the game featured fairy tales and their vast casts of characters, all mixed together in the magical lands. Enchantia. Rhoswyn. Loloria. You could design and build your own kingdoms, battle others for theirs, or compete in tournaments for special prizes.

Even after Cookie had branched out, leaving the company to play on her own, she'd chosen to remain in Oklahoma. She'd forged a family here. A real one. Weird, sure, but beloved.

Once, Nick had been part of it. In a single hour, they'd gone from being a happy couple in life and supportive teammates in the game, to enemies in life and foes in the game. He'd wanted to do something, she'd wanted to stay home. A fight erupted, and he'd blamed the entirety of their problems on Cookie. She *never* wanted to leave the house. She ignored him. The sex sucked because he had to be too careful with her. In other words, she had more online followers.

On his way out the door, he'd told her, "Fix yourself before the next guy comes along, yeah?"

That one still burned. In the game, she landed a particularly nasty blow. Just not nasty enough. Dang it. Time was running out. In twenty…nineteen…eighteen seconds, the hat would time out. If Cookie failed to drain Nick of his life essence by then, the match was as good as lost.

Pushing her dexterity to the limit, she played harder and downright filthy, upping the speed and veracity of her strikes. Nick got too busy defending himself to launch a counterattack and soon hemorrhaged energy.

"Yes!" she shouted when Prince Charming took a savage blow to the head. Down he went. Where he stayed, too weak to rise. A triumphant grin bloomed. "That, ladies and genitalmen, is how you deal with a pouty man-baby who thinks he's ready to spar with the big girls."

"Keep it down out there. I'm napping." The grumpy voice came from the hallway, courtesy of her sixty-two-year-old roommate, Pearl Jean Levitt.

They'd met two years ago in the lobby of their cardiologist's office. Cookie had insta-loved Pearl Jean for the same reason she considered roller derby one of the greatest sports in history. Both were brutally honest and absolutely bonkers.

"Good news. I won." She tossed her controller and ended the feed. *Enough of that.*

"Yes, you won," Pearl Jean replied, unimpressed. "Barely."

A win was a win, right? "So you watched?" She switched off her dual screens and removed her wireless headset.

"Only because I couldn't sleep. My sciatica is flaring. The gout is probably next."

Cookie snorted. Pearl Jean excelled in three things. Complaining, illness, and expecting the worst.

Her cat, Sugars, jumped from the couch. His throne. He leaped onto her station and butted his head against hers, a demand for pets. Her chest swelled with love for the ridiculously spoiled feline as she scratched behind his ears. Her little house panther had watched the entire game, silently judging her for ignoring him and praying she failed.

"Your sciatica, huh? You went to bed for a headache."

"A person can't have three ailments at the same time?" Pearl Jean retorted.

"Can that same person be a medical miracle who's contracted every disease known to man and even some that aren't?"

"Hmph. Today's youth. Too much sass, not enough class."

"You know you love me."

"Occasionally," the old bat grumbled. "Perhaps."

Grinning, Cookie anchored a nasal cannula in place and took a hit of the good stuff—oxygen. The tube connected to a portable tank. She'd needed this for half an hour, but she'd needed to not lose against her nemesis more.

Nick streamed for *The Fog A.E.*, too. People loved to

watch him practice. More people loved to watch her in combat.

"This boy, Nick," Pearl Jean called, restarting the conversation.

"Why don't you get up and march your butt into the living room so we can chat like civilized adults?"

"Is he the one who thought you were too sloppy to date?" her roommate continued, acting as if she hadn't spoken.

"No." That guy had taken one look at her T-shirt and yoga pants and laughed. He hadn't gotten a second chance. He almost hadn't gotten to take his next breath, either. In her mind. Only in her mind.

"Is Nick the one who said you're fun to look at but terrifying to hang out with because you're so bad at connecting with other people?"

"Nope. And how am I supposed to connect with someone who's never lived my life, anyway? No, seriously. Why am I expected to share my baggage with someone who'll never understand the constant terror of having a bomb in his chest? Besides, time is limited." For her, *very* limited. "Why waste a minute considering a past I can't change?" She was panting when she finished her speech. Climbing on her soapbox du jour took effort.

A pause. "Is Nick the one who complained about Cookie Standard Time and your constant tardiness?"

"No, that was Paul," she grated. Her only other long-term relationship. The same guy who'd temporarily razed her self-confidence with his "horrible to be around" barb. "And no need to remind me of another reason I've been cast aside. Nick is the wannabe hero who said I needed to stop thinking about game strategy 24/7 and start living for the future." Easy for him to do, since he had one.

Cookie had here and now.

When Nick had posted a one-on-one challenge via social media, she probably should have declined. Sometimes opportunities were like the *Titanic*. Big, luxurious and pretty, but destined to sink. Debuting a new hat during a livestream—a great opportunity. Losing a game because she couldn't suck down oxygen—an iceberg. Physically, she hadn't been at her best or even her most mediocre for months.

Her male counterparts still let their mothers cut the crust off their sandwiches. Yet, she had to maintain double the kill rate or viewers lost interest. Their interest helped pay her bills.

Forget the money, though. Forget the sponsorships and influencer deals. She played because she had no other choice. Her heart wouldn't let her.

Oh, the things she'd do, if ever she got a transplant. Finally, she'd experience the spark—the zest for life—everyone else seemed to have. A burning intensity for more. For better. Then, her real life adventures could kick off. Nothing and no one would stop her.

As Cookie chugged a bottle of water, she realized she'd forgotten to give shout-outs to her sponsors during the battle. "Well, crap." *Four* dozen emails now waited in her inbox, guaranteed.

Sighing, she toed empty snack bowls aside and climbed out of her game chair to stretch. Her back protested, and she winced. Maybe she should be more understanding of Pearl Jean's supposed sciatica?

Think of the she-beast, and she will appear. Pearl Jean marched down the hall, a woman on a mission. "I hope you're happy with yourself." She wagged a finger in Cookie's direction. "All your chatter made it impossible for me to sleep."

The old biddy stood at five-foot-seven, an inch taller than Cookie. They were both plump in the bust and the butt, and could easily pass for a hot young granddaughter and her thousand-year-old grandmother. A fact Cookie loved to tease her friend about. Although they didn't have very similar features.

Cookie possessed shoulder-length brown hair, smooth pale skin and gray eyes; Pearl Jean had a cap of silvery curls, lined golden skin and navy eyes. An older Marilyn Monroe, she liked to say.

With a wry undertone, Cookie said, "Next time take out your hearing aids. Problem solved."

Pearl Jean sputtered a moment.

Sugars jumped to the floor and wound around Cookie's legs, letting her know he expected his evening meal. She'd found him in her backyard last year, injured and freezing to death. With a little online help, she'd nursed him back to health. They'd been together ever since.

He meow-meowed with the whiniest voice. Sugars-speak for *Faster, woman.*

"Okay, okay." She saluted Pearl Jean before heading to the kitchen, dragging the oxygen tank behind her. Strands of fur clung to yoga pants in desperate need of a wash. One day. Soonish. Laundry required energy, and Cookie had burned through hers to slaughter a digital enemy.

A floorboard whined when she passed, and another groaned as if collapse was imminent. Because of course it did. She'd scrimped and saved to purchase this old farmhouse, eager to fulfill a childhood dream of living in a big, boxy home with acres of land, a white picket fence and a massive oak tree with a tire swing. Visions of neighbors offering welcome casseroles and borrowing eggs for last-minute baking emergencies had danced in her head.

She'd craved a community similar the those she'd seen on TV. Everyone shopped at the same grocery store, despised the same high school football team, and shared way too much personal information with each other.

She'd thought, *Get the house. Spend the money. Enjoy your life while you can.*

Translation: *All aboard the* Titanic.

Opportunity. Crash. Sink.

Now the house slowly crumbled around her. Small-town Wi-Fi came straight from the pits of hell. In a cart. Without wheels. Thousand year old Mr. Benson, the only neighbor within walking distance, had never given her the time of day, much less a culinary masterpiece.

Whatever. Cookie had better things to do than lament failed reveries. She concentrated on preparing a bowl of nibbles according to Suggy's specific demands. Wet food in the center, dry food forming a perfect circle around it, with ABSOLUTELY NOTHING TOUCHING THE EDGES OF THE BOWL. If a single kernel made its way outside the circle of acceptable morsels, her precious A-hole refused to eat.

When she finished, he looked over the offering and issued a meow of approval. As he ate, she set course for her bedroom to steal a quick power nap—nope. Pearl Jean stood guard in the living room.

Her roommate stepped directly in her path and motioned to the couch. "Have a seat. We're going to talk. In case there's any confusion, I'm not asking."

"What's wrong?" Without the aid of war-spawned adrenaline, fatigue seeped into Cookie's bones. Have a seat? No problem. She released the tank and plopped onto the cushions. "What do you want to talk about?"

"Your reactions were slower than usual today, and you struggled to maintain your focus. I could tell."

So the old bat had watched due to more than boredom, huh?

Needing a moment to consider the best response, she pitched her gaze over the well-worn floral furnishings, a huge plasma screen TV, portraits of smiling families she and Pearl Jean had found at various yard sales, and a coffee table scattered with all her must-haves: a bottle of water, iPod, earbuds, a bag of crackers, ChapStick, an iPad loaded with true crime and romance novels, and more snacks.

From this vantage point, she had a view of the bay windows across the room. Outside, clouds rimmed in rose and lavender smeared the sky, the sun setting over her neglected acreage. Fruit trees no longer produced and weeds abounded. What she wouldn't give to have the energy to garden. Or at least the money to pay someone to do it.

Here goes. "I'm fine today, Pearl Jean, and I'll be fine tomorrow. Honest. You don't need to worry. You're not going to wake up and discover I'm dead."

"Are you sure? Because you look like death *right now.*"

"Yeah, but I always look like death lately." Twelve months ago, her doctor guessed she had eleven months to go, unless they located a new heart. *Living on borrowed time now.* "It's coming, just as we knew it would."

"No. There's got to be something else we can do. Have you pursued ads on the darknet wide webs?"

"That isn't what it's call—"

"I don't care what it's called. Use it. You might get lucky and find someone who's selling a perfectly acceptable pre-owned organ."

Cookie blinked back tears. No emotion. If she broke down, Pearl Jean would break down.

"No, I'm not going to search for a preowned heart on the quote-unquote darknet wide webs," she said softly, evenly.

"Is money the problem? Because I'm willing to donate my Social Security."

Lying there, fatigue got the better of her. Cookie fought to keep her eyes open. "Can we postpone this conversation?"

"No, we cannot," her best friend cried. "This is life-or-death."

Guess she'd have to end this the Cookie way. Brutally. "All right, then. Let's talk about the fact that I'm not going to get a new heart. I'm going to die sooner rather than later. Before I go, I want to ensure you and Suggy have someone to take care of you." Preferably someone willing to attend to the house panther's smallest whim, exactly as he deserved, while this same paragon resisted the urge to stab themselves in the ears anytime Pearl Jean convinced herself she'd rung Death's doorbell.

In other words, Cookie needed to find the unicorn of people. The champagne of friends. A generic brand, maybe. Cheap didn't always mean lower quality.

"Okay, yes," Pearl Jean said with a nod. "We can postpone this conversation."

Finished with his meal, Suggy jumped onto the couch, pranced across Cookie's legs and curled up on her chest.

As she reached out to pet him, she caught a flash of light from her cell phone. Next, her ringer activated. How odd. Before the match with Nick, she'd turned off the sound.

Wait. She'd programed the cell to make a single exception.

Her jaw went slack. No. No way. This couldn't be happening. But was it?

Riiiing. She jerked her gaze to Pearl Jean. "I think…

that might be…a heart." The last two words emerged as a squeak.

"Well? What are you waiting for?" Pearl Jean vibrated with excitement. "Answer it. Answer the phone right now."

"All right, all right." She grabbed the phone, doing her best not to disturb the cat, trembling as she placed the device to her ear. "Hello? Yes?"

"Chantel Bardot?" a jubilant voice asked.

Hearing her birth name threw her for a loop. "Y-yes, this is she. Her. I mean, the first one. The first one I said. She." Her gaze remained on Pearl Jean. *Please, please, please be the news I've waited so long to hear.* "And you are?"

"I'm the one who gets to tell you that we found a match. Your surgeon and transplant team have been notified." She continued spewing facts, but Cookie could no longer hear her.

This was truly happening?

I'm going to live?

CHAPTER FOUR

Six Months Later

COOKIE DARTED HER gaze as she walked Sugars on a leash. The backyard appeared normal. Morning sunlight filtered through a canopy of branches, courtesy of massive oaks. Birds chirped from twisted limbs. A family of rabbits observed her little trio from behind a bush blooming with flowers, despite the winter season.

Everything seemed normal. Sugars stalked a billowing leaf, and Pearl Jean puttered beside her on a scooter. But nothing was normal for Cookie.

For 26 years, she'd felt as if she'd existed rather than lived. Never as fast or as strong as other kids. Kept on a strict diet and a never-ending medication regimen. Myriad doctor visits. Then, suddenly, the heart her parents had sparked at her conception was gone, cut out of her chest. Now, someone else's heart powered her body. Someone who'd died, selflessly giving Chantel Melissa Bardot a chance to live. And yet...

She still lacked zest. For so long, she'd expected to die. She'd resigned herself to it, growing comfortable with her worldview. But her vantage point had shifted. Now she was supposed to live for herself, as well as the woman who'd saved her. No doubt her family expected Cookie to do great things with the gift she'd been given. The pressure!

And how many other patients had been more worthy of the heart? What if Cookie screwed up, the sacrifice wasted? She had no idea what to do with this second chance.

The worst part? Paranoia had reset her brain. She couldn't shake the feeling she was being hunted. She felt it all—the—time. Even now, a cold sweat glazed her palms.

Along with the paranoia came a sensation of being both unstoppable and as fragile as glass, capable of everything and nothing at once. Presurgery, she'd had motivation but no energy. Postsurgery, she had plenty of energy but a confused motivation. It was galling, and it kept her imprisoned on her property.

Did other—normal—people feel this way, as if they didn't know up from down or in from out?

Had she gained a heart only to lose her mind?

She might ask her therapist, if ever she garnered the courage to leave the farm.

"You look ridiculous, by the way," Pearl Jean said, mist puffing in front of her face. The woman was a truth teller, no matter what.

"Me?" Cookie took a sip of her steaming coffee…inside a wineglass, because dish day was tomorrow…then readjusted the ginormous sunglass perched on her nose. "*I* look ridiculous?"

"Yes, you."

"I'm wearing clothes you knitted for me." She spread her arms to show off the sweater and scarf Pearl Jean had given her last Christmas, paired with a T-shirt that read "Stay-at-Home Cat Mom," black yoga pants, and fuzzy house boots with rubber soles. Only the world's greatest attire. Well, that and Daisy Dukes paired with cowboy boots, her gonna-snag-a-good-time outfit. Oh, and also the gowns she sometimes donned for cosplay. Those rocked, too.

"I thought you'd be smart enough to bury the sweater and scarf in a drawer," her friend said.

"What can I say? Comfort and warmth trump style, every time." Undergarment-wise, she'd gone with a minimizing sports bra and her favorite granny panties. *The* must-haves for every woman's lingerie drawer. This was a hill she would die on.

Except, lately she'd been eyeing sexy lingerie online with great interest, wondering how the silky material might feel against her skin and how a boyfriend might react. Even though she didn't have a boyfriend, or even want one. Guys required work, and they always bailed.

There was a higher likelihood she'd get a tattoo. Her first and another recent desire. Sometimes she imagined strands of ivy etched in rich hues of green around her wrists, stretching over her hands and fingers.

"And the Cheetos in your hair?" Pearl Jean asked. "Is that part of your *style*?"

Locks of hair fell from her sloppy bun as she skirted around a plant, avoiding contact in case something freaky happened. Sometimes, with a brush of her skin, flowers instantly bloomed. But she wasn't going to think about that. New panic would rise.

"Just so you know, you look ridiculous, too," she said with a snippy tone.

"Please. Your Pearl Jeanlousy is showing." Despite the chill, she sipped iced sweet tea from a squeeze bottle. Because "the hot stuff sucks" and "sometimes a girl needs to forget she might be coming down with diabetes." A big yellow beach hat topped her silver curls, shielding two sunspots she believed looked more suspicious today than yesterday. As usual, a muumuu and bathrobe draped her plump frame. "I've always thought of myself as a good single malt. Better with age and able to knock anyone flat on their face."

"I absolutely agree you're a good single malt—older than time. Fingers crossed I'll get to see you served on ice."

Pearl Jean snorted. "Morbid brat."

"Old crone."

Sugars turned his attention to a bug, chasing it— No. Sorry. He *ate* the bug. How nice.

The scent of mesquite wafted through the air. Mr. Benson must have fired up his grill. She breathed deep without the aid of an oxygen tank. A truly wonderful experience, until her belly twisted with hunger. Ugh. She needed breakfast. Correction: she needed *fourth* breakfast. Since waking in the hospital with tubes everywhere, she'd experienced bottomless pit hunger without gaining a pound.

In an effort to clog said pit, Cookie had consumed her weight in powdered donuts, the aforementioned Cheetos, and mint chip cookies earlier. Guess she'd have to keep trying.

Two butterflies fluttered past and— Whoa! They did *not* have *human faces*. Did they?

The mutant insects circled back, coming closer, and Cookie sucked in a breath. They did! Their very human-looking mouths moved as if speaking, but she detected no sounds. When she panicked and waved her hand through the air, her fingers disrupted their images.

They'd been nothing but mist?

Her stomach roiled. What did that mean? Was she asleep or insane?

She chanced a glimpse at Pearl Jean. "Did you see the butterflies?"

The other woman wrinkled her brow. "What butterflies?"

Maybe Cookie should start taking her medication again? "Never mind," she muttered.

"No, not never mind." Her friend jerked the wheel of her scooter to avoid a rock. "I've been noticing some strange happenings around here, and I think we should discuss them."

Uh-oh. Pearl Jean must want answers about Cookie's more personal changes. *Not ready.* She shrank into herself, as if becoming a smaller visual target might stop the conversation mid-track. "Let's agree that unusual things *have* been happening and leave it at that, okay? Please?"

"Save your pleas. This is *not* okay. You recovered from major surgery in a matter of weeks." The words spewed from Pearl Jean. "You don't even have a scar. Six months ago, your sable hair reached your shoulders. Now half the strands are pink and they reach the middle of your back. A length you've grown twice! Yes, I know you shaved your head the other day. Before, your eyes were gunmetal gray. Now, they're green with only specks of gray, and plants miraculously flourish in your presence. So? What's going on?"

Every accusation hit her like a punch. Her friend didn't even know the half of it. Without her medication—a supposed death sentence for someone in her situation—she had thrived.

Maintaining a neutral expression was difficult, but she managed it. "Here's an idea. You're finally fully senile?"

"Oh! And you always smell like fresh-cut roses, especially when you sweat. It's nauseating."

"I'm wearing too much Chantel N°5?"

"Don't get cute with me, hon. You might look like your avatars with those big round eyes and bigger red lips, but you've got darkness in you, and it's only intensified since your surgery. No," she interjected when Cookie opened her mouth to respond. "Don't tell me I'm imagining this stuff. Tell me what the new heart has done to my best friend."

She wanted to. She did. A couple hundred times, she'd almost done it. But what if someone listened to their conversation? Yesterday morning she'd mentioned a jones for pancakes with homemade strawberry jelly. By noon, ads for pancakes and special jellies were popping up on every website she visited.

Call her a conspiracy nut, but spies were everywhere, eavesdropping always. If word about her changes ever spread, she might end up imprisoned in a government lab. One of the many reasons she'd skipped her last few medical checkups. Sticking with silence struck her as the best option.

Return to me.

Cookie gave an involuntary jolt. The deep, husky voice had drifted through her head, seeming to rise from a long-buried memory. That timbre…more sensual than a caress.

This wasn't the first time she'd heard those three little words. Like every time before, she *yearned* to obey. But return where? And why? How? Who was the speaker?

Feeling as if she were being watched again, she cast a glance over her shoulder. Soft, lush grass greeted her. Trees with swaying limbs. The farmhouse remained in view, an adorable travesty of peeling paint and broken boards she still hadn't gotten around to fixing. The perfect metaphor for her old life. Neglected, forgotten, and beaten to heck by storms.

Everything looked well, no one openly following her. But. Dude. Unease skittered down her spine.

She needed to shake this stupid paranoia, and fast.

"Pay attention to me," Pearl Jean snapped. "What do you know about the donor?"

Right. "Not much," she admitted. "I'm told she was my age and involved in some kind of accident. The family doesn't want to have contact with any of the organ recipients."

Seriously, was someone watching her?

"Be honest. Do you have superpowers or something?" Pearl Jean hit a bump, the lid popping off her squeeze bottle, sweet tea splashing over the rim and overflowing from its holder. "You can tell me. And you don't have to worry. I'm sure I'll probably learn to accept your freakishness in the future. After all, home is where heart is, and heart is where Cookie is."

Her throat tightened. Dang this woman. "Did you just speak Cookie Monster to me?" *Winning another little piece of my heart.*

Pearl Jean humphed. "Maybe."

"Fine. You want to talk, we'll talk." After throwing another suspicious glance over her shoulder, she picked up Suggy. "But only when we're in the house."

"No. No more waiting." Pearl Jean drove the scooter in front of Cookie, stopping her. "We're not leaving this spot until you explain what's happening."

Was there anyone more stubborn?

She looked over her shoulder. Left. Right. The unease amplified. "One way or another, we're going inside. Move it or lose it."

Her urgency proved as contagious as an imaginary disease. For once, Pearl Jean didn't argue. "Yes. Let's go inside."

In unison, they hustled toward the house. Halfway there, the butterfly people reappeared, zooming past Cookie, then backtracking to fly circles around her. When she drew up short, the two stopped with her, hovering nearby. Watching her.

She noted other details. Human faces, around twenty years old…human *bodies* the size of her index finger. Both beings were clad in clover leaves. The female had shoulder-length blue hair and white wings, while the male had white hair and blue wings.

"Please tell me you're seeing this," she croaked.

"Seeing what?" The scooter beeped as Pearl Jean backtracked, returning to her side. Worry clouded her expression. "Cookie! *Seeing what?*" she insisted.

"I don't know. Yet. But I'm ready to find out." Trembling, she passed Suggy to her friend, then reached out. The butterfly people didn't mist upon contact this time, but they didn't appreciate her action, either. They hissed at her, revealing sharp white fangs.

Danger! Her fingers heated in an instant. The sizzle started in her bones and radiated through her pores.

She jerked backward and snapped, "Take Sugars in the house, Pearl Jean." She'd never used such a harsh tone with her friend, but she meant business.

"You can't—"

"Go. Now." The heat spread over her palms, and she groaned. She shook her hands, surprised when literal flames failed to ignite. Wait. What was *that*?

Her jaw slacked as green leaves budded from her fingers. Coffee spilled as the wineglass slipped from her grip. Horror and confusion bombarded her. Vines uncoiled, extending past her nails. Growing. Twining together and slithering over the ground.

"Only a hallucination, only a hallucination," she chanted.

"Then why am I seeing it, too?" Pearl Jean screeched. "Can't rationalize this…"

Up ahead, the vines sprouted up, up, as if reaching for the sky. At the seven-foot mark, the ends grew together, forming a thorny arch still connected to her hands. As thick fog filled the space between the stalks, an incredible force wrenched her forward. She stumbled and tried to dig in her heels, then fought to disconnect from the vines. She failed on both counts.

The vines only pulled faster. Soon she was choking on fear and being dragged across the lawn.

"Help us! Someone help us," Pearl Jean shouted behind her. "Cookie!"

"Pearl Jean!" No! Her heart thudded as she flew through the fog.

CHAPTER FIVE

DAZED, PANTING, COOKIE jumped to her feet. She surveyed her surroundings. What the—how—*what? Can't process*... Her sunlit backyard was gone. In its place was…something else. And it wasn't her imagination. This was all too real.

She spun, her heart thudding faster, gaze darting. Pink-and-white trees abounded. Rainbow flowers appeared as fluffy as cotton candy, releasing ethereal petals into a warm breeze. More butterfly people flew about, raining glitter. At her right, a babbling brook rushed over glowing crystals. On the other side of the water, shadows slipped over gnarled trees and brittle grass. Jagged leaves snapped together, as if chewing on something. Maybe they were. Bloodred crumbs/drops fell from the corners.

Cookie gulped as she focused on something moving at her feet… Screaming, she hopped around to avoid hundreds of tiny spiders charging out from beneath her house boots.

The butterfly people—fairies?—remained at eye level, zigging and zagging around her.

As soon as she quieted, she picked up the buzz of their wings and the squeak of their voices.

"She's her, yes?"

"Oh, yes. And no."

"Her but not her."

This couldn't be right. *None of this* could be right. It was time to go home.

Cookie whirled around, determined. She'd dive through the portal or doorway or whatever it was and—"No!" The vines had disconnected from her and withered, the remains drifting away on a gentle breeze.

Frantic, she patted the stalkless air. "Pearl Jean?" she shouted, going still. Tremors wracked her. "Sugars?" Where were they?

She licked her lips. Maybe she could create another... portal? with those vines? What you did once, you could do again. Right?

A humorless laugh escaped. Re-create something she didn't understand? Yeah. No big deal. Still, she had to try.

Cookie extended her arms and shook her hands. Nothing happened. She shook with more force, but the heat never reignited in her fingertips.

"Come on, come on." She wiggled. Flapped. Jumped. Still nothing.

Hysteria bubbled up, making a mockery of the panic. How was she supposed to get home? She *needed* to get home. Pearl Jean and Sugars— A vicious roar tore through the forest, and she sucked in a breath.

Currents of rage crackled, prickling her skin. The fairies zoomed off as fast as lightning.

Cookie gripped her throat in reflex, calling, "Wait. Come back."

Alone in a strange place? This was fine. Everything was fine. Her knees knocked, threatening to fold. What should she do? Stay here or venture out for help?

She executed another spin, scanning her surroundings more carefully. The trees weren't actually pink, she realized. Hundreds of ants with glowing bellies crawled over the trunks. Briar patches grew along the edges of the brook, warning visitors away. Purple mushrooms oozed on a fallen log. In the distance, a deer with mother-of-pearl horns munched on nuts and examined her without concern.

Even as another bloodcurdling roar sounded, making her shudder, the deer continued eating, unfazed. *Because he knows I'm slower and more likely to be dinner.*

Breathe. Just breathe. Light-headed, she clasped a branch, hoping to steady herself.

"Ouch!" A thousand needles seemed to prick her palm, and she hurriedly released the lifeline. In seconds, large red welts popped up on her hand and forearm. Queasy, she hunched over.

What the— A thick tree root curled around her ankle and yanked.

Cookie crashed to her butt, air bursting from her lungs and stars winking before her eyes. Then. That moment. The nausea won the war. Twisting to the side, she vomited the contents of her stomach.

When she finished, she clambered to her feet, unwilling to stay down any longer than necessary. She had no experience with…stargates? wormholes? But her avatar had plenty. In the video game, she remained ready for anything always. Here, now, the stakes were a thousand times higher. Relax her guard, even for a moment? No.

Another roar erupted, and birds took flight. Branches bounced and slapped her. Though she wobbled, she didn't fall. Thankfully, the roarer—whatever it was—sounded farther away.

Crickets chirped with relief, and locusts whirred. A frog croaked. Normal sounds in an abnormal situation.

She drew her arms around her middle, shrinking into herself. Before she figured out her next move, she needed to understand her previous one. Somehow, she'd…what?

Opened some kind of transport to a different location on Earth? Another dimension? Planet? Alternate reality?

The hysteria threatened to spike. She inhaled and exhaled for calm. For now, she accepted the fact that she'd left Oklahoma, and that she hadn't traveled by normal means. No more, no less. Now, she needed a plan to get home.

Okay. All right. This, she could do. Every quest she'd ever won, she'd tackled the same way: one step at a time.

Cookie slipped into game mode, her tasks aligning. Search for a nearby town. There, she could figure out the monetary system, acquire cash, food, shelter, weapons and answers. If someone drew her a world map, even better.

She couldn't allow fear to derail her, as if she were some kind of—Cookie shuddered—rookie.

In her experience, the biggest mistake new players made remained the same, no matter their age or skill. When fear of the unknown invaded, they disregarded their endgame. Rather than working to achieve a goal, they focused on quieting their sense of urgency, which only ever led to desperation.

Today's trials, tomorrow's strengths. A mantra she'd repeated over and over again as a child. If ever there'd been a time to bring it back...

Another roar left her reeling. Because it was *closer* than the first one. The creature, whatever it was, must have doubled back. She expected a hungry predator to breathe down her neck any second. Even the deer reacted, dashing away.

Time to blow this joint. Cookie plunged forward, following the same path as the deer. Dangers lurked all around. Not just the fairies and the roaring animals, but the plants. Anything could be poisonous.

No! She had lost sight of the deer.

To her surprise and relief, her feet seemed to know where

to go next, guiding her around this and that tree with no assistance from her mind. Resisting seemed foolish, since she had no idea where to go.

Optimistic she would stumble upon help, she waded across the brook…

LOST. STARVED AND dying of thirst. Exhausted and filthy. Too cold one minute and too hot the next. Beyond sore. Bruised and injured. Cookie was all of those things and more. Had she escaped the roaring monster, only to perish alone in a strange land?

As she trudged around a tree, she imagined an avatar somewhere safe and cozy, controlling *her*, making her go and go and go, no matter her feelings on the matter. She was pretty sure she'd used up all her pretend power bars. Remaining on her throbbing feet required energy she didn't have, but resting had been scratched out on today's list of activities. Her body refused to obey her mind, so on and on and on she walked. Resistance was futile.

Mud caked her from head to toe. She'd lost her beloved scarf and sweater somewhere along the way. Her hair had fallen from its bun, the too-long strands in tangles. At least she still smelled like flowers, blending in with nature, preventing predators from adding "tasty pink-haired snack" to their menus.

She gave a humorless laugh. Yeah, what a marvelous silver lining to her living nightmare.

Hours ago, she'd been forced to simplify her plan: keep going until she stumbled upon help or passed out. What else could she do? A thousand different times, in a thousand different ways, she'd tried to switch directions. Holding on to branches. Digging in her heels. Hugging tree trunks. Always her legs won the battle of wills and maneuvered her away from the obstacles, taking her nowhere.

Hours bled into each other, more and more fairies following her through the woods. Anytime she broke down and begged for answers or aid, they whispered among themselves and cast her furtive glances. No one ever responded to her directly.

A blessing in disguise, she supposed. "Now I can eat you little pricks without guilt," she snapped in their direction.

With a collective gasp of horror, they shot into the trees to hide.

Something she'd noted: the fairies came in all colors, everything from the lightest pastels to the brightest neons to the darkest shades. Which made her wonder…what if they weren't fairies, after all, but pixies?

In Rhoswyn, her favorite level of *The Fog A.E.*, there were nonplayable characters or NPCs known as pixies, and they came in all colors, too. Which made her wonder if she were maybe, possibly, still on the operating table, and this was a medicated delusion after all, her mind firing off scenarios as she died. Or if she'd already died and this was a type of Hell. Sometimes, when she was too exhausted to correct herself with logic, she even wondered if she'd somehow, well, opened a portal into a world based on her video game. Kind of like *Jumanji*, but also not like *Jumanji*.

That was dumb, right? A figment of her overactive gamer's brain trying to make sense of a bad situation. But, what if she had somehow entered a real life version of *The Forest of Good and Evil*? *Ready, player one.*

More than the pixies, the land and the animals bore a wealth of similarities to Rhoswyn. In both locales, rabbits were stripped like zebras. Frogs had the most endearing cat whiskers. Most of the snakes she'd come across had possessed two heads. Foxes used their nine-point tails like a whip.

What if the designer of *The Fog A.E.* had visited this land?

Once, she'd caught sight of a cluster of ogres who'd looked just like a painting hanging in the game's main HQ. Huge, furry and beastly, with tusks and a tail. They lived to kill invaders.

Cookie had braced for an attack as they'd snorted and stomped with boundless aggression. However, not a single ogre had ever even taken a step in her direction. As if she were marked with a shield of protection, the way avatars were often marked. For the right price, anyway.

Twice she'd passed an enclave of trolls. Big, muscled brutes with horns. In the game, they often beat and enslaved weary travelers. They, too, had exuded aggression at the sight of her. Like the ogres, they'd kept their hands to themselves.

What if her heart donor had come from this land? What if the organ had unlocked a door between the two worlds? It was an idea, anyway.

In the game, pixies coexisted alongside fae. Mystical beings with a variety of magical powers. Which explained her sudden ability to grow ivy beneath her skin, in the rich soil of her veins. Magic also explained her inability to halt her steps—she was being led by an invisible chain. Step. Step. Step. This way. Pivot. That way. Where would she end up?

What if Cookie's donor had been…fae?

Everything had changed after the transplant. The way she'd healed with supernatural speed. Her total lack of scars. The Miracle Grow Rapunzel hair. Skin ivy. What she knew beyond a doubt: a new world meant new rules. If *The Fog A.E.* was based on this land, magic was the norm. She might be able to do more than vine harvesting or whatever.

And dang it, was someone following her? The unease returned.

Hand unsteady, she smoothed hair from her damp brow and glanced over her shoulder. A pixie hovered mere inches from her face. A pretty pink Thumbelina, who decided to perch on her shoulder.

Cookie's nerves sharpened as the little beauty clasped her ear with a surprisingly strong grip and spoke directly into it. "Turn right."

"I'm sorry, but my feet don't want to go right."

Thumbelina tugged on her lobe, shouting, "Turn. Right. Here. Human. Fool."

She helps me? Was the current direction too dangerous for the "human fool?"

Adrenaline spiked. Gearing up to resist again, Cookie reached for a branch. Once again, her feet rebelled, continuing to march forward. She gritted her teeth and twisted, straining to grab a sturdier branch. That one right there. Almost...

White-hot pinpricks seared her skin as ivy budded from her forearms and hands. Vines uncoiled and propagated, wrapping around the tree's trunk and jerking her to a stop. Except for her feet. Step, step, step. Going nowhere. To her great relief, the foliage proved stronger than the invisible chain and she remained in place.

Wait. Her ears twitched. Was that a rush of water? A whimper escaped.

Smacking her dry, chapped lips and envisioning a pool of fresh, delicious, amazing, wonderful water, Cookie used the stalks of ivy to push her body forward, despite the objections of her feet. The farther she ventured from the undesired path, the less her feet fought her mind. Soon, she no longer required the vines. When they withered, she remained on her current route.

I did it? I won? Branches grazed her cheeks, a pinprick of heat here, a pinprick of ice cold there, but she didn't care anymore. Victory felt good, and water awaited.

Thumbelina flew ahead of her, disappearing in a wall of foliage. Cookie pushed through the tangle and stumbled into a clearing with a small, crystal-clear pond. Tears welled, blurring her vision as she waded into the water. Cool liquid engulfed her, easing the worst of her aches.

She ducked under the surface; on her way up, she swallowed drink after drink, moaning with delight. How clean it tasted. Cleaner than anything she'd ever consumed at home.

Return to me.

The husky voice echoed inside her mind, a remnant of that long-forgotten memory. A dream. Part of her heated, part of her chilled.

Though she would love to linger in the pond, she exited, lumbering to the shore. Time to find a town. Between one step and another, the flash of an image invaded her mind, arresting her. A man. Naked. A tall, pale-haired brute, with rough but handsome features and a crapton of tattoos. The sides of his head were shaved, the top locks long and thick. Very Viking-y and utterly delicious.

Sculpted muscle packed every inch of his powerful body. Golden skin glistened with moisture. He wore an expression of murder and malice as he faced off with another man, who stood in shadows.

Cookie's heart leaped with excitement, as if shocked to life for the very first time. Even without a glimpse of the second guy's face, she responded to him?

He was as tall as the Viking, and equally muscled, with gorgeous, dusky skin. He wore a shirt and leather pants.

Metal claws tipped his fingers. Who was he? Danger emanated from him.

In the memory, a woman with long pink hair hurled her body in front of the second man.

Another heart leap. The woman had long pink hair. Pink. Cookie instinctively reached for a lock of her own cotton candy tresses.

The Viking waved his hand, mist curling from his fingertips as thin shards of ice shot out. Those shards cut into the pink-haired woman, who cried out with anguish.

He'd attacked her? Cookie's eyes narrowed. *He will pay.* Thanks to years of murder mysteries and true crime, she knew dozens of ways to get the job done. And hide the body afterward.

Groaning, the woman toppled to the ground—no, she was eased there by the second man. The dangerous one from the shadows.

As he moved, he entered a beam of light, providing Cookie with a glimpse of his features. Breath suddenly smoldered in her lungs. Tousled dark hair framed the most beautiful face ever created. He had thick, prominent brows and a proud nose, the perfect contrast for his soft lips. Deep amber irises reminded her of iced whiskey, framed by lashes long enough to curl. A strong jaw boasted layers of jet-black scruff.

He couldn't be real, but there he stood, front and center in her mind, dressed in all black and loaded with weapons as if he'd stepped out of a video game. Besides the claws, she spotted a crossbow, two short swords and several daggers.

Bringing deadly back.

The image faded, and she frowned, again wondering

who he was. And what about the killer Viking? The pink-haired girl?

Somewhere in the immediate area, a rustle of noise yanked Cookie from her thoughts. Someone or something approached, but were they friend or foe?

She dashed into a cluster of vines, similar to the strain she produced. The leaves were big enough to conceal—"Ahhhh!" A thorn ejected from a stalk and pierced her shoulder. Her limbs seized, rendered unworkable as pain rocketed through her.

She collapsed, unable to catch herself, and ate dirt. Though she fought internally, she couldn't move outwardly.

"I told you she'd tire herself out soon enough," a male bragged from somewhere nearby.

A moment later, a shadow fell over her. Horse hoofs stomped near her face.

Hard fingers gathered a handful of her hair and lifted her into the air. Panic owned her as she ran her gaze over her captor. A centaur? He had the torso of a man and the lower body of a horse. Thumbelina perched on his shoulder, smirking at Cookie.

I was set up?

Horror iced her, but rage seared her.

The centaur smiled, a cruel twisting of his lips. To others she couldn't see, he called, "Our hunt is a success, boys. I caught our dinner."

CHAPTER SIX

KAYSAR SWIPED A dagger from his dresser, his mood worse than usual. He turned on his heels to… He couldn't recall. He'd probably planned to kill someone for daring to do something he didn't like. But who? Oh, what did it matter? He huffed with irritation and tossed the weapon to the floor.

As he paced through his bedroom, his thoughts strayed to Princess Lulundria. His obsession. Where was she? Why hadn't she returned to him? Had her injuries healed without the elderseed? They must have. He'd ordered her return, and she had no choice but to obey.

But why wasn't she here? In his home. His bed. He should be tempting her beyond reason and cuckolding her husband in every way imaginable. Where, where?

Roaring, Kaysar swung his arm over the surface of the dresser. Jars flew to the floor. Glass shattered, clear liquid gushing out. The sharp, pungent scent of preservation fluid saturated the air, stinging his nostrils.

"Noooo!" *What have I done?* Each jar contained a tongue he'd cut from King Hador's mouth. His most prized treasures. Now they rested on gold-veined marble, unprotected, as if they meant *nothing* to him.

He rushed to crouch and gather. *Mine!* He protected what was his. Always. Without exception. He must. If he didn't, who would?

As he scrambled about, streams of red trickled from his

palms, staining the floor as well as the tongues he held. He must have cut his fingers on the glass shards. Kaysar shrugged. Pain registered as vividly as pleasure—hardly at all.

"Eye," he bellowed. Where was his seer? Shouldn't she know what he wanted before he knew he wanted it? Right now, he required unbroken jars and preservation fluid. "Eye!"

A flurry of noise sounded behind his door. The seer rushed inside a moment later, holding out a single jar, liquid sloshing over the rim.

"I'm sorry, I'm sorry," she called. "I tried to carry more, but I dropped them. Why don't you cram—I mean *store* your collection in here for now? Yes, like that. Stuff the horrid blobs inside. You're doing an amazing job, majesty."

He glared at her. "I want to know where my princess is. Why haven't you found her? Why hasn't she returned to me? Why can't you tell me if she's dead or alive?" Why, why, why?

Eye sealed the lid on the brimming jar. "Do you think I'd come to your private bedchambers without answers, majesty?" She humphed, as if insulted, the hem of her yellow gown swishing around her ankles.

Excitement and dread collided, igniting a noticeable tremor in his hands. "Tell me."

"You'll be pleased to know your princess has returned to Astaria at last."

Kaysar's dark mood dissolved in an instant. He grinned as he clasped Eye by the shoulders. "She is healed?"

A firm nod. "She is. Completely."

How wonderful. His grin widened as he rocked to his heels. So much to do. Kaysar wished to look his best for their reunion. Her seduction commenced *today*.

"Where is she?" he demanded, already stripping for a shower.

Jaw slack, Eye spun and faced the wall. "I'm still working on that part, majesty."

"You aren't working fast enough. I know this, because *I do not have her with me.*" He flittered into the bathroom and showered in a hurry, then carefully selected a white tunic and black leathers before arming up. Two short swords. A pair of daggers. He bypassed the bow and quiver of arrows. Not today. Too bulky.

He donned his favorite rings. Those bearing molars he'd wrenched from an enemy's mouth. Last, he secured his best set of metal claws to his fingers.

He didn't need to glance in a mirror to know this was a panty melting day for him. Women loved his face. And his body. A rare few even loved his evil.

Kaysar stalked into the bedroom. Eye sat in the chair at his desk, the jar of tongues beside her.

She popped to her feet, words exploding from her. "I know where she is."

Anticipation stole his breath, his lungs burning. "Well?"

For a moment, she chewed on her bottom lip. "I won't tell you," she said, nearly losing her head in the process. "Not until I explain something else. The princess did die in the mortal world, Kaysar."

What? "You told me she survived."

"And she did. But she also died. Yet now she lives."

He tried to make sense of her claims. When he failed, rage drove him directly in front of the seer. Glaring, he gripped her delicate shoulders and shook. "Did you lie to me, Eye?"

Despite her tremors, she craned up her head to meet his gaze. "I didn't lie, I swear it. As if I would dare."

Only slightly mollified, he lightened his grip. "Explain, then. How is Lulundria both dead and healed?"

"I don't know, but she is." Eye used her most appeasing tone. "She died, but now she lives. Her heart beats..." Her voice trailed off as her expression glazed over, a vision overwhelming her. "You'd best hurry, majesty. The centaurs... their village. She's soon to die. Again. For good."

The centaurs thought to slay his princess, ruining his vengeance? Kaysar's rage returned, igniting a fire in his soul. He flittered to the outskirts of the centaur village, hidden in the heart of the Nightlands.

A field of wildflowers stretched before him. Beyond it, hundreds of half horse, half fae creatures went about their days. The men were bare-chested, the women covered by leather vests.

Kaysar flittered throughout the encampment, scanning. Here, soldiers trained for war, combatants battering each other with spears while riders practiced galloping, dodging hurdles and shooting arrows at the same time. Onlookers cheered every success and booed every failure. Over here, workers tended pots of soup and stoked firepits.

When he found no sign of Lulundria, his control frayed. Where had she— Ah. There she was. A soft wind carried a faint hint of her sweet perfume.

Like a stallion in heat, Kaysar tracked his chosen female, alternating between sprinting and flittering. He leaped over rocks and raced around trees. Carnivorous foliage shrank from him, eager to avoid his touch. Little wonder. Aggression charged his every action. Scanning, searching... Nothing had ever been so important to him.

Laughter rang out. Multiple sources, both male and female. The princess's scent strengthened, coating his breath.

Glee replaced Kaysar's rage as he reached a well-worn path, marred with hoofprints.

Spying the head of a centaur procession, he flittered to a thick branch, high in a tree, and crouched. Twenty warriors trotted in the path he'd traveled toward the village. Some of the soldiers were dark, some light, some spotted. All were armed, maintaining a steady trot and constantly hunting for predators.

Kaysar studied the tail end of the procession, where the prisoners were kept. Two males led a wagon bursting with fae, forest nymphs, and a handful of mortals. Dirty faces pressed against silver bars, bleak eyes peering out, seeking a savior.

Soon enough, they would learn a harsh truth. You could count on no one but yourself.

The centaurs hoped to use the mortals as servants, the forest nymphs as sex slaves, and the fae as food. A culinary horror meant to extend the eaters' lives.

Unlike the fae, who often lived an infinite number of millennia, centaurs usually expired after fifty or sixty years. However, the consumption of a fae—any fae but a royal—could buy a centaur an extra ten years or so. The royals were a different breed entirely. Eat one of them, and you gained an immortal's eternal life. The reason Eye had warned the princess was soon to die?

Kaysar released a soft snarl. The centaurs thought to *eat* his vengeance?

Oh, the pain they were soon to suffer...

Where was his princess? He drummed his claws against the tree trunk, impatient as he studied the rest of the procession. In the middle of the pack, two warriors carried a log between them, an end resting upon each male's shoulder. A woman hung from the center. Filthy rags clothed her, the length of her pink hair dragging over dirt and rocks.

Relief punched Kaysar, every fiber of his being assuring him of her identity. He had found Princess Lulundria.

Nothing could stop his vengeance now.

The centaurs had tied her wrists and ankles, dangling her from the beam like a prized hog. A tunic was stuffed inside her mouth, its sleeves knotted at her nape to secure it in place. *They practically gift wrapped her for me.*

Perhaps she'd be so overcome with gratitude after his rescue, she'd forget the little skirmish he'd had with her husband, the day she'd run from him.

Trying not to smile, Kaysar flittered to the start of the convoy.

The leader reared up, then raised a fist, calling, "Halt." As he settled, Kaysar's identity clicked, and the color drained from his golden skin. "King Kaysar." The centaur bowed his head in acknowledgment. "How…blessed we are to see you."

Though the soldier stood several feet taller than Kaysar, he quaked with fear. As he should. A pink pixie sat on his shoulder, watching Kaysar warily.

The centaur asked, "How may we serve you?"

He'd dealt with this colt before. Race, the cocky son of the centaurian emperor, considered himself a formidable foe. He wasn't.

The male had seized a Frostline, against orders. Now, he paid the toll.

"It's come to my attention that you failed to pay this month's Heartbeat Tax." Monies owed for Kaysar's willingness to let him *have* a heartbeat. "You'll be happy to know I'm feeling benevolent. I've decided you may apologize with a gift. I'll hear your thanks now."

Blink, blink. "Th-thank you. But…" The warrior inched backward. "The next payment isn't due for another week."

"Which means you're already two days late, doesn't it?" Kaysar chided, enjoying the man's discomfort. "For this unforgivable blunder, I'll expect double your usual fee. Also, at your insistence, I'll be choosing my own gift."

"Of course, but—"

"But? I don't recall requesting a debate about this. Now, what shall I choose?" With his hands clasped behind his back, Kaysar meandered through the ranks. No one wanted to die, so no one attempted to halt him. Not shoving everyone aside and rushing to the princess required immense effort. By some miracle, he sustained a slow, unhurried pace.

Race trotted to his side. "Perhaps you'd allow me to aid your selection? I'm happy to have my men show you everything we own while you sit and rest." He clapped his hands in command.

"No," Kaysar said simply, no one daring to rush over. Finally, his patience received its reward. The log came into view…and there she was. Princess Lulundria of the Summer Court, with marital ties to the Winter Court.

Pleasure unfurled. *So close to my goal.*

As she struggled against her bonds, their eyes met and— she stilled. Kaysar stutter-stepped. To remain upright, he flittered his next step. Once steady, he paused. His heart thundered in his chest.

This wasn't Lulundria.

Oh, she had the requisite pink hair, but the strands were intertwined with sable. And her skin…she glowed with radiant light, a beacon. Would he instigate an eclipse if he stood between her and the sun?

She had the most delicate features, reminding him of Drendall, the doll his sister had carried. Such imperfect perfection. A treasure trove in need of further study. A wide forehead led to thicker than average eyebrows. Big eyes. Exquisitely big. Long black lashes surrounded irises the color of a forest at sunset.

He pulled at his collar. Looking into those eyes did something to him. Shifted something. He didn't understand or like it. But he didn't want to stop it. Frowning, he forced his attention to her next features. Pink cheeks. A button nose. Lush red lips parted around the gag. A tiny dimple dotted what looked to be a stubborn chin.

She died and yet she lives.

Eye's words played inside his head. Lulundria had died and…this girl had eaten her heart, somehow *becoming* the fae princess? No. Wrong. The centaur did not become the royals they ate.

Could she be another Summer Court princess?

No again. He *sensed* Lulundria.

Had she worn a magical illusion before? It was possible. Some fae possessed such an ability.

"You don't want her," Race said, then forced a laugh. He rubbed the reddened marks littering his chest. "She bites."

Even better. "Give her to me." No longer could he mask his eagerness, the words spilling from him. "I want her. She's mine."

Tone hardening, Race told him, "Ask anything else of me. But the girl, I keep."

Did the centaur realize he'd rested a hand on the hilt of his sword?

Around them, soldiers stiffened. The males might not wish to challenge the King of the Nightlands, but they'd obey their leader. They wanted what he wanted, after all. A couple bites of the girl, ensuring their eternal life.

New sparks of rage ignited, burning through Kaysar.

"You may be the son of an emperor, but you inhabit the Nightlands. *My* lands. Have you forgotten my rule?"

Race bristled but gritted out, "I have not."

"Say it. Tell me the rule."

The centaur heaved every breath. An attempt to control his temper? "Do not unsheathe a weapon in Kaysar's vicinity unless we plan to kill him," he said, pushing the words through clenched teeth.

"That's right. So, you will remove your hand from your sword and gift me with the girl, or I will kill you and every member of your hunting party. I might turn my sights to your families next." Kaysar did not threaten. He vowed. "Decide. Now."

CHAPTER SEVEN

THE DARK-HAIRED HOTTIE from Cookie's vision! He was here, he was real, and he was horrifying. Beautiful and terrible at once, with a threatening glint in his eyes. An angel merged with a devil, both haunting and haunted.

He would look super-hot in a mug shot.

In her vision, she'd compared those dark eyes to iced whiskey. In person, they were set ablaze. Before, he'd had scruff on his jaw. Now, he had a full beard. He was even taller than she'd realized. At least six and a half feet of pure warrior, with the most sublime muscle mass.

Two elaborately detailed swords crossed at his nape, precious gems glistening from the hilts. The kind of weapons she utilized in the video game.

A white shirt molded to a broad chest, veeing at the collar to reveal a dusting of black hair and a hint of tattoos. Lines and dots. Torn leather pants stretched over powerful thighs, the ends tucked into scuffed combat boots. Metal claws tipped his fingers. He wore half a dozen rings topped by…teeth?

If anyone could pull off an impossible win against the centaurs, it was this man. Especially considering he owned the land. Home court advantage, baby. Talk about the perfect ally for a fish out of water. But what did he plan to do with her after the battle? Anytime he glanced her way, he lit up like a little kid at Christmas, eager to tear the heads off his new toys.

Christmas…home… *Will I ever see my family again?*

Poor Pearl Jean. Poor Sugars. They didn't know what had happened to her, where she was, or even if she even lived. How lost they must be.

What are you doing, lamenting? The game isn't over. Fight!

Cookie's top priority had stamped itself in her brain—get home by any means necessary. If she had to defeat an army, she'd defeat an army. If she had to kill, she'd kill. Without question. She used to practice stabbing people. The motions, only the motions. And only to gain a better understanding of her avatar. But…

In a deep, secret part of her, she'd maybe kinda sorta… enjoyed it. That same deep, secret part of her yearned to kill her captors and leave their corpses rotting on the ground. An hour ago, Cookie had awoken like this, tethered and engulfed by the scent of horses and sweat as she dangled from a pole. The constant pressure inflamed the joints in her shoulders, ankles and hips. Her body screamed protests. Ants and other abominations crawled all over her, making her itch. If she could have peeled off every layer of her skin, she'd be nothing but raw muscle right now.

The centaurs had trussed her up into the perfect appetizer for any outdoor barbecue, planning to feast on her all-you-can-eat-buffet-style.

Hope you taste as sweet as you look, girlie. Soon you'll roast on a spit, and I'll pick your bones clean.

The earlier taunt echoed, sparking fury. As the horsemen had carted her through Nightmare Candyland, they'd speculated about the spices to use on her charred remains. They'd discussed owning nymphs as pets and claiming mortals as servants. She'd flowed from hysteria, to rage, to game mode, doing her best to think of an escape.

How many others had the centaurs harmed? How many others would they harm in the future, if they were allowed to live?

Oh, yes, she *yearned* to kill them. A desire that sprung from a place far deeper than the petty, vengeful side of herself that delighted when she witnessed a bad guy's downfall. A place she'd never had the guts to face before. But face it she would.

For whatever reason, she'd never felt more alive.

"I'm done waiting," the hottie with the incredible voice said. His name was Kaysar. He was the one who'd issued the command to return, and every time he spoke, she shivered.

He struck her as a man who murdered without hesitation, breaking a sweat or regretting his actions.

So why is he more *attractive by the minute?*

"Respond," he said. "Before I start singing."

Every centaur issued a rushed protest. Actual, flesh-and-blood centaurs. A fact that might forever blow her mind.

Why did the newcomer want her? Why fight an army to claim a stranger?

Unless he had nefarious plans for her, too?

Apprehension shook her. Before she embraced her panic, she should weigh the facts. In the vision, the pink-haired woman had jumped in front of this man, as if to shield him from the Viking. If she'd loved him enough to save him, he might not be such a bad guy. But what had happened to Pink after she'd gotten hit by those ice daggers? Had she survived? Did this man seek her out?

Cookie's heart leaped at the thought, another question rising. Did she share a connection with the woman? She'd felt a leap during the vision. Now, she felt an undeniable tug of kinship. A knowing she shouldn't be able to discern…

I have her heart.

The knowledge dawned, bright and sure. Did the man know the truth, too? Could he sense it? Had he come for the heart of his…lover?

Had he adored the pink-haired beauty?

If he could take on twenty centaurs and live, he could help Cookie. Out here, there were threats she knew nothing about. And never would she forget the two threats she'd learned about firsthand—treacherous pixies and poisonous vines. She needed an ally. A teammate. Someone who knew the lay of the land.

Hottie moved into a brighter beam of sunlight, as if stepping up to bat, and her breath caught. His jet-black locks gleamed with shades of cobalt, his dusky skin glimmering with flecks of molten gold. He had the most adorable pointy ears of all time, studded with metal.

"Your silence tells me you'd prefer me to make the decision for you, Race." Confidence clung to him, a second skin oozing arrogance. "Is this true?"

His voice had dropped, awakening cells she hadn't known she possessed, pleasure suddenly superseding each point of pain. The sensation lasted only a moment, and she hungered for more.

Wait—what? *More?* Mortification scorched her cheeks. Getting turned on because of a stranger's voice—in the middle of a life-and-death situation—was so not okay. Even for Cookie.

"I… You…" Looking from Cookie to Hottie, the centaur named Race maintained his grip on the sword hilt. "I am keeping the girl?"

Race was the one who'd found her at the pond, and she

delighted when his inhalations shallowed. Let him experience some of the terror he'd dished.

"You sound unsure," Hottie replied, as smooth as silk. He smiled pure evil. "I must admit, I hoped you'd choose this path."

He seemed to shift from one boot to the other, nothing more, but a bloody organ appeared in his hand.

Whoa. He'd attacked so fast she'd missed it? He'd teleported? *What?*

Race clutched the gaping hole in his chest, red pooling between his fingers. Eyes widening with pain and an ever-increasing awareness of his coming death, he collapsed. His body jerked once, twice, then sagged over the grass. A pool of crimson formed around him.

Which wasn't nearly as disgusting as expected. It wasn't even upsetting.

It was *deserved.*

Mutters of shock erupted as the other centaurs comprehended their leader's fate. The soldier in front of her startled, rearing up, tilting her alignment. She slid down the log. The other soldier couldn't maintain his grip, and the log slipped off his shoulder.

Both the trunk and Cookie slammed into the ground. Air burst from her lungs and dirt plumed around her. She coughed, desperate for oxygen, and—"Argh!" A centaur tread on her ankle, crushing her bones.

Cookie screamed behind the gag, lights flashing, blinding her. Nausea churned in her stomach. She wheezed her breaths, the agony threatening to shut down her mind. *Stay awake, just stay awake.*

Won't be a sitting duck. She blinked, shook her head, willing herself to heal. Her vision cleared, and she craned her head to search for Kaysar…

One by one, the centaurs collapsed, each gushing blood.

Or missing a head. Every other blink, she caught a glimpse of Kaysar as he moved through the ranks. Crimson soaked him, his expression ecstatic.

He loved this.

Terror gripped her and squeezed. Okay. Maybe she didn't need his help, after all. If she'd misread the vision, if ever he focused his murderous sights on Cookie, she would lose. For now, she was better off navigating the forest and its survivable dangers on her own.

She bucked and contorted, doing her best to free her arms from the rope while pushing her way up the log. If she failed to succeed this way, she planned to succeed that way.

Slow down. Think. Fear is at the wheel, urgency setting in.

She ignored the warning. Cookie wanted out of this— Yes! See? Success. One hand free, then the other. Whipping upright, she yanked off the gag, then worked on the rope around her poor damaged ankle. To her amazement, she'd already begun to heal. In a matter of minutes, she might even be racer ready.

Come on, come on. What if Kaysar focused on her next?

Finally, the rope gave. Cookie lumbered to her feet and threw a swift glance over the battleground, tensing as realization set in. Only two centaurs remained. Time to go.

She launched forward, losing her houseboots as she zoomed past a line of trees—"No!"

Kaysar appeared, towering in front of her. Unable to slow, she crashed into him and bounced back, stumbling but remaining upright.

Breathe. Just breathe. This was fine. Everything was fine. Yes, okay, he looked a bit insane right now, his eyes maniacal as he surveyed her from top to bottom. But. He hadn't retaliated when she'd slammed into him. His intentions toward her might not be terrible.

She backed away, step by step, but kept her gaze upon him, just in case. Blood drenched a powerful body humming with aggression. After all the damage he'd caused, he wasn't winded. If a centaur had managed to injure him, she found no evidence of a wound.

Voice a rapture-inducing growl, he asked, "Where do you think you're going?"

Far from here? Forever? Fingers crossed.

She paused a good distance away and held up her hands, palms out. A gesture of innocence or an attempt to ward him off, she wasn't sure. Either way, so far, so good. "Hi. Hello. First, I can't thank you enough for the save. While I'm not a fan of being a damsel in distress, I'm glad I'm not dying." *Very smooth.* But true. "Right? I'm not dying?"

Eternal seconds ticked by without a response.

Okay. Moving on and trying again. The Cookie way. "I'm Cookie Bardot. Well, my first name is actually Chantel, but friends call me Cookie. Apparently, *cookie* was my first word, and also all I ever wanted to eat. But I'm babbling, sorry. I do that when I appear in a strange world, where mythological monsters eye me with mental forks and knives and a guy with sexy ears comes along and murders everyone." She forced an airy laugh, her cheeks heating. Had she told a homicidal maniac he had sexy ears? "Anyway. Short story long, you can call me whatever you want."

He fingered his ears before shaking his head and scowling. "Chantel? Cookie? No. Your name is Lulundria. Though I can be persuaded to use the name Drendall upon occasion."

Uh-oh. She detected a note of anger. Anger. From an unashamed killer who'd displayed zero anger before gutting the centaurs. "Sure. I'll answer to Lulundria. Or Lulu. Even Lue. Or Drendall. Dren is nice, too." Who were these women? "I'm easy. Easygoing, I mean. Not easy—never mind. You get it."

He narrowed his eyes. "You are her, but not her."

The same thing the first round of pixies had said. Not that she would be stupid enough to trust a pixie again. In fact, if ever she got her hands on the pink one, she'd stop being murder curious and start being murder happy.

Cookie proceeded cautiously. "Did, um, Lulundria—the *other* Lulundria have pink hair and green eyes?"

His chiseled features darkened. He gave a sharp incline of his head. "She did."

Lulundria. The name clicked, and once again she knew. Her donor. The woman she'd seen in her vision. Who she recognized on a cellular level, though they'd never met.

To tell this man or to not tell him? What if he'd only saved her to gain answers about the transplant? Once he knew the truth, he'd have no use for her. Worse, what if he believed she was somehow responsible for Lulundria's death?

On the flip side, what if the information bought her a protector and guide home?

Amid the silence, he prowled closer. Closer still…

She remained in place, motionless, her heart pounding harder and faster, as if she were in the middle of a marathon. When he stood only a few feet away, she caught his scent and liquified. What *was* that? Sweet, but spicy. Intoxicating.

He walked a circle around her, and she let him do it without reprisal, remaining rooted where she stood. Partly in fear. Partly in…not fear, a desire to nuzzle into his strength growing.

So desperate for a teammate, you'll enter the bear's cage?

He paused behind her, and his warm breath brushed her nape. The most delicious shivers of all rippled over her.

"You are far more beautiful than she was. An object of desire few have the strength to resist." He purred the words straight into her ear, wrapping his powerful arms around her waist, crowding into her. Tap. Tap. The tip of his metal claw kissed her belly again and again without cutting her clothes. "Tell me, girl. Do I make you apprehensive?"

The feel of him... "You do make me apprehensive," she admitted, earning a start of surprise from him. *Among other things.*

Cookie hadn't pressed against a hard, masculine form in so long. How she'd missed the warmth. The sense of closeness. The safety. For once, she didn't feel oppressed by loneliness or impending doom.

Tap, tap, tap. "You alone have no reason to dread your time with me, female." Tap, tap. "Not at the moment."

What about later?

She decided to roll the dice. *The truth will set you free.* "I'm sorry to tell you this, but I believe your Lulundria is... dead. I'm sorry," she repeated. "My heart was defective, and I was dying. She didn't need hers anymore, so doctors transplanted it inside me. After the surgery, I began to change. My hair. My eyes." The vines.

The brutal warrior tensed. She braced for a shout of denial, or an accusation of dishonesty.

He appeared before her, and she yelped. How was he *doing* that?

"You hold Lulundria's heart in your chest? She lives on in you?" He set two knuckles under her chin and tipped her head up to his, unveiling a stunning smile. He was temptation made flesh. "This is wonderful. This is wonderful indeed."

CHAPTER EIGHT

KAYSAR HAD DETECTED no lies in the beauty's confession, the truth hitting him with all the finesse of a cannonball. Lulundria *had* returned to Astaria. She'd come back as this living doll—this living Drendall—whose finely boned face both mesmerized and unsettled him.

One woman the same as any other? Hardly.

He could stare at this female forever and another day, and it wouldn't be long enough. And her body... All that pale, radiant skin. The top of her head reached his shoulders. Barely. She was short but curved, wearing a pink tunic with text scribbled over the center. "Stay-at-Home Cat Mom." On her legs was black material seemingly poured onto her skin. A mortal fashion?

He frowned as the unthinkable happened—he hardened without permission from his mind. But why would he do this? People responded to him; he did not respond to people.

Despite the unprecedented reaction, she aided his cause. The heart of a Frostline-by-marriage beat in this former mortal's chest, ensuring Lulundria lived on. Ensuring her connection with Jareth and Hador lived on.

The princess wasn't the first royal fae to extend her life this way, but there were few others who'd dared to venture down this particular path. A mind was a gateway to the heart, the battery for any glamara, and all were different, no two intellects the same. The longer this Chantel carried

Lulundria's heart, the more her thoughts and personality shaped it. For better or for worse.

Whether she realized it or not, she was unerringly immortal, incredibly powerful, and unarguably fae. Each of the five courts now recognized her as a royal Summerlander *and* Winterlander. Lulundria's own parents would welcome her with open arms. Jareth, too. His marriage vows commanded it.

The prince had no choice but to accept this stranger as his wife—and the de Aoibheall babe soon to quicken in her belly.

A babe Kaysar would never know.

He…wasn't sure how he felt about the idea, now that victory was so close. What belonged to Kaysar belonged to Kaysar. Always. Without exception. He didn't share with anyone. Ever. He *refused* to share. And yet he planned to give this princess his seed? His child? An innocent babe, handed over to the Frostline prince? Placed within Hador's reach?

Fury rose at the incongruity, ever at the ready, the need to kill someone, anyone, nigh irresistible. Instead, Kaysar stroked his claws over his forearm. The slight tickle reminded him of his maps. His sister. His safe harbor in any storm.

He centered and calmed, certain he could solve the conundrum tomorrow. *Vengeance first, everything else second.*

Today, fate *wanted* him to oversee the punishment of the Frostlines. Unlike the original Lulundria, this woman hadn't spent her childhood hearing horror stories about the Unhinged One. What reason did she have to resist him?

No doubt her seduction would be laughably easy.

"Who are you to me?" she asked, an uneasy little thing. First she shifted from bare foot to bare foot. Then she smoothed pink and sable locks from her brow. *Then* she massaged the abrasions marring her wrists. "Who were you to Lulundria?"

Her accent was soft, liquid and wonderfully lazy, like the warm maple poured over his mother's berry cakes. A delicacy he hadn't considered in centuries. Now, his mouth watered.

A pang sizzled in his chest, but he ignored it, honing his focus, schooling his features. *Let the princess's seduction begin.*

Today he chatted with her. If he received encouragement, he touched. But nothing more than a few light caresses. To keep her glued to his side long-term, he must earn her trust before he claimed her body. "I'm Kaysar de Aoibheall from the Midnight Court, and I'm at your service." No reason to mention his designation. "Unhinged One" might be a jot difficult to excuse in the beginning.

"Kaysar," she repeated, her slow drawl turning the *zar* sound into *sir.*

The pang only intensified. *Disregard.* "As for the other question, you alone know who I am to Lulundria. You must only remember." Filtering the eagerness from his tone, he asked, "Have you relived any of her memories?"

She rocked on her heels. "Only one, and only a fragment, but it was enough. A man hurled ice daggers at her. He *hurt* her."

Well, well. Her quiet rage was utterly delicious. Even better, she had referred to Jareth, her husband, as "a man." A stranger. She considered the prince a merciless killer.

The first hint of satisfaction teased Kaysar. *As good as mine.*

He pretended to think the matter over and nodded.

"Perhaps it's best not to seek any other memories. What if they're worse?"

"I definitely do not want to remember another woman's memories. I barely handle my own."

That, he understood. He stalked another circle around her, inspecting his prize once more. But once wasn't enough. There was too much of her to enjoy, so he kept going. With each loop, he increased the distance between them to take in more of her. No woman had a right to smell sweeter than poisonvine. Especially this woman.

Unfamiliar needs battered him. *Kiss. Lick. Touch.* For pleasure.

Ire forever at the fore, he scowled. Kaysar experiencing pleasure with a Frostline, doing things he considered a chore?

"You're sending me mixed signals, and I'm not a fan." For this perusal, she moved with him, her gaze firmly attached to him, no matter where he stood. "Are you planning to do foul things to me or not? I honestly can't tell."

He answered without thought. "Tell me your definition of *foul*."

She blink-blinked, a *pfft* of air parting her lips. A bright smile spread. "Dang, you're hot. I'll be honest. I think you're into me. And I admit, I might be a little into you, too."

That smile stopped him in his tracks and robbed him of breath. *Exquisite.*

He met her gaze and forced a smile of his own. He'd paid the realm's finest concubines to teach him how to charm and intrigue, and he utilized those skills now. "You aren't wrong... Chantel. I am very much *into* you."

Relaxing further, she asked, "Where are we?"

"This is Astaria." *Your new home.*

"Astaria," she echoed, surveying the land around them. "Not Rhoswyn? Or Loloria? Or Enchantia?"

"There are five fae kingdoms, also known as courts. Midnight or Nightlands. Summer. Autumn. Spring. And Winter." He grated the last. "There's also a territory known as the Dusklands. We are currently in the Forest of Many Names."

"Fae," she squeaked. "I knew it. But are we talking Seelie and Unseelie? Or does it even matter?"

"Fae are fae." Dissatisfied with the distance, Kaysar eased closer, reentering Chantel's flowery force field. His blood heated slowly, simmering…boiling.

Her scent reminded him of poisonvine—no, not poisonvine, not exactly, but a far more potent and pure strain. His head fogged.

"Shall I tell you how Lulundria and I first met?" he asked silkily.

"Yes, please," she rasped, licking her ruby lips.

Tension coiled inside his muscles as never before, a shock to his system. "Six months ago, I came upon Lulundria in this forest with her husband, a Winterland prince. The evil man you saw in the memory. With my aid, the darling Lulundria escaped, running away. I've sought her ever since. I've *craved* her ever since." He observed her expression, saying "Now I crave you."

Her features softened, any lingering stiffness evaporating.

Oh, yes. This seduction was laughably easy indeed.

She searched his gaze. To his consternation, her stiffness returned gradually. When the metamorphosis was completed, she straightened with a snap, stepped back to widen the distance between them. "I may have Lulundria's heart, but I assure you, I'm not her."

He snapped, "What use are you to me, if you aren't Lulundria?"

She took another step back. Good. Let her dread the temper of the man who decided her fate. As a Frostline, her every breath was a gift from Kaysar. Let her see the blood of the enemies he'd slaughtered on her behalf.

Her behalf? No. Every murder had served his master, vengeance. Nothing mattered more than her husband's pain and suffering.

"Also," she said, as if his outburst meant nothing to her, "I don't want to be a princess. They're the weakest characters."

He had no idea how to respond. Deep breath in. Out. Kaysar offered the princess his best imitation of a reassuring smile. "You *are* Lulundria in every way that matters. You are also married to the prince who killed you." To further increase her distrust of the prince, he told her, "Jareth pierced Lulundria's internal organs with ice directly in front of me. I fought him and chased after her, intending to heal and protect her. But in her pain, fear got the better of her, and she created her vines. The stalks dragged her through a doorway, and she vanished."

"Vines dragged me through a doorway, too." In her fervor to learn more, she lost her reluctance and sidled closer. "The second I went through it, the stalks withered."

Like a teacher to his student, he told her, "Because you are a doormaker. You open and close doorways into the mortal and fae worlds."

"So I can go home?" Relief poured from her in great, sweeping waves, rousing a confusing tide of…something inside him. "I can go home!" She bounded the rest of the way and gripped his tunic. "How do I open a doorway? Do you know?"

He wished to respond, but his voice had ceased working, speaking suddenly an impossible task. His mind whirled with wild, unfettered thoughts he couldn't quite grasp. Her body was flush with his. So warm. So soft. Breasts. Breasts were smashed against his chest. Plump ones.

Pleasure lashed him like a whip with a thousand tails, wrenching a groan from his innermost being. His shaft reacted with no prompting from his mind again, shooting iron-hard. The urge to rub against her was nearly impossible to resist.

"You can't," he rasped. He barely stopped himself from wrapping his arms around her. First he must temper this strange and unappreciated reaction to her. "The opening of a door always drains the maker. While you're probably able to create vines, you won't be strong enough to craft another door for weeks or months."

Months. Hmm. He'd lived thousands of years, and he would live thousands more. How could he obtain lasting satisfaction through this woman's connection to Jareth with so little time? And what if she failed to conceive before her ability recharged?

Other than chaining her, a temporary solution and a hindrance to his goal, he had no way to contain her.

"Are *you* a doormaker, too?" she asked.

Calm. Steady. "I am not. Few are."

"Well, that's just great," she huffed, resting her forehead against his sternum. A pose born of dejection or a need for comfort? "A mandatory cooldown for an ability I didn't know I had and didn't mean to use."

Cooldown? Yes. He should cool down. Should flitter out of reach and escape the heat generating between their bodies and shed the awful, wonderful things she continued to make him feel.

He wrapped an arm around her instead, holding on tight. The pangs he'd experienced earlier must have caused some sort of residual damage in his chest. Left cracks. Something. Because some long-buried instinct resurrected, rising to the surface. *Need...more of...her. Must protect...*

She lifted her head, and he knew. She hadn't been dejected; she'd sought comfort from him. *From him.* "Well. No matter," she said. "One down doesn't mean all down, right?"

"Obviously," he said, having no idea what she'd meant. Kaysar could not stop himself. He traced two claw tips gently over her cheeks and tucked a lock of hair behind her ear, careful not to nick her skin. "Which of Lulundria's plethora of abilities have you exhibited?"

Eager, she jumped up and down a little. "How many is a *plethora*?"

"I'm not sure. More than a dozen, less than a throng?" New urges fought for dominance. To hear her babble more nonsense. To deepen her excitement. To knead her softest places and see her eyes glaze. To push her against a tree and tear off those skintight pants. Things he'd never fantasized about doing to others.

How was she affecting him like this?

"Every fae has a glamara, their strongest ability," he explained. "But some also travel great distances in seconds or mesmerize with a glance. Others cast illusions. And on and on and on the list goes."

"*You* are fae." Chantel retained her clasp on his tunic and searched his eyes without reservation. Most people averted their gaze within seconds, unwilling to stare into the abyss. A shame, he used to think. He'd paid a high cost for the seething pools of hatred, and he enjoyed showing them off. Now? He thought he might be unnerved. "What can you do?"

"More than a plethora." He cupped her cheeks. "Say you'll come with me to my home. I'll see to your protection, I swear it."

Her good humor faded. "I'm sorry, Kaysar, but I want to return to *my* home as soon as possible." She extracted herself from his hold, and he could do nothing but let her. "I'd love it if you helped me find another doormaker, though."

Help her return to the mortal world? No. She would come to his palace. Where she could leave anytime she desired, once she learned to flitter. Which she could do, long before she recharged her glamara.

He stroked a claw over his arm, grazing his skin. Map. Sister. Calm. "The evil prince will hunt you. He might hunt you even now, Chantel. And he'll find you. All royals employ seers. Those who peer into the past, present and future. But I can hide you from him and his seer. Let me. I was too late to protect Lulundria, but I'm not too late to protect you."

His vow only bolstered her resistance. She shook her head, firm. "Fear won't keep me from action. There's no guarantee my glamara will ever fully recharge. I need a plan B."

Laughably easy, Kaysar? "You no longer belong in your old world," he cajoled. "Stay here. You'll experience every comfort in my castle."

Her shoulders squared, and her spine straightened. She elevated her chin as those forest-sunset eyes frosted over. "I don't want to go to your castle—wait. Like, it's a legit castle, with towers and dungeons and stuff? What defenses are— No. Don't answer that. It doesn't matter. I'm going home. My best friend and cat are worried sick about me.

Pearl Jean does *not* need another illness, and Sugars has…
peculiarities. I will return to them. Nothing will stop me."

"You'll never find another doormaker." He would make
sure of it.

"Are *you* a seer?" she asked, a little too sweetly for his
liking.

Because he knew where she was headed with her line of
inquiry. "No," he grated, resentful over the answer. Over
her insight.

"Then you can't know whether I will or won't find a
doormaker."

He worked his jaw. She truly meant to leave him. "You
won't succeed without my aid," he warned.

"Maybe, but I'm still going to try. Will you at least draw
a map in the dirt before we separate, and point me to a
safe town?"

A map. Yes. Automatically, he scraped his claws deeper,
using the blood to craft a swift crimson outline of the surrounding miles. When he finished, he extended his arm to
her without thinking.

She peered at his wounds, pensive. Horrified?

His cheeks heated as silence stretched between them.
Even the pixies had gone quiet, no longer whispering in the
trees. With a growl, he dropped his arm to his side.

"Wait. I wasn't done memorizing." She clasped his wrist
and maneuvered his arm into a brighter beam of light. The
cuts had already woven together, but the blood lines remained. "Correct me if I'm wrong, but this is the pond.
This is the carnage we abandoned. Which means we're
here." Her brow furrowed as she tapped a spot near his
wrist. "This path seems to lead to a town, yes?"

She could read his blood-map? How was this possible?
No one could read his blood-maps.

"Kaysar?" she prompted, peering up at him. A warm breeze twirled between them, swirling leaves and lifting a lock of pink hair.

She was too beautiful. Too soft. Too warm. Too singular. Kaysar bit his tongue until he tasted the metallic tinge of blood. "Even with a map, you won't find a doormaker on your own. If you survive the forest itself, you might die at the hands of its inhabitants. You think the centaurs are bad? Wait until you meet ogres and trolls."

"I have. They left me alone."

Yes. Well. Of course they had. They'd sensed her connection to the Frostlines, and they'd heeded his rules. Not even a scratch on the royals. "Have you come across a goblin yet?"

She shuddered, as if she knew what horrors to expect from the ghostly fiends. "No, but I'm not calling off my hunt for a doormaker."

Stubborn female. "Very well. I will accompany you." He pieced together a new plan. Forget seduction at the castle. He would lead Chantel through the forest and into the Dusklands.

The journey would prove exhausting for her—because he would make it so, forcing her to rely on his knowledge and depend on his strength. Nights spent under the stars guaranteed she sought his body for warmth.

As soon as he got her in his arms, she would forget all thoughts of her former home. *I will have my vengeance. All will be well.*

"You'll help me? Really?" she asked, suspicious. "For what price?"

Oh, they would discuss his price soon enough. "I'm sure I'll think of something." He looked her over with their com-

ing travels in mind. "For now, you require shoes. And supplies."

"And weapons of my own."

This little dollop of strawberries and cream wished to
wield weapons? When she quirked a brow in challenge, he
merely replied, "Naturally. I will gather everything you
need."

"And the price for all of *that*?"

How much was she willing to pay?

He decided to push in the direction he wished to end
and gauge her reaction. "Tell me, Chantel. Do you fear I'll
demand sex from you? Or do you hope I will?"

CHAPTER NINE

KAYSAR'S QUESTION HUNG in the air, a sultry caress against Cookie's overheated skin. His whiskey eyes gleamed with some concentrated emotion. The need to kill her? To kiss her? Excitement or resentment? More anger than any person should be able to contain? Longing? Hope?

Insanity?

During their brief interaction, he'd displayed all of those things and more, weaving between the contradictory mess seamlessly. Sometimes, especially when he stroked those metal claws over his arms, he reminded her of a lost little boy...with dreams of burning the entire world to ash.

During those episodes, she actually felt a kinship with him. Weird, right? Proof *she* wasn't quite there, maybe.

His voice was the vocal equivalent of kerosene, and his intensity a lit match. In a handful of minutes, he'd set her ablaze with a thousand different desires and fears. His every touch electrified her, as if she'd been preprogrammed to react to him. His scent drugged. The greedy way he watched her, as if he'd never observed a more fascinating creature, bolstered her confidence. *I can survive this.*

What's more, she'd kind of enjoyed chatting with him, despite their ups and downs. He'd offered information she'd desperately sought, and every so often, he'd made her feel gloriously safe. Even—shockingly—normal.

Did he truly wish to help her?

"Look. Sex is one hundred percent off our table." For starters, she had never used her body as payment for anything, and she wasn't starting now, probably. Second, sleeping with someone you needed was stupid. He might lose interest afterward. Or obsess. He was a killer, and she had enough trouble controlling her own dark side. She didn't need to go and add his to the mix, muddying the waters of self-control further. "That's never going to change."

"Should I escort you about this realm for free?" He used his silky tone again. She didn't know if the danger had passed or escalated. "I do have duties to attend to. I'm sure there are other damsels in distress I can save. Those who are more amenable to my requests."

Oh, that burned. "Do you plan to proposition them all?" she snipped, irritated that he'd lumped her into the same category as the helpless maidens of lore. "If you're ready to get realistic with your payment options, I'm ready to bargain. But ticktock, Claw Man." She tapped the wristwatch she wasn't wearing. "I'm only wasting two more minutes on this conversation. Then I jet."

He executed a slow blink. "Did you refer to me as *Claw Man*?"

Yeah. So? "My teammates get nicknames, or they aren't my teammates. We'll need a uniform, by the way."

He narrowed his eyes. "The word *teammate* implies we are equals. We are not. I make demands, and you obey them. That is how our relationship will work."

Cookie bristled. "You can't just decide you're team leader." The nerve! "My tough-as-nails, decisive manner and no-nonsense approach to battle inspires confidence in others. When I have a vision, I make fast decisions, and I never veer off track, mostly. I should be *considered* for co-captain at least."

Kaysar was better suited as the muscle. The perfect meat shield. With him, she'd have the best chance of finding another doormaker. And also convincing said doormaker to aid her, free of charge.

"Clock's about to run out, Kaysar," she said, impatient to get this partnership sealed and the show on the road. Or to just get the show on the road. Either way, she was getting some action.

Behind him, the sky darkened as suddenly as if someone had flipped a switch. Lightning blazed, a flash there and gone, illuminating her companion's impossibly sexual face and war-god body—her heart skipped a beat. Dang. He was beyond sexy-scary.

Thunder boomed, a sudden storm rolling in. The instant change in weather startled her, though she wasn't sure why. This kind of thing happened in *The Forest of Good and Evil*, too. The designer *must* have lived here.

Yes, Mother. Video games did *provide me with a proper education for my future.*

Her companion's anger—if that's what he currently displayed—dissipated as icy raindrops descended. "Fate is trying to tell you something, princess." He offered a tight grin. "Traverse the Forest of Many Names during a storm without my protection? Tsk-tsk. Do you *want* to die?"

"So it's raining. Big deal." Droplets splashed her face... the rest of her. In seconds, she was chilled to the bone. Teeth chattering, she said, "Rain or not, I'm finding a doormaker, and I'm not sleeping with you. And don't call me princess."

The day she signed on as Cinderella or Sleeping Beauty was the day she retired. Hero complex? No, thanks. She'd rather not be burdened with one of those.

Even as a child, she'd gravitated toward characters like

the Mad Hatter and Maleficent. Actual role models who'd gotten things done.

"But you *are* a princess." Amid another flash of lightning, Kaysar appeared a whisper away. She gasped as his hot palm seared her nape and his hard body pressed flush against her curves. "You are *my* princess."

The claim and the contact thrilled her for all the wrong reasons.

Focus. "Did you teleport?"

"We call it flittering."

"Flittering," she echoed. Why did he have to be so deliciously warm? So wrong for her?

He "craved" Lulundria. Oh, yes, and this Drendall, whoever she was. Another princess? Whatever. Bottom line: Cookie wasn't Lulundria. When Kaysar accepted the truth, he might revolt. Best to curtail all sexual thoughts and urges with him.

"I'm not your anything right now, Kaysar." Good. She used a rational tone. "But I could be your partner, if you'll give a little, working with me instead of against me."

The reasonable request ticked him off. He peeled his lips from his straight, white teeth in a parody of a smile. "You'll be pleased to know my price isn't sex. That, you'll give me for free. No, what I demand of you is a vow never to run from me. And Chantel? There is a steep penalty to pay if you break your word. Liars do not fare well in my presence."

She gulped, a hard lump dropping into her stomach. *And we're back to lethal.*

Did she need Kaysar's help? Yes. Obviously. Maybe? She didn't know anything anymore. But she wouldn't lie or trick him into anything. Honesty mattered to Cookie, too. It was her thing, the line she refused to cross. How many times had her mother and father promised to take her to some event or another, getting her hopes up, only to bail?

She might suck at a lot of things, but she always kept her word.

"I'll always be truthful with you, I promise." The raindrops continued to fall, and she caught herself teetering closer to him. "That is why I won't vow to never run from you. Never is too constrictive." And had he really confessed his belief that she was a sure thing? "There should be exceptions."

If he tested her vow, and she ran because she felt endangered, he would have the perfect excuse to harm her. Why set herself up for failure?

The look he gave her said, *darling, please.* "Unfortunately for you, I have no need to bargain. This is a Summerland shower, and it will last all night. You'll do what I demand or you'll freeze."

Irritating man! He had no give. But spend all night in the rain? The droplets had begun to prick like needles. "Look. I always do what I say I'll do. So, you either add some exceptions to your request, or I walk despite the danger. No," she said when he opened up to protest. "Think about it. What if I need to run from you to save my life, for whatever reason?"

He did think about it, then nodded. "You make an excellent point. But there will be no exceptions."

Argh! He was bluffing. He must be bluffing. But *she* wasn't. When she'd told him she meant what she said, *she'd meant what she'd freaking said.* "Very well. I decline your offer. Thanks for the assist. Now, good day, sir." She wrenched from his clasp and stepped around him.

Nope. Not around him. He moved with her, continuing as

if she hadn't spoken. "To pay for the supplies, you'll give me an hour to show you why I demand you remain at my side."

Finally! A concession. But was it a trap of some kind? His unholy glee said *yes*.

He looked beyond her and brightened further. "I'll have a pair of shoes for you within minutes." Then he vanished without giving her a chance to respond, leaving her in the chilling rain.

Okay. Message received. He preferred to discuss the vow thing later. Same. But, uh, where had he gone? Should she wait for his return? Or run while she had the chance?

A pair of boots versus her own agency?

Ugh. Maybe she could steal the shoes from him, *then* ditch? *Could* she ditch him without an opportunity like this? He wanted the woman he thought she was. He'd made that clear. She had leverage, but how much?

What other superpowers did the frightening centaur slayer wield?

Better question: *What other superpowers do I wield?*

Colder by the second, Cookie sprinted for an area shielded by a dense canopy of leaves. Along the way, her clothes gained a hundred pounds of water. Freezing mud splashed her bare feet. Her teeth-chattered with greater intensity and spread through the rest of her body.

When a continuous click of metal against metal rang out, she frowned. Kaysar's doing? Was he crafting the shoes from swords?

Curiosity and misery got the better of her. She braved the storm, racing onto the field of slaughter, where the noise originated, her gaze scanning. There. Kaysar slammed a dagger into the lock that trapped the prisoners inside the cart. He'd removed his soaked shirt, his muscles bulging and flexing with his movements. Raindrops sluiced over his tattoos. Oh! The lines and dots created an intricate map she could stare at for days.

As he toiled, women dressed in threadbare rags mewled and begged for mercy.

Maybe he wasn't such a bad guy. He'd decided to aid the others before procuring those shoes.

"Quiet," he snapped, "before I add your tongues to my collection."

Well. He wasn't a good guy, either. But a good deed was still a good deed, right?

Did he really have a collection of tongues?

They seemed to think so. They hushed in an instant.

Hinges squeaked when the door swung open. He regressed into the shadows, allowing the prisoners to spill from the cart. Until—with superfast reflexes, he snatched a woman by her garment, yanking her to his side.

"Your shoes," he said, his voice as hard and cold as steel. "Give them to me."

The tearful woman squeezed her eyes shut and nodded, bending down to unstrap her sandals.

Oh, no, no, no. "Stop," Cookie shouted, rushing over. "Keep them." Steal an innocent's property to save herself? Big nope. Not outside of a video game, anyway.

The owner of the footwear paused, hopeful as she glanced from Cookie to Kaysar.

He met Cookie's gaze. The rain picked up, washing away the evidence of his earlier battle. "The woman will give me the shoes or I will take them. Which is it to be?"

The prisoner ripped off her sandals as swiftly as possible.

Cookie forged ahead. "I will go barefoot if I must, Kaysar. I'm not accepting those shoes."

"Accept them or I'll—" He pressed his lips together. "You *will* accept them. No other option is available to you."

Okay. He clearly operated under the misassumption that she'd cave to his demands, if only he fronted long enough. To make him understand the depths of her stubbornness and the strength of her determination, she was going to have to call *his* bluff. And actually follow through if necessary. *Bring it.* "If you force this, I'll leave you at the first opportunity."

"You dare to threaten me with your abandonment?" he demanded, his lethal side making another appearance. "Me?"

All right, then. Time for that follow-through. "Forget the sandals," she said, and humphed. He needed to learn a valuable lesson. Screw with Cookie and lose. But man, she thought she might actually miss him. Not his sterling personality, but the connection she'd felt when he'd wrapped his arms around her. An elusive sensation she'd craved for years. "I'm leaving with the others." Perhaps the better choice, regardless of his next response. "Goodbye again, Kaysar."

Head high, she followed after the females he'd sprung from the cart. Maybe her would-be protector would do the kind thing and call her back, ready for a genuine bargain. Maybe he wouldn't. There at the end, his thunderstruck expression had been satisfying. The undercurrent of his rage even more so, despite the danger.

Did she actually *want* him to call her back? He might not be stable.

Well, so what? She wasn't known for her rationality, either. And dang it, Kaysar was the best option to protect her from hidden and not-so-hidden dangers—because he was her only option. How could she navigate the world without another blood-map? How would she know the difference between a doormaker and an ordinary fae without his help?

Wait. Were any of the escaped prisoners doormakers? "Hey, guys, wait up," she called, kicking into a jog, moving farther and farther from Kaysar—who didn't call her back. The rain lightened at least.

No one waited up. They disappeared beyond a line of trees.

Still no callback. Whatever. She and Kaysar were parting. No big deal. Most people opted not to hang out with her at some point or another. Apparently, she was "abrasive." Pearl Jean and Sugars were the only stickers. The pair she'd been unable "to unconsciously drive away," as her therapist once said.

This was for the best, anyway. Why team up with a domineering, commanding male who might snap at any moment? Surely someone would let her tag along, ask questions and—

"Stop," Kaysar bellowed, power crackling in his voice.

Oh, thank goodness. Cookie's feet froze while her heart raced faster. Any woman still visible froze, too, as if too frightened to move.

"Return to me," he commanded. "All of you. I agree to your terms, Chantel. I'll fetch you another pair of shoes."

He would? Shock hit her first, nearly knocking her on her butt. She'd won their private war?

"I believe I issued an order to the rest of you." He bellowed again, but the crackle was missing, replaced by impatience. "Why is no one standing at my side? Shall I start hunting?"

In unison, the women raced for Kaysar, many exiting the line of trees. Wow. He spoke and everyone obeyed, as if the price of disobedience was too high.

Was it too high? Would he actually stoop to harming the women if they refused him? Cookie enjoyed a bloodbath as much as the next person, but come on! These prisoners had done nothing wrong.

As the ladies passed her, one muttered, "He's king of the Nightlands and ruler of the Dusklands. Do what he says or die."

Wait. He was an honest-to-goodness king, with a crown and a throne? He *had* mentioned owning a castle and claimed to own the land. His master-of-all-I-survey attitude certainly fit. But why leave out his title when he'd introduced himself?

As a king, he had more resources at his disposal than the average fae. He definitely had more power. What doormaker would have the stones to refuse his bidding, if ordered to help her?

She trudged back, growing warmer only when she stood at his side.

As she met his gaze, his irises blazed with satisfaction. Had she made a terrible mistake?

"You're a king, huh?" Wait. "Do you have a queen?" Cheaters were liars who'd leveled up; they made the worst teammates. The worst everything.

His face scrunched with distaste. "I will *never* have a queen."

"Commitment isn't your thing, huh?" Very well. Cookie was going to do it. She was going to hitch her wagon to his.

"You may have your exception, as well," he grated, ignoring her question. "You will not run from me…unless you feel I'm endangering your life. Me. I can protect you from any other threat." He had a caveat of his own, apparently. "But. Before you run, you will tell me you feel as if I'm endangering your life. Only after I have confirmed that you are in fact in danger may you run. I'll even give you a head start."

"What do you want for the supplies then?" Since he wouldn't be giving her that hour long tour to convince her to agree to his terms. Best they be clear.

"You will not naysay me again."

Uh... "I'm going to need exceptions. But other than that," she added before he could complain, "I agree to your terms."

He traced his tongue over his teeth. "I must leave you here to source other shoes." Rather than celebrating a mutually beneficial arrangement, he projected irritation. "You will stay here, in this exact spot. You will not move. These women will stand guard around you. If they flee, they die. If you are injured during my absence, they will die badly." With that, he disappeared.

Cookie glanced at the terrified faces around her. *What have I gotten myself into?*

CHAPTER TEN

"EXCEPTIONS," KAYSAR GRUMBLED, materializing in his bedroom. "The audacity of the chit!" He stomped to his closet and grabbed the bag he used to cart around a severed head or organs whenever necessary. The magical, self-cleaning cloth couldn't be ripped, even with his metal claws.

Did Chantel know how close she'd come to losing *her* head? "I bow to the dictates of no one."

Since escaping the Frostlines, Kaysar had done what he wanted, when he wanted, with *zero* exceptions. Until today, when a former mortal dared to walk away from a powerful king she desperately needed on her side.

The wily beauty had certainly astonished him. She'd planned to leave him for good, jeopardizing her life and his vengeance, forcing him to capitulate to her demands or go to war with her. A choice between bad or worse.

But then, he'd given her an equally miserable choice. *Help me destroy your husband or suffer.* Not that she'd known it.

For some reason, the newly resurrected instinct to protect issued an increasingly loud protest. *The princess must never suffer.*

Protect and coddle Chantel—a Frostline—from his schemes? So she possessed the face of a doll from his most treasured memories? So she offered him a chance to be a savior at long last? Laughing a maniacal sound, he slammed his fist into the wall. Stone crumbled. Skin split, and bone cracked.

He was no one's savior. Yet still the tug-of-war persisted. Use her. Protect her. Use. Protect.

He thought he might...admire her a little. Her stubbornness seemed to rival his own. She'd toed up to a pitiless opponent, consequences be damned. Despite her fear, she'd sought his embrace. Twice. But not with the hopes of luring him into bed, as others had done in the past, thinking to tame the unhinged king. No, she had pursued comfort. From him.

That fact might forever baffle him.

His conflicting objectives hardly mattered, though. *Vengeance first.* Chantel demanded a search for a doormaker? Very well. She'd get one. And she would despise every second of it. He would do more than make her uncomfortable. He would push and push and push until she reached her breaking point. She had one; everyone did.

Eager to return, Kaysar stalked through his bedroom, stuffing anything he thought she might need into the bag. As he riffled through his belongings, his mind strayed to Jareth. Would the prince balk when he met the stubborn beauty unwilling to back down from a battle of wills? Or rejoice?

I want you this much, he'd told Lulundria while stroking his shaft. How much more might he desire this one, a woman who appeared created from carnality itself?

Old bitterness merged with new. What if the prince took Chantel to bed as soon as Kaysar finished with her, too relieved by her return to care about her pregnancy?

Jareth, daring to enjoy her curvy little body night after night... The outrage!

He deserves no pleasure. Kaysar punched the wall again.

And again. And again and again and again. Skin split.
Knuckles shattered like glass. But his rage failed to cool.

Perhaps he'd keep Chantel for years.

Slightly mollified, he flittered to a treasure trove in the
catacombs of his castle. Eternal torches illuminated a door-
less room, casting muted golden light over a sea of gold
coins, gemstones and weapons. A thousand maps hung over
the stone walls. In the center of the chamber was a massive marble water fountain topped by a likeness of Prince
Jareth's dead mother.

In here, Kaysar kept the material goods he'd stolen from
the Frostlines. Trunks filled with clothing they'd worn during special occasions. Invaluable family jewels. Swords
they'd commissioned from the most skilled blacksmiths.
He'd even taken furnishings, paintings and—his personal
favorite—the urn containing Prince Lark.

One day, Kaysar would decide how best to desecrate
the ashes.

What did Chantel require? She'd need clothes, of course.
He shoved several gowns into the bag, unconcerned by size
since fae garments magically fit the wearer, whoever the
wearer happened to be. Although… She'd be too comfortable in these.

He wanted more than her misery—he wanted her de-
pendent.

Kaysar removed the gowns and selected much lighter
ones with nearly transparent material. Basically night-
gowns. He grinned. Until the heat in his groin reignited,
and his shaft hardened.

Spontaneous desire for the princess needed to stop. What
did he care about a woman's attire? Especially garments he
planned to peel from her body as soon as he bedded her.

A groan sprung from him. Chantel…naked…

What color were her nipples? Did she have pink or sable curls between her legs? Would those emerald irises with their silver flecks go soft as he brought her to climax?

He pressed a hand to his aching length—wishing it was *her* hand.

With a growl, he blindly crammed something into the bag. *What else, what else?* This, this, and this. Yes, yes. This. Elderseed. He carefully set the large black brick-like object in the folds of a gown.

If someone mortally wounded Chantel anytime in the future, Kaysar now had the means to heal her right away.

What else? As he stalked across the chamber, the soles of his waterlogged boots squeaked. He should change into dry— Shoes. He'd almost forgotten. Where were the shoes?

He flittered to Eye's bedroom, took a step forward, and paused. His seer lounged in a clawfoot tub before a blazing hearth, enfolded in a thick veil of steam. She'd piled her dark hair on her crown. In a reclined position, with her eyes closed, she presented a picture of total relaxation.

Envy scorched the cracks in his chest. "Give me your shoes," he demanded.

Her eyelids popped open, and she screamed, scrambling to her feet. Water droplets slicked down her nakedness. Nakedness she attempted to cover with her hands before scrambling again, reaching for a towel.

He rolled his eyes. "You are of no interest to me in that regard." Kaysar didn't see people. He saw pawns and obstacles. "Where are your shoes?"

"Y-your majesty," she sputtered. "How did you enter without—never mind. Now isn't a good time for anything. You should leave. Please."

He offered a cold laugh. "Aren't you amusing today?

Attempting to eject me from the bedroom I allow you to breathe in."

Her fingers clenched on the edge of her towel. "Perhaps you should be nicer to me. I've had a vision about your princess."

He acted without thought, flittering to her. So close the tips of their noses brushed together. "What did you see? Tell me."

Words tripped from her tongue. "She is more than Lulundria. She is the skin she wears."

He waited for her to say more. She didn't. Confusion drew his brows together. "What does that even mean?"

"I don't know. I only sense this is similar to the heart issue. The skins are her, but they are also not her, both a part of her and separate from her, not yet fully formed." She bent her head and rubbed her temple. "Chantel is still figuring herself out. She hasn't chosen a path."

"You speak nonsense." Useless female. He moved away with a huff and shuffled through the room, searching for slippers, sandals or boots. In the closet, he found books. Hundreds of volumes stored in a private library.

He scanned the contents of every dresser drawer. Nothing. His fists turned heavy as fury collected there.

He raised his arm to strike something. The room didn't have what he wanted? Very well. The room was coming down, to be nothing but a pile of stones. At the last moment, he spotted a shelf of varying footwear on the balcony outside and flittered over.

Grinning now, Kaysar grabbed a pair of bejeweled boots a portion of his brain recognized. Where had he seen them before?

As he readied to rejoin his princess, Eye called to him

from inside the bedroom. "Your majesty, wait! You must see what I see." She pushed a new image into his mind.

Like every instance before, a scene took shape, making him feel as if he peered at a painting come to life. Chantel, sprinting through the forest, panic etched into her features.

Hundreds of emotions welled up at once, none of them good. Muscles tensed, and bones vibrated. He primed his claws. "When does this occur?" he demanded.

"About five minutes ago."

In danger? Or had she seized an opportunity to escape him, as boasted?

Whatever the answer, someone died today.

Temper redlining, Kaysar flittered to the field of carnage. Frigid raindrops sizzled on his skin, white-hot rage coating him. No sign of Chantel. The fae and mortal prisoners he'd commanded to remain noticed him and rushed over to plead for mercy.

"Be silent and step away," he shouted. Immediate obedience. "Did someone attack?" He thought he scented— Kaysar belted a curse. *Jareth.*

As if he'd issued a summons, the prince lumbered to his feet a short distance away. Fresh blood coated his mouth. He shook his head, as if to discard a daze, and caught sight of Kaysar. Jareth, too, belted a curse.

Hatred slithered down Kaysar's spine. "Hello, princeling."

"She's mine," Jareth snarled as the women promised that they'd fought the prince to prevent him from following the princess. "You won't touch her."

"She is yours, yes," he agreed. *For now.* The thought threw him, and not in a good way, but he quickly recovered, unveiling the smile he reserved solely for the Frostlines. A cruel twisting of his lips as much a warning as a promise. "But who do you think will bed her first?"

About Five Minutes Ago

COOKIE WIPED THE raindrops from her face. "Come on, guys. Can't you give a girl a little space?" she pleaded. The moment Kaysar had vanished, the group had drawn a tight circle around her.

They faced away from her, on the lookout for any possible threat. As if they could actually fight off a soft breeze, much less an attacker. They looked like they hadn't eaten in months.

No one responded to her, the air ripe with apprehension. She could throw an elbow or two, forcing a portion of the group to back off. The others would only rally. Because they feared Kaysar would do as threatened and slay them all if harm befell Cookie.

She suspected he…might. The worst part? She didn't know how she felt about it anymore. And she should. These women had done nothing wrong. They were innocents, and they didn't deserve to die.

Idiot. As soon as the others were safe, she should ditch Kaysar without hesitation. It was the right thing to do. Maybe. Probably. Personally, she wasn't afraid of him. Not really.

Sure, when he went all still and quiet, hissing his words, he evinced sheer terror in everyone around him. But, she sensed the danger wasn't directed her way. His high-handed tactics sucked, but they weren't a deal breaker. The pros outweighed the cons.

"Lulu?"

A voice both familiar and unfamiliar caused her to cross her arms over her belly. An instinctive, protective gesture. The Viking stood in the distance, his gaze locked on her.

Big, blond and handsome, able to kill a woman at twenty paces with ice.

Her heart thudded with realization. He'd found her, exactly as Kaysar had warned. Here he was, the evil prince Lulundria must have despised.

Calm. Steady. He rushed over, and her guards tightened the circle.

Anger sparked, dousing Cookie's fear.

He reached the outer wall of women. Though they fought him to the best of their abilities, he had no problem shoving them aside, two at a time.

Like Kaysar, he towered over her with muscles galore. His weight must be double hers. She would lose a physical altercation, no doubt about it, but she wouldn't go down without a struggle.

"You wanna come at me?" *Kill or be killed, winner takes all.* "Okay, let's do this."

In front of her, he paused. And frowned "I don't understand." He pinched a lock of her hair between his fingers. "You are her. But how can you be? You are not her."

He'd killed his own wife. What wouldn't he do to Cookie? She punched him in the throat. Twice.

He wheezed as he gripped her shoulders. Oh, no, no, no. This wouldn't do. With a snarl, she kneed his junk, hard. *Shake* that *off, prince.*

He hunched over, spittle spraying from his mouth. No hesitation. No risks, no rewards. She slammed the palm of her hand into his nose, his own momentum giving the blow more steam. He roared and released her, dropping to his knees.

Had the bones in her hand shattered on impact? Yes. Did pain and nausea roil up? Also yes. But she didn't pause. He'd murdered her donor and now suffered a little of her hurt. *Worth any agony.*

"Let's go, girls. Run," she commanded, grabbing two of them by the dresses and shooting off.

Both women resisted. They even latched on to her wrists and forced her to stop...then they slowly dragged her in the opposite direction. Cookie grappled for purchase in the mud.

"Kaysar will understand, okay?" Rain blurred her vision, and she shook the droplets from her eyes. Tugging. Wiggling. Failing. "We're not running *from* him. We're running *to safety*. The Viking is a wife killer."

A wife killer already straightening and refocusing on her, his eyes narrowed.

Fear and fury rammed together, heat collecting in Cookie's arms. Vines licked out and rolled back in, whipping her captors before vanishing. Both women yelped and released her, falling.

A lash of soft leaves caused so much pain, they lost their hold on the prize? Seriously?

A living bullet, Cookie sprinted toward the trees. Mud puddles splashed at her feet.

"Noooo," the Viking shouted. "Do not hurt her."

A stampede sounded behind her. Had her guards given chase?

A quick look back—argh! A hard weight slammed into her, throwing her face-first into the ground. For the second time that day, she ate a mouthful of dirt. Air exploded from her lungs, and stars winked over her eyes as the women dog-piled her.

"Lulu, please," the Viking called, running over.

"That's not my name," Cookie grated, squirming and fighting. The rain helped, slickening her skin. Yes! Freedom. She came to her feet and sprinted off once more, barely dodging the Viking's clasp.

Her tasks crystalized. *Get to safety. Find Kaysar.*

CHAPTER ELEVEN

THIS MUST BE my origin story. A real-life hero quest or whatever.

Cookie hated hero quests. She mumbled under her breath as she tripped through the forest of pain. Her fight-or-flight response remained in high gear, whipping her blood into fuel. Not that it did her much good. The numerous gashes on her feet left trails of crimson for any would-be detective to follow.

She'd fled from the prince, her donor's abusive ex, what? Twenty-four hours ago? A thousand years? He'd given chase. Because of course he had. Somehow, she'd managed to evade him throughout the night and survive the freezing wet. She'd even evaded him throughout the morning. Now afternoon sun streamed through a colorful canopy of leaves, spotlighting her every move.

How much longer could she go on? The rain she'd lamented, she now missed. *So thirsty.* She still hadn't eaten, her empty stomach protesting. Her clothes had dried, but they were stiff and dirty. Itchy.

She'd lost count of the trolls and ogres she'd stumbled upon. They'd reacted like the others, snorting and pawing, ready to charge, only to let her pass without incident. With the exception of one. That particular ogre had barreled over and pinned her against a tree trunk, his beefy hands caging her in as he huffed and puffed his big, bad breath all over her face. But in the end, he, too, had let her pass. The whole lot of them had done the same thing to the evil prince. She'd doubled back a time or two, hoping to witness his comeuppance.

Why hadn't Kaysar found her yet? Were fae males like humans? Had he already given up on Lulundria, the woman he supposedly craved? Well, good riddance. Cookie didn't need him. No matter how much she'd once thought otherwise. She wasn't the damsel in distress or the princess in need, as he believed. She had skills. Good ones. And she would remember what they were as soon as she unearthed a safe—semi-safe—halfway decent spot to rest.

Which direction to go? To the left, trees, bushes and flowers flourished, a breeding ground for pixies. To the right, shadows ghosted over gnarled limbs that were littered with thorns.

Left—anything could be poison. Right—those thorns probably sliced like razors.

"Lulundria?" the Viking called. He'd gotten closer. "Please, sweetheart. Kaysar will recover from his injuries any moment."

The two had fought, and the Viking had won? Dang. That sucked for her. And Kaysar. If the Viking prince was strong enough to incapacitate the centaur slayer, the fiercest warrior she'd ever met, what kind of harm could he cause Cookie?

An image of his ice daggers flashed, and she shuddered. Rephrase. How much *more* harm would he cause her?

Despite protesting muscles, she quickened her pace. *The thorns it is.*

As she advanced, branches slapped her. A sharp rock sliced the bottom of her foot. She muffled a shout of pain with her hand. Sweat beaded on her skin, stinging every wound, but she didn't slow.

Keep going, don't stop. Breath sawed in and out of her mouth. She jumped over a procession of fireants, her knees nearly buckling when she landed. Halfway there...

A twig snapped somewhere behind her. Cookie chanced a glance over her shoulder, her gaze darting. He wasn't within sight yet. A relief. But it was only a matter of time. A worry. She plowed ahead, pumping her arms faster. Harder. Blood rushed in her veins, her hands heating. Suddenly ivy budded from her fingers.

The vines slithered away from her, as before, but they didn't go far, and they didn't create a doorway. What the— Ever-thickening stalks coiled around her, knitting a cocoon of foliage, covering every part of her body and rooting her in place.

Her heart continued to race. How had she created her branchy, leafy prison without thought or practice?

As she fought to control her breathing, the leaves eased off her. The ones in front of her eyes parted, providing a slit for viewing. Forget breathing. The Viking materialized roughly fifteen feet away. Frantic, he searched high and low.

"Lulu? Please, sweetheart. I know you're here. The trail has stopped." He shoved branches out of his way and kicked rocks, closing in on Cookie... "I love you. I've missed you so much."

Closer still... Tremors sped through her. When his attention shot her way, blood rushed to her ears, and she froze, even her racing heart seemed to stop. But he merely cringed and moved on, skirting around the vine to avoid contact and continue his hunt.

He hadn't noticed her beneath the leaves?

"Lulu, I know you're nearby. Sweetheart, I'm so sorry I

hurt you. I won't let Kaysar win again. He will pay, I swear it. Where are you? Have you remembered me yet? I can't flitter you to safety if I can't touch you."

A new image flashed. The Viking, poised above Lulundria, his features strained but blissful as his baby blues peered at her. That look…what was it? Love? Adoration, maybe. It was the kind of look Cookie had never received. An expression she'd yearned to see her entire life. She just hadn't known it until now.

Her mother and father had usually only demonstrated disinterest. Boyfriends had mostly conveyed horniness. Pearl Jean and Sugars had come close to adoration, but the pair had their own defenses to overcome, and Cookie had refused to push.

How could the prince look at Lulundria like that, then kill her? *He's worse than I realized. As bad as the centaurs.* How many other innocent, defenseless women had the Viking harmed in his lifetime? How many would he harm in the future, if someone didn't stop him?

If only Cookie could command her body with a remote control right now. His mutilated remains would be splayed at her feet already.

"Lulu, please," he whisper-yelled, growing desperate. "You're injured. The thought of your pain… You need my help, and I need to help you. Sweetheart, I know what happened to your heart. The pixies told me. Please, don't worry. We can navigate this together."

The pixies— Those wretched gossips!

The burst of temper reminded her of one in particular, and she scowled. Give her five minutes alone in a room with Thumbelina, and Cookie would be picking pink pixie out of her teeth.

"I might be a stranger to you right now, but I'm a stranger

willing to die to protect you. Lulundria? Please." The Viking spun this way and that. "Kaysar is fast on my heels. If he discovers you—"

"Too late," a familiar voice announced. "He's discovered you already."

Kaysar. Her knees wobbled. He'd come for her, after all.

"When will you die?" the Viking snarled.

Her dark knight stepped into her field of vision and grinned. "Come now, Prince Jareth. Is that any way to greet a treasured foe?"

Sweet goodness. He grimed up good. Gaze voracious, she drank him in. Tousled dark hair fit the gleam in his eyes. Controlled aggression flushed his skin, his muscles straining. His clothes were dirty and torn in numerous places, his boots scuffed.

"I won't let you near her a second time." The golden-haired brute braced for battle. He and the king were close in height and muscle mass: size Hulk. The demon versus the demon, both experienced killers. But only one of them made her go liquid.

"How about a third?" Kaysar exuded more of that disturbing patience, a jot of amusement and a dash of satisfaction, each liberally coated in malice. "My Eye is better than yours. I had the princess's location long before you did."

Whatever damage the prince had inflicted earlier had healed, the king ripe for his next battle. She almost whispered his name to let him know she waited nearby, but prudence kept her quiet.

"Go on," Viking taunted him. "Strike at me."

Kaysar arched a brow, amused. "You truly think you can win against me?"

"I did before."

"You?" Kaysar scoffed, a casual action that belied the

bombs of fury exploding in his irises. "There you go, lying again. A pink pixie sliced my Achilles tendons," he explained, so patient he was terrifying. "The pink pixie won. At least temporarily. I believe I still have bits of her on my boots."

Cookie's pulse fluttered. He'd taken care of Thumbelina? *Hat tip. Next round's on me, majesty.*

"You kill and kill and kill," the other man snapped, his daggers glinting in the sunlight. "How are you any better than the Frostlines you hate?" Dust motes swirled around him, a gentle contrast to the tension that fizzed the air. "Why can't we end this war between us, once and for all?"

"Tsk-tsk. If you didn't want me addicted to your misery, Jareth, you shouldn't have made it taste so good."

The Viking lunged at him. Kaysar winked and vanished before contact.

Cookie silenced a shout of denial as she pressed against the front of her leafy cocoon, a visceral need to grab hold of the king choking her. He didn't know she was here. He didn't know he'd left her behind, that she—

Amazing heat flamed from her nape to her ankles. She attempted to turn, but there was little room. Less than before. Strong arms wrapped around her from behind, a hand tipped by razor-sharp claws flattening on her belly, the fingers spread wide. Another hand cupped her throat, cold metal resting on her rushing artery.

Cookie's heart raced a thousand times faster than before, frissons of awareness pinging her nerve endings. Kaysar *had* known she was here. He'd come to her. She wasn't alone anymore. Breath left her as she sagged against him, relieved.

With his thumb under her chin, he forced her head to slant and rest against his shoulder. Despite the shadows enveloping them, she had no trouble meeting his gaze. His eyes glowed, a beacon in her storm.

Kaysar bent his head, putting his lips at her ear. He whispered, "Have you missed me, sweetling?"

His low rumble filled her head, rousing sensual smoke, fogging her thoughts. How easily he wove a spell over her mind. And her body. Her nipples drew tight, and her belly fluttered. A warm ache bloomed between her legs. She wanted…*she wanted!*

The intensity of her desire for the man frightened her in a way Jareth's violence had not, and she gulped. Kaysar had spoken of craving her. But *she* craved him, even though she knew better.

What you craved, you focused on. What you focused on, you magnified. What you magnified had the power to erode your resistance.

She needed her resistance to prevent herself from making a stupid mistake. Her defenses were already down, her ability to filter emotion on the fritz. It must be. Her senses remained heightened, her nose saturated with his delicious scent, her skin tingling, desperate for his touch.

Afternoon heat? What afternoon heat?

Realizing he'd lost his foe, the Viking—Jareth—released his aggression, using a tree trunk as a punching bag. She flinched with every blow. How often had he used those fists on Lulundria?

When he finished his temper tantrum, the tree had a nice hidey hole for cat-size squirrels.

Cookie tried to maintain a strict watch on his whereabouts, in case he neared again. But her mind had other ideas, tracking Kaysar's every breath. Every point of contact warmed her.

Jareth stomped around. Kaysar continued to hold her, as

if they had all the time in the world, gliding, gliding, gliding his thumb over her hammering pulse, leaving a trail of fire in his wake.

When Jareth finally bailed, Kaysar smoothed a leaf from her cheek. "Someone is enjoying her new powers, I see. As she should." A husky chuckle fanned her lips, and she wanted to tell him to shut up and never stop talking. To be still and move against her. To let her go and hold on forever. "Lulundria created ivy. What you created is poisonvine. The difference is telling, don't you think?"

"Telling?" she said, biting back a moan when he rubbed a massive erection into her crack.

"Mmm-mmm. Telling." He nuzzled her cheek. "One was made for light, one for dark." Holding her gaze, he slid the hand on her throat up and over her jawline, then traced the tip of a claw around her lips. The lightest of grazes, yet streams of pleasure arced to her core. "How perfectly you fit against me, princess."

Concentrate on what matters. Survival. Knowledge. A ticket home. "What is poisonvine?" Would she hurt others with it, as she'd hurt the two women during her escape? Would she harm loved ones like Pearl Jean and Sugars? That—no. That couldn't be allowed to happen. She would rather die than injure her family.

"Poisonvine is dangerous to most fae. It weakens them. But you, it will strengthen, I suspect."

"What does poisonvine do to *you*?"

"Tickle," he breathed. He nipped her earlobe and goose bumps erupted over her limbs. "Tell me, Chantel. What is this power you wield over my body, hmm?"

She had power over his body? Her? "None. Some?" Tons? "I don't know." He certainly wielded power over hers. As he held her and bestowed those gentle caresses, her muscles melted like butter. *Focus*. Right. "What's your beef with Jareth?" And they did have a beef. A big one.

What had Jareth said? *Why can't we end this war between us, once and for all?*

Kaysar tensed. "That is none of your concern."

Six words, unbending command. If she asked again, he intended to retaliate. But how? She still wasn't afraid of him.

Think this through. The battle between the two men hadn't started with Lulundria. Kaysar only met the princess the day Jareth iced her. So why had the king risked his life to aid an enemy's wife?

"Maybe you should let me go now?" she said. She needed a moment to think *without* him nearby.

Another chuckle. "Does my proximity bother you, sweetling?"

"Yes," she burst out. "And I'd prefer an endearment like Machete or Chops. Now be a good boy, and let me go."

He moved his hands over her arms, so gentle, almost tender, never cutting her with those vicious claws. "Little doll, I'm not the one holding you captive. You are."

Little doll? Breathing became an activity of the past. "How do I get rid of the stalks?"

"You haven't learned to hold on to the stalks mystically," he said, "so you must release your connection to them physically." When he tapped his fingers on hers, she remembered the vines. Oh, yes. Right again. Yesterday, the stalks had withered when she'd ceased needing them. To her knowledge, she'd done nothing special.

As she eased her grip, the leaves withered, like the few times before, freeing her and her guest from their emerald prison. She sucked in a mouthful of clean, crisp oxygen that lacked Kaysar's carnal sweetness. Finally, she could think again. Kind of. Mostly. A thrum of desire lingered…

He flittered in front of her, and she yelped.

"At the very least, give a girl a warning first," she grumbled.

Too beautiful for anyone's good, he removed a pair of boots from an overstuffed cloth satchel. "For you."

She accepted without hesitation, clutching the shoes to her chest. "Thank you so much."

He smiled at her as he removed the bag's leather strap from his chest and offered it to her. Disconcertingly gleeful, he told her, "Your provisions are inside. You will carry them, of course."

She frowned, the weight of the bag a little worrying. "Why *of course*?"

"*My* provisions aren't cradled inside. Why would *I* carry it?"

Uh… "Because you're a gentleman or whatever?"

Amused, he softly chucked her under the chin. "What a silly thing to say."

Good point. Okay, trying again. "You should carry it to tick off Jareth." He delighted in the prince's misery. Was that why he'd aided Lulundria? To hurt Jareth? "He'd probably be super bummed to know his enemy helped the woman he believes to be his wife."

He scanned her face, as if he needed to double-check the intent behind her words. "You will carry the bag, Chantel, or we will leave your provisions behind."

Ugh. His flat tone promised friction if she protested. But so what? "I'm already weak and tired. I've been on the run forever because you didn't find me fast enough." She couldn't mask her whine as her fortitude wavered. "And I'm starving."

His eyelids lowered a tad. "You're the one who insisted on our current arrangement," he reminded her. "I'm your paid-for guide through the forest, nothing more. Though you broke your promise within minutes of giving it, didn't you?"

"No way. I exercised my caveat. What was I supposed to do, anyway?" she huffed. "Stay put and let Jareth nab me?"

He thought for a moment. "I made sure to pack you clean clothes, toiletries and even the weapons you begged for."

Weapons? "Really?" she squeaked. Finding new strength, she hooked the satchel's strap across her chest. "Okay, yes, I'll carry the bag."

"That's my princess," he said, his lips twitching. He reclaimed the boots and knelt before her. He clasped her ankle, his gentleness surprising. "First, let's prepare your poor feet."

As she gripped his broad shoulders to steady herself, he secured the boots in place. She expected pain, but her gashes must have healed. A welcome development. Though she would have endured *any* amount of agony for these boots. They were the most exquisite pair she'd ever seen, studded with sapphires, yellow diamonds, obsidian and pearls to create a *Starry Night* effect.

None of her footwear at home compared. "To be clear, these boots are mine to keep forever?"

"They are." The moment he tightened the laces, the boots warmed and shifted, conforming to her feet, as if made specifically for her.

She moved around, testing out the fit as Kaysar straightened. Perfection.

"We are ready." The gleam in his whiskey eyes did odd things to her insides as he offered his hand to her. "Come then. Our journey begins."

CHAPTER TWELVE

KAYSAR LED HIS charge through the Forest of Many Names, pretending to be the gentleman she'd hinted about wanting. Being solicitous didn't come naturally to him, but his mood remained bright.

A novel experience for one who existed in a haze of fury.

He thought he might even hover at the edge of giddy. He had his princess again. The day and night without her had been torture of the worst kind, his mind constantly on the verge of a breakdown.

Now, here she was, alive and well, panting her breaths and mumbling her complaints as she trudged behind him. She struggled under the weight of the bag. Possibly because he'd added a rock every few miles, but who could say?

He hadn't forgotten Eye's warning. *She is the skin she wears.*

He simply didn't know what it meant or how it affected his plans. *Nothing will affect my plans.* Every step impelled him closer to Jareth's endless suffering.

Once the prince and his bride were dealt with, Kaysar would focus on King Hador for a while. Rumors suggested the old king desired a wife of his own.

I can take her, too...

"How far are we going to walk today?" Chantel asked, no longer content to mumble.

Do not grin. "We're almost there."

She puffed a breath. "That's what you said an hour ago."

"And now we are even closer." Her misery had only begun. Soon she would realize her complete dependence on him and beg for aid. "Isn't that wonderful?"

"My feet are sore," she whined. "These boots are the best, yeah, and I love them dearly, but they are also the worst, and I hate them with the heat of a thousand suns."

"You'd rather go barefoot?" On alert, he maneuvered around trees, ducked under gnarled branches and avoided webs of any kind. They currently meandered through Autumn Court territory, where the Frostlines had many allies.

Trolls and ogres kept their distance. Pixies, too. Understandable, considering what Kaysar had done to the pink one. He'd been in the midst of a battle with Jareth when she'd swooped in and hobbled him, running the edges of her dagger-sharp wings through his Achilles tendons. Her version of retribution for slaying Race.

Had she flown away immediately afterward, she might have survived the encounter. Instead, she'd circled back to finish him off. Though pixies appeared fragile, they were incredibly strong. Even still, he'd had no trouble catching and crushing her in his fist, then stomping on what remained.

Remembering her attack renewed his fury. He almost wished someone did hide nearby, thinking to attack him. If nothing else, he'd have an opportunity to test Chantel's fae powers. What more could she do? What were her limits? How would she react to his song?

"Slow down already," she griped, and he cast a glance over his shoulder. Sweat dampened her radiant skin, glistening as if she'd been dusted with diamond powder. "The land is treacherous. The rocks are sharp, the tree bark is spiked, and what is that awful smell?"

Despite the clenching in his chest, there was no preventing his grin. "That, princess, is the stench of death. We near another field of slaughter. My enemies and their allies thought to invade my land weeks ago." Months? Days had blurred together for Kaysar. "I attacked first and left their bodies for all to see. Care for a viewing?"

"No, thanks," she said, but he thought he might have heard a note of curiosity rather than distress or disgust.

His grin widened. There was darkness in this woman. He'd realized the truth when she created poisonvine rather than ivy. A development Jareth was sure to lament. The fool. *No appreciation for the finer things.*

Perhaps that darkness explained Kaysar's inexplicable pull to her? Throughout his endless existence, few had understood his drive to devastate the Frostlines. The citizens of Astaria called him evil, as if he had no right to entertain such malice. Of course, few knew the abuse he'd suffered.

Months of pain. Degradation. Endless loss.

The past rose from the mire of his mind, a treacherous tide intent on swallowing the present. With a hiss, he shoved his metal claws deep into his wrist and dragged the tips to his elbow. Blood gushed from the four furrows. Map. Sister. Calm.

Better.

"Kaysar! You're injured," Chantel cried from behind him. "There's a trail of blood—"

"I'm already healing." Her concern did something to him. He hardly noticed it, though. Yes, it was already forgotten.

Lying to yourself *now?*

He sliced a tree limb blocking his path, then ushered her along a line of azure bushes. A small, circular clearing overflowed with sunlight and wildflowers. The entrance to *his* territory.

"Shall we rest here?" he asked and commanded in unison.

"We—" She gaped at the terrain, suddenly speechless, and his chest puffed with pride. He'd paid for every square inch of the Nightlands with misery, countless battles with monsters, and starvation, often going weeks without food or even comfort of any kind.

As she looked everything over more closely, her lustrous skin reveled in the sunlight, aglow with life and vitality.

When can I hold her again? How will she react?

He couldn't wait to find out. Remembering how her body had trembled against his, how her pulse had jumped and her soft curves had melted over him, he throbbed. Throbbed. For her. A Frostline. As if she controlled his body, and he did not.

Kaysar scowled, frustration entwining with anger and desire. His stance hadn't changed. Women were tools to be exploited for his cause. They were useful until they weren't, and they weren't worth any effort otherwise.

Did the princess release a special plant pheromone that heightened his senses and unlocked a wanton nature he'd previously known nothing about?

Too often in their short acquaintance, he'd caught himself deliberating what sex with her might be like. How it might vary from the sex he'd had with past targets. How she might prefer it. Hard or soft?

He'd always tailored his seductions to the individual, taking no thought for his own pleasure. He'd simply done whatever he'd known the other person wanted. Some had feared violence. Others had begged for it. Some had required demands, and a few had felt inclined to issue them.

But which had *he* favored? He didn't know. His broken mind had never cared, his body's sensations dulled.

But they weren't dulled anymore.

"That tree." She pointed to a massive okatriva. A tricolored sapling with a black trunk, white leaves, and red fruit. "That looks like a Tree of New Beginnings found in *The Forest of Good and Evil.*"

Tree of New Beginnings? Forest of Good and Evil? No doubt she referred to her former mortal world. Key word: former. Meaning, the information mattered not at all. She had a new home now.

During their trek, she'd asked numerous questions about different landmarks, poisons and animals, using names he'd never heard of. She'd asked questions about everything—except Kaysar himself. The insult of it all. As her guide, her safety was his responsibility. Shouldn't she wonder about him? At least a little?

He definitely wondered about her. Did a mortal husband or lover await her at her former home? How did she like to spend her days?

Irritated, he told her, "I suppose those who eat its fruit do receive a new beginning." He shrugged. "Since they die seconds later."

She grimaced, but cast the fruit a longing glance. "Is the death permanent or is there wiggle room?"

"Yes." Hungry, was she? Good. He'd devised the correct strategy. Her needs would herald her capitulation.

Except, the instinct he'd combatted intermittently whispered once again. *Feed. Satisfy. Protect.*

The conundrum threatened to incite his rage. He gnashed his teeth, then gnashed harder when he noticed more of her hair had pinkened. The light shade lent an undeniable illusion of vulnerability to her delicate features. *My own personal doll.*

Still, he missed the rich sable locks. Were the strands as silky as they appeared? He almost reached out, when Eye's warning echoed inside his head, stopping him. *She is the skin she wears.*

"What?" Chantel gave herself a self-conscious pat. "I have bugs in my hair, don't I?"

Her irises. They'd changed, too. A golden starburst had exploded around her pupils, spilling deeper into her emerald irises. The effect was startling. Stunning. Mesmerizing. And oh, the scent of her. Her innate perfume had developed a spicier undertone. A powerful drug meant to lure unsuspecting males to their doom.

"Seriously," she said, chewing on her bottom lip. "What is it?"

"You are—" He clenched his teeth until his jaw protested. Compliment her, while he orchestrated her misery? No.

Movement pulled his gaze to the left, where a two-headed snake unfurled from a tree limb, nearing Chantel. A bite wouldn't kill her, only make her wish she'd died, accelerating her reliance on him.

Do not reach out. Do not.

Kaysar reached out, raking his claws through the reptile's body. Both heads plopped onto her shoulder, then tumbled to the ground.

Fool. He'd wasted an opportunity.

"What the—" She peered at the bodiless heads and screamed, then darted behind him and grabbed fistfuls of his tunic. "Save me!"

She feared snakes to such a degree, she was willing to

use him as a shield? He stood in shock. The last person to use him this way had been Viori.

The pang returned to his chest, and the sensation was not unpleasant. Rather than resist it, he leaned into it just as he leaned his body into hers, winding an arm around her. "*No one* will save you better," he told her. The vow sprang from the depths of his soul, unstoppable.

"Oh, um…I misspoke. I don't need saving." She scrambled away from him, her cheeks flushed a deep red.

Too prideful?

Her hair had grown, and she tripped over the ends. "Argh!" She lifted her fists high and shouted indecipherable words. "I hate this world."

She could not have been more adorable.

Adorable? He frowned as he approached her, saying, "Allow me."

She froze as he gently collected her hair and twisted the mass in his grip. The red returned to her cheeks and spread into a rosy flush as he unsheathed a blade with his free hand. Her incredible eyes rounded, and her breathing quickened, but she didn't fight him.

He sawed through the pink mass, careful not to apply pressure or pull.

"Oh, thank you," she moaned as the shorter hanks fell into place. She rolled her head over her shoulders. Longer locks framed her face, reaching her collar, while other strands stacked over her nape.

The uneven style amplified her delicacy, which amplified his pang. He cleared his throat, keen to look away from her or stare forever, he wasn't sure. Either way, the beauty refused to release his gaze, peering into parts of him he'd never wanted another to see.

A flush burned *his* cheeks. When he unearthed the

strength to tear his attention from her, he plunged forward, resuming their trek.

"Come," he called.

She caught up with him, huffing as she stayed close to his heels. "And I thought I was bad at peopling. You have to be the worst peopler in history."

Whatever that meant. He still held her wealth of hair, he realized. That might be…disturbing? He should release it.

But he didn't want to release it.

Disgusted with himself, Kaysar pried his fingers from the curls one by one, letting the silken mass slip away. At the last second, he snagged a sable lock and stuffed it in his pocket.

On they marched. Chantel chattered away, asking more questions about foliage. Still no queries about him. "Shall I tell you the entire history between mortals and fae?" he sniped.

"Let me guess." How bored she sounded. "Your kind lived in harmony with mine until we persecuted you. Some ancient fae banded together, using magic to create a new world. Without a common enemy, fae kingdoms are now divided against themselves, always at war."

"We never lived among you," he grumbled. Not for long. His ancestors *had* visited the mortal world to offer aid, and they'd died for their efforts.

"So, what's the biggest danger out here? To me personally, in case I wasn't clear."

Me. "Some would say a stickypit."

"Stickypit?"

"Trees like the one ahead. They bleed when they're wounded. Watch." As he passed it, he raked his claws through its trunk. Thick red liquid oozed out. "Once a trickle begins, it can't be halted. Soon a pool will form at the trunk's base, and anyone who comes into contact with it will remain glued there for the rest of their life."

"What?" She threw herself against him to escape the sap. He'd expected the action—had hoped for it, at least—and coiled an arm around her, pulling her to his side. As he continued walking, he kept a tight clasp on her hip.

He liked the way she fit his grip.

"I would have believed you without an example," she stated. "Why'd you have to go and murder an innocent tree?"

"Because your husband is following us, and I will relish his bellows if he's caught." Oh, yes. The prince had found their trail a few miles back.

"What!" she cried again.

"If you have a message for him, thirty-eight pixies are hiding nearby, happy to carry it to him."

"Pixies suck. Oh, yeah. Speaking of, I overheard you tell Jareth you killed the pink one."

Would she dare complain about his savagery?

"Thank you," she said, flicking him a glance laden with…something. What *was* that? Awe? As if he were some kind of hero? "I owed her a whole lot of nasty."

Forget the pangs. Kaysar's chest *blistered*. "You're welcome?" He didn't know what else to say. No one had ever thanked him for ending a life.

When the hairs on his nape stood up, he realized an outpost neared, a place where fae purchased food, lodging and supplies. Chantel would never know. Outposts were pocket realms hidden by an invisible curtain or veil.

He would thrill in her ignorance, of course. The worsening pang meant nothing.

Miles beyond this particular outpost was the waterfall.

The entrance to the Dusklands. His home away from home. A desolate kingdom with few other inhabitants.

Though he hadn't visited in, what? Twenty years? He loved the kingdom few others dared to enter. Or rather, he liked it. Kaysar wasn't sure he was capable of loving anything. But he did enjoy the solitude he found in the Dusklands. The few remaining citizens always hid from him, and the monsters who usually tormented them always provided an outlet for his worst rages.

He quickened his pace, forcing the princess to jog to keep up.

"Speaking of Jareth," Chantel said, bringing his thoughts back to the present. "That man disgusts me."

Shock. Tenderness. Both hit Kaysar, and he slowed, basking in their warmth. Then a worry sprang up, as cold as ice, ruining everything. Would Chantel feel the same disgust for *him*, when she learned the truth about what really happened to Lulundria?

Could he win her back when he had yet to win her in the first place? Maybe. But she'd want to leave him first, and he'd have to go more days and nights without her. He didn't want to go more days and nights without her.

Faster. His stride lengthened.

"So, how do you spot a doormaker?" Chantel asked.

Why. No. Curiosity. About. Him? They were teammates. She'd said so. She should care about his interests. "You don't spot a doormaker. You hear rumors, and you pay him a visit to perform a test."

"And you've heard rumors?"

"Oh, yes." Centuries ago, he'd heard *many* speculations about a male living in the Dusklands, someone who opened doors to the mortal world using a fire-based glamara. Had

Kaysar killed him a short time later? Yes. But he'd still heard the rumors. "Do you have no other questions for me?"

"Well, I'm interested in learning more about flittering," she said, panting as he lengthened his stride yet again. "I'm guessing you can't flitter a non-flitterer like me by holding my hand? What I mean is, Jareth mentioned holding my hand to whisk me away. Is that something *you* can do but for some reason you're choosing not to?"

"I'm offended you must ask, sweetling." Suspicious of him already? His gut tightened. He lifted her feet off the ground and sped into a light run. "Of course I can flitter you. I can flitter anyone. My powers are vast."

She scrambled to throw her arms around him, trying not to teeter from his hold. "Why haven't you flittered me already? I'm so ready to *not walk*, Kaysar."

He liked his name on her lips.

He might like Claw Man better.

"Do you wish to pay for additional services from me, princess? If so, I find I'm keen to bargain." He slowed. What would he demand this time?

Her gaze dropped to his mouth before she wiggled to her feet. He kept an arm around her, ensuring she remained at his side. "Right. Walk-running it is." She gave a nervous laugh tinged with fatigue. "Although, fine. Call me curious. What *is* your price for flittering? Since we took sex off the table."

"We took sex *as payment* off the table. So what are you offering?"

Her chortle pleased him, his pace slowing. "Not a danged thing," she said, and if he wasn't mistaken, a teasing light shimmered in her eyes. "You truly believe you'll convince me to sleep with you?"

"You've seen my face, yes?" Her amusement spurred

his own, and he flashed her another grin. "Wait until you see my body."

"I'll tear off my clothes to get to it, will I?"

"Piece by piece." His voice dipped. "I will have you, sweetling." Many times, in many ways.

"Do you have a shot with me? Certainly. I'm telling myself to resist but… I mean, I endured a yearlong relationship based on less, and you are definitely hot." Quick glance. Hooding eyelids. "*Really* definitely hot."

He basked in her admiration for his appearance until her other words registered and a terrible, frothing fury descended over him. She'd spent an entire year with the same person? An *eternity*. "Did you kill him? Did the relationship end with his death?"

She shook her head. "He ended the relationship and blamed me for it while I blamed him. But now I think he might have been right. I think I feared being with him. Ugh. That's so embarrassing to admit. But for most of my life, I believed I was going to die. Some nights I wasn't sure I'd wake up the next morning. Sometimes I didn't *want* to. My body had become a prison. I didn't think Nick would understand. I was certain he'd leave me if he knew the full extent of my condition."

Voice gentling, Kaysar told her, "I know about prisons and wishing to die so the pain will stop, but needing to live anyway. Always wondering what will happen next. Hating your lot and resenting others for theirs."

"I—yes," she said, her eyes going wide. Liquid. *Molten.* "You get it."

That look… He wanted to stare and bask in it forever. He needed to look away. So he did. Kaysar pulled at his collar and forged ahead, as he always forged ahead. Vengeance mattered. Nothing else.

CHAPTER THIRTEEN

COOKIE MARCHED BEHIND KAYSAR. She'd begun to lag behind as he and his impossibly long strides pushed through tangle after tangle of limbs. Begging him to slow down wasn't an option. He only increased and decreased his speed according to his mood. The faster he stalked, the more agitated his mind.

According to the exercise chart Pearl Jean had tacked onto a bathroom wall at home, Cookie and Kaysar currently maintained a level six "mall walk." He was mad about something but unsure about it.

The only bright spots to her endless cardio? Every step carried her closer to the farmhouse. And, well, she kind of enjoyed watching the king's butt. That thing had pop. There was no shaking it, even when he shook it.

She needed to enjoy the glorious work of manly art while she had the chance. Never see it again? A total travesty. And yeah, okay, his butt wasn't the only lure. She'd begun to think that maybe, just maybe, leaving Kaysar behind was going to be a real bummer. They'd known each other a hot minute, but he got her in ways no one else ever had, and she thought she got him, too. As they'd talked, they'd had a moment of bonding, accepting that their baggage came in similar makes and models.

What awful trials had he endured in his lifetime? Oh, what she wouldn't give to learn.

Was this how Nick had felt when they'd dated? Desperate for answers but stifled by his partner at every turn? Yikes. Perhaps she'd send him an apology basket when she returned to Earth.

If ever she learned to open doorways on command, she could maybe, possibly return to Astaria and visit Kaysar. Upon occasion. When she didn't have something better to do. Or want to nap.

Would he even desire to see her again? They'd had that moment of bonding, yes, and she felt as if she knew him. But she didn't know him, not really, his objectives a mystery. One moment she suspected that yes, he did crave her, whoever she was, and he couldn't get enough of her. The next she firmly believed he loathed her very existence. That, too, depended on his mood.

The current mood blew chunks. Everything annoyed him.

Asking more questions about the realm might work as a distraction from whatever bothered him. Or heat his temper another fifty degrees. Totally depended on which side of his personality responded. The besotted stalker or the surly king.

The truly sad thing? She was attracted to both.

Whatever his mood, he remained strong and capable. A fallen tree in the way? No problem. He tossed it aside. Nothing deterred him from anything he decided to do, and nothing frightened him. No, he deterred and frightened everyone else. The guy had cut her hair and saved a lock as a keepsake. She'd noticed the dark strands sticking out of his pocket. Any fae, ogre or troll they came across paled before fleeing at top speed.

Each time it happened, she'd gone all ooey gooey inside, feeling like a silly schoolgirl with a crush.

"Ow!" A limb grazed her shoulder, slicing her shirt and drawing blood. When she hopped to the side, she stepped on a rock, and her poor feet seemed to swell in her boots. Then another limb sliced her. And another. Ugh! She hated this world. Hated feeling helpless and lost, not knowing up from down. Mostly she hated hiking and everything and everyone everywhere. And she wasn't being dramatic right now. They all deserved it.

"Worst fantasy resort ever," she grumbled. "One star." The review for her guide might not be any better. Not once did he do what she secretly wanted and carry her.

He walked faster, making her walk faster.

As they trudged up another hill, her lungs cooked to well-done. Her thighs cooked. *All of her cooked.* "I'm never joining a gym. After this, I'm never exercising another day in my life."

Jumping over a thick tree root, she whimpered. When she skirted a cluster of snapping flowers, the satchel slammed into her side, and she winced. Stupid bag! What was she lugging around, anyway? Anytime she reached for the tie, Kaysar—

"Do you enjoy going nowhere?" he snapped, increasing his pace.

That. He prevented her from finishing the task and pushed onward. So frustrating, but probably for the best. If she dropped an item, she lost it forever, guaranteed. The king pausing to allow his lowly partner to collect it? Please. But oh, she wasn't sure she possessed the stamina to go much farther. Lack of food and water had taken their toll. Utter fatigue ruled.

Crush? Dwindling fast.

"What?" Kaysar said, pivoting to wag a finger at her

face. "What is this look? We're doing as you demanded. Where are your smiles? Your thanks?"

He actually wondered why she lacked *smiles*? Her nerves frayed beyond repair. "Are you referring to my Resting Serial Killer Face? Because I'm nearing a snap, and I'm not sure there will be survivors. Slow down a little."

"You are the one so desperate to find a doormaker, Chantel," he chided, as if she needed another reminder.

To her astonishment, he slowed to an amble before acknowledging her silent pleas and sweeping her into his arms. He redistributed the weight of the satchel, taking the burden upon himself.

"You're so strong." Cookie snuggled closer, molding her body to his.

"The strongest," he said, as if her praise mollified whatever had angered him.

Her animosity seeped away. Mmm. He smelled so good. Though she'd lamented the heat only moments ago, she reveled in it now. His warmth delighted her.

She opened her mouth to ask him a personal question. She knew so little about him, and curiosity was a thorn in her side. Before a single word escaped, she clinked her teeth shut. Nope. No antagonizing her guide when he'd only just begun to carry her.

There were only two directions that kind of conversation could go.

Scenario #1

Cookie: *Asks the question.*

Kaysar: *Snaps at her for daring to ask and puts her back on her feet.*

Scenario #2

Cookie: *Asks the question.*

Kaysar: *Refuses to answer and puts her back on her feet.*

Besides, the moment she inquired, he would learn he possessed knowledge she wanted. *Personal* knowledge. He could use it against her. No, thanks. Already she relied on him more than she wished to admit.

Just get home.

"Do you have nothing else to ask me?" he demanded, getting worked up again.

"Well, yes," she said, testing the waters. If he was amenable, she'd asked him a non-personal question.

His breath hitched. With eagerness? "Ask, Chantel."

"If the fae are immortal, how did Lulundria die from her wounds? I mean, my powers came from her, and I healed a broken bone in minutes."

He grated, "Immortality doesn't mean we live forever. It just means our bodies generally regenerate faster than they die. However, some injuries are too severe and heal too slowly."

He ducked under a long branch without a hitch in his stride, keeping her secure in his arms. As he straightened, the temperature dropped. Noises changed, too. Rushing water drowned out chirps, croaks and buzzes, though she saw no sign of a river. Even the atmosphere changed, the air electric, as if another storm brewed.

"What is this place?" she asked. No flowers grew, yet the bushes were seemingly placed by intelligent design, strategically creating a pathway to lead to a tree dripping with blue fruit.

"There's nothing we need here," he responded, his voice tight and his posture stiffer than before.

Not really an answer, but okay. She surveyed the tree. Pink bark, purple leaves. Those fist-size sapphire fruits. Her mouth watered, heart rate increasing. In the center of the trunk was a swirling symbol—one she recognized.

Chantel barely contained a squeal. Rhoswyn *was* inspired by Astaria. Any remaining doubts dissolved, a torrent of excitement ripping her next words from her. "This is an outpost."

Her companion cursed and hurried on. "So? We need no goods."

Cookie squirmed from his arms, her feet dying a thousand deaths as she backtracked to examine the area. Oh, yes. Definitely an outpost. The sapphire fruit acted as an edible key, but you couldn't pluck one until you'd issued payment.

A muscle jumped beneath Kaysar's eye as he joined her. "Did you recall another of Lulundria's memories?"

She'd tell him about her job later. A fae who'd never encountered a computer might not be able to comprehend her meaning. For now, she shrugged away the question. "I'm entering the outpost, one way or another." In Rhoswyn, outposts allowed players to recharge, eat—food!—pick up cool weapons and switch paths, if they so desired. Well, Cookie so desired, please and thank you. "A doormaker might be inside."

"And I haven't heard rumors about him?" He scoffed, then beckoned her closer. "Come. Soon we reach the waterfall. The entrance to the Dusklands, where rumors suggest the doormaker resides," he explained.

"What's the rush? I'm starved." She ran her hands over the tree's shockingly velvet-soft bark. "Why do you always get to make the calls, anyway? We're a team. Technically, I'm paying you. You insisted on a price, and I'm delivering. Look at me, staying by your side. That makes you my *employee*. Guess what? At my company, we have a saying. 'The boss is always right.'"

He made a little noise of annoyance. "I should have charged more."

"Well, it's too late now. We already agreed. The only remaining question is whether you're going in with me or waiting out here."

"Is that so?" His brows winged up, his smugness as irritating as it was sexy. "How do you enter?"

"You offer payment, and you receive a key." In the game, you paid with blood rubies—also known as credit cards. Maybe Kaysar had packed some coins in the satchel? "Am I right? I'm right, aren't I?"

He glowered at her.

Cookie dropped her gaze to the bag. He noticed. Of course he noticed. She dove for it anyway. He flittered, and she swiped nothing but air. Dang him.

He appeared a few feet away, still holding the bag and scowling. "You want to visit the outpost? Very well. We'll visit the outpost." He reached inside the bag and withdrew a diamond choker. "The worth of this far surpasses the cost of a key, yet we'll receive no reimbursement. I hope you're happy, Chantel."

Her eyes nearly bugged out of her head. She'd carried *jewels*?

Complain about the weight of the bag? Never again. *Worth every ache.* "That is…" What word would do that masterpiece of glittering stones justice? Oh, yes. "That is *mine*," she said, making grabby hands. She'd never owned anything so fine. *I'll wear it every day, no matter which yoga pants I select.* Heck, she might even decide to be cremated in the thing.

Kaysar regarded her with a curious look before lifting his arm, ensuring the magnificent stones remained just out of her reach. "Since you have indicated this is a price you are willing to pay…" He slapped the necklace against the symbol carved into the tree.

The diamonds vanished, a piece of fruit plopping to the ground.

"Tell me I have more necklaces in the bag," she beseeched. Ugh. What was wrong with her? She'd never reacted to *anything* this way. But the necklace… She wanted it back.

The curious look returned. He watched her intently as he announced, "You have a *collection* of necklaces in the bag."

"I do? Really?" In that case… She squealed with happiness and swooped down to pick up the fruit. As soon as they found a safe spot to rest, she'd examine every jewel and figure out why she had a sudden hard-on for gemstones.

"You do know you'll have to part with more jewelry to pay for your meal, yes?" Kaysar asked, never removing his gaze from her.

Hmm. Maybe she'd settle for a light snack. Like the fruit she'd already paid for.

Her mouth watered again, her taste buds reawakening. In a daze, she dusted off the smooth flesh and bit into the soft center. Warm sweetness ran down her throat, reminding her of piña colada.

Her eyelids slid shut. The worst of her hunger pangs eased, sparking an urgency to gorge.

"No," Kaysar said, confiscating the fruit. "One bite, and you can keep a clear head. More, and you'll become drunk. While I think I'll enjoy an intoxicated Chantel— which I *will* experience—I'm unwilling to share the event with others."

"Right. Clear head." Very important during a mission. "So? What happens next?"

He narrowed his eyes as he sank his teeth into the fruit

and…a whole new world appeared, as if they'd teleported to the edge of a Victorian Wild West, Fae Edition.

How amazing. They stood at the beginning of a cobblestone path; it extended before them, leading to dozens of shops, where vibrant murals adorned the outer walls and flowers grew from the roofs, spilling over the sides.

Different scents left her drooling. She thought she detected fresh baked bread. Spices. Meat? Her stomach *pleaded* for a feast.

Fae moved in varying directions at varying speeds. Some entered the shops, some exited. Hundreds of voices rang out, conversations blending together. The clothing styles differed as much as physical features. Different species wore different clothes, everything from warrior-chic to the peasant drab.

Envy hooked her and reeled her in. Spend more money at the outpost? *Watch me.* She'd go broke for a shower and clean clothes. Something made of leather, maybe.

She could acquire more jewels. A desire born from the depths of her being…or Lulundria's? Did the other woman gain territory in Cookie's mind, as well as her exterior?

The very idea repelled her.

At some point, you lost those you loved. One day, she would even lose Pearl Jean and Sugars. She refused to lose herself along the way.

As if he sensed her turmoil, Kaysar anchored a strong arm around her waist and tugged her closer. "You will stay by my side the entire time we are here. Do you understand?"

"Sir, yes, sir." Currently without defenses, she snuggled into the big, hard body as comforting as it was maddening. Wait. Why had the shoppers and shopkeepers gone still and quiet, staring over at Cookie and Kaysar with something akin to horror?

"Um," she said, growing uneasy. "Maybe we should go?"

Whispers rose from the masses, then shouts. "King Kaysar?"

"The Unhinged One invades!"

"Run!"

Unhinged One?

With those shouts, pandemonium reigned. Fae burst into motion, grabbing their things and flittering away, vanishing one by one. Others sprinted in the opposite direction.

Well. At least they hadn't attacked. "You have a reputation, I see."

"Perhaps I do," he said, urging her forward faster than she wished to go. Not this again. "You would do well to remember their fear the next time you think to test me."

"Is that a threat?" Why wasn't she afraid?

"Merely an observation."

"Are you trying to tell me you'll kill me in cold blood?" Oops. A personal question.

He didn't seem to mind, though. "Cold blood? I assure you, sweetling," he said, with his first smile in forever. His steps slowed to a crawl. "My blood always boils white-hot."

CHAPTER FOURTEEN

WITH THE OUTPOST abandoned by shopkeepers and patrons alike, Kaysar procured the best room at the best inn, as well as any dish in the kitchen he and Chantel desired, without having to threaten, maim or murder anyone. A novel experience indeed.

His plan to keep his companion in abject misery until she called off her search for a doormaker had derailed. Temporarily. Letting her go hungry appealed less and less. Meanwhile, having to watch exhaustion settle deeper into her doll-like features bothered him more and more.

He didn't know what to feel with Chantel. Which he didn't understand. He *always* knew what to feel—murderous—and he always knew what to do. *Hurt everyone.*

She was a Frostline, yes, but she also wasn't a Frostline. She'd never harmed or abused him. No, oh, no. Not his princess. She'd merely irritated him in a thousand different ways. And challenged him. And infuriated him. And amused and confused him and inflamed him as no other. But so far she'd earned none of his wrath.

Unlike Lulundria, she had no interest in Jareth. The prince "disgusted" her. A part of Kaysar believed she would understand and applaud his plans to destroy the Winter Court royals. The other part of him remained a jot…concerned about her reaction to being misled, if ever she discovered the truth.

At the moment, he sipped iced whiskey in front of a blazing hearth. Night had fallen, fierce winds howling outside. Not because of nature, but magic. The outpost was situated at the edge of his land, but operated on behalf of the Spring royal family. An allowance he made for their continued rejection of peace with the Winter Court. The owners manufactured frigid temperatures to ensure overnight guests paid extra for thicker blankets and a fire.

He'd chosen a suite with mahogany trim, gilt marble and mirrors everywhere. No matter where Chantel stood within the confines of the two-story room, he was able to watch her. His new favorite pastime. The sensual way she moved. The many expressions she revealed, none of her emotions hidden. Her body... He couldn't get enough of it—or her.

The satchel rested at his feet. He wasn't ready to remove or reveal the rocks he'd dropped inside it. As soon as she spotted them, she might comprehend his purpose. Part of him wanted her to, and he didn't know why. Warn an opponent of the actions he took against them? Was he truly so foolish?

Her misery began anew tomorrow, no matter his feelings on the matter.

"Taking a shower," she mumbled and sealed herself in the bathroom, the only area closed to his viewing pleasure.

He said nothing, letting her, his fingers tightening on the glass.

Earlier she'd eaten her weight in meat pies and lemon tartlets. Before that, she'd convinced him to use his "own money" to purchase a brand-new tunic. There'd been no need for pants, since he'd packed two pairs. Actually, he'd brought a tunic, too, but she'd wanted the one with roses and ivy embroidered around the collar, not the plain one he'd offered.

She'd pointed, batted her lashes at him and said, "I want that. Buy it for me?"

How could he refuse? With the garment secured behind an invisible blockade, he'd needed only to fetch a coin from his treasure trove and flitter back to insert the gold in the proper slot. Besides, he thought he'd begun to piece together Eye's riddle and desired a test.

She is the skin she wears...

Chantel's eyes had developed the golden starburst after she'd donned the bejeweled boots—boots he now remembered stealing from King Hador's second wife. A woman obsessed with jewelry, who'd once visited Kaysar in his prison tower, curious to scrutinize the "whore" the king used on special occasions.

Kaysar had begged for help, and she'd sneered. Sneered. She'd also left him to rot. A mistake she'd later paid for. Dearly. Only a handful of years after his escape, he'd followed her through a market. He'd known Hador needed the greedy woman, because she came with a hefty allowance from the Autumnlands, with all payments ceasing upon her death.

Kaysar had sent half of her to Hador and the other half to her family. A memory he cherished. He'd kept the boots for sentimental reasons.

Would Chantel's personality change with her garments? He would find out. Tomorrow. Tonight, he was too busy aching.

An hour ago, he'd showered and stroked himself off. Something he'd never had to do before. Even still, his wanting remained. When he'd dressed in a clean tunic and leathers, he'd barely gotten the zipper over his straining erection. Chantel's lock of hair remained in his pocket, mocking him. Why had he wanted it? Why did he keep it?

He thought he might murder anyone who tried to take a single strand from him.

When the water shut off, he tipped his glass and drained the contents. Decisions had to be made, and fast. What would he do to Chantel tonight? Kiss her? Caress her? How would she react? Welcome him eagerly? Rebuff him? *Must know.*

No. Bad Kaysar. He should do nothing to her. She required rest. So he would not advance his seduction of her. Not yet. Even if he wished otherwise. Even if she begged.

He licked his lips and growled at the thought.

A single decision remained then. Should he lie beside her in bed or force her to sleep in this chair?

Again, one question led to others. How would it feel to hold someone in his arms without choking them or stabbing them repeatedly? Good? Better than good? Awful? He'd never spent an entire night with a woman. Or anyone. After sex, he'd only ever stayed long enough to get what he'd planned to get. Secrets. Information. Ammunition.

He despised having someone's skin pressed against his. Usually. Too much did the sensations remind him of his time with Prince Lark and Hador. Then Chantel came along. Kaysar worked his jaw. They had traded touch after touch, yet he'd rarely harkened to his past. The wonder of her reactions and the shock of his own had kept those thoughts at bay. Which meant...

She had sway over him.

He gnashed his teeth, a habit he'd developed since meeting the princess. What was he going to do about her? About Jareth?

The prince hadn't followed them inside the outpost—yet. Kaysar should be the one to remain in the chair, at the ready. On the other hand, shouldn't he *try* sheltering his living Drendall up close and personal, his body acting as a shield for hers?

He masked a hoarse groan as Chantel exited the bathroom, accompanied by a cloud of steam. Though he hadn't moved, she startled when she looked his way, executing an abrupt stop. Those magnificent eyes widened, driving him crazy.

"Um. Hi," she said with a wave.

Kaysar barely stifled another groan as he drank her in. Blood pooled in his shaft. She wore the tunic, and only the tunic. Plump breasts crested by puckered nipples strained the material. Pale, slender legs stretched beneath a hem that stopped mid-thigh.

Breathing became impossible. He balled and opened his free hand, imagining kneading all her soft places. Her damp cheeks possessed a deeper rosy flush than usual. Was she aroused? Damp hair streamed to the middle of her back, the strands longer by the hour. Perfect for fisting.

Her lips parted under the weight of his perusal.

Will. Not. Kiss. Her.

She appeared fully recovered from their excursions, yet he sensed the depths of her exhaustion, and his chest ached. She'd been through much these past few days. Transported into a different realm. The development of unnatural powers. The attentions of a vengeful king.

With slow movements, lest he alarm her, Kaysar set the glass next to the satchel at his feet and rose.

"Get in the bed." The command rasped from him. But what else should he say? No other words filled his head.

No, not true. Four others sprang to the surface. *I'm sleeping with her.*

COOKIE BURROWED UNDER the velvety covers, getting comfortable on the soft mattress. Fatigue owned her, one hundred percent. Or maybe ninety. Apprehension had a piece of her, too. But she had no fight left, too exhausted to think, much less resist Kaysar's commands. She couldn't even ready her best or worst defenses against his appeal.

Cookie wanted to cut herself a little slice of Kaysar.

After Nick, she'd considered herself invulnerable to romance, her heart locked in a stronghold, protected by dragons. Somehow, the enigmatic and ferocious Kaysar was scaling her towers, making her wonder and want and wish. What would a relationship with him be like? Or at least a roll in the hay?

Hunger abated for the first time in days, she should have no trouble sleeping. But each time her mind began its shutdown, a thought about Kaysar popped up, inviting others. She alternated between being too cold and too hot.

Her dark king remained near the hearth, breathing with force, as if he struggled with a choice.

"Are you planning to watch me sleep?" she asked, curious.

"Maybe."

He'd been mostly quiet since they'd entered the outpost. Now, firelight bathed him, outlining his powerful body and illuminating the lines etched into his forehead. He was opening and closing his hands at his sides. An action he had performed before.

What thoughts tumbled through his mind?

"Kaysar?"

"I'm sleeping with you. Only sleeping." He stalked across the room, stopping here and there to snuff out the lamps. As darkness thickened, she thawed, glad for the reprieve. "Tonight," he intoned, "you rest, nothing more. So rest hard. You might not get another chance."

A warning? Or a promise? She couldn't tell.

He paused at the side of the bed, and she held her breath. Would he strip?

Clothing rustled. He unfastened his belt. Dang it. He *was* stripping, but she couldn't see. Why hadn't he left at least one lamp on?

The mattress dipped as he stretched out beside her, his drugging scent filling her nose.

Would he make a move, despite his claim? Did she hope he would?

Either way... "Don't expect cuddles," she warned. "I *hate* cuddling, snuggling, canoodling, and everything in between."

"I would rather die," he replied with a shudder.

"Good." Right?

"Good," he echoed.

Minutes passed, neither of them moving. Outside, a great wind blustered and a shutter slammed.

Remembering how amazing she'd felt in his arms, she inched toward him. Not to cuddle, just to...touch. Connection with another. At the last second, she thought better of it and rolled to her back. But the desire only magnified, until she tossed and turned, miserable.

When she could stand it no longer, she whispered, "Kaysar?" Was he still awake?

"Yes, Chantel?" The rough rumble caressed her ears.

"Try to survive this, okay?" She draped her body over his. He hissed in a breath as she rested her cheek over his heart. His *racing* heart. He wasn't immune to her nearness. She burrowed closer.

"Chantel?" he said, the tightness of his voice rousing dread.

Ugh. Was he about to order her to move?

"Do your best to endure this, all right?" He tentatively wrapped his arms around her, holding her close.

Oh. Ohhh. His heat lured her to total relaxation at long last, her muscles suddenly the consistency of jelly. The trials of the day faded. This. This was far better than tossing and turning. From now on, she never wanted to sleep any other way.

So much had happened to her these past few days, she'd *needed* an anchor in a storm.

"Mmm. You feel amazing," she said, embarrassed that she slurred. Not just exhausted. Drunk on him.

"You feel…" He hesitated, toying with the ends of her hair.

Her eyelids grew heavy, attempting to slide shut as she awaited his verdict. She fought the deluge of lethargy with everything she had. *Will squeeze every drop of enjoyment out of this.*

"Necessary," he whispered, filling the silence.

Sleep? Suddenly impossible. Had she *ever* been necessary to another person?

Longing as potent as newly popped champagne fizzed inside her, going straight to her head. Wait. Necessary? To a man she'd known a handful of days? No way. He didn't need her, and she didn't need him. She didn't need anyone, and that was that.

Why would she let herself need a man? *Nothing* lasted forever.

Needing a distraction, she asked the first question to fill her head. "Are you a terrible king? The way those people ran…"

Tension invaded their little haven. "Finally, you show interest in me, and this is what you seek to learn?"

Finally? He'd *wanted* her to get personal? An unexpected

wisp of pleasure unfurled. One wildly invasive interrogation, coming up.

"You've spent the day with me," he said, grumbling a little. "What kind of king do *you* think I am?"

Easy answer. "Cunning. Expectant. Difficult. Complicated. Liberal with orders. Quick with complaints. Unafraid of consequences." Everything he'd been with her. Perhaps a bit…mad at times, too.

More than once but less than a baker's dozen, he'd sliced his own forearm to ribbons, leaving a blood trail a mile long. Sometimes he'd muttered, "Study the map," over and over like a mantra.

"I am all of those things and more, so of course there is no better king in the realm." He sounded prideful, and it was amazingly sexy.

If exhaustion hadn't ruled her, she might have done something about that sexiness. But only might. Despite the other reasons to remain platonic, one-night stands weren't her thing. Or however-long-night stands. She and Kaysar wouldn't be together more than a few weeks. A month or two tops. Maybe? Probably?

She'd grown up hanging out online with much older gamers. Too often, they'd bragged about their conquests, all *man is god, woman is whore*. If they acknowledged the woman at all. Most they'd *dismissed* as unimportant. Forgettable. No, thanks. Cookie had wanted—still wanted—more. To be essential to someone. If only for a little while. Even if she didn't let the other person become essential to her.

"How old are you?" she asked.

"Thousands of years."

"Ah. That wonderful age when you start counting in

adjectives. I believe you've reached what's known as decrepit."

"I am not decrepit." His tone suggested he currently pursed his lips.

"Denial is the first sign that you are, in fact, decrepit."

The cutest little puff of air left him. "How old are you?"

"Twenty-six very mature years."

"Also known as infantile," he said, and she chuckled. "Tell me how you spend your days in the mortal realm."

"I play games." She racked her mind for an understandable explanation, but her thoughts grew dim...dimmer. She began to drift off, even though she continued to fight. "Don't want to sleep. Want to learn more about you..."

Her exhaustion won the war. A final thought wafted through her mind as darkness swallowed her whole. *He might be a* little *necessary.*

COOKIE SLEPT LIKE the dead. One second she knew nothing. The next she was blinking open her eyes, greeted by a wealth of sunshine. Groggy, she stretched under the covers. Had she ever been so wonderfully warm and pliant?

Ohhh. *What is this?* An ache here, an ache there. Arousal simmered inside her, a delicious heat unfurling between her legs. Well. Her mind might have shut off last night, but her body certainly hadn't.

Perhaps she and Kaysar should—"Kaysar!" She jolted upright, fighting a sudden swell of panic. Where was her gorgeous guide? Because he wasn't beside her. Or beneath her.

Her jaw dropped when she noticed the state of the room. Furniture was overturned and splintered. Fist-size holes littered the walls. Only the bed was safe. Had there been a battle she hadn't heard? Or had he done this in a fit of rage?

Pearl Jean and Kaysar believed Cookie carried darkness within her. Looking at the devastation inside this room, she could say the same about King Kaysar.

So why wasn't she afraid of him even now?

Without exhaustion coloring her thoughts and actions, the truth shone so brightly. The man hurt, and something inside her commanded, *Soothe*.

Her? When she couldn't even soothe herself? Should she even try? Soon, they'd find a doormaker and say their goodbyes. Maybe. Hopefully. If not, she'd get herself home once she recharged. If she did. *When* she did.

She shuffled from the covers and padded to the bathroom, where she splashed her face and brushed her teeth. Despite last evening's feast, she had no need to use a toilet. A wonderful and hopefully permanent development. Now that she considered it, she realized she hadn't experienced an urge to go since her arrival.

As she reached for the leather pants Kaysar had left out for her, her reflection caught her attention. Her hair contained more brown than pink today. Her eyes were gray with green specks. Not exactly the attributes her parents had given her but closer.

Would she ever be plain ole Cookie again? Did she want to be?

Was she always meant to be a Cookie-Lulundria combination?

She tugged on the leathers and gave her reflection a final glance—whoa. Had her eyes changed color again? Leaning in, she tilted her head this way and that. From gray with specks of green to green with specks of gray again. But why? What had changed? All she had done was dress.

The leathers, then? She removed the pants and studied her eyes. Gray. Pants back on. Green.

Okay. So. Obviously the garment was responsible. But why the leathers and not the tunic? When she'd donned the top fresh from its pristine packaging, she'd undergone no changes. The pants were clean but used. Was that the difference?

What did this even mean? Would other used garments affect her appearance?

Wait. What if more than her appearance was affected? When she'd worn the boots, she'd developed that hard-on for jewels.

What happened if she mixed and matched her outfits?

Cookie donned her boots and called, "Kaysar?" They should have a conversation. She rushed out of the bathroom and skidded to a stop.

He sat at the bottom of the bed, fully dressed in a white tunic and black leathers. Their uniform? He wore it better, no doubt about it, gorgeous beyond imagining. In his hands dangled a pair of ugly but comfortable-looking slippers.

A kernel of sexual desire broke through her anxiety when he dropped the shoes on the bed and jumped to his feet, his big muscles flexing. He bowed up, preparing for battle, the gleam in his eyes as turbulent as the destruction around him.

He looked capable of any vile deed, and she...liked it.

"Someone dares threaten you?" He readied his claws. "Someone dies."

She closed the distance to clutch his shirt as she explained what she'd witnessed. He evinced no confusion, only awe.

"I was right," he said with a slow grin. "You are the skin you wear."

Oookay. Cookie couldn't look away as he traced his gaze over her form. She couldn't catch her breath, either. "I don't understand." *You are the skin you wear.* Like, an avatar? "Explain to the rest of the class, if you please."

He pinched a lock of her sable hair between his fingers, rubbing the strands together. "Tell me. Do you feel any different right now?"

Did she? "I don't know. Why? Should I? Is this good or bad? Is this a fae thing?"

"Not a fae thing," he said with a slow shake of his head. "A Chantel Cookie Bardot thing. I believe you'll experience physical and emotional changes whenever you don clothing or shoes once owned by another."

Was he right? Would she undergo more changes every time she, well, changed?

"I don't want to be someone else," she griped. She already contended with Lulundria. Throwing other people into the mix sounded like the perfect recipe for disaster.

Not yet ready to consider all the ramifications of this development, she switched her attention to a subject of equal importance. "What happened last night? Why did you *Hangover* our room?" She motioned to the damage to help him translate her meaning.

His features chilled and heated, the inconsistency bewildering. Perhaps even heartbreaking. He looked almost needy and lost. "Oh. That. I had a bit of an argument with myself. I won." His shoulders lifted in a shrug. "Are you sure you wouldn't rather luxuriate in my palace as your doormaking ability charges?"

"Positive."

He pursed his lips and bent over to pick up the shoes he'd dropped. "These are for you."

If ever he decided to share his reasons for tossing furniture, she'd listen. For now, she examined the gift. Thick rubber soles. Rounded toes. Plain. The fae equivalent of tennis shoes? Perfect for hiking.

"They have no jewels," she remarked. "I'd rather wear the boots."

He looked confused. "But the boots hurt your feet."

"And they have jewels." Comfort paled in the light of their beauty.

"Fascinating creature." Amused, he dropped the shoes on the floor and offered his elbow to her. "Shall we break our fast and continue our journey?"

"We shall."

CHAPTER FIFTEEN

KAYSAR LED CHANTEL through the Forest of Many Names once again. As they wound through a maze of bushes, nearing their destination, they remained quiet. She carried the satchel, straining under its weight after a mere two hours of hiking. Already she wheezed her breaths. Her much-needed rest and a hearty breakfast had done little to aid her stamina.

He didn't feel guilty about her growing discomfort. Or the new rocks he'd slipped into the bag.

Last night, as he'd held her soft body in a tight clasp, clinging to her as if she were some kind of lifeline, he'd had to remind himself of his mission. Fury had consumed him, and he'd erupted.

Vengeance first. Her comfort wasn't and would never be his objective, no matter his feelings on the matter—a decision he'd made and accepted, even as he'd demolished their room.

"Are you sure you wouldn't rather spend the next weeks at my palace?" he asked for the hundredth time.

"Dude. Get the hint. No doormaker, no luxuriating."

A flash of anger. Very well. She would suffer the consequences of her refusal.

As always, he forged ahead. Sunlight spotlighted their path, the sound of rushing water growing louder with each step. No sign of Jareth. Had the poor princeling run into trouble?

Soft limbs and leaves brushed him, and Kaysar imagined grazing Chantel's silken skin in such a way. He hissed with need. He *must* caress her.

So this is lust. Continual, desperate wanting. An inescapable needing. Insatiable, all-consuming hunger, capable of disrupting the best-laid plans. The sweetest, most excruciating battle he'd ever waged.

Had he been drifting through his life before this, only half-awake?

He scrubbed a hand over his face. He could have killed the princess a thousand different times this morning, and two thousand different ways last night. But she'd slept so peacefully, trusting him to see to her protection. He hadn't wished to disturb her. In a mere handful of days, her life had been turned upside down and inside out. And yet she'd continued to find comfort with him.

He'd never wanted her to *not* find it.

He…liked her. If she had a problem, she complained about it, letting him know. He didn't have to wonder or ask. Did she have any idea how refreshing that was? And her ability to transform into another because of her clothing—that, he thought he might love.

How he envied her. To become anyone, if only for a little while. To feel what they felt. To experience their greatest desires and later exploit them.

Wonderful. He was erect again. Obscenely so.

Thoughts of Chantel had hardened him again and again throughout the day. He'd been inundated with unfamiliar urges, requiring every ounce of his restraint to resist her. He wasn't sure how he managed it.

Noticing a tangle of thorny vines ahead, he acted with-

out thought, lifting Chantel off her feet and dragging her
to his chest, then urging her to nestle her face in the hollow of his neck.

Another missed opportunity for her discomfort. With
his arms banded around her, offering protection, the thorns
wouldn't scratch her. Now it was too late to switch positions. He'd have to see to her suffering later.

"You should always carry me," she muttered against
his skin.

Always. Holding her tighter, he pressed through the
mess, shielding as much of her as possible. When they
came out the other side, reaching the waterfall at long last,
he exhaled with relief.

"Behold." He motioned to the waterfall with a tilt of his
chin. "The doorway we seek. The dividing line between the
Nightlands and the Dusklands." His home away from home.

"Wow," she said, gaping as she settled on her feet. "This
is lovely."

Ahead, a ten-foot cliff with glistening stones poured
pink-tinged water into a pond with two sides separated by
a rocky path. One side turned blue as the water crashed,
while the other darkened to a rich purple. Pixies flew about,
raining their sparkling dust in air perfumed with jasmine
and lavender.

The rocky path cut through the center of the water, providing a walkable path to the waterfall.

Kaysar scanned the area, remaining on alert, as usual.
Did he hear footfalls? "Stay here." He bit out the command,
hating to leave her. As soon as he did, she would find the
rocks in the pack. Either she would deduce the truth or
convince herself of a lie. Either way, she would react, and
he'd have to deal with the fallout. *Avoidable* fallout. He had
only to clean out the bag before he left.

His vengeance demanded he remove any obstacles. The truth was an obstacle. But...

His instinct. *Protect*...

Gnashing his teeth, he plunged his hand into his pocket to sift the lock of her hair between his fingers. Inhale. Exhale. He told her, "I'll give you an hour to do whatever you'd like while I secure the perimeter."

Then they would enter the Dusklands, whether she wished to or not, and her true misery would begin.

No excuses. No more wavering.

COOKIE SAID NOTHING as Kaysar flittered...somewhere else. Did he know he'd stroked her lock of hair as he'd spoken of leaving?

Developing an attachment to her? Oh, the very thrill of it. Until she recalled her newest dilemma. The tweaking of her personality, caused by clothing. So far, the ability tallied only two marks in the pro column. Potential for taking cosplay to a new level, and overriding negative emotions with positive ones through a simple wardrobe change. But both pros added a con, too. Overspending money she didn't have on those cosplay outfits and encouraging emotionally unhealthy decisions she might regret later.

Kaysar liked this development, she could tell. Did he *not* like her personality without the tweaks?

Could no one accept her for *her*?

Sighing, she searched for a comfortable spot to unwind. There. A flat, dry rock next to the pond. A landmark she believed she recognized. In the game, there was a pond/waterfall doorway, too, and it led to a treacherous land brimming with traps and treasures. Were the two locations the same?

She lugged her satchel over and plopped down. Without Kaysar's interference, she could finally examine her loot.

Trembling with anticipation, Cookie unfastened the bag and removed the item on top of the pile. A stunning emerald gown too sheer for hiking. Material crisscrossed over the breastical area for maximum cleavage, ensuring her navel would remain bare. What had Kaysar been thinking to grab this—uh, never mind. Men. Although, yes, it was perfect for cosplaying a concubine—or becoming one, if ever the urge struck—and it cost her zero dollars.

Okay. All right. Maybe the clothing ability wasn't that bad. Cookie the Vixen might be able to do what Cookie the Jewel Collector hadn't: win a kiss from a fae king. So badly she craved his mouth on hers.

What would Pearl Jean think of the man? Would Sugars hiss and scratch him, as he'd done to Nick?

Ugh. Why did it matter? Cookie and Kaysar were from two different worlds. They had no future. Not that anyone did.

She turned her attention to the second item from the bag. A pink dress with less material. The skirt appeared gossamer, as if paper-thin scarves had been sewn together, with slits here, there, everywhere. *Love!*

Next she found a tunic and another pair of leathers. Ugh. Enough garments. Where was the good stuff? She dumped out the rest of the items. Maps. Toiletries. A flask with—she unscrewed the lid and sniffed. Oh, wow. Her eyes burned and watered. *So dizzy. A flask with the most potent alcohol ever.*

When her vision levelled, she resealed the container and stuffed it in her back pocket for safekeeping, then resumed her investigation. Another diamond choker. A double-looped ruby necklace. A plethora of rings with stones the size of walnuts. An emerald armband. *Mine, mine, mine.*

Oh! She found two daggers with bejeweled handles. A black brick of...tree bark? Rocks he'd collected on their hike? Thirteen, to be exact, each weighing a pound or more. But why had he added the rocks? A fae custom, maybe? Magic?

Her sixth sense—Lulundria—told her, *No.* The rocks served no purpose...except to weigh her down and wear her out.

The words echoed, her heart doing its *you are on the right track* leap. Suspicions whirred. *Weigh down. Wear out.* She remembered Kaysar's reluctance to visit the outpost, to buy comforts she'd desperately needed. His outright denial of the outpost's existence. *Nothing we need here.* His high price to flitter rather than walk. His suggestion that she never remember Lulundria's memories. His hatred of Jareth...whom he considered Cookie's husband. His war with the man.

Confusion gave way to anger. Had Kaysar kept her miserable on purpose? Had he *made* her miserable? How many times had he accidentally led her into a briar patch? The few times they'd stopped to rest, some kind of critter had attempted to bite her. Her. Not him. Every. Time. As if she'd been purposely led to the animal.

But why would he do this to her? Just to strike at the Viking prince? Or did he not wish to find a doormaker and simply wasted Cookie's time until she capitulated to his demands and signed on for a temporary vacay in his palace? Because both explanations fit both sides of him.

Her nails sharpened into little claws, her own personal thorns. A shock as much as a delight. But why had Kaysar allowed her to discover the rocks? Had he forgotten them?

Not likely. Did he think her too foolish to uncover his ill intent, once she'd rested?

Cookie zoomed her gaze to the lingerie—sorry, the gowns he'd provided. They offered no protection against sharp limbs or bugs. Or weather. Another method of controlling her?

He absolutely wanted her miserable.

She couldn't believe she'd ever considered the possibility of sleeping with the prick.

She practically dislocated a shoulder as she tugged off the boots. "Pretend you desire me? Make me carry rocks? Fine." She stood and stripped with more force than necessary. "I'll *make* you desire me. You'll be as *hard* as rock with no outlet," she muttered with clenched teeth. The fool had given her an arsenal to use against him. Sexy clothes and scented lotions.

Cookie would take him to the brink and leave him there.

Motions clipped, she gathered her bundle of toiletries. A girl should look her best when she dished her payback.

In the water, she used the fancy soap, scrub and oil, the sweet perfumes complementing her unique scent. When she finished, she dried off and peered at the two gowns. Pink or green? If her outfits affected her personality, it mattered. She had a pretty decent mad going right now, and she refused—*refused!*—to cool off.

Justice would be served hot.

Her tasks aligned. *Wind him up, let him down, and get the heck out of Dodge.* After she'd made his body as uncomfortable as hers, she would snatch up her things and bail.

You couldn't team up with someone you couldn't trust.

With more and more similarities popping up between Astaria and Rhoswyn, Cookie could figure out the Dusklands terrain on her own, thank you.

Maybe you shouldn't play with the killer's affections?

Please. She *still* wasn't afraid of him. In fact, there was no one else's affections she'd rather play with. The idea of kissing Kaysar, of revving his engine and leaving him wanting more, excited her in ways *she* craved. Or Lulundria craved? How could she know? Did it even matter anymore?

She darted her gaze between the two gowns. The green. Something about it called to her...

For once, she didn't startle as buttery material tightened on her curves. Though she waited, expectant, she noticed no change in her mood or mindset. Did that mean anything? Or nothing? Breathing deep, she donned matching jewelry.

"Chantel?" Kaysar choked out from somewhere nearby.

He had returned.

Her heart skipped a beat as she lifted her gaze and discovered him mere feet away. She looked him over and cut off a whimper. Blood splattered him from head to toe, and it was a good look for him.

Sexy good.

But then, she looked sexy good, too.

A spring of simmering confidence poured through her, and Cookie imbibed of its waters deeply. The dress's doing? Oh, who cared? Self-assurance had fused with her bones, gifting her with a core of iron.

She smiled slowly. Coldly. "Tough day at the office, dear?"

He perused her, his eyes blazing and his jaw clenched.

A bead of water dripped from the tip of her sable locks to her nipple—a nipple drawing tighter as he watched, enthralled, wiping his mouth with the back of his hand.

He swallowed. "I found no sign of Jareth, only a band of centaurs who followed our trail. Naturally, I slaughtered them."

"Naturally. And I'm sure I'll love to hear all about it... after we've chatted about your treatment of me and you've apologized sufficiently." Not that she'd change her mind about bailing.

The pile of goodies scattered at her feet captured his attention, specifically the rocks, and he stiffened. "Well." Resigned—relieved?—he refocused on her. Wait. Had he *wanted* her to know and actively *sought* this standoff? The notion gave her pause. "You have questions, I'm sure."

At least he wasn't playing dumb. "I do."

He looked her over again, radiating a mix of satisfaction and fond remembrance. "You selected Princess Tatiana's dress to face me, rather than a garment previously owned by a royal concubine. How intriguing. I recall Tatiana well, now that I see her clothing drizzled over your luscious flesh."

Luscious? Sometimes he said the sweetest, hottest things. Other times he cut to the quick. "Do tell."

"Tatiana was Jareth's third betrothed, celebrated by many for her unflappable stubbornness. No one expected me to win her from the prince. But I did."

And he expected to win Cookie from the prince, too? By exhausting her? "Tell me why you did this to me." Let him defend his rationalizations.

"I seek Prince Jareth's punishment," he said, confirming her suspicions. He raised his chin, his pride unmistakable. "Our war has lasted eons." The ferocity in his tone proclaimed, *Not long enough.*

"So you abused *me* to punish him?" she demanded.

"I did." He offered the words without a hint of remorse. "I *live* to punish him."

Punish. Had Jareth the wife killer harmed someone Kaysar loved?

And he thought it made his actions okay?

Forget leaving him hard and wanting. Beneath her anger, hurt seethed. If she punished him for punishing someone else, then Kaysar had a right to punish her. A never-ending cycle. She sank to her knees and stuffed her belongings into her satchel—she'd earned these items. "I owe you a warning, so here it is. I'm leaving you."

Whoosh. Cookie blinked, her entire world suddenly upside down. No, right side up. Kaysar had flittered over and tossed her to the ground, pinning her beneath him. He loomed over her, one hand restraining her arms over her head, the other gripping her throat, the tips of the metal pressing into her skin.

The savagery in his face intensified the vulnerability of her pose. Those whiskey eyes glittered as he wedged a massive erection between her thighs.

"You will *not* leave me."

Her heart thundered, even as her blood heated. *Not even the slightest bit afraid.* Rather, her confidence reached new heights. This lethal king might wish to strike at Jareth, delighting in his petty retaliations against the prince's "wife," but he did crave Cookie. That, he hadn't lied about.

Hurt receded.

Unflappable? *Watch me.*

"What's the matter, Kaysar?" she purred, cradling his body against hers. "Has your raging hard-on for me left you cranky?"

He flinched but recovered quickly. "You will not leave me," he repeated. "Until I'm finished with you, we stay together."

Finished? With her? Dream on. "Stop me from leaving you in my dust. If you can." Her smirk slipped free, suddenly on full display—because she let it slip free. "If I fail to discover another doormaker, if I never recover the ability to open a door myself, I'll *still* find a way home."

Different emotions tinged his features, each one steeped in despair. "Leave me, and I'll hunt you. I'll find you, Chantel. Nothing will stop me."

Cookie smiled sweetly at him, wrenched a hand free and rammed the heel of her palm into his nose. Cartilage snapped, blood flowed.

"Go ahead. Threaten me again," she said, "and I'll hurt you."

Other than a whip of his head as he absorbed the impact, he displayed no reaction to her strike—which proved shockingly hot. "Lulundria is the key to my vengeance against the prince," he continued without a hitch. "Therefore, you are my key. You will aid me, Chantel. Willingly. That is not negotiable."

"I'm not your anything," she said, and she meant it. "I could have been your friend and your teammate, but you ruined it."

Had he just cringed? "You will stay with me, and I'll do better. I'll choose a different path for you. I've already strayed from the original."

From threats to false promises. "Too little, too late. I said we're done, and I meant it."

"I…made a mistake," he rushed out. "I didn't know you when I fashioned my first plan. It was an eternity ago."

"An eternity," she said, rolling her eyes. "And you think you know me now?" Days later?

"I know you better." He nodded for emphasis. "I know you would be *very* upset if I harmed or misled you again."

Realizing he couldn't keep her without her cooperation? Or did his burgeoning desperation stem from a different source? As he'd spoken, he'd gently rocked against her, as if he'd lost the battle to remain immobile.

To her consternation, the soft bump and grind coaxed an embarrassing amount of wetness from her. She stifled a needy gasp.

"You had a chance with me, Kaysar. You blew it."

"You hope to leave your Claw Man?" Rock. Rock. He applied more and more pressure, until suppressing a gasp was the least of her worries. "Or come on him?"

"Neither? Both?" So good! Cookie couldn't stay still. She undulated her hips, meeting his next grind and groaning. Her gaze dropped to his soft lips. So badly she wanted his mouth on hers.

Maybe...maybe she should stay a *little* longer? No, he'd done her wrong! She shouldn't do him right. "You won't seduce me into changing my mind."

"What if I only wish to seduce you for now?" he asked above her, fierce and carnal. Fatal to a woman's resistance. He smelled like sunshine, soap and sandalwood, and every inhalation left her light-headed. "You make my body want things it's never desired before."

"That means *my* plan is a success. Your body can suffer as mine did." She'd meant to make a bold statement. She'd uttered a raspy taunt instead.

"You seek the suffering of my body? Mission accomplished, little doll." He swooped down, as if to slam his mouth against hers. A split second before contact, he stopped, as if he dared not take what wasn't offered. Warm exhalations fanned over her face, tickling her sensitive skin. "Are you pleased to know I've *never* suffered like this? That I hunger in ways I didn't know I could? With your need and your trust and your everything, you've frayed my control as no other." He revealed a grin far smugger than hers. "But you hunger, too, don't you, sweetling? I scent your arousal. It is the sweetest perfume."

Heady admission. Sumptuous ferocity. Dangerous question. "Maybe I do." Time for Kaysar to learn a hard truth about her. "I'm petty enough to deny myself pleasure, as long as you're denied it, too."

His pupils dilated as if she'd uttered the most provocative invitation. He appeared spellbound. Enthralled. "Pleasure. Yes. I want it. Give it to me." His inhalations grew ragged. "I gave you my truth, after all. Now you are supposed to offer me a reward."

He nearly enthralled *her*. He…his tone. Agonizing need saturated every note. He *had* instigated this showdown. This was his version of a confession. Maybe even an apology. Because he expected—pursued—a do-over with her?

Not good enough. Her eyes slitted. If he sought absolution, he'd picked the wrong girl. "Reward you for finally giving me what I'm owed? No." But oh, the wanting refused to fade. Heat poured from him, cocooning her more surely than her vines ever had.

"Let me go," she rasped.

"Pleasure," he repeated, as if the word had gotten stuck in his brain. "I've never tasted of it, and I want to. With you." He brushed the tip of his nose against hers. "If you tell me to let you go again, however, I'll do it."

He'd *never* tasted of pleasure? Impossible. But intrigue remained. He *did* appear entranced by the thought of a simple kiss, staring at her lips as if they held the key to life's greatest mysteries. No other man had ever looked at her like that.

Confidence merged with vulnerability, creating… something else, and her breath shallowed. She imagined being the first woman to ignite passion in Kaysar, and oh, the challenge appealed. So did the power. Would any triumph be greater? Afterward, she could walk away, as planned. Because he was right. She did hunger for him, and it wasn't going away.

Why should she pass up an opportunity to rid herself of her curiosity?

"You want a taste of pleasure?" She licked her lips and rasped, "Come get it, your majesty."

Need thrummed from him. Little by little, he eased his lips to hers.

She waited, suspended on a cloud of eagerness and uncertainty...

Contact.

Her breath caught. He applied the barest pressure, there but a moment and so gentle she had no defense against him. He...he...

What was happening to her? With a brush of his mouth, he depleted her anger.

He didn't pull back, but hovered his face over hers as he rocked against her. The barely-there caresses hastened her to the edge. She arched and—friction!

Cookie whipped her hips, grinding against his shaft. They cried out in unison. But he didn't speed up or rock harder. He kept her wanting...addicted.

They breathed each other's air and panted. She grew wetter, trembling and aching, her arousal unfathomable. How much longer could she bear the acute sharpness? Every part of her remained aware of every part of him.

"Twelve months of torture, yet you are becoming my greatest torment." He appeared dazed—or crazed. Did he even know what he was saying right now? "I never want you to stop."

Twelve months of torture? The reason for his war with

Jareth? No wonder Kaysar demanded retribution. No matter who he had to hurt.

A need to comfort him drew a ragged moan to the surface. Voice breaking, she commanded, "Kiss me, Kaysar. Kiss me and don't stop."

He dove down. Blessed contact. A man possessed, he thrust his tongue against hers. He devoted himself to the kiss, claiming her hard. Claiming her well.

The decadence of his flavor left her reeling. They fed from each other, as if starved. How did such soft lips deliver such powerful bliss? Beneath the gown's flimsy fabric, her nipples throbbed for him. Between her legs, a sublime ache intensified.

He rocked against her, the friction better than before. Divine. Then he did it again. And again. Rubbing.

She broke his hold on her wrist to scrape her thorn claws through his hair.

He closed his eyes a moment, enjoying the contact. Slowly, he glided his hand from her throat to her breast.

"Yes," she cried as he kneaded her. With his thumb and forefinger, he pinched her nipple. Moaning, she arched into his hold. Worked up so intently, so quickly? "More, Kaysar."

His touch roughened. His kiss became wonderfully aggressive. When he lowered his head to tongue the rushing artery he'd threatened only seconds ago, she gasped.

"You want more? I will give you *everything*," he vowed fiercely.

Mmm, that voice. The pure, undiluted authority of it. She rocked her hips, driven by raw instinct. Feeling more vulnerable and raw with every new sensation he elicited, she fisted his tunic, only to frown when she realized what she'd done. As a child, she'd grabbed her parents' clothing to capture their attention. A habit she'd conquered years ago. Why did it resurge now, with him, a temporary diversion?

A worry for later. *Must get rid of the tunic. Yes.* The source of her trouble. Pulling at the material, she commanded, "Off."

After Kaysar wrenched backward, she expected him to clasp his shirt's hem. He remained immobile instead, panting and stiff. He searched her gaze, his own teeming with horror and shame, as if terrible memories danced behind his eyes.

Golden glass shards seemed to shimmer around pupils the size of dimes. Lines of tension branched from the corners of his mouth, where his skin pulled taut. A hated contrast to his red, kiss-swollen lips.

The sight of him like this hurt something inside her.

"Did I harm you, sweetling?"

Harm? Why would he think so? She shook her head. "No, not at all." Just before he'd ended the kiss, she'd used the word *off* in hopes of undressing him. Was it possible he'd mistaken her meaning? That he believed she'd ordered him to stop?

The horror-tinged shame roused terrible suppositions.

She must have made a face he perceived as pitying. His cheeks flamed, and he reared further back. But he didn't stomp off. He stood before her, a muscle jumping under his eye. As he examined her, his expression iced over. A corner of his mouth tilted in a sneer. "Your husband will be displeased when I describe this indiscretion. I think he'll be particularly interested in the way you begged me for it."

Oh, that cut. Did she understand why he'd said it? Yes. He was lashing out over the misidentified pity. It sucked—he sucked, too, kind of—but she did understand. She had probably done the same to others. If probably meant definitely. But what sucked the most—he meant those words. He wanted to tell Jareth; an undercurrent of glee had given him away. Which made her speculate about other things...

Had he attempted to save Lulundria from Jareth simply to hurt the other man?

"How original," she said with a roll of her eyes. "The big, bad man-boy brags about his prowess over the easy conquest." Cookie eased to her feet and arranged the folds of her skirt as if she hadn't a care. "I hope you enjoyed your first taste of pleasure with me. Because it was also your last."

"We do not split up," he grated.

Right now? No, they didn't. If she fled, he'd chase and catch her. But she could bide her time... "Trust me, Casanova. We won't be together much longer."

He scrubbed a hand over his face. His shoulders sagged. "I'm sorry for the way I treated you. I'm more sorry for my outburst. You didn't deserve it. I just... I don't like how *needy* you'd made me feel, and I reacted poorly. This is all so new to me. I'm floundering. I've never wanted a woman the way I want you."

His honesty about his emotions astonished her. No other boyfriend had ever apologized or copped to feeling needy. Not that Kaysar was her boyfriend. But maybe she should give him another chance as her guide?

Argh! How did he do this to her? One second she wanted to leave ASAP, the next she wanted to glue herself to his side.

"The time for misleading and threats is over," he said. "I'd like... I think we should be teammates. Real ones."

"Excuse me?" She sputtered for a moment. "The killer has jokes."

He pursed his lips. "Jareth is a vile male. He and his family did vile things to me as a child. You can help me hurt them." Angry, hopeful and hesitant, he ducked his head and lifted his gaze to her. "Will you help me, sweetling?"

Oh, he's good. There was a hundred percent chance he was toying with her emotions right now. Because there was no way, just no way, a man as powerful as Kaysar could be as vulnerable as he currently appeared.

But what if he'd spoken the truth? What if Jareth and his family *had* done vile things to young Kaysar?

Could she really let the murderer of an innocent off the hook? Didn't she owe Lulundria a debt? What better gift could Cookie give the woman than delivering total retribution to her killer?

Kaysar could help *her.*

Once again, she switched directions. "All right," she said with a nod. Decision made. "I'll give you a second chance, and I'll willingly team up with you. Out of the goodness of my heart, I'll even help you hurt Jareth. But you better treat me right, Claw Man, or I'll ditch you at the first opportunity."

"Yes." He clasped her by the waist and drew her close for a hug. "I will treat you right. I'll learn how."

His earnest expression did strange things to her insides. "There'll be no sex, of course." He'd ruined the attraction when he'd sneered. "I've forever removed the option from our table."

A harsh denial burst from him. "Sex is pleasure, and we both need pleasure. But sex is also vengeance. I demand it."

Hardly. "Hate to break it to you, bud, but your war plan just got tweaked. Jareth is gonna die badly." For Lulundria.

A deadly, unholy rage descended over Kaysar. "No one kills Jareth. Not even you. Do you understand?"

The malice he projected...yikes. "You want to torture

him while we search for the doormaker, fine, let's torture him instead of killing him. I can aid you without putting out. And don't tell me I have nothing to offer but my body. In my world, I'm a gamer, and I play a video game set in yours. If the kingdom beyond the waterfall is the one I think it is, I know the terrain's traps, tricks, and poisons. I'll ensure Jareth *pleads* for death." There were ways…

With her words came a new influx of confidence. With the confidence came clarity and acceptance. She had a marvelous weapon at her disposal, too—the ability to change personalities at will. It wasn't a burden, after all, but a tool to be utilized.

Utilize it, she would.

Cookie smiled at Kaysar, who watched her warily now. Finally, she knew what she was doing. This was a team sport. Her specialty. Jareth didn't stand a chance.

Game on.

CHAPTER SIXTEEN

WITH HIS MIND a war zone, Kaysar stripped to his skin and dove into the pond. The cool water did little to temper his frenzied emotions. Only short moments ago, he'd been consumed with need as he'd kissed Chantel, feasting on her lips, his every thought attuned to her, and her alone. His past? His vengeance? Forgotten. He'd disregarded everything but the stunning woman in his arms. How sweet she'd tasted. Sweeter than her scent had promised. The softness of her silken skin was a revelation. Her breasts had filled his hands, her hard nipples abrading his palms as he'd kneaded. His control had dissolved.

Her kiss had breathed life into him, his body no longer his but hers. Theirs. What she'd desired, he'd longed to give. He'd felt *compelled* to give, as if he'd uttered the order to himself.

At the time, he'd thought he'd loved the heady sensations. Now he had doubts. Neglect his vengeance, even for a moment? How could he dare?

He couldn't get lost in the princess again. But keep his distance from her? When her curvy little body all but wept for his? Impossible. His shaft throbbed unbearably for her. Impaling her topped his agenda for the day. He just had to convince her to put sex back on their table.

Could he?

He must.

He would.

Kaysar whipped his gaze to her for the hundredth time, unable to halt the action. She perched on the shore, barely covered by the pink dress he'd insisted she wear after he'd noticed the blood he'd deposited on the green one. Her beauty robbed him of breath.

After donning the garment, she had softened immensely, becoming shy and playful—battering his defenses with stronger force.

The gowns meant to punish Chantel only punished Kaysar.

She drew his gaze—compelled it to return to her. The sight of her struck him like a blow.

At the moment, she snacked on the breads, cheeses and fruits he'd confiscated from the centaurs, a contingent of mercenaries Jareth had paid to attack him.

Kaysar had fetched the food for her before his bath, relieved the misery portion of their relationship was over. He'd had no thirst for it, anyway. He liked the idea of working together to oversee his goal.

What to do about the doormaker, though? He owed her a way home, so he should deliver. Something an honest partner would do. But he didn't want Chantel leaving Astaria. Ever. Which meant he had to convince her to stay with him *before* he presented her with a doormaker. But how? What else did she need from him?

When no answers were forthcoming, Kaysar stomped from the pond. He shook out his hair, flinging water in every direction, then dressed in the clean tunic and leathers Chantel had "gifted" to him.

Upon his return with the food, she'd told him, "You said everything in the bag is mine, and I carried nothing of yours. Rather than let you traipse about naked or in dirty clothing, I'll gift you with a shirt and pants." She'd beamed the sweetest smile at him. The same smile she'd beamed before she'd punched his face. "For a price."

When he'd balked, both affronted and savagely turned on, she'd only smiled wider, a temptress no man had the strength to resist. "Do you think I'll demand sex," she'd asked throatily, "or do you hope I will?"

How he'd hoped! In the end, she'd merely requested information about "the bark." The elderseed. When planted, it grew enchanted trees. When ingested, it healed any injury and strengthened any fae exponentially for a short period of time. Her eyes had widened with excitement as hc'd explained, and she'd muttered, "Just like the elderseed in the game.

"If I eat the elderseed, I'll power up, right?" she'd asked. "Will I recharge enough to open a doorway?"

Of course her mind had gone there. "You won't," he'd replied, and it was the truth. "Creating vines and opening a doorway come from two different sources of power. The glamara merely utilizes the vinemaking as a bridge from which to manifest. The elderseed will fuel any ability *but* your glamara."

"Are you hungry?" she asked, drawing him back to the present. She motioned to the picnic she'd set up, rubies sparkling on her throat, biceps and fingers. "I saved you half...after I ate the original half."

"No, thank you." *No, thank you?* He frowned, confused. When had he taken lessons in gentlemanly comportment? "We should go." They would enter the Dusklands as originally planned. He would put his ear to the ground and seek a *living* doormaker he probably wouldn't find. Chantel would be satisfied with his efforts. At least for a little while. He could use the time to learn her better. To win her affections.

"Very well." From her perch on the ground, she gathered her belongings. As soon as she finished, he offered her a hand. With a sigh-worthy smile, she fluttered her fingers over his. "How kind of you. Ohhh. Look at us. So polite to each other. It's like we've *both* become new people."

Her softness. Her warmth. Struggling to rein in his sharpest desires, he tugged her to her feet. Guilt seared him when he anchored her satchel to his chest and the heavy weight strained his shoulder.

Disregard. They moved forward from now on, not backward.

Kaysar laced his fingers with hers, marveling at the differences between them. The smallness of her bone structure compared to the largeness of his. The paleness of her silken skin next to his darkness. The delicacy of her pink nails, with her black thorn claws retracted, pitted against the sharp metal tipping his.

The guilt conquered more territory, and he scowled.

As he squired her across the path that divided the pond, stepping from one mossy rock to another, she made the sweetest little noises. Blood continued to rush to his groin, his shaft nearly ripping free of his leathers.

"I'm surprised Jareth hasn't found us yet," she said.

"I expect your husband to—"

"Uh, he isn't my husband, thank you very much. This perma-bachelorette isn't getting hitched."

"You are a Frostline. He is a Frostline." Would she change her mind if she remembered Lulundria's love for Jareth? The idea nearly stopped Kaysar cold. He didn't like the thought of Chantel kissing and touching the prince. Ever.

"Wait." She yanked her hand from his. "Are *you* in a relationship with someone? I mean, I know you aren't married, but what about a girlfriend? A mistress? A harem?"

Did the thought leave her frothing with jealousy?

He grinned at the mere possibility and flittered behind her. Kaysar molded his body to hers, just the way he liked, crowding her. The instinct demanded it, and he obeyed.

As he slid his hands over her hipbones and clamped down, she held her breath. When he applied pressure, pressing her against him, she didn't try to escape—no, she melted closer.

She loved her pleasure.

He nuzzled his cheek against hers, a gesture of affection and gratitude. Unstoppable. "I have no girlfriend. Nor do I maintain a stable of mistresses as Jareth does." He rasped his words, delighting as goose bumps broke out over her arms. He would never choose to permanently bind his life to another. Become responsible for another's well-being? Give the Frostlines something else to steal from him?

Though, he shouldn't allow anyone, especially the Frostlines, to keep him from taking something he wanted, either. The incongruity would bother him tomorrow, after he'd secured Chantel.

"In the eyes of the fae," he said, "you *are* wed to Jareth, which is why he hopes to take you from me."

No one takes her from me! His rage blazed, ever at the ready.

A breathy puff of air suggested he squeezed her a little too tight—or that she enjoyed being squeezed a little too tight.

Just like that, intrigue overshadowed his anger. He nipped her earlobe, rewarded by the softest mewl. What would she do if he tilted her head back and sucked on her hammering pulse? If he slid his hands lower?

If he licked her skin. Kneaded her breasts. Tore off her clothes and—

"Well," she said, clearing her throat. "You can let me go now."

Do not shout a denial. She wasn't like anyone else, and he couldn't treat her as such.

Wait. Sounds in the distance. He canted his head, listening, honing in. Jareth had found their trail. Was about five minutes away.

Kaysar cursed. The Frostlines ruined *everything.*

"We're about to have company, sweetling." With a furious huff, he flittered in front of Chantel, clasped her hand once again and tugged her forward. "Come."

"Jareth?"

"No doubt."

As he stalked forward, she followed. At the other side of the pond, he navigated the slippery stones with ease. Cool mist dampened the air, reminding him of the first time he'd ever ventured here. He'd been a boy then. Only fifteen. He'd spent a fruitless year searching for his missing sister, then another year learning the various royal courts and preparing to conquer the wild Nightlands most other fae avoided, hoping to find Viori there. He'd been sick from yet another brush with poisonvine when he'd collapsed near the water.

Upon glimpsing his reflection—seeing Viori's eyes hidden within his own—he'd sung himself to health, exactly as he'd sung himself to health in the tower. The way he'd sung to Viori each night. The melody had quickly turned into a scream of pain and misery, and he'd broken into sobs. It was here, on this very bank however long later, that he'd decided to halt his search for his sister. To cease splitting his focus. To fixate on the only thing he *could* give his precious Viori—proper vengeance.

"Once we go through the water," he told Chantel, "I won't be able to flitter. No one can flitter in the Dusklands. The ability is neutralized by a mineral in the ground. However far we travel, remember we must travel it all over again to return."

"Ten-four. I'm happy to report the same is true in *The Forest of Good and Evil*." She nodded, her excitement seeming to catch fire, burning through the charming shyness the dress had highlighted. The clothes might influence her, but they didn't control her. "Don't worry. I won't be an anchor dragging you down anymore. I'll be an asset. You'll see."

Her ability to torment the prince outside of Kaysar's bed remained unconfirmed. Her ability to aid Kaysar in other ways did not. An asset to him? Shockingly yes.

Danger approaches. Almost upon you.

Even with the crash of the water, Kaysar caught the prince's footfalls. Jareth had quickened his pace.

He considered his next move, tossing a glance over his shoulder. His only goal at the moment? Keeping Chantel, his key, safe.

In a sprint, the prince burst through a wall of foliage before vanishing, reappearing halfway to the waterfall. Still sprinting, seeming to fly over the rocky path, already swinging his sword.

Kaysar flittered in front of Chantel, a dagger clutched in each clawed hand. He lifted and crossed the weapons, creating a metal V. His gaze clashed with Jareth's as the male's sword tip grazed a straight, shallow cut from the end of his nose to the underside of his chin before meeting the daggers. A clink and a sting registered.

Blood trickled into his mouth, coating his teeth and tongue.

Chantel gasped and clutched his tunic from behind, fueling the rage directed at Jareth. *The prince dares to frighten my princess?*

A single punch dislocated Jareth's jaw. A kick sent him careening into the pond with a splash. Jareth flittered to land, materializing on the other side of the pond, where he dripped water and violently forced his jaw into place.

Behind him, pixies darted through trees, landing on limbs to witness the festivities.

Kaysar and Jareth glared at each other from their respective sides. This intrusion grated. Kaysar hadn't yet secured Chantel's affections, and he resented the prince's interference. He didn't want the male looking at her. Much less speaking to her, reminding her of a past she hadn't lived and didn't wish to remember. Lusting for her mere minutes after Kaysar had kissed her—perhaps an hour before he kissed her again.

He flicked his tongue behind his teeth. Jareth had been unable to keep his hands off Lulundria. How much less would he control himself around Chantel? The woman whose touch had elicited indescribable pleasure in Kaysar. The man who'd never before known passion. If she affected *him*, how much more must she affect those like the prince?

How much more would the prince affect *her*?

Foreboding choked him. The odds were stacked against him. One way or another, Chantel would learn the truth about Lulundria's murder. How would she react then? She hadn't forgiven him for his other misdirections, but she'd agreed to help him anyway. He sensed she didn't offer such clemency often or easily. Now he…feared. Could she ever pardon him for his part in the death?

Would the truth propel the prince and princess back together?

A risk Kaysar might have to take. Not knowing was a burden he couldn't bear. Like the rocks, he needed Chantel to know what he'd done—to understand and stay with him anyway. He required this as much as air.

"Did you come to say goodbye to your wife, Jareth?" He threw the words across the water, unwilling to back down.

"I'm not his wife," Chantel retorted behind him. "If I'm ever eager for another ice dagger stabbing, though, I'll be sure to give the prince a call."

First she had denied being Lulundria. Now she claimed the woman's injuries as her own? Were the females merging? Cold sweat beaded Kaysar's brow.

"You misunderstand what you remember, princess." Jareth glared at Kaysar, his blue eyes frosty. He cast his next words to Chantel. "I would never purposely hurt you."

"Go spin your lies somewhere else," she snapped, and Kaysar reached for the lock of hair he'd transferred to the pocket of his new pants.

"I would *never* purposely hurt you," Jareth repeated. "But the king would. He arranged Lulundria's suffering, pushing her into my ice."

Kaysar could have stopped the prince. He could even refute the male's claim with more carefully spun truths. And Chantel would probably believe him. For a time. Instead, he remained quiet. *Let's get this over with.*

If Chantel fled him, he would…he…didn't know. For the first time in too many years to calculate, *he didn't have a next move.*

Aiming the tip of his sword in Kaysar's direction, Jareth bellowed at Chantel, "The king is a madman. You realize this, yes? He looks at maps that aren't there. And his song." He shuddered. "You'll believe your head is about to explode. You'll pray it does. He kills without mercy and attacks the Winterlands on a whim. His evil knows no bounds." He swung his gaze to Kaysar once more. "Deny it, your majesty. Lie to her."

Kaysar was many things, but he was not a liar or a coward. "I deny nothing. Yes, I pushed Lulundria into the path of your ice. No, I didn't care that she was injured. Actually, that isn't the full truth. I *required* her pain. I planned to heal her immediately afterward, becoming her hero. She would have fallen straight into my bed. But she fled me."

"You did *what*?" Chantel dug her claws into his back.

In a secret part of him, he perceived the tiniest flicker of shame. And he resented it. He had done *nothing* that hadn't been done to him. "If you consider the variables, this is actually an extension of the crime you've already almost forgiven me for. Therefore..."

Despite his logic, her anger persisted. "Obviously, our partnership is over. For good and for real this time."

He silenced a denial. *Breathe in. Out.* He'd done her wrong. He'd admitted it. Now he owed her more than an apology. He should offer some kind of appeasement. Yes, yes. What could it hurt?

But what was he to offer? The last female he'd attempted to appease was Viori. "I... I'll do better from now on. I'll try, at least. No one will ever try harder. I'll give you more jewelry. A sea of it."

"Good for you, but no, thanks. Scratch my name off your roster. You go after innocent bystanders. That means you're no better than the one who hurt you."

Was she right? Was she wrong? He didn't know! "What if I limit my targets from now on?"

"I'm sorry, but it's too late."

Different impulses warred. Face her. Pin her against the rock wall. Touch her hair. Touch *all* of her. Kiss her until *she* forgot what he'd done. Beg for another chance. Just one more.

Who am I? Kaysar de Aoibheall did not beg for anything. Ever. But he *had* promised to be better for her, and he always kept his word.

"Come to me, Chantel," the prince called, extending a hand in her direction. "Let me take you from this awful place."

Kaysar glared at the prince, telling Chantel, "You wonder why I target him, sweetling? Allow me to share." To Jareth's credit, he held Kaysar's stare, even as he flinched, because he knew what was coming. "Lulundria's darling Jareth once watched with a smile as his father cut out my tongue. I was only twelve at the time. Too young to heal from such a severe injury."

Chantel gasped with horror.

"I grew a new one only because of my glamara."

He couldn't see her face, and she didn't retract her claws, but her expression must have softened, because Jareth shouted, "You're *wavering*?"

"Maybe? I don't know, okay?" she retorted, and Kaysar's knees nearly buckled with relief. "It didn't happen to me, but *I* want to punish you for your reaction."

Kaysar floundered, some unknown emotion *ravaging* him. This woman…

Jareth tried again. "He made you think your own husband was a monster out to kill you."

"Tsk-tsk. You know there's more to the story, Jareth." Chiding tone. Deepening rage. Unwavering determination. Chantel deserved to know *everything*. "You witnessed your father and your uncle locking me in the tower after the removal of my tongue. Did you know they took me from my five-year-old sister, leaving her without a protector?" His voice hardened, and his insides roiled. "For a year, I remained chained to a wall while you enjoyed freedom. Your uncle visited me every day. Your father preferred to wait for special occasions."

Jareth closed his eyes. Opened them. For a moment, he looked ready to vomit.

"They. Did. *What?*" Chantel plucked her claws free and patted the punctures. "I'm so sorry that happened to you, Kaysar. I am. But." The claws pierced him once more. "I'm so furious with you, too. I want to scream and rail at you. And I want to hug you."

Had there ever been a more fascinating creature?

"I need a moment to deliberate which reaction to embrace." Claws out. "I mean, what you did to the royal family is justified. But what you did to Lulundria and me is terrible. I should slap you." In. "But I get it. The royal family sliced open your heart. Now you bleed all over them." Out. "I want to hug you *harder*. You know what? I'm not resisting the urge anymore. I hope you're ready for me." Quaking, she flung her arms around him, clutching him from behind. Her scent muddied his thoughts. "I'm so sorry that happened to you," she repeated softly.

The gentle hold nearly broke him. The understanding finished the job. "You'll stay with me? You forgive me for my crimes?"

"I forgive some of it. Most of it. Maybe. I mean, I forgive-ish. I'm fifty percent there, bordering on forty-nine or fifty-one. The number teeters depending on reasons." She sighed. "But stay with you? I don't know. I don't trust you. How can I?"

"I won't use you again," he vowed in a rush. Oh, how he'd needed her forgiveness; he just hadn't known it until this moment. That she'd offered to clear half his crimes against her… A weight eased from his shoulders. The fore-boding and anxiety he'd carried since meeting her began to evaporate. Trust could be earned.

"You consider me a Frostline," she reminded him. "How can you *not* use me again?"

Jareth listened to the conversation, but Kaysar didn't care. To him, the outcome was vital.

"You are *anything* but a Frostline, Chantel. You alone are safe with me. And innocents. Hurting you or others like you will never again be my goal. That, I swear to you. Give me a chance. I only need one more. I'll prove myself worthy this time. We'll work together, just as we hoped. Jareth's father, King Hador Frostline, requires punishing." He wondered… Was it possible…

Was Chantel his woman? The one Eye spoke of?

He remembered telling the oracle, *I have no mate, I want no mate, and I seek only vengeance.*

Now, as he imagined Chantel in his bed, naked and spread for him and him alone, he nearly roared, needing her there as soon as possible.

"Lu—Chantel." Jareth appeared agonized. "I love my wife. Her love for me burns bright in her heart. You'll re-member our relationship, and you'll love me, too. Please. Remember me," he beseeched her. "As soon as you're away from the king, you'll return to normal."

Normal? "Shut your filthy mouth." Kaysar withdrew and tossed a dagger, too fast for another to track. The blade sank into his opponent's shoulder, silencing further re-quests. Chantel would *not* be remembering her time with the male. He forbade it. "She's perfect, just the way she is."

"Thank you, Kaysar," she said, humphing at Jareth the way he adored. "I happen to like myself just the way I am, too."

With a bellow, the prince yanked the bloody dagger free.

She thanks me for defending her honor?

His chest clenched.

"You'll pay for this," Jareth snarled.

"Will I?" Glamara heating his throat, he called, "Ogres. Come."

Insects went quiet, and the soft breeze died. What started as sporadic tremors quickly became a constant quake, every ogre in the vicinity rushing toward the clearing. A tree toppled as several of the massive brutes arrived.

"You will not kill Prince Jareth," Kaysar said, the command hot enough to sizzle. "But you may do anything else to him if he attempts to enter the waterfall." He smiled at his glaring foe before offering his elbow to a wide-eyed Chantel. "Allow me to show you the Dusklands, sweetling. There's a marvelous oasis I'm keen to explore with you. The golden roses are lovely this century."

She accepted without hesitation. "Golden roses, you say?"

He led her through the water, his self-assurance mounting with every step. All would be well. He would make sure of it.

CHAPTER SEVENTEEN

COOKIE REMAINED AT Kaysar's side as she emerged from the spray of water. The deluge did little to douse her fiery thoughts.

In a five-minute span, she'd gotten a Kaysar 101 crash course. The abuse he'd suffered was a thousand times worse than she'd imagined, and her heart broke for him. The raw agony she'd heard in his voice had devastated her. Now he sought retribution for all he'd lost. It was his right. But he'd hurt innocents to achieve it—could he, would he truly stop? There were ways to punish people who deserved it without harming those who didn't. Already her mind whirled with an idea...

Was she ready to offer Kaysar her full trust? No. She'd meant what she'd told him. But she understood him better, and ditching him was no longer a long- or short-term goal. No, before she returned home, she planned to aid his vengeance, exactly as promised. Hador Frostline had a thorny green reckoning coming. But Jareth himself? She wasn't sure. Was he a monster as Kaysar believed, or a halfway decent guy?

You'll return to normal. As if Cookie wasn't good enough in "as is" condition.

Maybe half monster, half decent guy?

Whatever. Kaysar seemed to like her better than ever. Maybe something would happen between them at some point, maybe it wouldn't. She wasn't putting sex back on the table or anything, but she wasn't storing her casserole dish in another room, either. As long as she managed her expectations, enjoyed him with no deep commitments, they could maybe, probably, possibly do...other things.

She really, really wanted to do other things.

His kiss had been a shock. The intensity of it. The intensity of *him*. She shivered even as she heated. Her body hungered for his, desire simmering in her veins, ready to boil over every time he cranked up the heat.

Kaysar drew to a stop a few feet in front of the waterfall, and she wiped any lingering water droplets from her lashes. Oh, wow. Though she'd logged thousands of hours in every level of *The Forest of Good and Evil*, and the new terrain fit her expectations, the extreme change in scenery proved shocking.

She'd gone from a lush, sunlit paradise with vibrant colors to a wasteland filled with ghostly smoke that curled from a fire-scorched ground. A dark cloud lingered overhead. There were no trees or flowers here. No weeds, even. Mountains consumed the distance, a fortress carved into the side of the largest.

She and Kaysar poised at the edge of a floating rock. A gaping chasm of nothingness provided the sole path to flatlands.

A bloodstained garment tumbled between the two turfs.

"In my game, avatars cross the chasm on a cloud bridge, but I see no sign of *any* bridge," she said, shocked by her calmness. "Oh, yes, and no big deal, but did you happen to notice what seems like millions of armored soldiers sitting atop centaurs, waiting on the flatlands, aiming arrows at us?" Each word contained a scooch more hysteria than the last. Her confidence in her abilities remained high, even though she'd changed into the pink dress, but she couldn't pretend to be indestructible.

"I did notice," Kaysar replied, unveiling a you're-going-to-die-screaming smile to the waiting soldiers. His easy tone possessed the sharpest edge, meant to draw blood internally. If ever a voice could kill...

"I have no plans to harm you, King Kaysar, as long as you cooperate." The statement boomed from the army ranks. A rough, husky timbre with a slight accent. The leader? "And do not think to sing your song to madden us as you have done to so many others. There is but a single hearer here. I made sure of it."

Kaysar's song? What was so bad about his song? Jareth had freaked out about it, too.

"As you can see," the leader announced, "I have been expecting your arrival."

Wait. Back up. Had the guy insinuated that he and his men purposefully deafened themselves? To avoid a song?

The army formed a half circle at the canyon's ledge, blocking the left, right and center paths of escape, if Cookie and Kaysar ever crossed over.

"You will leave or you will die," he added, confident. Smug.

Just got here, and it's already game over?

Kaysar couldn't flitter. A bridge hadn't magically appeared. Either they retreated or they cliff dived without a chute.

Many of the soldiers held torches, soft amber light illuminating the warriors with arrows nocked and spears lifted.

"Do not worry, sweetling." Kaysar clasped and lifted her hand to kiss her knuckles, sending shivers down her spine. "These lands are mine. No one keeps me from what's mine."

What else did Kaysar consider his? No, silly question.
How did he think to defeat this many soldiers?

Heat blazed in Cookie's hands, traveling up her arms
to collect in her shoulders. Vines prepared to sprout. The
speed of her reaction astounded her, but the urge to protect
her newly minted teammate was undeniable.

"How kind of you to welcome my return with a gift.
One of my favorites, no less. Foes to slaughter." Kaysar's
eyes gleamed with delight, boosting her confidence. Perhaps the vengeful king knew tricks?

A male in the center of the horde, maybe the biggest
male in the batch, directed his mount forward. Though everyone else wore gleaming armor, creating a living, breathing Terracotta Army, he sported a plain black tunic and
leather pants. Standard attire. No helmet shielded his features. And what incredible features they were. Dark eyes
currently smeared with black paint and pale skin. Straight
nose and full lips. Jet hair spiked from his scalp.

The fae certainly grew their men right.

Without looking back, his men recognized the correct
time to move from his path. They returned to their original spots as soon as he passed.

The warrior giant kept his attention fixed on a female
who stood before the entire army, with two torch-bearing
soldiers posted at her sides. She used hand signals to communicate Kaysar's words?

A sudden icy wind brushed her nape, and Cookie spun.
Ambush? Oh, yes. A blood soaked Jareth flew from the
waterfall, his dagger aimed at Kaysar.

Strike her partner from behind?

Not on Cookie's watch. In reflex, she dove at the prince
with her arms outstretched. She intended to crash into him
and knock him aside before contact with Kaysar. Her vines

burst forth first, coiling around his wrist. He reacted as if she'd hit him with a wrecking ball, convulsing.

As he plummeted, a spear whooshed past her, mere inches from her fingers, then embedded in Jareth's shoulder, flinging him backward and pinning him to the rock wall. He never hit the ground.

Everything happened so fast. Too fast for Cookie to disengage from the prince. Connected by a vine, she was dragged toward the rock wall herself—until a hard clamp on her nape and a harder tug hauled her against Kaysar. He snaked a powerful arm around her waist, trapping her body against his.

"Let go." He squeezed her hand, forcing her to release the vines.

Leaves withered, ending her connection to Jareth.

Heart galloping a hundred miles an hour, she spun and gripped his shirt. *My hero!* "Thank you, Kaysar."

"You meant to save me," he told her, his voice nothing but gravel and smoke. He maintained his grip a moment more, the hand on her nape gentling. He roved his fingertips over her cheek. "You didn't hesitate to risk your life for mine."

For a moment, she forgot their audience, her attention enraptured by his beautiful face. "I told you I'd be an asset to the team, and I meant it."

He tenderly swiped the pad of his thumb over the rise of her cheek, searching her gaze. "You are *magnificent*."

Admiration from a guy like Kaysar curled her toes.

Jareth bellowed curses, struggling to free himself.

Impatient, the leader of the horde called, "I am King Micah the Unwilling, ruler of the Dusklands and sovereign of the Forgotten Court, and you *will* heed my commands."

"What did you say?" Soft voice, homicidal tone. Kaysar lowered his chin, his mouth resetting into a vicious sneer as he focused on the leader. "Did you refer to yourself as *king*? Of my lands and a nonexistent court?"

Okay. Cookie now understood how she and Kaysar could survive a battle. He would kill everyone in a rage.

People gonna die.

King Micah watched the interpreter. "You have not walked these lands for over two hundred years, King Kaysar. No longer do they belong to you. Everything you see is mine."

Each sentence seemed to toss a log onto Kaysar's internal inferno. Undercurrents of hostility pulsed from him. "Twenty years or two hundred and twenty centuries matters little. What's mine remains mine. Always. I won these lands. I *own* these lands."

"And I took them," the would-be royal responded, his archers nocking their bows tighter.

The pissing contest had just escalated into a DEFCON 2 situation, stage critical. Unless...

Cookie flattened her palm over Kaysar's thumping heart. "Put me in the game, coach. Give me the elderseed, and let's see what I can do. Create enough vines to get us over the canyon? Maybe. Block any attacks? Surely." A power boost couldn't hurt. "Getting to safety and regrouping will be a piece of cake when we don't have hundreds of weapons trained on us."

"I am weary of waiting," Micah called.

Kaysar ignored him. Sporting an indulgent smile, he anchored a finger under her chin and tilted her face higher. "You wish to fight as my teammate?"

Her fluttering stomach flip-flopped. Her first real-life battle. With a pro, no less. "I do."

"Very well. We'll do this your way. At the moment, I find I can deny you nothing." Amid Jareth's protests, her dark king pressed his lips to hers...

CHAPTER EIGHTEEN

MOUTH-TO-MOUTH CONTACT with Kaysar, in front of their enemies? A doubt surfaced: What if he did this for Jareth's benefit?

Cookie should care, right? But a ragged moan burst from her. The feel of this man.

Her sexy king took full advantage of her surprise and thrust his tongue against hers. One second her thoughts raced, reminding her of cars on a highway. Just zoom, zoom, zoom. The next her mind quieted, fixated on the most amazing sensations. His taste was a rich dessert wine, intoxicating and addictive, and she had no defense against it.

To her disappointment, the kiss ended far too quickly. He brushed the tip of his nose against hers, as if he wanted to apologize for the brevity, and rasped, "You are the most glorious female in existence, and I must have you."

Man, when he decided he wanted something, he went all out to obtain it. His ferocity attenuated her doubts, and she peered up at him, a little too dazed for her liking and a lot too vulnerable.

Noticing something strange on her tongue, she frowned. What—the exotic flavor exploded at first crunch. Mmm. *Delicious*.

"I hope you enjoy the rush, sweetling." He kissed the tip of her nose. "I know I will."

Rush? Wait. The morsel on her tongue. He'd used their kiss to pass her a slither of elderseed? Uh, when had he reached into the satchel?

Oh, who cared? She swallowed and prayed the minute portion of elderseed worked fast. In the game, results were instantaneous. But...

She waited.

And waited.

"Do you think I will hesitate to slay you?" Micah demanded. "I assure you, I'll do what I must."

"Give her to me." The second Jareth freed himself from the wall, he lunged for Cookie, attempting a grab-and-nab. As if she wouldn't poisonvine him again. "You *will* come with me, wife. We tried this your way. Now we'll do it mine."

Gone was the loving husband intent on protecting his bride. This man expected absolute compliance.

With graceful, catlike reflexes she'd rarely never displayed, she danced out of reach. Well, well. Perhaps the elderseed had kicked in, after all.

"You think to touch her?" With awe-inspiring speed, Kaysar swiped his claws at Jareth's outstretched arm. "You dare to touch what's mine?"

He *did* think of Cookie as his. How did she feel about that, after everything that had happened?

The prince's hand flew into the chasm, severed from his wrist. A gruesome sight she found oddly satisfying.

As if he'd known such pain before, Jareth clutched the bloody stump to his chest and wheezed. "I'll rejoice the day I kill you, Kaysar."

Protective urges pitched and swelled. Harm her teammate? No. Oh, no. She'd end Jareth first, despite her companion's protests.

"The female may stay. The king and the prince have thirty seconds to take their feud elsewhere," the one named Micah shouted, his voice a lash of anger.

Another threat to her teammate. She saw red. Here was the thing about Cookie. She valued her partners, whoever they were. At game time, any bad blood between them got benched.

In a flash, the burn returned to her arms. Hotter and hotter and oh! Her blood fizzled and sizzled in her hands, the tips of her fingers on fire. Shockingly, she saw no flames.

The elderseed had *really* kicked in.

When leaves budded from her pores, their tips vibrated, eagerly awaiting her command. She *sensed* their desire to obey. To conquer.

Power filled her head and flowed through her veins. As promised, she had charged like a battery—a ginormous battery with stores and stores of strength.

Her thoughts realigned and smoothed out, the chaos that had lived in her mind for so long suddenly eased. For the first time, she knew who she was. What she was. She knew what she wanted and how to get it.

Nothing could stop her.

"Your time is up. We attack on three." Micah raised an arm. Aggression and malice pulsed from his army, the soldiers shifting. "One."

"Oh, Kaysar. Isn't this *amazing*?" Never had she felt so giddy. So alive. "My first actual battle. They threatened us, and now I get to kill them all by myself."

"Lulundria," Jareth croaked. "Don't do this."

"I'm looking at the real you, aren't I, sweetling?" Kaysar appeared entranced.

Micah's determination remained unfazed. "Two."

"Will you keep count of my kills?" she asked her partner, clapping. She could hardly wait to begin. These men weren't innocents; they were enemies. Enemies paid a steep price. Unlike Kaysar, this army and its king weren't getting a second and third chance. "I want to make sure I share the correct tally with Pearl Jean and Sugars when I recount my tale of victory."

The barest hint of a smile teased the corners of his mouth. "There are three hundred and seven men before us. Something tells me your count will be all of them."

Even more wonderful.

"What did you do to her?" Jareth screamed at Kaysar.

"Three," Micah called.

A volley of arrows whizzed through the sky, whistling on approach. Knowing what to do as if she'd trained her entire life, Cookie lifted her arms. Vines shot from her fingers, branching into hundreds of other vines in seconds, forming a large wall.

The arrows embedded in the stalks, and she felt every strike. But she liked it.

"There is no more perfect creature." Kaysar grazed the shell of her ear with a metal claw.

She preened for him, because she couldn't not. When she released the vines, the stalks withered to ash, but a sweet scent remained.

The arrows plummeted into the chasm, useless, and the soldiers took a collective step back, one word rising from their ranks. "Poisonvine."

"My turn to attack." She smiled her sweetest smile at Micah—and produced hundreds more vines.

SOME MOMENTS FOREVER altered your existence. This was one such time for Kaysar. He knew it, sensed it. And he wasn't sorry.

For the whole of his life, he'd considered himself incapable of passion. He'd *lauded* the inability. But it hadn't taken Chantel long to coax his deepest desires from hiding. Now, Kaysar stood transfixed, desperate to worship at the feet of the hauntingly beautiful princess who had turned his world upside down.

In her sexy pink dress and jewels, wielding her gift and poison, Chantel was every dream he'd never known he possessed. Wise. Discerning. Fierce. His doll to dress up and play with. His sweetest weapon. The war prize he deserved for surviving a year of agony and a hundred lifetimes of misery. His mate.

She *was*. He knew that, too, all questions assuaged. The knowledge lit him up, pride infusing his spine. Fate had selected this warrior woman for him and him alone. Eye had predicted it. Whatever Chantel's last name was, she belonged to Kaysar. He had decided.

He dared *anyone* to contradict him.

More and more vines flourished from the princess's delicate, bejeweled hands. Those thorny stalks matured fast and bred others, splitting here, there, everywhere. Each end sharpened as it uncoiled and slithered.

Rule my *lands, Micah? Think again.* So Kaysar had been absent from the Dusklands longer than he'd believed. So what?

The false king's soldiers panicked as the vines descended, a row of archers unleashing another volley. Once again, Chantel stopped the assault midair. Vines grew over the chasm… Chaos reigned, centaurs rearing, dumping their riders. Men retreated, but they were slow, weighed down by their armor.

Within seconds, Chantel constructed a wide, sturdy bridge, connecting the cliff to the flatlands. Still her vines grew, coiling around the first line of soldiers—and squeezing. Armor crunched, caving in, and blood gushed from every metal joint.

She laughed, the sound of it lovelier than Prince Lark's screams for mercy. "Do you see, Kaysar? I made fae in a can. Chicken of the siege."

Hair swaying in the breeze. Irises like mercury and gleaming. Skin aglow. She was more radiant than the sun, her every motion a study of grace and elegance. Rosy color painted her cheeks as red and pink flowers bloomed from her vines.

A vessel of vengeance and woe.

He had no defenses against her. Desire burned him. Scorched him—branded him. He wanted her more than he'd ever wanted anything.

I will give her jewels. All the jewels. He would give her *everything.* Just as he'd promised. But he would expect everything from her, too. Her loyalty. Her devotion. Her presence. She would stay with him *always.*

Supply Jareth with one of her children? *One of mine?* No. Kaysar devised a new plan. He and Chantel would have no children. Since the citizens of Astaria considered her a Frostline for the rest of eternity, the name would die when he tired of tormenting Hador and Jareth.

An acceptable outcome.

Chantel would support his agenda, of course. *Look at her.* His Briar Rose, the embodiment of destruction and the most breathtaking sight in all the lands.

"Do you happen to know if Micah has been slain yet, sweetling?" he asked, curious. Soon, the battle would end, a vast majority of the army annihilated as easily as breathing.

"I'm not sure." Her pout only kindled his desires. "I lost sight of him fifty or so deaths ago."

The unseated men shouted as they ran. Other warriors stayed to fight, stabbing and hacking at the poisonous stalks. Venom leaked from the punctures, rendering many of the fighters immobile.

Arrows flew at random, embedding in different parts of the vines. Kaysar scowled when Chantel winced. She felt each strike?

Pain fanned her eyes with the next volley, a bead of sweat trickling from her temple. Her shoulders hunched ever so slightly.

She did. This was *unacceptable.*

You know what you must do.

Oh, he did. But he hesitated, unsure. For centuries, he'd used his song as a weapon to cause madness and death. He hadn't attempted to heal anyone but himself since Viori's loss.

He sank his claws into his palms. Emotions mattered, affecting tone. If he caused Chantel a moment of agony or furthered her injuries…

He took an honest look inside his heart. What emotions currently seethed there? Fury, yes. Always. Hatred? Malice? Bitterness? All were present and accounted for. But beneath them, he thought he sensed…affection? A well of it. More than he was comfortable carrying for someone—anyone.

Could he utilize it? Should he?

More arrows plugged her vines, and she mewled. Some of her strength dwindled. Kaysar stopped musing, his answer suddenly clear. Yes, he should.

He moved behind her and clasped her waist. *Will never get enough of these curves.* Concentrating on the affection wasn't as difficult as expected. As his throat heated, he placed his mouth at her ear.

The heat built…and he released the first note of his song.

Chantel's eyes hooded as he crooned to her. Even as she wielded her vines, she leaned against him, swaying from side to side. She began to sing along. "Death has come for you. And you. And you. Hmm-hmm. You can run, but you can't hide. My vines pursue."

She gives words to my melody? Satisfaction slaked some previously unknown desire. Was there nothing this treasure of a female couldn't do?

The louder he sang, the faster her vines bred. More and more thorns emerged, protruding from the stalks, cutting through armor as easily as a knife through butter.

Having a partner might be…nice.

"Stop." Features scrunched with agony, Jareth crumpled into a fetal ball. He pressed one ear to the ground and covered the other ear with his remaining hand. Blood ran between his fingers. "You have to stop."

The prince reacted this way, despite Kaysar's affectionate tone?

Ever better. Kaysar didn't stop until the soldiers got the message—attack Chantel and her vines in any way and you would die worse than your comrades.

"Let us cross the bridge, sweetling," he told Chantel, a plan forming as the numbers thinned. Get to the other side. Make their way to the mountain fortress. Reclaim his crown. Figure everything else out. "Jareth, you'll accompany us, of course." The prince was stubborn, certain to follow no matter what. Kaysar wasn't ready to divide his focus between two enemies while his female remained out in the open. He also didn't trust Micah around Jareth. If the would-be king were to kill the prince, what of Kaysar's vengeance then?

Jareth unrolled and lumbered to his feet. A bull contemplating a charge, he glared at Kaysar. "She'll remember being my Lulundria. She'll not remain this abomination."

His hands balled into fists, the need to strike escalating. Abomination? When there was no female more perfect?

But what if Chantel felt the same way as Jareth tomorrow, when the elderseed wore off? What if she awoke and regretted the slaughter of this army? Would she blame Kaysar for her actions? He'd fed her the elderseed and encouraged her kills.

And what if she remembered Lulundria's past sooner rather than later, as Jareth taunted? What if she fell for the prince all over again? What would Kaysar do then?

He'd wondered before. He worried now.

Unsheathing a dagger, he snapped, "Keep up, prince, or I'll remove your feet and carry you over my shoulder." He placed his empty hand on Chantel's lower back, urging her toward the bridge.

A good little puppy, Jareth trailed after them with loathing in his eyes.

Micah must have escaped the field of destruction. There was no sign of his armorless body as they passed the first, second and third lines of corpses. No sign of the male's centaur or interpreter, either.

A soldier leaped over a thick, slithering vine and charged the princess. Kaysar spun in front of her, shielding her. With sadistic glee, he minced the attacker's breastplate. Metal sparked against metal, the male losing his footing. Kaysar shoved a dagger through a gap in the armor. Dead.

Two other soldiers approached from the opposite side, their swords already swinging at Chantel. Despite Jareth's injuries, the prince reacted with halfway decent reflexes, stopping the pair.

More soldiers came. The number of kills stacked up as their little trio moved forward once more.

Doing battle alongside a Frostline. How novel. Jareth's wounds didn't affect his skills—skills he'd never displayed with Kaysar. The prince's reflexes were faster and more fluid than usual.

Had he *hesitated* during their private skirmishes?

The mere possibility boiled Kaysar's blood. He *deserved* to pit his best against his foe's. For someone to pull their punches... An unforgivable insult.

Kaysar slashed another soldier. He blocked, spun and ducked whenever needed, always advancing while guarding Chantel as needed.

Felling enemy after enemy, he adopted a rhythm. Calm came when he realized a wonderful truth. Chantel was witnessing his ability to protect her. His ferocity. When the elderseed wore off, her desire for him might be stronger than ever. Why fear Lulundria's affections for the prince?

Strike. Slash. Duck. Kaysar's gaze returned to Chantel again and again, her pull too powerful to deny. A beauty assured of her power. *My beauty.* Her hips swayed seductively, her steps sure, her posture steadfast.

She kept her arms extended, even when her stalks reached full maturity, attached to her hands by a mystical connection rather than a physical one. Golden smoke swirled around her fingers.

"The survivors are running away," she pouted. "I sense their movements through the vines."

"That's a wonderful thing, sweetling. Now we have targets for later."

"Well. I doubt there's ever been a better silver lining," she said, brightening. "There will always be another bad guy to crush."

"And claw."

The prince spit a mouthful of blood at Kaysar. "You rejoice over the death of innocents?"

Innocents? "They attacked your ex-bride, hoping to kill her, Jareth." He slew a soldier hiding in the shadows. "This is more than deserved."

A choking noise drew his attention back to the Frostline. Kaysar stopped and blinked. Chantel stood before the male, her vines wrapped around his wrists and ankles, stretching his limbs past comfortability as he dangled in the air. A vein bulged in his forehead. Though he struggled, he couldn't free himself.

"We saved your life and you dare complain?" she asked quietly. Her eyes were molten, the light around her fingers brighter.

Kaysar flittered—no, he stalked, only then remembering the ability to teleport was negated in the Dusklands. "He isn't yours to kill, Chantel." She was his mate, yes, but his priorities had not changed. Vengeance first, Chantel second. Best she learn and accept. "You will release him."

"I won't." Her attention remained fastened on Jareth. "Because I don't want to."

"Release him," he repeated, the command firm. "I won't tell you again." But what could he do to her, if she failed to comply? His instincts shouted louder and louder. *Protect.* "Please? For me?"

"Fine." Huffing, she stepped back and released her hold. Kaysar breathed a sigh of relief. "But only for you, and only because you're so sexy when you're angry."

She found his anger sexy?

Without the strength of the vines to hold him up, Jareth smacked into the ground. He attempted to catch himself, an instinctive action, but he only injured his mutilated arm further. His bellow of agony filled Kaysar's ears with a melody as sweet as ever. "You think...I wasn't...as much a victim...as you were?" He threw the words at Kaysar between panting breaths. "I assure you. I was."

A victim? Hardly. "Perhaps you shouldn't have laughed as your uncle decapitated a servant girl and batted her head like a child's ball, Jareth." But even as he spoke, dismay chilled Kaysar's nape. What if the prince had spoken tr— No. No! Frostlines lied. That's what they did. They were deceivers by nature, willing to do anything to hide their crimes. "Not another word from you, or I'll add your tongue to my collection."

Torment stripped the prince of civility. "I'm sorry for the abuse you endured at the hands of my family. I hate what happened to you. But what do you think happened to me when I didn't go along?"

Rage iced his chest. "So you exchanged your misery for mine? Today you dare seek my mercy?" Something he did not possess.

"Kaysar?" Chantel asked, her voice reedy.

Something was off. He whipped to her side. "What's wrong? Tell me." If he knew, he could fix it. He *must* fix it.

"I feel funny." Her cheeks were pallid. She blinked rapidly, as if to stave off dizziness. "Weakening fast...so tired."

Ah. The elderseed was wearing off. "Shh, shh, it's okay, sweetling." He draped an arm around her waist, holding her up. "Release the vines and cleave to me. I'll take care of you. I will let *nothing* harm you."

Her gaze searched his before her lids sank over her eyes. Resting her head on his shoulder, she breathed, "Promise?"

"You are mine, and I take care of what's mine. Remember?"

"Oh, yes. It's nice to be wanted." She obeyed at last,

wrapping her arms around him. Foliage withered as her body went limp against his.

Sleep had claimed her.

He swept her up, clutching her slight weight against his chest. This felt…right.

Jareth hadn't attempted to rise yet. He panted, "She isn't yours."

"She wasn't." Kaysar grinned with staggering satisfaction. "But she is now." He would be securing her agreement posthaste. When in trouble, she'd turned to him.

"You're a monster, and you're going to ruin her. You know that, yes? Do you even care? She's already poison—because of you."

Ruin her? When he planned to give her the world? Kaysar laughed, but there was no humor in it. "I am merely what your family made me, Jareth. You know *that*, yes?" He resumed his journey to the mountains, done with the conversation. For once, he had something more important to do than torment a Frostline.

CHAPTER NINETEEN

"TIME TO WAKE UP, sweetling. You've slept long enough, and we have much to discuss."

The sexy voice roused Cookie from a deep, sublime sleep. "Just ten more minutes," she muttered. "Fifteen if you have a heart."

A heavy sigh greeted her words. "Once again, it seems I can deny you nothing. Sleep, then. And sleep well." Sexy Voice hummed the most beautiful song, and she slipped into the darkness...

However long later, the barest shaft of light pierced the fog that encompassed her mind. She tried to blink open her eyes, but her lids remained glued shut. Oh, well. She rolled to her side, getting more comfortable. Huh. Her memory foam had amnesia.

"You've been sleeping for three days, Chantel. An endless eternity." Sexy Voice had returned. The bed dipped, as if he stretched out beside her. "I have so much to tell you. So much has changed." His tone effortlessly glided from firm to irritated.

She'd taken a three-day snooze?

"I insist you wake, Chantel. Micah has destroyed my playground. The goblins are missing, and the lack has encouraged people to move here. Willingly. He's made the Dusklands *habitable*. The outrage of it all!" The bed shook, as if he'd shuddered. "I suppose there are a *few* welcome developments. I'm able to flitter in and out of the palace. Which I sacked. Jareth is my prisoner, of course." A weighty pause left her suspended. What would he tell her next? "Do you hate me now? Do you hate *yourself*?"

I know him. Who... Lights switched on in her mind. Memories crystalized, and she let them. "Kaysar," she breathed.

She recalled his betrayal. Learning about his tragic past and the Frostlines who'd held him captive. She remembered the sweetness of his lips. The elderseed. Unleashing her vines and— Whoa. Her body jerked, as if shocked by a live wire. She'd killed. She'd killed *a lot*. Now, Kaysar feared she blamed him, *hated* him, for encouraging her to do it?

Did she? She thought... No. How could she? Miss Murder Curious had enjoyed every minute and scream. Every death. And hate herself? No again. Anyone who endangered her or her loved ones—er, or rather, her companions, whoever they happened to be—earned a bad end. But...

A part of her feared what she was becoming. Because there was no going back. That, she knew.

Cool metal glided along her cheekbone, sending warm shivers cascading over her. "You don't *mean* to tempt me to distraction, do you, sweetling? You just do."

Sexy voice, sexy words—very sexy man. Lust welled, as if it had only waited on the sidelines. She longed to touch her dark king, to be touched by him, but she couldn't open her eyes. Her lids were too heavy.

Though she fought, she failed. The fog in her mind only thickened, snuffing out the lights. All too soon, she drifted back to sleep...

However long later, Cookie's eyelids popped open. She blinked into focus, lights switching on in her mind once again. How much time had passed since—"Kaysar!" She jolted upright, various candles flaming to life.

Heart like an anvil, she surveyed her surroundings. A spacious bedroom straight out of a fairy tale, with marble walls, wispy white curtains that draped a massive bay window with colorful stained glass, and elaborate gold furnishings. Across the way, a crackling hearth blazed with cerulean flames, seeming to burn sapphire bricks. The opulence shocked her.

Remembering the things Kaysar had mentioned, she thought she might be in Micah's palace. The fortress carved into the mountainside, perhaps?

Once his, now mine. No, not hers. Kaysar's. She owned the farmhouse filled with her and Pearl Jean's thrift shop finds and Sugars's toys, and she wanted it back.

Only last week, she'd lamented her unwillingness to leave the run-down home. The epicenter of her childhood dreams. Today, homesickness churned in her belly. Mostly, she just missed Pearl Jean and Sugars.

What would they think of the new Cookie?

She shied away from the answer, calling, "Kaysar?"

When no response was forthcoming, she crawled from the warmth of the covers. Air kissed miles of bare skin, shocking her. Well. Someone had stripped and bathed her, then left her in her original packaging. Had that someone also provided a note about where he might be and what she should do next? No.

Cookie sighed and rummaged through the bedroom, on the hunt for a piece of clothing. Any piece of clothing. No, not *any*. She had to be careful now. What she wore affected her moods.

Ugh. The ability she'd first bewailed as a curse, then lauded as a weapon, was currently an inconvenience.

Maybe one day she would make a decision and stick with it—the way she wished people would stick with her.

Atop the dresser she discovered an empty jar. Bemused, she pretended to dump out invisible contents. Something her avatar was forced to do upon occasion. A silly action programmed into the game, whether a reward filled her jar or not.

Focus. What if Kaysar returned to find her naked?

She paused midway to the closet. *Yesss. What if he did?*

He wanted her. He'd made his desire clear. And she wanted him. Enough to put sex back on the table?

She checked her mental ledger to re-examine his crimes. The man had praised honesty—insisted on it—while purposely misleading her. Worse, he'd punished her for something she hadn't done, dumping rocks in her bag to exhaust her. He'd also kissed her as if she was oxygen required for his survival and stopped far too soon. Not a terrible offense, but still. Offense!

Had she forgiven him for everything? Maybe? A one-time deal, never to be repeated?

What if he used her as Jareth's substitute again?

Jareth, who might not be the villain she'd originally considered him to be. The torment he'd sported as he'd confessed his own trials had rung true. Had he suffered abuse, too?

Memories of his mistreatment at her hands sparked guilt and regret. Maybe she should apologize.

And how would Kaysar react to *that*?

As always, her thoughts swung back to her ruthless companion. The magnet to her metal. In a way, Kaysar reminded her of her bejeweled boots. Beautiful to look at, but extremely uncomfortable and better suited for special occasions. And what was more special than a trip to a magical land?

Before, she'd wondered if she should enjoy him while she had the chance. The question surged once more. Shouldn't she take this opportunity to explore the rare heat between them? They had a pre-determined expiration date, so she wouldn't do something foolish and fall for him. She would remain prepared for their inevitable split.

Could she *ever* return to the mortal world, though? She'd stopped taking her "necessary" drugs and healed supernaturally. She grew vines from her skin. How long before she was captured and studied? And that wasn't her former paranoia or game-brain talking, either, but cold, hard logic.

But the most important question: What happened when she murdered a mortal who wronged her or her loved ones? What then?

A hefty weight settled atop Cookie's shoulders. Why let herself get down over this stuff? Hadn't she yearned for a different life? Well, here it was, hers for the taking. She could make it better or worse, depending on her actions.

What if Pearl Jean and Sugars came here, after all?

Tears burned her eyes, and she rubbed them away with her fists. Homesickness was a real disease, and it sucked. She was only surprised Pearl Jean hadn't contracted it first.

If Cookie learned to unleash a torrent of vines without elderseed, she could protect her loved ones from anything. Wait. Was she still able to produce vines upon command, without the aid of elderseed?

She peered down at her hands and willed it so. *Buds. Come.*

Tiny green sprouts broke the surface of her skin, and she grinned. Faster and easier than before. *Nice.*

If Kaysar helped her protect Pearl Jean and Sugars, even

better. He certainly possessed the means. Not to mention the will. But how long would his willingness last? He desired Cookie, yes. For now. What happened when a shiny new toy caught his eye and he bailed?

People always bailed.

Great. Her mood had soured without the aid of clothing. Speaking of, she needed to dress ASAP.

Jutting her chin, Cookie entered the closet. Three gowns hung on the racks, awaiting her perusal. The first was an adorable mix of an evil queen and a cat woman. Black, sexy and super tight. Basically a long-sleeve bodysuit with an attachable train.

The second gave off a Little Bo-Peep vibe, with its pink ruffles and purple bows, while the third gown had been designed with a schoolmarm in mind. Cinched waist, with a slightly flared, ankle-length skirt. The harsh gray color would wash out anyone's skin, and the stiff collar probably itched like crazy.

It was the most magnificent ensemble she'd ever beheld, and it called to her on a cellular level.

"Mine!" She snatched the gown from its hanger as if someone lurked nearby, ready to pounce on the deal of the century. Fingers crossed Kaysar had left her a pair of panties with core-to-kidney coverage to complete the outfit. The perfect accessory for a persona like this.

Dang. No panties. Although… Going commando under such a prim and proper dress struck her as highly provocative, and she grinned.

In the private bathroom, she stumbled upon her satchel. Giddy, she dangled the dress on a robe hook, dropped to her knees and rooted through her belongings. Her jewelry. Her flask. Her toiletries. Everything remained but her elderseed. Which she'd be getting back. She'd carried it through the forest, so she'd *earned* it.

Wait. She didn't recall seeing this amethyst armband before. Or this pearl brooch. Or this tiara with crystals shaped like roses. No doubt the pieces were double the worth of her farmhouse, and she marveled. Looked like her love of jewelry hadn't faded, even without the boots. Which meant it came from Cookie herself.

Maybe the clothes highlighted different aspects of her own personality. Hadn't Kaysar alluded to that fact?

Kaysar, who had just *given* her the jewelry? For free?

She really needed to speak with him about…well, everything.

Her tasks gelled. *Shower and dress. Without panties. Find Kaysar.*

With new purpose, Cookie gathered her toiletries and entered the shower stall. But, uh, where were the knobs? She searched this way and that, up and down, but…no knobs. There wasn't even a spout.

"Help a girl shower on her own, while awake," she complained.

And just like that, water spilled from the ceiling, raining over her. The icy liquid made her squeal. "Too cold. Need heat."

Again, her words caused instantaneous action, the spray warming until it scalded like acid. Her preferred temperature.

Cookie scrubbed from head to toe, then exited the stall, saying, "Off." As hoped, the waterfall ceased.

Standing on a bathmat, she scanned for a towel. But there was no need. Warmth wafted from the mat, drying her from head to toe. *A girl could get used to this.*

At the sink, she discovered a note from Kaysar. Only,

it wasn't written on a piece of paper or even blood. The words appeared on the steamy mirror. *Drink me. You'll like it.* An arrow pointed to clear, minty-smelling liquid in a small glass decanter.

A type of mouthwash? A drug? *Bottoms up.* Like Alice in her Wonderland, Cookie drained the glass. The minty liquid fizzed against her gums and on her tongue, seeming to scrub every inch of her mouth. The fizzy sensation spread through the rest of her, infiltrating her stomach, then her chest, then her veins, and oh, that felt nice.

As the fog faded from the mirror, Kaysar's note disappeared, and her reflection came into focus. Her hair had darkened to a stunning black. And her eyes...the left was green, while the right was silver.

But, she was naked. Did her appearance change with her moods as well as her clothes? With her actions? Was the elderseed responsible? Or something else entirely? Would Pearl Jean and Sugars even recognize her? She looked different, smelled different. Acted different. Her very DNA had changed.

Ignoring her dismay, Cookie anchored her hair into a severe knot at her nape, with no strand out of place. No other style would complement her amazing dress. Which she donned, amazed all over again as the garment cinched to her curves, creating a seamless fit.

The desire to square her shoulders and straighten her spine proved undeniable. A desire she heeded, feeling as if she'd exchanged a worry-prone avatar for a military general. Or head mistress.

Madam Cookie.

Her thoughts cleared and sharpened, the dismay fading. She almost smiled, but humphed with disapproval instead.

Which jewelry should she don? The pearl brooch caught her notice. She pinned the beauty over her heart.

As unhurried as any stern matron, Cookie headed for the door. Which swung open before she reached it.

Kaysar strode inside the bedroom, the sight of him arresting her. He wore all black, his dark hair was gloriously windblown and spiky. He'd trimmed his beard, a thick shadow dusting his jaw.

For some reason, metal claws adorned only one of his hands today. Combat boots and an assortment of weapons added to his drool-worthy appeal.

Even as her body reacted with a dizzying rush, the dress served her well, helping her maintain a stoic expression. If she was going to sleep with this man—and she might—she required a level head about the matter.

"You are awake, as Eye predicted." He glided closer, sweeping his gaze over her and stopping midway. Hot, blatant desire glittered in his eyes. *As smooth as whiskey, twice as intoxicating.* "You chose the disciplinarian."

She didn't fidget, just allowed him to look his fill, revealing nothing.

"If you're curious to know whether or not I examined your naked body as I bathed you, allow me to put your mind at ease," he said. "I did. The entire time. I have no regrets."

"As if you are strong enough to resist this." She waved a hand to indicate her curves, certain she presented a picture of grace, elegance and sophistication. Most likely perfection, too.

Well. The schoolmarm had game and a healthy ego. Good to know.

"What happened after I fainted?" she asked.

A flicker of…something darkened his expression. "Jareth fought off the remaining soldiers as I carried you. We reached the fortress later that evening. Once I realized I could flitter, the guards stood no chance. I kept the servants and fetched Eye. She—"

"She?" Apparently the "disciplinarian" possessed a nasty jealous streak. "Who is Eye?" *And how soon can I kill her?*

"She's an oracle who sees into the past, present and future," he said with a dismissive wave. "Hardly worth mentioning." Cautious, unsure, he approached Cookie once again. "Do you regret what happened with Micah's army?"

"Not even a little," she admitted, her jealousy eroding. "Why? Should I?"

"You should not." He lifted a hand, snapped his fingers, and stepped aside. "Starving, sweetling? Allow me to satisfy your hunger."

A procession of servants entered the room, no one daring to glance in her direction. Were they cowed by Kaysar or Cookie? Or were they simply following orders? Two men carried a small round table. Two others marched in with chairs, and six women followed with food and drink. The accompanying scents proved divine, and Cookie's mouth watered.

As the servants set up a romantic meal near the hearth, Kaysar stared at her, hard. Her nipples tightened beneath the dress.

Reveal nothing.

The group retreated, shutting the door behind them, leaving Cookie and Kaysar alone.

His countenance changed dramatically right before her eyes. From reserved to fierce, as if a mask had slipped. He bared his teeth in the semblance of a smile. "We have many things to discuss."

CHAPTER TWENTY

KAYSAR HAD BEEN miserable these long, torturous days without Chantel. He'd missed her the way he would miss a vital organ. He'd craved her company, complaints and praises. There were so many things he ached to do with her. To her. Things he *needed* to do.

The moment he'd spotted her starched, somber dress, he'd feared the worst. That Jareth had proven correct, and she'd mourned her previous behavior. That she intended to punish Kaysar. He should have held fast to his certainty: he knew her best, and he was never wrong about anything ever. Except when he was wrong.

She'd chosen the stern maiden to help herself *resist* Kaysar. But she would fail. There was no one more determined, and he already scented her arousal.

He motioned to the table. "Shall we sit?" Something had occurred to him as she'd slept off the effects of the elderseed.

Desires beyond the physical seethed inside him—desires only she could assuage. But she couldn't know what he required of her unless he told her. The same was true of him. He couldn't know what she needed unless she explained. He *yearned* to know.

A slight nod revealed no hint of her emotions. "We shall."

For her, he could pretend to be a gentleman—he wanted

to be. He swept over to ready her chair. "Please, sit here." When speaking to a woman you hoped to entice into your bed for the rest of your lifetime, you did not issue demands. You offered requests. Or so he believed he'd witnessed from other males.

Something he knew beyond a doubt. When you failed to respect something, you lost it. If you accepted its loss, you were never worthy of it in the first place.

A silent Chantel eased upon the cushion, as graceful as a swan. He scooted her forward, gently but firmly, before claiming the seat across from her.

He wanted this matter settled as soon as possible. Acting nonplussed, he flipped his napkin to unfold it, and said, "I've made no secret of my desire for you."

She arched a brow the same shade of obsidian as her hair. The darkness enhanced her pale skin and rosy cheeks, her delicacy. "Diving into the deep end right at the beginning? A bold strategy. Very well. I'm game to play." A imperial wave of her fingers. "Please, do continue."

Actually, his strategy was much simpler. Honesty, no matter the consequences. And lavish gifts, priceless in value. He wasn't above bribery to secure this woman. "I'm determined to have you at my side and in my bed. Forever. I'm willing to take the necessary steps to acquire your complete surrender."

"My complete surrender. Forever, no less." Again, she gave nothing away. "You wish to bargain for sex, after all?"

"I do. But also your future," he said. Let there be no misunderstandings between them.

He waited for a response… She selected the choicest of berries from the bowl and bit into half of it. Red juice wet her lips.

I will not lean over. I will not lick those plump lips clean.

Unless she begs me to.

He gripped the arms of his chair. "You'll find I'm *very* keen to acquire you."

"Acquire me, hmm? As if I'm a possession."

"A treasure," he corrected.

"But you don't take care of your possessions and treasures, do you, Kaysar?"

The simply asked question set off hundreds of alarm bells.

He bristled, barking, "Explain." *You wish to keep her, Unhinged One, or lose her faster?* "Please," he added with a softer tone.

"You claim this land is yours, and yet you abandoned it for two hundred years."

"I never abandoned it. I lost track of time. Which I would not do with you," he added. "The land is nice, but it doesn't offer such..." He dropped his gaze to her breasts. "Stimulating conversation."

"What of my connection to Jareth?"

Did she pine for the Frostline prince? Kaysar reached for his wine to moisten his dry mouth. The glass shattered in his grip, dark red liquid pouring to the floor. "Have you recalled more of Lulundria's memories?" he asked as if nothing had happened.

"I'm sure you'll be pleased to know I haven't. Though I do wonder if you wish to keep me in ignorance because you fear the uncovering of another lie." She leaned over to offer her napkin.

"I have admitted to each of my crimes." Kaysar accepted the cloth and dabbed his hand before filling a second wineglass. He'd requested extra of everything, just in case. "I merely dislike the thought of my Chantel feeling affection for Lulundria's prince."

She double-blinked, nothing more, but he sensed the admission pleased her. "You'll understand if my trust in your motives remains shaky, yes?"

He opened and closed his mouth twice before settling on a response. "Your lack of trust in my motives is a matter I can rectify with time." Sweat broke out on his brow, his next words paining him, even before they emerged. "There's no reason for us to rush to bed. I'm happy to wait until I've proven myself."

"You are *happy* to wait? Yes, I can see how eager you are to acquire me."

"I am happy to wait because you need me to be. I will wait however long you require, the end worth any hardships." Even throbbing, aching hardships.

Again, he sensed his answer pleased her.

She popped another berry into her mouth, thoughtful.

He decided to carry the conversation to the next plateau. His bribes. "You'll be overjoyed to know I've captured a doormaker's apprentice. He awaits you in the throne room. While he cannot open a doorway to the mortal realm himself, he's well able to train you to do so. He knows tricks." A loophole he'd considered after sacking the palace.

He scrutinized her, expectant, hopeful…disappointed when her expression failed to soften.

"You want me forever, but you also wish to teach me how to leave you? Help me understand." Her level tone belied a slight twitch from her fingers.

A tell. But of what?

Did she notice the way his hands trembled when he placed the softest breads and most delectable puddings on her plate? "You must learn to open doorways to retrieve your loved ones. Pearl Jean and Sugars, yes? I assume you'll wish to bring them to Astaria. I'm eager to meet them.

They'll live with us, of course, and receive the full protection of my name. Does the royal feline prefer to knock priceless vases from counters or shred irreplaceable antique furnishings? I'm able to acquire both within the hour." He shook his head. "Foolish question. I've already deduced the answer. He prefers both."

She double-blinked again, and his heart tripped. Another tell. His plan was either working better than he'd dreamed or failing miserably.

His next gift was sure to please. "I've decided to bequeath you this fortress, along with everything inside it. The moment you accept, you become Queen of the Dusklands." He took a sip of the rich, woodsy red. "I believe you'll approve of the treasury as well as the defenses. The curtain walls and flanking towers are extraordinary. The machicolations more so."

Her knuckles whitened on the wineglass. "Machicolations, you say? Used for pouring boiling oil over attackers? I employ them in my Rhoswynian castle." An ember of arousal flickered in her mismatched eyes, and he sucked in a breath.

Emotion must *seethe* beneath that stern maiden exterior.

Or not seethe. That ember of arousal died too quickly. An arctic cold etched grim lines into Chantel's features. "I'll be a queen, yes, but also a lowly princess in your eyes, irrevocably bound to Jareth Frostline. Perhaps that's even part of my appeal, eh?"

Kaysar shouted an inner curse. He'd nearly had his prize within his clasp, then logic had snuck in and ripped her from his reach.

He wondered about his plan no longer. He was failing miserably.

He couldn't retreat now. He'd vowed to be honest with

her, no matter the consequences. If he wavered in that regard, he would be as bad as a Frostline. "When we first met, I planned to get you with child, allowing my seed to rule from the Frostline throne."

"And now?" Her voice contained the barest rasp. Of outrage?

"I've decided you will bear no children at all." He used his flattest tone, leaving no room for argument. Tapping a spot on his shoulder, he told her, "I've added a tattoo. Mystical birth control."

"*You've* decided." Her eyes narrowed. "You have. You. Decided. For me?"

"My vengeance demands it." They had reached a dangerous dividing line between them. How could he make her understand his side of it? "You are precious to me, Chantel, and I have no wish to act otherwise. I wish only to give you the world."

"The world. But not children."

Ignore the burn in your chest. "Do you even want them?"

"Not right now. But one day. Maybe. I'd like the option, at least."

He gripped the edge of the table. *Losing her.* "I will keep you so satisfied, you'll never miss them. For the rest of my life, I will devote myself to your pleasure."

"And if my pleasure gets in the way of your vengeance?"

He wouldn't deny the truth. "She is my master, and she will always come first." Vengeance fed him. He liked his meals cold and often.

Chantel revealed nothing—at first. "Before you entered the room, I debated the merits of sleeping with you for a few weeks before going home. Now you demand obedience for eternity. That's a big nope, by the way. I won't submit to you, and I certainly won't rely on you. The moment I do, boom, you'll decide you're done with me, and good ole Cookie will have to pick up the pieces yet again."

The more she spoke, the more hurt she projected.

His chest pinged as never before. He'd been so focused on his own past, he hadn't given hers a thought. What had branded such anguish in her eyes? "I will *always* need you," he told her, his certainty unwavering.

"I thought we'd established the fact that you aren't a seer. You can't know the future."

"In this, I can. I do." He sensed the truth in the deepest part of himself. Looking back, he realized he'd experienced a glimmer of her importance to him the moment their gazes first locked. "I've lost *everything* of importance to me. My parents. My sister. My innocence. For most of my life, vengeance has been my sole pleasure. Before you, sex wasn't something I deemed essential. But you affected—*affect* me. The things you make me feel, every hour of every day, whether you're with me or away from me…"

Desire scraped him raw, even now. He ran his gaze over her, and his timbre dropped. "Your mind and body are most definitely essential."

Emotions spun inside her eyes, reminding him of the wheels on a cart, going around and around, delaying her reaction. As if she couldn't know how to feel until the wheels stopped.

He pressed his advantage. Confusion had opened a door; he needed only to slide in. "My affections are yours, Chantel. I will see to your every need and slay your every dragon."

Her eyes narrowed. She came to her feet with that awing grace. Leaning over, languid but intent, she gripped the sides of the table. "I don't need you to slay my dragons, Kaysar." Those mismatched eyes glittered as she displayed a cold smile. Vines unwound from her fingertips, slithering around his throat and squeezing—lifting him out of his chair. "I'm perfectly capable of killing *anyone*."

Savage arousal choked him as surely as her vines, and he shot as hard as stone. *Want her. Need her.*

"In case it isn't obvious," she said, severe and pitiless, "I'm keeping the apprentice and the palace, but I'm declining your offer."

Perhaps he should modify his strategy? A small tweak, nothing more. "Allow me to stay and help you defend your palace against the coming attacks," he said, slowly, gently wrapping his fingers around the stalks.

Pressure eased. She retracted her vines and returned to her chair. Wineglass in hand, she reclined. "Go on. I'm listening."

He openly adjusted his erection, not trying to hide the action, and returned to his seat, as well. "Micah and his army want this palace back. They'll return. As queen, you'll be responsible for the defense of every person, door, window and trap. To achieve victory, you'll require an army of your own filled with loyal soldiers—or a king able to fell thousands within seconds." Because he had no moral compass, he added, "Think of Pearl Jean. Sugars. Guarding their lives will be a high priority for me. They'll be my family, too. I'll protect them with my life. No other king, teammate or lover will vow the same, and mean it."

A moment passed without the slightest hint of a reaction, both endless and agonizing for Kaysar. Then she swirled and swirled and swirled her wine, and he longed for the inactivity of yesteryear. What did the swirling mean? What would she say or do next?

Finally, she spoke. "Micah and the bulk of his men are unable to hear your voice. How will you defeat them?"

"No, sweetling. They *were* unable. The effects of the drug they used have since worn off."

"And if they use the drug again?"

"I can sing to you." Did she feel anything for him? She must. When she kissed him at the waterfall, she'd lost herself in the throes. Her body had clung to his, desperate for more.

But what if she had changed her mind?

He shifted in his seat, agitated by her stillness, his thoughts fragmenting. She must, she must, she must.

"Stop that," she snapped, and he jolted into focus. "I will not have my meal ruined with unnecessary bloodshed."

He realized he'd dug his claws into his arms and slashed. Blood trickled from the wounds. "My apologies for maiming myself at our table," he said. "I find I am…uneasy about your unwillingness to respond to my gifts. Do you leave me in suspense to punish me? If so, I accept it as my due. But you must explain what I've done. I cannot guess your thoughts if—"

"I'm not punishing you," she interjected with a softer tone. "I need a moment to process, that's all. Your last offer both intrigues and confuses me. You'll remain in my palace and act as my family's personal bodyguard. That, I understand. But what do I get in return for allowing you to do so?"

Cunning seductress. So assured of her control. And oh, he liked her. Calm replaced his panic, tempering his posture. She *did* feel something for him. Otherwise, the treacherous beauty would be drilling a vine into his head right now.

He told her honestly, "You will get a devoted lover who will pleasure you in every filthy way you desire, help you slay any enemy you wish and lay his heart at your feet, if ever you ask."

Her red lips parted. "You think repeated orgasms will bind me to your side. That I'll do whatever you command, if only you keep me drunk with pleasure."

"I'm staking a lifetime of happiness on it." Kaysar dropped his chin, the corners of his lips curling into a predatory smile. His glamara heated. Not enough to compel, just enough to singe. "The things I'm going to do to your body..."

Beneath the fabric of her severe gown, her nipples drew tight—he watched it happen. When she wiggled in her seat to assuage her aches, he almost roared with triumph.

She pulled at the stiff collar, softly asking, "What kind of things?"

He held her gaze. Throat suddenly raw, he told her, "There is *nothing* I won't do to you. If you have a desire, I will fulfill it." Menace seeped into his tone. "I will do this. There will be no other for you."

Her features shuttered. With a flat tone, she told him, "There will be no other for you. For *any* reason, even vengeance."

"Agreed." He couldn't release the word fast enough. She was considering his offer because of jealousy. She nearly frothed at the mouth at the thought of him with another. She must! The queen of the Dusklands was delightfully possessive, refusing to share her male with another.

Placing the glass at her mouth without tilting her head, she drained her wine. Closed her eyes. Drew and released a deep breath.

He shook, wanting to push his advantage. But he didn't do it. Somehow he found the strength to tell her, "There's no need to provide me with an answer today." As long as she deliberated, they stayed together.

Her eyelids popped open, and he frowned. She appeared…
disappointed. Had she *hoped* to bed him today—now?

Perhaps he would push his advantage, after all. "Answer a
single question for me, sweetling, and we'll reserve this line
of conversation for another day."

A stiff nod. "Very well. Ask."

"Are you wet?"

CHAPTER TWENTY-ONE

COOKIE WAS STRIPPED to the studs while still fully clothed. Kaysar had destroyed her with his heart-wrenching confessions and earnest promises. He craved her *bad*. The guy claimed to want forever with her, and he might even possess the stones to actually stick around.

The problem, for Cookie, was his priorities. She'd been second, third and fourth choice all her life. Every forgotten birthday, broken promise and missed dinner had gutted her. To willingly sign on for a pre-ranked relationship—when you started off as the loser—was utter stupidity. The fact that she scored below his ideal of vengeance rankled.

They hadn't known each other long, but their chemistry was off the charts. Their connection more so. Maybe, over time, his priorities would shift. But maybe not. Yeah, probably not. There was no one more stubborn than Kaysar.

And yet, despite every reason to bail, she remained seated, stewing. The problem had an obvious answer. Win him away from his vengeance. A battle of desires. Claim Kaysar's heart in victory, and she would become first place.

Before their negotiation began, she'd considered him a candidate for a temporary fling. Now? Some of her barriers were reduced to a pile of rubble, and she saw the truth. He was a coveted war prize. One kiss, and he'd become her drug and her dealer. She craved another hit of the good stuff—connection.

Falling asleep in his arms every night. Waking beside him every morning. Conferring over battle plans. Dispensing their brand of justice throughout the land. Redecorating this castle and making a real home together. *Their* home. Yes!

Could she win the Unhinged One, though? Did she want to try?

Their courtship, for lack of a better word, wouldn't be easy. Two hardheaded royals, each with a point to prove? *Are you kidding me?* Fights were a guarantee. Knock-down-and-drag-outs that were sexually charged to the max.

And yes, she thought of herself as a fae royal now. No, it wasn't a big deal.

"I asked you a question, Chantel." Kaysar reclined in a pose of total relaxation. Those whiskey irises told a different story. An epic fantasy of war and seduction. He was a warlord soon to demolish any obstacle in his path.

The barest whimper escaped. She shifted in her seat. Reeling…steadying. As she locked gazes with him, she centered. He was right. There was no reason to agonize over this decision today. He wasn't asking for a commitment right this second, only a chance to do those filthy things to her body.

Why hadn't she said yes already?

Cookie flowed to her feet and strolled to his side, admitting, "You did ask me a question, Kaysar, and I desire to show you my answer."

His pupils consumed his irises, his aggression spiking. "Yes. You will show me. I will see." With a violent sweep of his arm, he sent dishes clattering to the floor, food spilling here and there. Liquids gurgled. "I will see your answer *now*."

His urgency was kerosene to Cookie, her aches catching flame. Her tremors worsened as she gathered the hem of her skirt and eased upon the table's edge, then swung a leg over Kaysar, placing her feet on the arms of his chair. Lace trim stretched over her thighs.

With slow precision, he stroked his claws over his mouth and slid his gaze from her chest to her toes. On the way back, he lingered on the shadowed spot between her knees.

"Show me." A raw entreaty.

Emboldened, Cookie widened her thighs bit by bit, forcing the skirt to lift, more and more light chasing the darkness away. Cool air kissed her feverish need. She groaned as Kaysar moaned.

The most delicate vines budded, growing over her hands as she traced the pierced edge of his pointed ears. "Am I wet, Kaysar?"

Appearing stunned, he shackled her ankles with a vise-grip and stared at her. "You are soaked. Pink and pretty. *Beautiful.*" His throaty tone thickened. "You are perfect. And I am undone."

He moved his gaze to hers. Never had she seen such ferocious determination. Eyes glittering, he released her…and rolled his shirtsleeves up to his forearms. Muscles bunched with each movement. Ligaments pulled.

"Soon, Chantel, you will be undone, as well."

The carnal promise battered her remaining defenses. She panted for the massive erection pressed against his leathers, the scent of her poisonvine perfuming the air. He traced the cold tip of a claw against the underside of her knee, dragging it back and forth, back and forth. Not once did he cut her. His masterful control rendered her mindless.

"Do you know what I'm going to do to you, sweetling?" He purred the words.

"I do, darling." She curled an emerald vine around one

side of him, urging him to his feet. She used the same vine to glide upright. "Anything you want."

He heaved his next breath.

He was bent over, hovering above her with his body cradled between her legs. The width of his hips kept her legs spread for him. His eyes were hungry, smoldering, their lips separated by a sliver of air. Lust torched her every thought.

"I will," he swore, white-knuckling the table edge. Longing ravaged his features. "I will do anything I want, and you will scream your satisfaction."

Yes. "Over and over and over and—"

He slammed his mouth into hers. Cookie eagerly met the thrust of his tongue with a thrust of her own. His ferocity worked her into a frenzy, a series of mewls spilling from her. She kissed and licked and bit him with abandon, exactly as he kissed and licked and bit her.

As her vines withered, she wound her arms around him, needing him closer. He palmed one of her breasts. Squeezed it and pinched her nipple through the dress. Exquisite pleasure constricted her lungs.

"Getting wetter by the second," she panted into his mouth.

He kissed her harder, reaching up to cup her nape.

Fevered and desperate, she whipped her hips, attempting to grind herself on his length. Yes! There. The friction she sought. She whipped her hips again and— Noooo! He'd drawn back.

"Kaysar—"

He yanked her closer, forcing her legs to spread wider as his shaft pressed flush against her core. Leather against flesh, and she gasped for more, tempted to beg for it. He didn't grind against her, and she really, really needed him to grind against her.

"Do you hunger for me, Chantel?" he demanded, slowly reclaiming his grip on her nape, winding the claw-tipped hand through a thick lock. He angled her head further and further back, until she teetered, forced to rely on him for balance. "Say it. Say, 'I hunger for you, Kaysar.'"

Did he need to hear the words? "Yes, Kaysar. I'm *ravenous* for you."

His intensity sharpened, beautiful in its brutality. Stripping her of more control. "My name on your ruby lips… I want to watch your beautiful face as I finger you deep. Would you like that, sweetling?"

"Love that." *More diabolical than I realized.* No wonder he'd worn only one set of claws. He'd planned this. How… delicious. "Do it. Do it, do it." As she command-pleaded, she undulated as much as possible, given her position.

He tightened his clasp on her nape and kissed her, his lips firm as his tongue swiped at hers. When he pulled back, he trailed his unencumbered hand up her inner thigh and under her skirt, watching her.

The light graze of his finger against her core set off a chain reaction. A cascade of shivers. Aches. Oh, the aches! Her nipples hardened. Her clit throbbed. Lost in pleasure, she writhed against his hand, seeking more, more, more.

He teased the edges of her sex with lazy up-and-down strokes, drawing closer to the heart of her need but never quite making contact… Those fingers. As hot as a branding iron, leaving a trail of fire in their wake. She moaned and gasped and moaned again.

"Your song commands my body." His words were hoarse, his eyes glassed with desire. The face she'd once touted as stunning proved savage in the firelight. Tension pulled his skin taut. "I hope you're ready for me, sweetling."

The words seemed to have more than one meaning. "Yes, I'm read—"

He plunged deep. Again and again. He worked and stretched her. The closer she came to climax, the more strangled her cries sounded.

"So tight." He slowed his pace, stroking her inner walls with every glide. Easing his fingers almost all the way out... watching her intently, gauging her every reaction. "Look at you, chasing my touch. You adore what I make you feel."

"I do," she rasped when he thrust his fingers back in. Out. In. Leaving her empty. Filling her back up. Innnn, outttttt. Incoherent mumblings tripped off her tongue. The pleasure. His obsession with her. That incredible intensity. It was all too much. But stop? She would rather die. "What are you doing to me, Kaysar?"

Inout. Inout. Inoutinoutinout. "Are you desperate for me to stroke your soaked little clit?"

Burning hotter... Sizzling. "Do it. You want to. You said you'd do whatever you wanted..."

"And I always keep my promises." At last he pressed the pad of his thumb against her clitoris. Her back arched, and she screamed. Sparks. The approach of bliss. Almost shattering. Almost, almost.

"More," she commanded. So, so, close.

He stirred the digit against her, rubbing an ultra-sensitive spot. Closer...

"I once told you I'd give you everything." He panted as he leaned down and brushed the tip of his nose against hers, always rubbing. "Do you remember?"

"You want to chat?" *Can't think.*

"I do, and we will." He removed his fingers, leaving her empty and aching. "I asked you a question, Chantel. Do you remember?"

"I remember, I remember. Fingers back in!"

He flittered her to her bed and the entirety of his weight came down upon her. Mmm. This was what she'd missed before. His weight and his heat.

She rolled her hips, grinding on him at her leisure. Hardness on top, a soft mattress beneath. The contrast was breathtaking. "Or we give your fingers a break. This is good, too."

Kaysar's harsh groan filled the room. He elevated her arms above her head, urging her to grip the headboard. As soon as she obeyed, he drew back to study her new pose in their new surroundings.

"Touch me," she said, licking her lips.

Satisfaction oozed from him. "Oh, I will be touching you. Extensively. Your climaxes are a priority for me."

Just not the top one.

The rogue thought dampened a tendril of her ardor. Then he reached over his shoulder and pulled his shirt over his head, slowly baring his chest—a sculpted chest heavily tattooed with map on top of map.

Cookie forgot everything else, tracing her gaze over lines, landmarks, words, faces, arrows, more lines that zigged and zagged, creating endless paths that led everywhere and nowhere at the same time.

"You should never wear a shirt. Ever," she told him.

"A request I shall take under advisement."

"The sight of your muscles makes me wetter." She caressed his legs with her own. "Does the royal no-shirt policy get a stamp of approval *now*?"

He smiled, almost sheepish. "It does."

She imagined sucking on every landmark and groaned. Why not use this opportunity as a cool down? "What do your tattoos mean?"

He moved his big hand over the maps. "Never lost." Then his bicep, and the snake eating its own tail. "Eternal war." His gaze slid over her, his eyelids sinking low. "Though I'm more eager for eternal pleasure at the moment."

Had she just whimpered? Forget any kind of cool down!

He smiled at her, a mere baring of his teeth. The irresistible rake knew his effect on her. On all women. "But I think you are equally eager."

"Oh, I am," she said, rolling her hips with more vigor. "If you give me what you want, Kaysar, I'll give you what you need." What they *both* needed.

Releasing a broken sound, he swooped down and kissed her.

CHAPTER TWENTY-TWO

KAYSAR KISSED CHANTEL with everything he had. He kissed her until she couldn't breathe without him. Until he didn't want to breathe without her. His first and last mistress.

He had desired her, and he had won her. For now. Could he keep her?

He would have to find a way.

How many queens, princesses and peasants had he seduced throughout the centuries? Countless. They'd hailed from different kingdoms and had wanted different things, yet he'd had no trouble charming them from their husbands and lovers. He'd had no trouble remaining unaffected.

His relationship with Chantel wasn't a temporary thing. Everything he did, everything he said, mattered. Because she mattered. He'd made mistakes with her that he now regretted. He refused to add new marks to his tally of wrongs.

Winning her for eternity was a requirement. The devotion Lulundria had showed Jareth, Kaysar now demanded for himself. There would be no rest until he achieved his goal.

Lifting his head to break the kiss hurt in a thousand different ways, but he did it. He kept his focus on the prize. Kissing was only the beginning…

She watched him with luminous eyes, her chest rising and falling as he gently unwound her hair from its knot.

Long ebony waves spilled over the pillows, a waterfall of splendor and temptation.

Kaysar sat back on his haunches to examine his feast of feminine delights. An image forever branded into his mind. The top three buttons of her bodice were open, the material gaping, hinting at cleavage he would slaughter thousands to explore. The skirt bunched at her waist, baring the pale length of legs spread by his own—revealing a glistening sex guarded by a tiny thatch of black curls.

A new kingdom to conquer. The most exquisite of all.

"You need me," he told her, in case she wasn't certain.

"Maybe I do, but you can't get enough of me, can you?" Clinging to the headboard, she undulated her hips. "Do you still carry my lock of hair?"

She knew about that? "I have it stored for safekeeping."

A heady scent emanated from her, signaling a spike of pleasure.

Passion in its purest form took hold. She *liked* his obsession with her.

Only moments before, he'd been two knuckles deep inside her, enveloped by slick inner walls. His fingers glistened with her arousal.

Ensnaring her gaze with his own, he licked one digit, then the other. His shaft jerked at the incredible taste. "Sweeter than poisonvine, and far more potent." *The things I'm going to do to this woman...*

Her lips parted. "You want more of me?"

"I want everything from you." He would give everything, too. Almost. "Show me more of this luscious body." Leaning forward, muscles flexing, he plucked one, two, three other buttons from her bodice. The material separated further, unveiling pretty pink nipples.

My own personal treasure trove. He had no words, rational thought erased.

A rosy flush spread over her breasts. "Am I everything you ever dreamed?"

"You are more than I ever believed possible." The admission left him without reservation. Remaining on his knees, keeping her open to his view, he stroked his throbbing erection through his leathers. "See what you do to me."

Her coarse whimper drew an answering groan from him.

With her prim gown so disheveled, her eyes alive with pleasure, she appeared wanton. "I will win you, my darling." She released the headboard to cup her breasts and pinch her nipples. "I'll make you mine. You *want* me to win you, don't you?"

He reacted to her words as much as the thrill of her body. She'd called him *my darling.*

Win him? Already done. And yet, he croaked, "Yes. Win me."

Intricate strands of ivy coiled designs over her arms, along her chest and around and around her legs. Those strands spread to him, binding his wrists tightly together.

She winged her brows, as if to say, *Go ahead. Try to escape me.*

As if he would ever want to. Once upon a time, he'd enjoyed a single fascination—his war with the Frostlines. With Chantel, he discovered many others. Earning more endearments. Being challenged by her mysterious mind. Watching a flush heat the flawless skin soon to burn his own. Playing with those plump breasts and nipples so like little berries. Filling a body made to glove his.

The sight of her at this moment...

She smiled, fully aware of her power over him. "Have I stolen your thoughts, your majesty?"

He went cold. Lulundria had spoken the same words to Jareth.

Forge ahead. Too late. Fear had taken hold. "You mastered your ability, even without the elderseed." If ever she remembered Lulundria's life, as Jareth expected, she might change her mind about staying with Kaysar.

What would he do then? *Can never lose her.*

"I did master it. Far too easily," she answered, all languid pride and sultry heat. As the foliage receded, she undulated her hips again. "We can discuss it, or we can continue your seduction of me. Which do you prefer?"

I will have her! He was King Kaysar the Unhinged One. Fiercer than any enemy. Mightier than any army. More dangerous and cunning than…anyone. He would win his mate, whatever memories returned.

Determination cut through his fear, as sharp as a blade. "We *will* discuss it." From now on, they had no secrets. No hidden agendas or conscious misleadings. "Later."

Heart pumping, breaths labored, he repositioned and leaned down to tenderly nuzzle the side of her thigh, just below her knee. As he licked toward her glistening sex, she encouraged him with irresistible pleas and demands.

"Please, Kaysar. Do it."

He did it, flicking the tip of his tongue over her needy little clitoris. The lightest of grazes. Her sweet honey went straight to his head, and he nearly fell on her to feast. But he forced himself to ease off, licking around the heart of her need, always halting just short of his target.

How needy could he make her?

"Kaysar! It—it's been too long since I…played." Tremors shook her, her confidence overrun by torment. "I need to come. Please."

"How long?" he demanded, so hard he thought he might explode at any moment. *Slow down. Steady.*

"Kaysar…"

He licked her clit and thrust two fingers deep. The tight fit drew a ragged groan from them both.

Though she rocked into him, he experienced a flicker of apprehension. Too readily he recalled the day he'd spied Jareth and Lulundria at the pond. The princess had teased her prince about being too big to fit inside her.

Sweat beaded his brow. Could this tiny channel accept his invasion without a hint of pain? If he ruined this experience for either of them… If ever she thought back and remembered that pain…

No! "How long?" he insisted, edging ever closer to worry. Thrusting his fingers. Slowly. Gently. Licking her clit.

She cried out. Arched to force him deeper. Gave her nipples another pinch.

A surge of primal satisfaction stole his breath. He had this effect on her. He alone. "How long, how long, how long?"

"A year? Don't know, can't think," she babbled. "Harder, baby. Faster. Make me come."

His next plunge shook the bed. A year. An eternity. He would prepare her, no matter how long it took. No matter the pain *he* endured. "Won't stop until you come *hard.*" At least a dozen times…

Throat burning white hot, he hummed against her slickness. Lick. One finger. Lick. Two fingers.

"Kaysar." She continued to chant his name, chasing his touch. "Baby, baby…yes. Right there." The radiance of her skin intensified, her irises like mercury. Shivers cascaded over her and goose bumps followed. "Don't...don't stop. You said you wouldn't."

"Never stop. Want this honey always."

When she bowed up, ready to snap, he thrust his fingers as deep as he could get them and licked her clit at the same time. A scream barreled from her, the climax swift but brutal.

No mercy. Before she had a chance to come down from her high, he flicked her little bud with more force, earning another moan from her. Music as sweet as her flavor. She'd grown richer with her orgasm.

Frenzied, he licked harder. Sucked. Fingered. In and out, until she was writhing against him once again.

He scissored his fingers, preparing her to take more of him, all of him, and—she petted him? He flipped his gaze up. She looked drunk with desire as she glided her thorn claws through his hair.

The rest of the world faded, instinct overtaking him. Only passion mattered. Chantel's. His. *Theirs.*

This scrumptious beauty belonged to him.

He removed his fingers and crawled up, pressing his shaft against her core. Upon contact, he hissed in a breath. He rocked.

"What are you doing to me, baby?" She thrashed over the pillows. Streams of black hair tangled.

"I'm stripping you of your control, making you insatiable. Obviously." He rocked against her with more force. Again. Pumping. "It's only fair, since you do it to me."

With his next forward glide, he nipped her bottom lip. She fisted the sheets, arched, and came with a hoarse cry.

The sounds she made... Sweat beaded his brow, and his muscle turned rigid. "Chantel," he rasped, needing... something from her. Desperate for it.

A femme fatale with blazing eyes, she rose to her elbows. Her breasts bounced between the split in her gown, her nipples begging to be sucked. "My turn to seduce you."

That. He needed that.

He traced the line of her jaw, adoring her. "I think you won me the moment you looked at me with those big eyes and a gag in your mouth." A gag like that gave a male ideas. Made him wonder what else he could fit in there.

The corners of her mouth twitched a split second before new vines shoved him to his back at the foot of the bed. She used the connection to pull herself to her knees, until she braced her palms at his temples. Ebony hair framed a hauntingly beautiful face flushed with brimming arousal.

Something inside him cracked—something deeper than before, as if he'd only shattered the surface last time.

Though he floundered, he palmed her breasts and swiped his thumbs over her distended nipples. He *needed* his hands on her. "What is my queen planning for me?"

"No sex. Not yet. But I still want to ride you." When she ran her tongue over her upper lip and eased back, reaching for the waist of his pants, his thoughts faded. Her breasts bobbed as she worked the tie, freeing his straining erection. The release of pressure was a mercy and a punishment, one indistinguishable from the other.

After wrapping searing fingers around his length and stroking, driving him to the brink, Chantel returned to her previous position.

"Do you want me to ride you, Kaysar?"

"More than anything." Truth.

"I'm glad. It's gonna be so good, baby," she rasped, before lowering. A slow sinking. Excruciating. "You're so big."

She pressed her bare sex against his shaft. Male to female. Flesh to flesh. A hoarse cry barked from him. "We're gonna do what I call a leisurely bump and grind," she said.

Another bark exploded from him when she rocked against him, rubbing, coating his length with her wetness. She glided up. Down. Up. Bliss as sharp as a blade and twice as dangerous sliced more of his control.

"The feel of you against me, sweetling…"

She rocked against him with increasing force, but it wasn't enough. He needed more. More! Kaysar cupped her nape with his clawed hand, holding her steady, and thrust up his hips. The firmer contact proved too much but still also not enough. The pressure, the pressure. So good. So necessary. Wonderful and terrible. Agony and rapture.

"Chantel…precious…" He didn't care if the fortress crumbled from the mountainside. He didn't care if the Frostlines or Micah invaded. This pleasure…*increasing, magnifying, overtaking*…the sensations…

He couldn't…

He wasn't…

She leaned down and licked into his mouth, feeding him raw passion, rocking against him harder and harder. Kaysar planted his heels and thrust up, meeting her, and they rubbed together. The bed shook. He lifted his hips again; she rocked hers. Lifted. Rocked. Again and again and again.

His heart thudded. His inhalations thinned and shallowed. Still too much, still not enough. Soon, something inside him might shatter for good. Might reach a part of him he wasn't ready to face. Yet he rubbed himself against his female, desperate to continue the ride.

Growling, he flipped her to her back and rose above her. Grinding. Pressure continued to build.

She thrashed and spread her legs wider. "Kaysar, I'm so close again."

"Let's get you closer, hmm?" He draped an arm around the top of her head as protection. Rocked against her. Faster and faster, until he hammered at her. With his free hand, he pinched her pretty nipples.

"Like that, like that, like that," she chanted. "Yes!"

Satisfaction swelled his chest as wonder glazed her exquisite features, her body coming for the third time. He'd done this. He had reduced this powerful queen to a creature of sensation, ruled by her body's demands.

"Want to *feel* you coming." He angled just enough to plunge two fingers inside her.

As her inner walls clenched around the digits, she clutched his wrist to ensure he remained there. Only when she sagged over the mattress did he pull them out, and wrap his soaked hand around his shaft.

The ecstasy and the pain. The duo ruled him. For the first time in his existence, he felt alive. But as he stroked himself while pinning his sweetling, his own climax remained at bay. Why, why? Stroking, stroking. Faster. Harder. Still no climax.

Frustration dulled the pleasure, the bliss slipping further away, and he roared.

Chantel lay beneath him — still coming. She lifted her head to lave his nipples. "It won't stop. It's so good. You're so good. Kaysar? Please, come for me. You said you'd give me everything."

As he pumped his length, the head of his shaft grazed her clit. Her back bowed, and she screamed.

Blessed euphoria ripped through him. The shattering he'd expected. A culmination thousands of years in the making.

Kaysar threw back his head and bellowed, climaxing over his female's dress.

CHAPTER TWENTY-THREE

COOKIE REMAINED BENEATH KAYSAR as he came down from his high. A sense of vulnerability proved as strong as a shackle. Usually she left immediately after a make-out session to discourage after-chatter. But at this precise moment, she longed to snuggle up and speak to Kaysar about anything, everything and nothing all at once. Her stern demeanor? In tatters.

Did he feel the same? Deep down, he must feel *something* for her. Something meaningful. Profound. The way he continued to react to her, the way he *looked* at her... It had nothing to do with vengeance. They shared a connection. The kind she'd never experienced with another—the kind she wasn't sure she could live without.

He wanted her to stay with him. And she would. But she would never be content with a second-place participation trophy. She would fight for him, as advertised.

You couldn't win the battles you forfeited.

Kaysar's eyes remained closed as she smoothed a lock of hair from his forehead. *Beautiful, broken king.* Her chest tightened. There was no denying she hungered for him as she'd never hungered for another. He excited her—fulfilled her—in ways she'd only thought possible in dreams.

She liked him and enjoyed the way his cunning mind worked. His dry sense of humor was warped enough to fit perfectly with her own.

Two Mad Hatters, spinning inside the same teacup.

He'd endured the worst kind of abuse as a child. As an adult, he'd known only hate. No one had fought for him, a tragedy all its own. He deserved a champion. Someone to slay *his* dragons—someone to save him from his big bad.

Hadn't she longed for adventure? But how much was too much? What if the two killers tanked? Honestly, they probably had a super high likelihood of failure. Could Astaria survive the end of their relationship?

The time to stop a breakup from happening was now. Only now. With a little work and a lot of selective amnesia, they could return to a businesslike arrangement safely. Probably. Fingers crossed, anyway.

But she wanted him. *Bad.*

She would give the battle everything she had and fight the only way she knew how—one day at a time.

And there was no better day to start. *Cookie Bardot, reporting for duty.*

She sized up her competition. Her opponent, Vengeance, had lived with Kaysar for thousands of years and provided his only source of joy.

What could she provide? What, exactly, did she offer? Something he could get nowhere else? Cataclysmic sex, if their bump and grind was any indication. Sass and trouble, definitely. Comfort? Maybe?

You had to work with what you had. So. Her strategy was clear. Her sexuality would just have to suck it up and take one for the team.

Kaysar opened his eyes and…smiled at her. His irises were animated. Had any man ever exuded such sublime fulfilment? "Oh, dear." He eased to the side and motioned to her clothing. "I seem to have ruined your dress."

Cookie's stomach fluttered. Sex made him playful. And

absolutely irresistible. Good to know. "Shall I remove it?" she said, playing right back.

"Most definitely. I'll have it cleaned." He raked his claws down the gown's center, splitting the sides from collar to ankle. Buttons flew in different directions, and the material fell from her curves. Material he removed from beneath her with only a flick of his wrist. Suddenly, she was naked, cool air enveloping sensitive skin. "And repaired."

He'd slashed precisely. His claws never scratched her skin.

"Thank you." Cookie rolled her shoulders, luxuriating in the lack of starch. The time for cold disdain had ended. "But you'll have the dress cleaned, repaired *and* replaced. I expect something even more matronly. I'm eager to discover which of my personas you're able to seduce." Only all of them?

He went still, his hand paused midair as he reached for her breast. "You're allowing me to stay in your castle? Am I *more* forgiven then?"

"Mostly." She sighed. "For now, you can stay. We can negotiate one day at a time, as needed."

"This pleases me." His smile returned—sparking one of her own.

Vengeance didn't stand a chance.

"Within the hour, your closet will brim with the finest garments in all the worlds." He brought her hand to his lips and licked between her knuckles. "Otherwise merchants, servants and guards will die painfully. You'll require something for every occasion, I'm sure."

He seemed to love that her clothes highlighted different aspects of her personality, while other men might have fled in terror. Which made her appreciate her new ability—

and Kaysar—so much more. They could have *fun* together. Something they'd both sorely lacked.

"You are too far away for my liking. Come closer to me." He lifted her, then draped her torso over his. The same position she'd cherished at the outpost, with her cheek resting on his tattooed pectoral, directly over his heart. He hadn't removed his pants. The fly gaped open, his shaft free and already semi-hard. The perfect complement to her own outfit—nature's lingerie.

The warmth. The comfort and safety. The connection.

Mmm, the scents... Every breath carried Kaysar's potent fragrance.

He combed his fingers through her hair. "Why did you never snuggle with someone before me?"

Going deep right out of the gate, sharing fears and insecurities. Okay, why not? They'd never done anything the un-weird way, so why start now? "Why get used to something you can't keep? People get to know the real me and leave. That's what they do. Pearl Jean and Sugars are my only stickers."

"I will not leave you," he boasted, and he sounded as if he meant it. "Fate did you a kindness with the others, sweetling. Anyone willing to leave you is a fool, and you are too precious to suffer fools. Also, if another male had snuggled you at any time, I would be killing him right now for daring to take what's mine."

She was only mildly embarrassed by her misty eyes. "That's kind of you to say."

"Yes, I am known far and wide for my kindness." He smiled when she peeked up at him from her perch on his chest, then grew serious. "Have you introduced *me* to the real Chantel Cookie Bardot, then?"

"I think so? I mean, I've never felt more like or unlike myself at the same time."

With the pad of his thumb, he traced the shell of her ear. "You are learning and accepting your own truths, perhaps."

Well, he wasn't wrong. "FYI—er, for your information, I like the real Kaysar." Cookie had a feeling she was the only person who'd received an introduction to him. A murderous teddy bear with a big heart and a bigger erection.

"I'm glad. I'm not sure how to be any other way."

Had he meant the words as a warning? "Then *I'm* glad."

Did he realize he flexed his fingers on her scalp?

"Who's Drendall?" she asked as the question popped up.

The combing paused for a moment. "My sister carried a doll. Very beautiful, this doll. Viori's most favorite toy. She took it everywhere she ventured." He paused as his gaze drifted to a faraway place. "Viori was such a happy girl. Smiles for everyone. Except those who insulted her magnificent Drendall. I don't remember where or how she acquired the doll, only that she clutched the little darling close at all hours of the day and night. You look like Drendall."

She did? "Is that why you responded to me at the beginning? Why you like me? Because I look like a doll?" She supposed there were weirder reasons. Right away, she'd noticed Kaysar's dreamy serial killer eyes.

"I *noticed* you because you look like a doll," he said. "I remain interested because you are…you."

Well. Okay, then. She ignored the lump in her throat. "What's your favorite memory of your sister?"

"The times I sang her a lullaby. She always fell asleep with a smile, her troubles gone."

Cookie kissed his heart, offering comfort and affection, and brushed her knuckles over his throat. "Your voice is the most amazing thing I've ever heard."

"My glamara revolves around it. I'm able to compel others to do my bidding or sing them to madness and health."

A super cool ability to wield, and a terrifying one to face. "I won't like it if you compel me to do something."

"Have no worries, sweetling. I'll never force you to do anything, you have my word. I covet your affection, freely given." He cupped her nape and kissed her brow, a gut-wrenchingly sweet gesture. "You respond to my song differently than everyone else."

She could tell he delighted in that fact, and yeah, okay, maybe she did, too. "I'll share a secret with you. Your singing makes me horny." In case he didn't understand human slang, she added, "Horny is when someone gets turned on." Wait. "Turned on is when someone wants to get laid." Moving on. "If I hadn't been busy murdering those soldiers, I would have thrown myself at you on that battlefield."

His fingers flexed on her. "Truth?"

"Truth."

He groaned and shot rock hard. "Allow me to reveal to her royal highness what I have planned for her this morning, before I become distracted," he said, playing with her hair again.

Oh! Her first official day as queen of her own castle. Bouncing against him, she squealed, "Yes, yes. You are allowed. Tell me."

His chuckle tickled her ears, unleashing a tide of shivers. "I've arranged for your subjects to pour into the palace. They will offer gifts to their beloved queen and beg for the opportunity to serve your every whim. Once you grow bored of the constant adoration, you'll begin your training with the doormaker's apprentice."

A thousand times yes. "What else, what else?" His delighted expression told her there was more.

"Our oracle, Eye, has been commanded to do nothing but await your summons. When you are ready, she will peer into the mortal world and show you Pearl Jean and Sugars."

What? "Are you for real?"

"I am very for real," he deadpanned.

"Oh, Kaysar." Cookie sniffled as she hugged him tight. "Thank you for arranging the most special day of my life for me."

He snaked his arms around her, lightning fast, holding on. "Will you do something for me in return?" he asked hesitantly.

"Yes. Anything."

"No caveat?"

"Within reason," she added, and he flashed a smile.

Appearing tormented a moment later, he said, "If you remember a portion of the princess's life, any portion in any capacity, or if you feel a single flicker of her emotions, you will let me know. Do not wait to tell me, even for a moment. Stop whatever you're doing and find me. Interrupt me, whatever *I'm* doing. Give me an opportunity to explain all the reasons Lulundria was wrong to feel what she did."

He *couldn't* need his vengeance the way he needed Cookie. He just couldn't.

Her chest squeezed. "Agreed. But Kaysar? I honestly don't think I'll remember anything else. If she's in here—" Cookie tapped her temple, then her heart "—she's not strong enough to show me anything else. I'm probably too powerful or whatever." To be honest, she kind of believed the two visions she'd seen had been Lulundria's last-ditch effort to warn her away from Kaysar.

The princess who died hating him had given Cookie a gift. For Cookie to shack up with her killer—yikes. A totally sucky move on Cookie's part. No doubt it had a top spot on the list of How Not to Be Appreciative of the Person Who Saved Your Life. But she wasn't backing down, reversing her decision, or giving Lulundria and Jareth Frostline a chance to change her mind.

"Are you sure?" he asked. "You learned to use her powers as naturally as breathing…as if she taught you herself."

"Maybe it's muscle memory? Or thanks to the elderseed?" Cookie hadn't wanted to discuss it before because she honestly had no idea.

A knock sounded at the door, and she jolted. Kaysar came to his feet, his single set of claws curled in—ready.

His aggression awakened hers. She crouched on the bed, covering herself in vines and preparing to strike.

"Whoever stands outside that door," he bellowed, fastening his leathers, "will be wearing their innards if I'm unsatisfied with the reason for this interruption."

"The ballroom is ready, your majesty," came the reply. A woman, oddly upbeat considering her life was at stake.

Kaysar's irritation vanished in a blink. He brightened. "Your subjects await you, sweetling."

"Wait," Cookie cried, hit by an unexpected and violent tsunami of misgiving. What should she wear? How should she style her hair? Did she plan to be a benevolent queen or a malevolent one? A girl should know these things before she assumed a role of leadership. First impressions mattered greatly.

And what if Micah attacked her mid-queening on day one? She hadn't yet honed her abilities—abilities he knew about. The element of surprise was gone. As a natural resident of this kingdom—and this world—Micah might know what weakened or stopped her. If he beat her in front of her own people…

No, no. Cookie needed training and a lot of it before she assumed control of her kingdom.

"I'm sorry, but I'm not ready, Kaysar. I won't go to the ballroom, and you can't make me. I'm staying right here, and yes, I will die on this hill. Don't try to change my mind." Her cowardice was humiliating. He was so strong, and she was being so weak. If he decided to ditch her because of this...

Good riddance.

"You will never die. You aren't allowed." He flittered to her side, sat on the mattress and cupped her cheek. He gentled his tone, saying, "Sweetling, the gathering was merely a suggestion. If ever I plan something that's disagreeable to you, you have only to tell me, and I'll gladly cancel it in favor of another. I can give you anything you want, but only if I know what it is."

Okay. All right. Kaysar was kind of being amazing right now. Her heart rate and breathing slowed. "Thank you. I think I'd prefer to train with the apprentice this morning."

"Of course." He kissed her brow. Rising to his feet, he called, "Eye! Send the people away immediately. Be sure they understand they have offended their queen with their impertinence, and they shall be punished if ever it occurs again."

Cookie pinched the bridge of her nose. *Malevolent it is.*

"I've left a gift for you in the closet." Kaysar smoothed his hair. Such a normal task for such an extraordinary man. He swiped his shirt from the floor, then tossed the material into the hearth. "I haven't forgotten the kingdom mandate for shirts. I hope you'll recall it, as well." He winked at her. "Dress and meet me in the throne room. Your training will begin as soon as you're ready."

Perfect. "Where's the—"

He vanished with a grin.

"—throne room?" she finished her question for an audience of zero.

Whatever. Gift! Cookie sprinted to the closet and flung open the door, soaring inside.

Everything looked the same, nothing added. Except... Head canted, she crossed to the built-in dresser. Something metal gleamed on the surface. A weapon?

Frowning, she lifted a thin line of links—metal claws tipped the ends.

Kaysar had given her the right set and kept the left for himself. One of the claws punctured a note. She freed the paper and read the flowing script.

Our team uniform.

Pressing the claws to her chest, she grinned and looked over her current dress choices. Whom did she want to be today? The evil queen or the innocent shepherdess?

CHAPTER TWENTY-FOUR

KAYSAR OCCUPIED CHANTEL'S throne room and perched on her throne, an elaborate monstrosity made from solid gold, with flowers carved throughout. He'd recruited a goldsmith to add them while she'd slept off the effects of the elderseed. Would his Briar Rose approve?

He eagerly anticipated her reaction. If she admired the throne even half as much as her jewels, she might dazzle him with another laugh.

Perhaps she would wish to return to their bed. His body *needed* more of her. And only her. No other living creature affected him so strongly. The cadence of her voice did things to him. Heated things. She teased and tormented him, leaving him desperate for more of her—for more of life. Who else filled his days with such stunning anticipation?

Her smiles lit a room. With Chantel, time had meaning again. A minute away from her was an eternity, but a thousand years at her side wasn't nearly enough. She possessed a staunch sense of loyalty and valued her partners and teammates. And she was brave, facing danger head-on. Both confident and unsure. Vulnerable with him alone. She told the truth, even when threatened.

If ever Kaysar hurt her, she had the power to skewer him with a vine. Did she even know how sexy that was?

Where is she? He'd left her in the bedroom an hour ago.

A true eternity. Now he awaited her arrival, his every cell humming with an unfamiliar mix of impatience and excitement. He suspected he…missed her.

A reminder surfaced. *Vengeance first, Chantel second.* That was the way it had to be. He could give and receive pleasure, but he couldn't allow her to become his reason for breathing. To trade one for the other…

No. He wouldn't. Viori was vengeance, and vengeance was Viori, and he couldn't let her go. But. Kaysar was unwilling to backtrack with Chantel, either. Even if it was the wiser path.

Fear of the unknown plagued him… End their association because of it, never exploring more of her depths? No. He'd already carved out a place for her in his life—where she would stay, despite his unparalleled reactions to her.

He should be careful, that was all. Grant her a certain amount of his time, energy and thoughts each day, but no more, and never before he contemplated another way to harm the Frostlines. See? Absolutely sustainable.

Kaysar stared at the throne room doors, willing them to open. Which gown had Chantel selected for the day? The dark queen or the gentle shepherdess? Would she wear his claws?

He'd never given gifts to a lover before. Or a friend. He'd never given anything to anyone except his family. And he'd never had a friend. But to those he'd once loved and respected, he'd presented songs.

His chest clenched as memories surfaced. He remembered how his mother used to close her eyes and hum along, just as Cookie had done. His father, a gruff farmer, had often attempted to secretly wipe a tear away mid-chorus. Anytime Kaysar had sung Viori a lullaby, she'd told him she loved him.

If he and Chantel ever decided to have a child—

He stiffened, gripping the arms of the throne overly tight. No children to further the Frostline legacy. Ever. No further thought needed on the subject.

Kaysar tapped his foot, faster and faster. To distract himself, he cast his gaze about the room. As she recovered, he'd ordered this space filled with things he hoped she'd like. What would Chantel think of the end result? Velvet chairs provided spots of color. Side tables displayed crystal vases overflowing with fresh flowers. He'd relocated tapestries and paintings from the royal treasury; they now covered the walls.

On the battlefield, he'd learned how much environment mattered. Opulence invited wonder and awe.

Why had she not arrived? He shook the ice in his third glass of sweetened lemon juice. A treat he'd only recently discovered. Oh, he'd consumed it before, but it had been as bland as everything else. The past few days, his taste buds had come alive.

Would Chantel be amenable to letting him pour the juice over her body and licking up the droplets?

He readjusted his hard-on.

"Did you bed my wife?" Jareth grated from a few feet away.

The second he'd assured Chantel's safety, Kaysar had shackled the prince to the edge of the royal dais, using an unbreakable chain mystically enforced, preventing flittering. He planned to torture the prince at his earliest convenience; he simply hadn't gotten around to it yet, his mind too chaotic.

"What I do with *my mistress* is none of your concern." The deceptively easy tone said what he did not: *You skate perilously close to the edge, Frostline.* Boast about the private things he did to Chantel? The world-changing things she did to him? He'd rather cut out his own tongue. Her passion belonged to him and him alone, and he would not share it, even in conversation.

A tug-of-war raged within him. He didn't like that Chantel was bound to Jareth, even by association. The only way to sever their tie, however, was to kill Jareth. But. Kaysar wasn't ready to cease tormenting the prince. On the other hand, he wanted Chantel free *now*.

The prince stood tall, seemingly unconcerned by the diamond collar that anchored him to the thick link of chain. He bared his teeth and fisted his hands. "In your own way, you care about her. I see that now. So why aren't you more alarmed about the horrors you're visiting upon the girl? The bleak future you've arranged? With you, she becomes more and more evil. You know that, yes? You are *ruining* her."

Kaysar sipped his juice as if it were a fine wine. "You wish to give her what you want. I give her what *she* wants. Learn the difference, and maybe you'll manage to keep your second wife."

After much internal debate, he'd decided to allow Jareth to train Chantel in the art of doormaking, teaching her everything he'd learned at Lulundria's side.

Kaysar worried the prince meant to trick Chantel into recalling him. He almost hoped the Frostline tried. Part of him *needed* her to remember as soon as possible. Then he would know the obstacles he must hurdle. The foreboding would go away and the wondering would stop. He could act, fixing things.

If she fell back in love with Lulundria's husband...

He recoiled at the thought. No. She wouldn't. She was strong. Very strong. Her emotions would remain her own. Forever.

Jareth sprinted for Kaysar, but the chain pulled taut, stopping him before he ever reached the throne. Having regrown his hand, he pointed an accusing finger at Kaysar. "You sit there with no regard for life other than your own, seeking to punish anyone you feel has wronged you. But what of your own crimes? Do *you* not deserve punishment?"

"Of course I do," he said, his honesty surprising the prince. He knew he'd done terrible things; one day, someone *would* make him pay. Chantel had already begun... He cast a glance to the door. "But I received most of my punishment in advance, did I not?"

The prince flinched, then retreated to sit dejectedly upon the dais steps. "By your logic, I received my punishment in advance, as well. I suffered the same abuse."

"Or you are lying, as all Frostlines do." As his snapped rejoinder echoed throughout the room, he realized he'd stood. Deep breath in. Out. He eased into the seat. "You forget yourself, prince. You are here to teach my woman how to excel at doormaking. Something you can do by example. Your tongue is unnecessary. In fact, I've already selected a jar for it."

The double doors swung open at last. He zoomed his gaze there, his heart thudding too fast. The moment Chantel came into view, his mind utterly blanked. He dropped his beverage, uncaring when the glass shattered.

Look at her. Pride squared his shoulders. She occupied the space between the double doors, her hands on her hips. A black bodysuit clung to her curves, a deep V displaying a wealth of mouthwatering cleavage. Silk flowers lined each side of the V. A ruffled train cinched to her waist, the hem pooling at her feet. Leather boots climbed up her calves.

She'd styled her hair in a series of elaborate curls and

knots. Rubies adorned her ears, throat, wrists and fingers, the bloodred stones a magnificent complement to her exquisite pale skin. Claws gleamed from her right hand, and he exhaled.

Worth every second of the agonizing wait.

This woman had wrung his most powerful climax from him, and she'd done it with a whispered plea. Now, she'd chosen to be his perfect queen, and Kaysar would *never* recover.

Spotting him, she grinned slowly, so stunning he knew no other sight could ever compare. "Hello, boys. Mind if I join the party?"

"You may do whatever you wish, sweetling." He stood, the urge to smile already sparking. She did that. She made him feel lighter.

But what did he do for her? Jareth's taunt resurfaced. *You are ruining her.*

Kaysar rubbed the sudden burn in the center of his chest. His efforts only made the heat worse. He didn't breathe easier until Chantel raked her gaze over him, following the dizzying, overlapping lines of his map tattoos. When she flicked her tongue against an incisor, as if she imagined tasting every spot she studied, blood filled his groin anew.

"I would have gotten here sooner, but someone forgot to leave me a map." Chantel blew him a kiss, making it clear he was already forgiven.

The urge to stalk over and claim a real kiss bombarded him.

"Hello…Cookie. I'm told that's your name of choice." Jareth regained his composure and stood, as well, his chain rattling. "I'm eager to begin your training."

Her eyes went wide. "*You* are my instructor?"

"He is." Kaysar flittered to her side. "And he'll be on

his best behavior, keeping his insulting opinions to himself." As her incredible scent engulfed him, he lifted her hand and kissed her knuckles. "You remember our bargain, yes?" If she recalled a single memory, she must tell him.

"I do." Without looking away from him, she told the prince, "You'll want to glance away and cover your ears for this part, Jareth." Stepping closer to Kaysar, her body flush with his, she rested her metal claws over his still-thudding heart. Whispering, she asked, "Do you remember the way I made you come all over my dress?"

"I do," he croaked, winding his arms around her. The interlude was branded into his brain. "Will I be receiving a repeat with *this* dress?"

"Only if I'm wildly turned on after my lesson." Her grin returned with a wicked slant. Something he wished to see every day for the rest of eternity.

"You will *ache* for me." He would make sure of it.

"Guess what?" Rising to her tiptoes, she placed her lips at his ear. "I'm *already* wildly turned on. I can't stop replaying what we did to each other..."

Perhaps her first doormaking session could wait? "You liked when I tongued you, did you?" The roughness of his voice surprised him. "You want me to tongue you again?" He would force everyone from the room and feast.

"I really, really do. But I'd rather tongue *you*," she admitted. "I thought I'd feel a little murderous in this dress, perfect for my lessons. Imagine my astonishment when I discovered I'm not an evil queen at all." A flush tinged her cheeks as she nipped his bottom lip. "You're looking at an evil seductress, baby, and she is *desperate* to suck you off." Another nip. "Do you want me to?"

"Yes!" He didn't mean to shout, but he would *die* if she didn't wrap those ruby lips around his length.

"Then I will…later. Probably."

He swallowed a groan. "Do not play with your male, Chantel."

"Baby, all I'm gonna do is play." A temptress like no other, she slowly eased from his clasp. Her eyes gleamed. "I told you. *Evil.*"

He shot out his arms to yank her back into his embrace. Pressed together again, he warned, "There will be consequences for teasing me."

"I'm counting on it." Her smile never faltered. "If you're a good baby boy, I'll let you come on my tongue while I drink you down."

The things this woman made him crave. "Today's lesson is officially canceled," Kaysar bellowed to one and all as he tightened his hold on his prize.

"Jareth," Chantel called, dancing out of Kaysar's hold. "You can look now. The lesson officially begins."

"I'm here, I'm here." Eye raced into the room, carting a tray of varying tartlets. "I bring the snacks you're soon to demand, your majesty."

Kaysar strove for calm as the whole world conspired against him. "Chantel, this is Eye the something or other. Our oracle. Eye, this is Chantel the Briar Rose. My…mine."

"Is she the one who will show me Pearl Jean and Sugars?" Chantel asked. "And did you call me Briar Rose?"

"My teammates get nicknames," he told her with a shrug.

"I can't do it, I'm sorry," Eye blurted out. "Kaysar didn't wait around to hear my response to his demand. I'm unable to see into the mortal world."

Kaysar rubbed the center of his chest again. First, "Chantel opted not to greet her citizens, now the oracle contradicted his claim.

Chantel returned to rest her head against his shoulder

and pet him where he'd rubbed, the simple actions calming him. She kept her gaze on the oracle. "Is Eye short for... something else maybe?"

"My given name is Ambrosine," the girl replied. "Ambrosine Adriene."

"Hmm. Do you have a nickname?" Chantel asked.

"Amber." Eye shrugged. "That's what you prefer to call me, anyway."

"How do you— Oh." Chantel gave a husky chuckle, and he kissed her brow, treasuring the sound. "Never mind. The seer sees. I shouldn't be shocked."

How much of her future had the oracle witnessed? Kaysar had refrained from inquiring or seeking images, because he was too...he wasn't sure. Not afraid. He didn't do fear. Discounting the times he had, in fact, feared. But he might be a jot...uncertain when it came to knowing how to be in a relationship. Did he really want the future interfering with the present?

"I'm Cookie." She cast Kaysar a pensive glance. "As I navigated this maze of a castle, I experimented with possible titles for myself. Chantel the Briar Rose is great, but I don't want everyone in Astaria calling me Chantel. Only you. So what do you think of Cookie the Uncrumbled?"

"A designation is given, not chosen," Jareth said, deciding to insert himself into the conversation. The barest hint of bitterness had infiltrated his expression. "Lulundria was known as the Kindhearted. A label to strive—"

Kaysar flittered and gripped the prince by the throat. "Perhaps you'd like to take a moment to rethink your comment to my honored companion, Jareth." Before, he'd noticed how much the barb about "normal" had bothered her. What was normal, anyway? "I shouldn't have to remind you that Cookie the Uncrumbled is perfect, just as she is."

Fury mottled the male's skin as he fought to breathe.

"No need to injure my tutor." Chantel glided over and folded her fingers around Kaysar's wrist to draw back his hand. "I get it. He misses his wife, and he seeks her substitute. We can't blame him for that."

He opened his grip at once, freeing the prince, who sucked in a mouthful of air. Chantel—his Chantel—had spoken kindly about a Frostline who had insulted her.

Eye and her tray of tartlets inched backward.

Was Chantel experiencing the princess's emotions, without realizing it? A development he hadn't anticipated.

He clasped his belo—beliked mistress's hand, linking their clawed fingers. Holding on, lest she escape him. Then he flittered her to the throne, wanting no one else to hear his next words. "You will begin your lessons," he told her, "but you will not treat the prince with kindness again." He forced the words from clenched teeth before he changed his mind about the training sessions altogether and another gift disintegrated before his eyes. The sooner she started, the sooner she finished. The sooner he could remind her of the things *he* made her feel. "All right?"

"Not all right. I'll treat him however I think is right," she said, blowing him another kiss and walking away. Over her shoulder, she told him, "This evil seductress isn't mastered. She masters."

He wanted to kiss her.

He met Jareth's gaze. The prince smirked.

"Let's get this over with," Kaysar grated.

CHAPTER TWENTY-FIVE

UNDER KAYSAR'S WATCHFUL EYE, Cookie trained with Jareth for hours. Her seething king observed from an ornate throne of gold—her throne, to be clear—as quiet as…things that were quiet. He never pulled his gaze from her. Did he even spare a moment to blink? More and more tension emanated from him.

His fear of Lulundria's memories marked the first obstacle in Cookie's campaign to win him from his vengeance. Operation First Place was off to a rocky start.

Fear of losing something only drove you away from it. She knew this firsthand. She'd lived this. His worry, if left untreated, would become a wedge between them. She would lose the battle before the war even started. She needed to act ASAP. Which meant she needed to actually remember Lulundria's life and prove Kaysar's concerns were moot. But how?

She hadn't lied to him. After those two flashes of Lulundria's last minutes in Astaria, when Jareth had tossed his ice daggers, and Kaysar had thrown the princess in the line of fire, Cookie had received zip, zero, nada from the other woman. Well, besides those heart leaps. And knowledge that she hadn't learned.

"Focus," Jareth snapped. He reached for her, only to stop himself before contact. Afraid Kaysar might remove his hand again? Smart. "I told you how to create and release vines without allowing the stalks to wither. You continue to disappoint."

She glared at her merciless instructor. "The problem isn't the student." Jerk. So far, the only bit of information she'd gleaned was dancing her fingers for faster vine growth. "You expect me to do everything Lulundria did, when I didn't grow up knowing what she knew."

"Apples!" Eye—er, Amber sat on the royal dais, near the throne. Whenever Kaysar neared his snapping point for whatever reason, she shouted her version of a warning. "Would you prefer an apple tart, majesty?"

Jareth shoved a big hand through his thick, pale hair. "Vines will preserve their vitality, even at a great distance from you, as long as you maintain a mystical hold on them. Think of every stalk you create as a member of your family. You don't have to be together to feel close."

Uh, she'd never felt close with her family. Pearl Jean and Sugars, though. Yeah. Kaysar?

She gulped. Did she already think of him as family?

"Let's try something else. With practice, you can throw thorns the way I throw ice. Observe me." He turned his big Viking body toward a far wall and waved a hand, ice daggers spewing from his fingertips. "Power flows from here—" he banged his chest "—to my fingertips. The conduit."

"Yes, but how do you force the power from A to B?"

"Force?" He bowed his head and muttered, "Do you *ever* listen?"

"Cinnamon!" Amber called. "I selected a delicious cinnamon cake for you, majesty."

"Never force," Jareth continued, glaring at Cookie. "Flow. *Flow*. F.L.O.W. Fuh-low."

Condescending jerk. Her temper threatened to redline.

"How do you *fuh-low* the power from A to B?" Even high on elderseed, she hadn't tossed thorns.

"You stop resisting. As I've told you *many* times."

"Chocolate strawberries!" The oracle increased her volume with every dessert. "The fruit is particularly sweet this season. Shall I prepare a batch?"

Cookie began to understand a harsh truth. Lulundria hadn't gifted her with a heart; she'd saddled her with a belligerent ex. The guy had no patience. His irritability had no borders. Granted, she'd rejected his claim on her hardcore. So, he had reasons to dislike her. But how about a truce? Or a little credit? Not once had she purposely stabbed him with a vine.

"Let's approach this from a different angle." Jareth mulled before nodding. "A spiritual heart is a battery for your abilities the way a natural heart is a battery for your body. It's the core of you. Your most primal state. Discover what drives you, and you'll access your power."

She paced as she thought back to the day she'd first created vines. A sunny morning in her backyard, feeling as if someone spied on her. She'd panicked and run. No, that wasn't entirely true. Before that, she'd urged Pearl Jean and Sugars to go inside. For their safety.

Was the answer so simple? Did her primal state revolve around the protection of her loved ones?

Except, during her first hours in Astaria, she'd created vines for herself, not her loved ones.

So, her primal driving force was self-protection?

Cookie blinked into focus, ready to find out. But as she continued to march back and forth, she realized both the king and the prince tracked her every move. Hello, distraction. Only one man's hot gaze branded her skin, reminding her body of the pleasure and connection awaiting her...

"Kaysar," she said with a pang of longing. He'd promised they could do whatever she desired today. Right now, she desired closeness with him, so, lesson over. She and Jareth could reconvene tomorrow and pick up where they'd left off. Getting Kaysar into bed had just become priority one.

Finally, he spoke. Leaning forward in the cathedra, intent on her, he inquired, "Yes, sweetling?" Hunger sharpened his timbre. "Is there something you need from me?"

She opened her mouth to invite him to Orgasm Hour when Amber butted in.

"Majesty," the oracle burst out. "It's King Hador."

He flittered to the girl, materializing in a crouch, his hands already on her shoulders, shaking her. "Tell me."

Cookie rushed over, worried. And annoyed. He was supposed to shake *her* shoulders. "What is it? What's going on?"

Amber looked past the king, past the room, a crinkle of concentration between her eyes. After a moment, she paled and blinked into focus. "Hador has invaded the Dusklands."

"He *dares*," Kaysar hissed as he straightened. The abrupt, jolting motion bumped his body into Cookie's, and she stumbled a step, mouth agape. "He must pay, and I must go."

He didn't spare her another glance before he vanished.

Her cheeks heated as Amber winced at her, all *he'll remember you eventually, probably*. "I'm sorry," the oracle said, "but he won't be returning for a few days."

"Trust my father to make everything worse," Jareth said.

So Kaysar had beat feet for battle, serving his vengeance—the one he considered his true wife. Leaving his mistress behind without bothering to give her a real goodbye. Expecting her to understand. Her, the one he'd studied with such fierce lust only seconds before. Forgotten. A promise broken.

Old wounds cracked open, the scabs oozing hurt. *He just* left *me here*. Was this what life would be like with him from now on?

The evil seductress had failed her first day on the job, just like student Cookie.

AS THE DAYS PASSED, one bleeding into another, Cookie developed a routine. Wake, dress in the gown of her choosing, train with Jareth, and tour the castle, learning its layout and defenses. She ate and slept alone. Kaysar had yet to return. Not even a quick flitter home to check on her wellbeing and make sure Micah hadn't attacked. He hadn't, but come on!

Every morning she woke and wondered, *Is today the day I get to see Kaysar?* Hope always ballooned, despite the inevitable pop when night arrived without word. Her nerves couldn't take much more. Her childhood nightmare had overtaken her adult life, and it sucked.

Today's trials, tomorrow's strengths. Right?

She laughed without humor. How about this: *Always have an escape plan*.

With Jareth's help and a few handy dreams, she'd learned to create different kinds of vines, both poisonous and medicinal. She could even produce certain fruit and nut trees. If ever she had to go on the run, she could feed and shelter herself. She wouldn't need anyone's artificial aid.

She fisted her hands. Due to his absence, Kaysar didn't know her doormaking ability had begun to recharge. She *felt* it, deep inside. In a matter of weeks, she suspected she'd have enough juice to collect Pearl Jean and Sugars.

Homesickness nearly doubled her over as she imagined

rubbing her face in the little house panther's fur and cracking Pearl Jean's ribs when she hugged her too hard.

Cookie wiped her eyes and turned her thoughts to the array of garments in her closest. A much safer topic, and a promise Kaysar had actually kept. Her racks overflowed with different personalities. She thought she understood the purpose of every garment—seduce, command, rebuke, punish, tease, submit—but one. A clinging ivory frock with both soft and sharp edges. A severe but hauntingly lovely… wedding gown? Maybe, possibly?

Except, he already had a wife, didn't he?

Argh! What did vengeance give him that Cookie didn't? She just…she missed him so much. And she shouldn't. Not if he made her feel this crappy. *Unwanted. Alone.*

Tears gathered again, and she sniffled. How many times had she watched the door at home, waiting for a parent to come get her? Or stared at a phone, willing it to ring so someone would tell her happy birthday? Oh, and how could she forget the evening she'd overheard her parents arguing about who had to keep her over a weekend. Had to. As if she were nothing but a burden to bear.

Did Kaysar think of her? Was she an afterthought? What was he even doing? They were partners. They were supposed to torment Hador Frostline *together.*

Jareth Frostline, as it turned out, wasn't such a bad guy. Even when his impatience got the better of him, which was almost always, he never insulted or hurt her. Not with real barbs. He'd stopped judging her for being different from Lulundria.

Every day, his circumstances bothered her a little more. Chained for a crime he hadn't committed, and ignored by the man responsible for his captivity.

When an opportunity presented itself, she planned to

broach the subject of Jareth's release. Gently. As an added bonus, Kaysar's reaction to the topic could reveal her current placement in his hierarchy of needs.

Whispers erupted behind her, and her step faltered. Servants. Gossiping again. They'd taken an instant dislike to her. Maybe because she'd slaughtered their guards? Possibly?

Too frazzled to deal with the malice today, she turned around and snapped, "Go ahead and keep talking behind my back. You never know when I'll decide to stab you in yours."

They paled and scurried off, leaving her alone, guilty and shamed on top of everything else. They'd done nothing worth such ire from the strange woman demanding they serve her. She needed to do better.

Cookie sighed. She would grow everyone their own personal apology plant. The Dusklands had been barren so long. A little color could really make the terrain pop.

Feet heavy, she continued on her journey. Another tour, checking the final group of bedrooms and...uh, where was she? Mind swirling, she spun in a circle in an effort to catch up with her thoughts. Seconds ago, she'd stood in a sunlit hallway with gilt-framed portraits, elaborate side tables and velvet settees. Then she'd turned a corner and boom. A dank, dark catacomb with a handful of torches anchored to stone walls surrounded her.

A surprisingly sweet scent wafted. Heart thumping, Cookie readied vines and strode forward. With every step, a staff clinked against the floor. The perfect accessory for the Little Bo-Peep's dress she'd chosen today. Why, why, why had the garment called to her? How could she find her missing sheep while *she* remained lost?

Cookie rounded a corner and— Whoa! A beautiful arch

made of metal shards stood anchored to the floor, the belly thick, blue and rippling. A doorway? Amber stood before it, dressed in a flowing white gown and peering inside, quiet and contemplative.

Sensing the invasion, Amber spun and pressed a hand over her stomach. She relaxed when she spotted Cookie. "How did you find me?"

"I don't know." The dress? Maybe *this* was why she'd chosen to be the shepherdess. She'd noticed Amber tended to vanish at certain points throughout each day. "What is this place?"

"A type of treasure room, I think. The doorway—" the oracle motioned to the metal "—never closes. I discovered it the day after Hador's arrival in the Dusklands."

Cookie wouldn't ask for an update about her boyfriend. She wouldn't stoop so low. Nope. She would keep those humiliating questions to herself.

"What's on the other side?" She had a right to know where her kingdom's perma-doorway led. *Part of the castle, all mine.*

"My guess is the mortal world."

Homesickness took another jab at her, silencing her response.

She and Amber stood in the quiet, both peering into the azure glow. For a long while, Cookie contemplated doing something wild and spontaneous and…going through. There was no better time for a discovery mission. But what if the doorway was a trap set for unsuspecting usurpers? Go through, and you ended up in a dungeon or something.

"Tell me about your visions," Cookie asked, and licked her lips. "Are they ever wrong?"

"No." Amber toed a pebble with her slipper. "I see events as if they are my own memories. Sometimes of things that have already happened. Other times I observe what's happening in the moment and even situations that have yet to occur. Forcing myself to look into specific times, places and individuals is straining but doable."

"Have you seen into my future?"

Amber's shoulders sagged the tiniest bit. "I have. And I don't need to be an oracle to know you crave answers about it."

Her emotions had run the gamut today. Apprehension decided there'd never been a better time to shine. *I'm doomed?*

Maybe, maybe not, but Cookie most certainly didn't wish to know about it.

And yet? "Yes," she croaked. "Will I crash and burn with Kaysar?"

Today's trials, tomorrow's strengths.

"Let me show you what he's doing right now. Then, you tell me the answer to your question," Amber said.

An image appeared in Cookie's mind, there and gone, but she had no trouble memorizing every detail. Kaysar, prowling over scorched earth, smoke billowing all around him. Shadows cloaked his powerful form as he approached a patrolling soldier.

With a slash of his claws, the soldier died.

"I'm confused," Cookie said. "Is that supposed to be a deal breaker for me?" She only wanted him more. That soldier had guarded Kaysar's abuser. Meaning, not innocent.

The ground shook with enough force to impel Amber in her direction. They crashed together, and Cookie bounced back, her shepherd's staff clattering to the floor. The oracle toppled.

"What's happening?" she cried when the shaking intensified.

A large stone fell from the ceiling, hurling straight toward the seer. Cookie unleashed a wall of vines, protecting the other woman long enough for her to roll out of the way.

As her leaves withered, dust plumed the air, tickling her nose and throat. She coughed and coughed.

Amber coughed, too, and remained on the floor. "My inner vision is hazy but…I think an army of goblins has entered the palace. They're out for our blood."

Ghost goblins, like the ones in the game? Foreboding creeped down her spine as she tugged the oracle to her feet. "Come on. Let's go kick butt." Hopefully.

"What? No! We stay here, where we have an escape hatch if we're found."

Cookie struggled to make sense of her refusal. Escape? "I don't think you understand. If we remain here, we can't fight the creatures and defend my castle." She pivoted, ready to run. "Let's go."

Amber latched on to her wrist, stopping her. "*You* don't understand. You've never fought goblins, and I don't yet see a path to victory."

Her stomach turned. "Do you see a loss?"

"Maybe?" the oracle hedged.

Maybe wasn't a guarantee. Good enough. "Sometimes you can't see the end until you get to the middle." A trick she'd learned sacking digital fortresses. "Imma go get in that middle." No one took her stuff, especially not goblins.

"Wait," Amber called as Cookie wrenched free and jogged off. "I see now," the oracle continued, and she slowed. "Others lead the goblins…"

Another image flashed into her mind, there and gone. A picture of Micah, his skin smeared in red paint. No, covered in blood. Beside him was a smaller man, who was in no way, well, small. He was older, though, with silver-blond hair and a barrel chest. He looked like an older version of Jareth.

A Frostline, then. *The* Frostline, most likely. The one Kaysar hunted.

The Winter Court king Chantel longed to kill.

Had the two men escaped Kaysar's wrath? Or something worse?

Fire blazed beneath her skin, and she raced for the exit.

CHAPTER TWENTY-SIX

KAYSAR SULKED THROUGH Hador and Micah's campground, enveloped by shadows, unseen as guards made their rounds and went about their evening. Irritation rode him hard. When had his vengeance become such a chore?

Again and again, his mind returned to Chantel—to his desperate longing. He continued to replay their last moments together and cringe.

Long ago, his father had kissed his mother goodbye anytime he'd journeyed to the Summer Court market for supplies. Though the trips had usually only lasted two weeks, they had embraced at length, clinging to each other as if they were to be forever parted. Always afterward, his mother had touched her lips repeatedly, seeking the comfort of a remembered kiss.

Kaysar had missed an incredible opportunity. He could have left his woman with his kiss.

Did she miss him, even a little?

He shoved his hand into his pocket and sifted her lock of hair between his fingers. He'd spent days away from her, his instinct to return slowly eroding his calm. *She slips away. Can't let her slip away.*

He sensed trouble, and quickened his pace. *Focus.* Five minutes ago, he'd watched Hador and Micah enter a war tent set in the center of their campground. Surrounded by

countless guards—Dusklanders in armor and Winter Court
mercenaries in fur—the enclosure had few vulnerabilities.

No flittering had occurred, the ability limited to the area
around the palace due to some kind of special rock Micah
had used. And yet, Kaysar no longer believed the pair occupied the tent. None of the twelve silhouettes fit the exact
measurements of his targets.

Yet how could the two kings have left the shelter? Unless Hador employed the same strategy Kaysar had once
used against him—an underground tunnel.

There hadn't been time to dig—except the two hundred
years of Kaysar's absence.

Kaysar cursed and launched into a sprint. Had Micah
constructed tunnels throughout the land?

Anyone who stepped into his path, he rammed, clawed
or stabbed, whatever proved necessary. He hurled his body
through the entrance of the tent, the flap ripping. Quick
scan. Twelve guards, no royals. He dispatched his foes
quickly and searched—oh, yes, a tunnel.

Tricked. Because he'd been distracted by thoughts of
Chantel.

Did the males approach her? The desire to gaze upon
her amplified as a gut-wrenching thought occurred. Kaysar had left her *undefended.*

Fear grabbed him by the throat and squeezed. If the
kings reached her before he did…if they harmed her… *Not
her. Anyone but her.*

Eye knew to provide him with a mental image if trouble
arose. But what if she couldn't?

Pounding footsteps registered, more guards rushing in
his direction. Kaysar had a choice. Take the tunnel wherever it led, hoping to catch the royals, or return to the castle, where the two were probably headed.

Castle, he decided, already speeding across the campgrounds, barreling past anyone in his path. When he cleared the tents , a cool wind resisted his momentum. He cut through the bluster with fierce determination matched by few.

Kaysar hated himself for leaving Chantel. His war could've waited another few weeks or months. Instead, he'd opted to prove to them both that he had the strength to stay away from his mate whenever his foes neared.

Fool. He flew along the plains. Leaped over naturally generated fires that sparked from the ground, throwing embers. Smoke stung his eyes and clogged his lungs. All had better be well at home. *Not one scratch on her.*

He'd never desired a female of his own. Now, he couldn't imagine his life without her in it.

A ragged bellow broke from him. *Just get to her. All will be well.*

The second Kaysar moved into range of the mountain, the ability to flitter powered up. Between one step and the next, he entered the castle. A unique but familiar charge electrified the air, and an emotion he hadn't experienced since childhood gripped him. Sheer, unadulterated terror.

Goblins. Hundreds of them. Where?

Where was Chantel?

His thoughts sharpened. Claws at the ready. Dagger in hand. Kaysar flittered through the rooms. No sign of Chantel. No hint of goblins. Not that he could see them unless they embodied. And they would embody. Their only means of feeding.

Goblins couldn't possess royals with Kaysar's power, his mystical superiority acting as a physical shield. Yet, despite his dominance, his glamara had little effect on the beings. Compelling one, much less an army of them, required time and toil.

A brush of putrid cold against his cheek—there. Kaysar spun and slashed, his claws raking through a goblin's throat as it materialized. The dagger finished the job; the body dropped with a thud. Thick black blood gurgled onto an elegant rug.

Goblins remained interconnected with a hive mind. If one caught sight of you, all caught sight of you. *Come and get me.*

As he waited, he surveyed his kill, his lip curling in disgust. A bag of rot and bones. It had pitted gray skin oozing with pus, razor-sharp teeth as big as sabers, and claws longer than his own. Unlike the others, this one had an oddly shaped patch of mold growing from the side of its skull. Four interconnected lines, creating a W. Or an M.

A waft of stink—Kaysar twisted, slashing again. Thud. More cold. Twist, slash. Again. Then again.

And so it begins. A cold stench enveloped him as the spirits crowded him. Usually he experienced glee as he warred. A temporary reprieve from internal struggles and obsessions. Today he sought the battle's end.

He flittered in and out, twisting and slashing as he reappeared. Frigid black blood splattered him as bodies toppled. Always he pushed forward, determined to find Chantel.

As he turned a corner, the number of goblins increased substantially, the hallway arctic. Every breath misted in front of his face. With a snarl, Kaysar attacked. Slashing—without—pause.

A vibrant green vine whooshed past him, snaring a goblin. Kaysar paused mid-battle, bathed in relief. Chantel lived! And she'd aided him, despite his abrupt abandonment.

Because she is my partner. My...friend.

Multiple vines snagged multiple goblins, popping off their heads as they embodied. As thick black blood spurted, Kaysar kicked into motion, slaughtering his way through the hallway. The emerald stalks propagated and attacked the goblins, but never turned on him.

Chantel appeared at long last, and he staggered under the weight of his relief. He kept his gaze on her but a moment, fighting, fighting, fighting, yet the sight seared itself into his memory. Hair no longer black, but pink and split into two curling ponytails. A pink-and-white dress covered in bows, lace and blood molded to her torso but flared widely at the waist. The skirt reached just below her backside. Torn white leggings led to stained combat boots.

Gut-punch. She opted not to wear the metal claws.

No longer a team?

She glared at him while wielding her vines, the embodiment of feminine pique. Silent, he worked his way to her side, killing any fiend who neared her.

When he moved to buffer Chantel from an incoming strike, she lunged to safeguard him, putting herself in the line of fire. A goblin raked its claws across her collar, and she cried out.

Fuel for *his* fury. Kaysar punched a hole in the offender's throat and ripped out its spinal cord.

"Amber told me she...saw no path to victory..." Chantel admitted between panting breaths. Her vines slowed as goblin venom weakened her. She would shake it off and heal. Any moment. "Think she might be...right."

Her injury wove back together at last, but her steps slowed. Without the elderseed, fatigue already set in.

Kaysar doubled already doubled efforts. "We won't

lose." *Will cross any line...* The glamara heated his throat. "You *will* survive."

A stronger stench came from his left—only a distraction. A goblin slammed into Chantel, knocking her to the floor with every intention of eating her there. Kaysar flittered and clasped the goblin by the nape—

His fingers slipped free, slickened by the pus. A vine grew over Chantel's face, the fiend biting into it. Relief. Another goblin glommed onto Kaysar, sinking its teeth into his shoulder and flinging him across the hall. Searing pain.

He shook off both the goblin and the sting, fighting to reach his queen as other opponents piled onto her. Two by two, he tore them off and tossed them aside, minus an appendage. She clashed with the others, but the creatures were far taller and a hundred pounds heavier, pinning her down and gnawing through her vines.

Goblins latched on to her arms and snapped her wrists to prevent her from pushing them away. Her hands dangled, useless, as she bowed her back, a scream of agony tearing from her. A scream that quickly deteriorated into a whimper.

Pure. Undiluted. Rage.

Kaysar fought as never before. Sharp pains erupted as more fiends swarmed him, scratching and biting. So many. More than he'd ever fought at once. He didn't care. He fought without ceasing.

Despite his skill and ferocity, he made no headway. *I am...defeated?*

A pathway opened up as every goblin reared back, flattening itself against a wall, granting Kaysar an unobstructed view of Chantel. Pinned to the floor, clutching her broken hands to her chest and struggling for freedom as a smiling goblin loomed above her, staring at Kaysar.

Denial, horror and terror converged.

With a husky accent, the goblin proclaimed, "King Micah and King Hador paid a hefty cost to ensure your deaths. But I would have done it for free."

The others chortled and huffed in encouragement, urging him—their leader?—to end the Briar Rose at last.

"Know this," Kaysar snarled. "Her harm assures yours."

"No, Kaysar. Her harm assures *yours*." The goblin reverted his gaze to Chantel, a long tongue unfolding from its mouth, licking over her cheek. "Fight if you want. I'll like it."

As she craned her head away, Kaysar saw red, the total annihilation of the Dusklands certain. He geared to flitter. Except, where were her tears? Why did she smile, exuding rage rather than fear?

"Scream if you want," she purred, a split second before a sharp green vine exploded from the top of the goblin's skull. "I'll like it."

My queen.

The remaining fiends lunged for her. Kaysar flittered over, stopping many but not all. "Chantel!"

A sword came out of nowhere, cutting through the lot of them, ending the immediate threat to his queen. Eye stood at the other end of the blade.

She's overdue a reward.

The rest of the goblins flickered in and out of view, as if unsure what to do upon their leader's loss. Kaysar exploded into action. Flitter. Gently tug Chantel to her feet. Her bones had begun to heal. Flitter. Kill. Kill. Kill. Every death flamed a spark of gratification. He protected his female, as instinct demanded.

Vines filled the hallway once more, a welcome sight as they cut through a cluster of fiends.

"My apologies for the delay," Eye said with another swing of her weapon. Two bodies slumped, both missing a head. "I had to cave in a maze of tunnels and traps where Hador and Micah had positioned an army of trolls. They were seconds away from breaching a trapdoor."

"Don't care about that. How do I keep Chantel safe?" His primary concern. Though the level of danger had decreased substantially since the death of the leader. "Why didn't you sense the attack?"

"You, a one-hundred-pound fluff of nothing, *caved in* a tunnel?" Chantel bellowed, squeezing a goblin with her vines until it popped. "How am I the only one confused by this statement?"

"Upon my orders, she keeps a ready supply of forbidden weapons, artifacts and tomes." He decapitated an opponent with a single strike. "To be employed when necessary."

Remaining mute, Chantel wielded her stalks, stopping two goblins from reaching him. She looked as if she had a thousand things to say, and none skewed in his favor.

Her muteness eked on, his clenching chest unbearable. He dispatched the next goblin to move into his path. "If you won't speak to me, sweetling, how can you tell me how wrong I've been?"

She lifted her nose in the air, flowing with her vines.

He swung his attention to Eye. "Well? I'll hear an explanation for our lack of warning."

"Since your departure, my head has been filled with thousands of inane images, and I couldn't sort through it all," the oracle responded. "But the battle is all but won, majesty, the number of goblins finally dwindling."

"What of Jareth? Has he escaped?" Before Chantel, Kaysar would have rushed to the prince's side first. He couldn't regret his defense of his queen, though.

"He's alive and uninjured." Grunting, Eye fended off a group of four. "His father made a deal with Micah, who made a deal with the goblins, who agreed to leave the prince and all servants unharmed during the raid."

"Amber, as *my* oracle I insist you charge a hefty fee before answering anyone's questions about anything," Chantel said, wielding her vines with lethal accuracy. "Only me, your sovereign queen, your favorite Little Bo Chantel, gets freebies. Starting today. This moment. By the way, I'm speaking to Amber and only to Amber. Anyone else in this hallway is receiving the silent treatment for crimes too numerous to list."

He stiffened as he made the next kill. Leaving without a proper goodbye might have been the most foolish thing he'd ever done. Females *needed* goodbyes.

Kaysar had to fix this. Whatever punishment Chantel chose for him, he would gladly accept.

"We *will* talk," he told her. He could withstand anything but her silence. "After."

The wait would be excruciating.

Eye swung and replied, "If I may offer a piece of advice, majesty—"

"You may not," he informed her sharply, adding another death to his tally.

Goblins toppled, one after the other, but not swiftly enough for Kaysar's liking.

No longer trapped in a battle frenzy, he could better control his emotions and tone. Why not sing? Letting his throat heat, he released the first note of his song. Chantel's eyelids dipped, going heavy.

Eye scrunched her features, shoved her hands to her ears and collapsed.

A thousand vines filled the hallway at once, impaling the remaining goblins. Fiends who writhed, gradually slowing. Stopping. Kaysar went quiet as the vines retracted and bodies fell.

Chantel rubbed her hands together, then helped Eye to her feet. "And you couldn't see my path to victory. Good thing I never doubted myself."

His shaft swelled with hot, blistering lust. Little Bo Chantel was battered, just as he was, but her eyes glowed bright silver. She'd loved the battle—but she no longer liked Kaysar.

"Chantel. Briar Rose. I… You…" He wiped a drop of blood from his eyes, but smeared another with his wet hand. What could he say to make this better?

"Well," she said, pivoting, then looking over one shoulder to catch his gaze. "Allow me to give you a courtesy you didn't grant me. Goodbye, Kaysar. I'm sure you can see yourself out of my castle." Walking on, she called, "Someone had better clean up this mess."

CHAPTER TWENTY-SEVEN

HIGH ON VICTORY and low on patience, Cookie shut herself in the master suite. Her bedroom. Hers. Kaysar had better not get any ideas about bunking up.

Shaky from battle and emotionally wrung out, she stumbled into the bathroom to strip and shower.

Her first IRL battle in her first IRL castle, and she'd won. Not easily, as evidenced by the blood that splattered her, but the best victories came with the greatest battles.

She was thrilled. Overjoyed.

Raw.

Seeing Kaysar for the first time in days had been a wonderful, terrible shock. He'd blasted emotion left and right, ruining her concentration. When he'd shouted at the goblin leader, he'd looked so...broken. During battle, there'd been no one more ferocious. Or protective. Time and time again, he'd willingly taken a wound to shield her. There at the end, he'd gazed at her with such incredible longing that her defenses had cracked. Then, afterward, seeing his sexy face covered in the blood of their kills... The Uncrumbled...had crumbled.

In that moment, she'd known two things. She was still in the running for top dog, and she would eventually forgive him for abandoning her.

If she gave up after every faulty start, she'd never make it to a finish line. With Cookie and Kaysar, the battle for gold had only just begun. So, despite their current discord, she would march onward with him. After she'd yelled at him. After she'd calmed.

Would he attempt to explain all the reasons she was wrong?

She finished washing and drying, then slathered herself with the most amazing lotion. After donning a buttery soft robe embellished with hand-sewn roses, Cookie padded into the bedroom, ready to find her boyfriend and chat.

She stopped short, her heart pounding. *Seek and you shall find.*

He stood in the middle of her bedroom, shirtless, a fierce scowl projecting all kinds of fury. He'd showered, the blood washed away. His chin was jutted, his shoulders rolled back, and his arms anchored behind him. A battle stance. A pair of leathers hung low on his waist, a belt partially undone. Bare feet.

Argument commencing in three...two...

"I'm sorry," he barked, as if he'd held on to the words too long. As if his lucidity clung by a thread. "I shouldn't have left without kissing you goodbye. Without saying the word at least."

Well, he'd definitely taken a different approach than her past boyfriends.

The outburst shocked her. But his misery shocked her more. "No, you shouldn't have," she said, deflating. So much for yelling at him. She sighed. His entire life revolved around war. Did she really want the same for their relationship? He deserved at least one safe space. Besides, Rome wasn't conquered in a day. "You hurt me," she admitted softly. She deserved a safe space, too.

He flinched, true anguish contorting his expression. "I

never wished to hurt you. Only to bring you smiles and laughter." His gaze beseeched her. "Tell me you forgive me."

She didn't tell him. "You endangered me, Kaysar."

He flinched harder. "That is my greatest sin, and I will never forgive *myself*." Thrusting both of his arms forward, he presented her with a magnificent tiara made of sharp crystals. "This is for you. Your first crown as Queen of the Dusklands. A mere token of my great affections."

A bribe? "This changes nothing," she griped, even as she tripped over to snatch her prize. She petted and admired the dazzling accessory before setting it on the nightstand. "Fine. It doesn't hurt your cause, either. Consider yourself seventy percent, bordering on seventy-five percent forgiven. And for your information, I expect you to forgive yourself when I do, okay? That is nonnegotiable. No caveats."

He relaxed some. "How can I get to one hundred?"

Letting all of her heartbreak glimmer in her eyes, she smiled sadly. "You do better next time. One minute, you claimed to want me, the next you cast me aside. You *abandoned* me, exactly as you abandoned these lands. You were my dream, until you became my nightmare."

He opened and closed his fists, determination hardening his muscles. "I will do better, I swear it. You are my most precious treasure, and I'll never abandon you again."

The headiness of his promise took her breath away. "Fine. You're at ninety-five percent." Most precious treasure? How could she deny this man anything? "Do you ever tire of the constant war? Or long to be free of your tie to the king?"

"Never." His vehemence…hurt.

With their relationship hanging in the balance, she might as well be brutally honest with him. "I won't ever be satisfied in second place. I'm not wired that way. When I play,

I go for gold, always. That's what I want with you. To give you my best. But I expect your best, too. I won't accept a repeat of my childhood. Waiting and waiting for my turn to matter."

"You matter," he burst out, taking a step toward her. "More than anyone else in the world, you matter to me."

Cookie pushed the hurt aside. "I'll give you a chance to prove your feelings for me...while I try to prove my feelings to you." She toyed with the sash of her robe, his hot gaze tracking every movement, driving her need for him higher. When her nipples drew tight, he sucked in air. Even that turned her on. "Would you like that?"

"Would *love* that."

His intensity lured her closer...

"Did you think of me while you hunted your foes?" Already humming with desire, she molded her body to his.

"I thought of you *constantly*." He gripped her waist, shackling her in place, then parted her legs with an insistent knee, ensuring her aching, empty core balanced on his thigh. He smoldered at her. "The moon rose and set, and I thought of your eyes. Every pink flower reminded me of your hair. The scent of poisonvine drove me mad."

Her pulse raced, the confession heady. She traced her nails over his stubbled jawline. When she reached a spot near his ear, she grew thorns and pierced his skin ever so slightly. Her eyes narrowed to slits. "You will not leave me so abruptly again."

His pupils exploded over his irises, lust sizzling in their depths. "I will not."

The fervent vow pleased her, the next stroke tapering into the gentlest caress. "I think you just topped ninety-eight percent."

His nostrils flared. Cupping her nape with a trembling

hand, he bent his head and pressed his forehead to hers. "I pleasured myself to thoughts of you. Did you pleasure yourself?"

"I did," she replied with a smile. "I thought of you *almost* every time."

"Minx," he said, and nipped at her bottom lip. "I want inside you. Tell me you're ready."

Their problems hadn't been fully solved, but she couldn't deny him the truth. "I'm ready, Kaysar." She'd decided to win him. So Cookie would have him. All of him. "I want to take you deep."

"Yes," he hissed. "I will *pour* myself into you, and you will love it." His fingers closed in her hair as he backed her into the nearest wall, where he ground against her. "Does my sweetling want to come all over me?" he asked, grinding harder. Faster.

"Kaysar," Cookie rasped, hit by a lightning bolt of lust. She clutched his shoulders to remain upright. "Yes, I want to come." Every night without him, she'd tossed and turned, angry and aroused and nearing desperation. "Want to come so bad."

A harsh sound left him as he smashed his lips against hers.

She met his tongue with a hard thrust, his ferocity kindling her own. In mere seconds, he worked her to a fever pitch.

Cookie kissed and clawed at him, ripping at his pants. *Need him naked.*

Before she succeeded, Kaysar tossed her onto the mattress. As she bounced, he undressed, watching her. A powerful tower of strength and desire. Aggressive, his every motion a marvel of soft, violent seduction.

He flittered on top of her, his naked body ruthlessly pinning her down. His gaze made demands. "You are mine. My one and only."

Heat spread low in her belly, and she groaned. "Yes."

"I am yours." Kaysar's face hovered over hers, candlelight dancing with shadows over an expression etched with pure menace. Danger emanated from him, yet she'd never felt safer.

"You are, you are. Kiss me."

He brushed the tip of his nose against the tip of hers instead. "Do you want to know how I would murder the goblin leader, were he still alive?"

Shivers rocked her against him. "I do," she told him with another moan, the excitement of his words leaving her breathless. "He dared to hurt your woman. How did you hope to repay the insult?"

"I had a particularly gruesome end in mind," he replied with an evil smile, easing to the side to open her robe's sash the rest of the way. He ran her bottom lip between his teeth. "After I sliced him open from nose to navel and emptied out his entrails, I would have donned his body as a coat. A mantle of victory."

"That is so…hot." She panted as he dragged a claw along the left edge of the robe, parting the material, baring her breast. Her nipple beaded tight, the ache almost unbearable. "Did you enjoy watching me skewer him with a vine?"

"I nearly came from the sight." He kneaded her plump mound and licked his lips. "Are you hungry for me, Chantel?" Growling again.

The truth spilled from her. "I'm *starved* for you, Kaysar. And I'm going to have every bit of you."

KAYSAR BLINKED AND found himself flat on his back, Chantel a grinning, confident queen above him. Had she flittered them into a different position?

He knew the ability should bother him. At the moment, he couldn't rationalize why. "Your power grows."

"It does. Daily." On her knees, situated between his legs, she pushed the robe from her shoulders. The material whooshed away, fully baring those plump breasts topped by their coral-pink nipples. She might as well have a tattoo saying Kiss Here. "I learned during yesterday's lesson. I have to concentrate and really, really want to relocate, but I can do it."

And he'd missed the excitement of a new accomplishment. Kaysar nearly howled.

"Shall I tell you more about what I learned," she purred, "or shall I continue?"

Beyond speech, he gave an imperious wave of his hand. What would she do?

When she wiggled to position her mouth mere inches from his throbbing shaft, he nearly howled for a different reason.

Anticipation seized him. Would she suck him off? Was he to know this pleasure?

"Oh, dear," she said, drawing those beautiful lips away from his length. "This is what I had planned for you *before* your trip."

A curse welled up, and he found his voice. With a gravelly tone, he said, "Do not tease me, sweetling." He reached back and clasped the wrought iron headboard. "Tell me you'll be good and drink every drop I can give you."

"I want to tell you…but I don't know if I should." She lowered again. Almost…

He held his breath. Would she…?

She glided her tongue over the head of his shaft, capturing a bead of pre-cum. A hoarse sound left him, the pleasure unfathomable.

Her eyelids went heavy. "Suck you off—reward you— after you abandoned me for days and days and days?" She blew where she'd licked. "Tsk-tsk. This mistress doesn't play that way."

He trembled, the severity of his need making him desperate. "Another taste then." The sight of this woman and her big silver eyes glittering with excitement kept him teetering on a blade's edge. "Just one. Because I learned my lesson so fast."

"Just one? I *suppose* I don't see the harm in that. You *did* learn your lesson, so you *did* earn a reward. Oh, all right. You talked me into it." Watching him, she dragged her tongue from his base to his tip.

His control frayed, base desire clawing at him. A piece of the headboard bent. "One more taste," he rushed out. "Three licks in total is hardly a reward. Some might call it a punishment. Yes, you should punish me more." He was panting, his heart thundering. "Nothing less than twenty licks. Twenty would be excruciating."

"Perhaps you're right." The cruel temptress offered a languid nod. "Twenty tongue lashes *does* seem like a fitting punishment for your great crime."

He was to experience this *fully*?

She smiled at him—then she devoured his length.

He did howl this time. There was nothing better than this. Sweat dotted his face, his nape, and a bead trickled between his shoulder blades. The searing heat. The dizzying need and wet pleasure and, and, and… "Yes, sweetling. Yes. Just like that." He rocked into her eager mouth, careful, so careful.

Another rock, a little less careful.

She didn't accept his length—she demanded it. He couldn't think…had never had this. Had never wanted it from another. But this…he *loved*. Chantel sucked and laved him, and he was losing his mind. *No sweeter torment.*

"It's good, sweetling." He braced his heels on the mattress and lightly pumped his hips. "So good. Your mouth is…my heaven."

She did things with her tongue and teeth, forcing him closer to the edge.

"Don't stop. Please, don't stop." He begged? He didn't care. Bliss beckoned. One arm moved of its own accord, his fingers weaving into her hair and fisting. Panting graduated into heaving, breath sawing in and out of his mouth. Heat built at the base of his spine, pressure increasing.

He tried to stave off his climax, to savor this. The sensations escalated, until one bled into another. His entire body became a live wire electrified by the slightest touch. He chanted her name. Moaned and groaned it.

Focus consumed by Chantel, Kaysar lost sight of everything else. For the first time, he had no troubles. War had no meaning, and vengeance had no place. Satisfaction had filled him, soon to overflow.

"Yes!" With a roar, he poured his pleasure down her throat. Loving it. Instantly addicted. Robbed of thought and breath, ready to throw the world at this woman's feet.

She swallowed every drop, humming with the power of her conquest. After giving his rod a final suck, she released it and eyed him with sultry demand. "I think someone enjoyed his punishment."

Already hard again, Kaysar cupped her nape, gripped her outer thigh, and flipped her to her back. "My first taste of such a pleasure has obsessed me for eternity. I'll want your mouth on me every day."

"What do you mean, your first? No other woman has…"

When he shook his head, she offered him a sultry smile and pinched her nipples. "I'm glad I was your first."

Carnal and wanton. *Mine.* "My only."

Her eyelids dipped the way he adored. "Do you have me where you want me, Kaysar?"

"I have you where you belong, sweetling. With me." He settled his weight on his knees and slid a finger into her core. A groan parted his lips. Soaking wet. Blazing heat. *Tight.* "You've ruined me for others."

"That's right. You're mine, and *only* mine?" She spread her legs further, arching as he pumped the finger into her. Then two. Slowly working and stretching her. Preparing her body for his invasion.

"All yours." He dipped his head to stroke his firm tongue against her clit, and she moaned.

"Not all. Not yet. Soon."

Will never get enough of her sweetness. When he thrust his tongue *in* her, mimicking sex, she moaned louder.

"Kaysar," she cried. "So good, so good, but I need something bigger. Give it to me. Give. Please."

Can't resist her. He set the head of his shaft at her opening and gently pushed, breaching her tight, slick walls. "Don't want to hurt you."

Groaning, she melted around him. "Hurts without you."

He delved deeper, his eyes nearly rolling back in his head. "Never felt...anything like this."

"Give more." The way she moved her body... She *owned* his.

As he gained another inch, sweat sheened his brow. His breaths shallowed. Halfway in, he stilled, letting himself go no farther. With the pad of his thumb, he stroked her clit. "Tell me you need me."

"I do, I do."

"Tell me you can't get enough of me."

"I can't. Only want more."

He brought his thumb to his mouth and sucked, then gripped the headboard once again to hold himself steady. "You want all of me?"

"Yes. You *promised* everything." She clutched at his back and rocked her hips, maddening him. "I waited so long, Kaysar. Don't make me wait anymore."

"No. No more waiting," he croaked. No one had ever wanted the real, flawed Kaysar. Until this female with her wide eyes and vulnerable heart changed his life forever.

With a hoarse cry, he thrust *deeeeep*, impaling her on his length.

Their cries crashed together as her inner walls gloved him, tighter than any fist, hotter than summer honey and softer than rose petals.

By sheer will, he remained motionless. "Hurt?"

"Perfect." Wrapping her limbs around him, she bucked against him, commanding, "Do it again. You can't hurt me. You can't be too rough. I'll like it."

Kaysar obeyed, pulling out and surging in. A frenzy took hold then. He pumped inside her again and again, slamming in, shaking the bed.

She mewled and thrashed, lost in the throes. Every thrust, sight and sound propelled him higher. Pleasure stacked upon pleasure stacked upon pleasure.

He would have more than her mouth every morning. He would have this—he would have *her*—every day in every way for the rest of eternity.

"Right there, right there, right there." Chantel ran his earlobe between her teeth. "It's so good, baby."

"Who makes you feel this way?"

"Only you."

"That's right. Only me." He did this. Him. Kaysar de

Aoibheall. Scraped raw, he vowed, "But I will make you feel *better*."

He reared up to his knees, spread her legs wide—wider—and thrust with all his might. Bliss beckoned with more strength than before...

Spine bowing, she threw back her head and screamed. Her sheath squeezed him, milking every rock-hard inch, *forcing* his release.

A suspended moment as he fought it...before his body broke, ceding his pleasure. Kaysar roared, his voice tearing at the edge, rapture pouring through him, overwhelming his senses.

After the last lash of his climax, he collapsed atop her. He heaved as though he'd battled an army of hundreds. Defenses he'd built for centuries crumbled. Triumph expanded, an unstoppable force. Unimaginable. Nearly unbearable. Waiting in the center of it all...contentment. Because he'd pleased his mate. He'd satisfied *her*. He'd satisfied her well. Because, with his Chantel, he had no hate to bridge his past to his future. He had only here and now and tomorrow, pleasure his for the taking.

And take it he would.

"That was amazing," she said, her voice slightly slurred. "Think I'm gonna take a little nap now."

He rolled to his side and fit her boneless body on top of him. Their favorite sleeping position. As if she were his shield, his pain no match for her. As if he were an anchor for her, preventing her from slipping away.

Confidence surged. He could make this relationship work *and* enjoy his vengeance. From now on, he simply had to take better care of both.

All would be well.

CHAPTER TWENTY-EIGHT

THOUGH COOKIE AND KAYSAR had gone to bed only hours ago, the weather had changed drastically, a storm brewing on the horizon.

She stood on the master suite balcony, surveying her kingdom. Below her, across from the castle, was a bustling market, fae and an assortment of mythological creatures buying, selling and hustling everything from fresh baked breads, to swords and unicorns.

She'd been here, what? A week? Ten years? Since the change in management, this was the first time Dusklands citizens had come out of hiding to continue living. Progress was slow but sweet.

Evening had come, the descending sun setting storm clouds ablaze as they gathered. Lighting flashed, announcing a clap of thunder. In the market, people raced for cover to avoid the first light splatter of rain. Wind blew in, damp and fragrant with smoke and sandalwood.

As people congregated under the tents, standing still as they crammed together, a large group noticed her high in the castle. In the silence between booms of thunder, she heard, "Lulundria."

"Summer Court princess."

"Prince Jareth's bride."

She blew a kiss, smiled and waved, hoping to curry favor. They didn't smile, but they did wave. At least she

looked her best. She wore a gown of poisonvine, pink flowers woven throughout the leaves. Pink locks of hair danced
in the breeze.

She drummed her thorn claws against the metal rail as
her audience lost interest in her. In the bedroom, Kaysar
slept like the dead in bed. She doubted he'd rested more
than thirty seconds at a time during his hunt. Or in the
years before her arrival.

Low-grade arousal heated her body as she remembered
every action responsible for his coma of bliss. That man
knew how to move. How to render her desperate but also
delight her. He made her feel like the predator—and the
prey.

Sex with him was out-of-this-world good. Mind-blowing.
The best she'd ever had. His touch had been reverent but
demanding. Perfect. He'd concentrated the full measure of
his intensity on her pleasure.

Control? She'd had none. Defenses? Gone. He'd stripped
her in every way imaginable, and she'd reveled in it, hun-
gering for more. She was overjoyed with him. She was…
worried.

Falling fast. With no safety net.

The girl afraid of being ditched fought to win the man
who loved another. Vengeance.

The word alone made her want to destroy something.
How did you win against a concept?

Kaysar materialized behind her, pressing his bare chest
into her back. He braced his hands beside hers, caging her
in, and nuzzled her cheek. "I didn't like waking without
you in my arms."

Past rational thought, she nuzzled him in return, leaning
into his strength. The sky chose that moment to open up,

rain pelting the land. In seconds, red dirt appeared black, becoming a sea of gleaming obsidian.

The muscles in his arms flexed, as if he braced for a blow. "What thoughts plague you, sweetling? Tell me what's wrong, and I'll fix it."

Desire me more than your revenge. "Sometimes I don't seek fixes, Claw Man. I just want to talk or vent or share," she replied with a small smile. "How about you, right this second? Would you like to talk, vent or share? You could tell me about your hunt."

He frowned. "A disappointing venture. I pared their army down a mere hundred soldiers or so." With a gentle brush of his fingers, he smoothed her mass of hair to one shoulder and rested his chin on the other. "Your turn. Tell me what troubles you."

She decided to go for it. To discuss the big bad. She would start off easy, though. "Earlier you called me your one and only. How do you know for sure that's what I am?"

A relieved breath seeped from him. "I know because I know."

"But how?" she insisted. Most guys kept close-lipped about their feelings. Kaysar put everything out there, and it was screwing with her head. "You probably never noticed this, since you're so besotted with me and all, but I can be a brat sometimes. Expect to be annoyed by me repeatedly. What if I'm ever too much to handle? You'll talk to me, right?"

He chuckled softly. "Do you think my wanting ever goes away, sweetling? There's a clawing right here, every time I think about you. See you. Breathe you in." He slid his arms around her more fully and lightly tapped her sternum. "There's also a sense of incredible peace here."

Her next inhalation burned her lungs. "What kind of

future do you envision us having together? I mean, we've only known each other for a short while. What if I don't fit into your life long-term?"

"We will fit into *each other's* lives because we will make it so." Anticipation fizzed in his voice, reminding her of champagne and celebration. "I see a bright future for us. I will tell you what I need, and you will do the same. Sometimes I'll strike at the Frostlines alone. Sometimes you'll come with me. We'll spend countless hours in bed, of course." He rubbed his erection between her cheeks. "I never knew such pleasures existed, and now that I do, there's so much more I wish to do with you."

"A bright future indeed," she said, her body singing for him. Yes, they could do this. They were learning each other, but they were also making room in their lives. As long as he remained motivated to succeed with her, she had something to work with.

All right. Time to bring up the beating heart of the big bad.

"Help me better understand your vengeance," she said.

He clasped her by the waist, lifted and turned her, then sat her on the rail. He fit his hips between her spread legs, putting her face above his, and linked his fingers under her backside. His strong arms kept her safe and steady, but she clung to him anyway.

He was naked. Gloriously so. A proud, powerful—irresistible—sight. Disheveled hair made him appear boyish. Honestly, slumber had helped him shed two hundred and fifty years. At least.

On his left shoulder was the birth control tattoo he'd given himself. Three black dots the size of pennies, and a stark reminder of the ruthlessness of his nature. He expected her to remain childless, even if she one day wanted kids, simply to satisfy a debt he could repay with a sword at any time.

"What would you like to know?" he asked, wary.

The storm charged the air. A flash of lightning illuminated a male with lost whiskey eyes. Her heart banged against her ribs. If those eyes were the window to his soul, Kaysar the Unhinged One desperately needed saving. He was a king currently drowning in tears he'd refused to shed.

Cookie nearly looked away. As she held his gaze, silently offering a life raft, if only he would grab it, his expression softened into tenderness.

Here goes. "You let the Frostlines live so you can torture them. What if King Hador harms other innocents in the meantime?"

A muscle jumped in his jaw. "I castrate him regularly, and I use a blade that makes his injuries more difficult to heal. Sometimes I take his eyes and his hands, too. I'm eager to show you my collection."

"And I'm eager to see it." She chewed on her bottom lip as she toyed with his hair. "If I asked you to let Jareth go, you'd tell me...?"

He reared back, but she held tight. Eventually he settled back against her, and she melted over him.

"It's just a question, Kaysar. I'm not actually asking you to do it."

"I'd tell you no, absolutely not," he said, a little panicked.

Yeah. She'd figured. "Jareth was as much a child as you were the day you lost your sister." *Tread carefully.* "What if the king and his brother abused him the same way they abused you?"

"No. The Frostlines lie. They're kind in public and monsters in private. I watched from my window, my ire sharpening every time a servant or guest gazed upon them with adoration and admiration."

"But you never saw Jareth in private. You don't know if he broke down every time he sealed himself in his bedroom."

"No!" A violent shake of his head as he attempted to step back again. "You don't understand." His volume rose with each word.

"It's okay, it's okay. We don't have to discuss Jareth, young or old." She petted his chest until he relaxed, then steered the conversation to the present. "What are you going to do about Micah and Hador? Will you leave the castle again?" Tomorrow?

"Not without you. As to what I'll do... I am unsure. I must think. My schemes require...adjusting." He kneaded her backside, his touch almost bruising. "Earlier you told me you needed to be first. What if I can't give you that? I can't lose you, Chantel. But I can't lose her, either."

"Her?"

"Vengeance is Viori, and Viori is vengeance."

He spoke the words by rote. An internal chant, no doubt. He believed he'd failed his sister and sought to offer her reparation. The only thing he had to offer? The pain of those who had separated them.

Win him from his vengeance, yeah, Cookie could probably do it. But win him from his sister? He might hate her for it. Forgiveness wasn't something he knew how to offer.

"I won't ask you to give up your sister," she promised. "Not now, not ever." Maybe one day, he would freely— happily—*let her go*. Because Cookie wasn't done fighting. "We've got time to figure this out, baby."

He released a shuddering breath, relaxing further.

She pressed a soft kiss into his lips. "Sing me a song?"

Minutes passed in silence, the storm pitter-pattering behind her. She assumed he refused her request. But, as he combed his fingers through her hair, he released the first note. A haunting melody she felt in every cell. Once again, she melted over him.

He sang as he swept her against his chest and carried her to bed.

"WHAT DO YOU think of this, Kaysar?" Chantel stood before an erotic statue of a naked couple lost in the throes. "Beside the door or on the dais?"

Kaysar remained nearby. Yesterday, she'd found a trunk full of mortal clothes and gadgets she'd claimed with a shouted, "Dibs!" This morning she'd washed the garments, then donned a "tank" top, "yoga" pants, and a hideous green "bath" robe. Curlers covered her head, keeping her hair in tight ringlets.

"I'm taking today off from my royal duties and doing a little spring cleaning," she'd told him, her gray-green eyes glittering with challenge. "The people will love the end results."

"An erotic statue looks spectacular *anywhere*, sweetling," he told her now.

"Oh, my gosh. You're right." She beamed at him and returned to her redecorating.

He ensured the servants obeyed her without hesitation as she ordered them to place this here and that there. Items she'd discovered in the treasure trove. Framed maps. Marble statues. Paintings. Furnishings and vases.

She'd requested a carpenter, and Kaysar had supplied her with the best. Someone able to make "kitty cities" and climbing posts for the royal feline, upon his arrival. The carpenter also built ramps for Pearl Jean's "scooter." Whatever that was.

Three days had passed since the raid. Kaysar and his queen made love at all hours, whispered in the dark and slept curled together every night. Having tasted of their connection, he could settle for nothing less than an eternity with her. He cherished every minute in her presence. More than he'd ever cherished anything.

The prince occupied his usual spot at the edge of the royal dais. Jareth stared at Chantel, his gaze intent.

That wouldn't do.

Earlier, Kaysar did the unthinkable and showed the male a kindness. But then, this particular kindness had been for himself, as well. The prince had stunk, and Kaysar had allowed servants to bathe him.

When Kaysar rotated on his heel to approach the prince, Chantel swung around and patted his butt. He stopped for a moment, a smile flashing and vanishing. The things she did. He shook his head and crossed to the prince, winding through piles of goods awaiting her decision for permanent relocation.

"Look at my mistress, nesting," he said to Jareth when he stood at the male's side. "Creating a home for us."

"You're a prick," the prince snapped.

"The great Frostline prince thinks poorly of me. However will I recover?"

To his great annoyance, Jareth got smug. "Enjoy her while you can. She doesn't need to remember Lulundria to flee you. You'll drive her away all on your own. I saw her face when you flittered to my father. You didn't—because you weren't here. That's her war line. Your days with her are numbered."

Rage. Unholy. Consuming. How *dare* the prince use

his own fears against him. "You will not even *speak* of her." Kaysar went low, grabbing and yanking Jareth's ankles, smacking him to the floor. The crash shook the entire throne room.

Jareth remained stretched out, grinning at the ceiling. "Worth it."

"Kaysar," Chantel called, her gaze on a second statue, "be a dear and play with your toys outside today."

Remove Jareth's collar? Give the prince an opportunity to escape? How could she even suggest such a thing? But then, she'd made no secret of her desire to set the Frostline free. She'd softened for the prince.

Kaysar balled his fists. His woman and his foe, working together to make him crazed. He— What was that? Familiar eyes stared at him from a trunk.

Servants had dropped a beaten leather chest near Chantel's feet, the lid falling off upon impact.

His heart stopped. He stomped over and swiped up a doll. It couldn't be *the* doll. It. Couldn't. But he knew every scuff and crack on this porcelain face. Had seen them in his memories a myriad of times.

Viori's doll. Drendall. Kaysar clutched the little darling close. His sister had been here.

CHAPTER TWENTY-NINE

THE NEXT SIX days lasted six thousand years or six seconds. One or the other, and nothing in between, passing too swiftly and too slowly at once. All because Kaysar had found his sister's doll, Drendall.

Forget being first or second place in Kaysar's life. Cookie had been demoted to third.

He hadn't left the castle, at least. Instead, he'd constantly hounded Amber about visions. Where was Micah *right now*? Why couldn't/hadn't/wouldn't Eye see Viori? Where had Viori been throughout the ages? For her incompetence, did Eye prefer to die swiftly or linger?

Amber's visions were currently on the fritz, and the oracle didn't know why.

Unfortunately, Cookie's abilities were on the fritz, too. Since the doll's discovery, her doormaking power had stopped charging and started draining. Her dream of fetching Pearl Jean and Sugars floated beyond her reach.

Her life was topsy-turvy again. Because of a doll. She hated this. Kaysar made her feel things she'd never felt before. Wonderful, terrible, amazing, awful things. She'd fallen deeper. Too deep. And she was trying, trying so hard, to *stop* falling. She was doing everything in her power to hold a part of herself back. And he was helping her do it! But it didn't matter. If they split, she'd…she'd…shatter.

All the king's horses and all the king's men, couldn't put Cookie back together again.

She sometimes imagined marrying this man—without vomiting! She thought she might want to tweak his vengeance plan and start a family with him one day. They could be deliriously happy together. Kaysar at her side as she ruled the Dusklands. She might even help him lord over the Nightlands. But, deep down, he would be miserable the entire time. The hatred was eating him alive.

He'd asked for a chance to fix her problems. Why wouldn't he give her a chance to fix his?

She knew she was special to Kaysar. Soon she thought he might do the impossible and...not forgive, but pardon Jareth for his part in their wretched past. The two had reached an uneasy accord. Oh, they swiped at each other, but they weren't out for blood, either. They would never be friends, but they were almost done being enemies. No, the problem was Hador.

King Hador was the one Kaysar had linked with Viori and his retribution on her behalf. As long as the royal breathed, he posed a threat to Kaysar's happiness. Cookie's, too. Pearl Jean and Suggy's, as well. Not to mention the debt Cookie owned Lulundria—to live her best life.

When Hador died, Kaysar's hate would die with him. Finally, her dark king could heal.

How can I help him want *to heal?* He didn't realize—or didn't accept—that killing Hador meant dealing with Viori's loss.

Cookie hurried toward the secret portal room she'd visited every day since unearthing it. Hadn't taken her long to sniff out a second secret room, which had led to the discovery of another and another and another. Each room contained a mystical item—everything she'd hoped to find when they'd first entered the Dusklands.

A coin-filled hot spring. A full-length, freestanding mirror. A glass coffin. A telescope slash spyglass. Most of which mystified her. What could they do?

She'd also found an enchanted tree growing inside a pot. She knew because the branches dripped with elderseed. Had Kaysar done this with her bark? For her?

A grin flashed and fell, and she sighed. What was she going to do about that man?

Servants smiled, waved and bowed at her. Someone uttered "Our maddened queen" with affection.

Cookie pursed her lips. Yesterday she'd pouted to Kaysar, "The servants don't like me." He must have…spoken with them, encouraging better behavior.

Guess she would need to deliver another round of apology plants.

Anytime she messed up with her people, she offered a bush, flower or tree of some kind. The fruit trees earned the best reactions—reverence and awe. For the trees, only the trees, but progress was progress.

Cookie soared past the invisible veil that separated the maze of treasures from the rest of the castle. She'd expected Kaysar to be over the moon when she'd given him a gold star tour, but he'd been too distracted to care, patting her head, kissing her lips and moving on.

As she bypassed the portal and navigated the winding hallway of mystical options, the skirt of her ball gown brushed the walls. On both sides. Today she'd selected the Glenda the Good-ish Witch dress. The pale pink fabric boasted embroidered roses across the bodice, with an accompaniment of razor-sharp leaves. Anyone dumb enough to grab her would receive quite the surprise.

She'd *almost* chosen to be the Sugar Plum Fairy. A magnificent creation and an attempt to lure Kaysar to her side, ready to grant his every wish. To gain his attention and his touch. To reaffirm their undeniable connection. Once she'd talked herself out of that, she'd reached for the white dress. Its mysterious meaning had stayed her hand. Instead, she'd gone for the eternal optimist. Hoping...

There's no place like home.

At last, she entered the room with the telescope. Her favorite! The massive piece of equipment stared at a crumbling wall, yet she could use it to peer anywhere in the Dusklands, the Forest of Many Names, and even the borders of the five courts. Once, she'd thought she caught sight of Kaysar's palace in the Midnight Court. The Nightlands. Though she'd searched and searched, she'd failed to locate Micah and Hador here in the Dusklands.

Maybe she'd luck out today.

Let the search continue. In position at the spyglass, she searched the wooded areas in the mountain, where tree roots slithered like snakes, on the hunt for Micah or the Frostline king. Flowers had begun to bloom here and there. Pink. Blue. Yellow. Red. Purple. The petals shimmered in sunlight. Beyond the woods was a swampland that cut into a butterfly garden, which cut into a desert-like clearing.

"Cookie! Guess what? I did it. I figured out how I've been seeing hundreds of random images of no importance, preventing me from seeing anything else."

Invader! With a yelp, Cookie whirled around and flung a handful of thorns. The intruder's identity didn't register until too late. Thankfully, Amber ducked and continued forward without a pause in her step. Or dying.

"Well, don't leave the rest of the class in suspense," Cookie said, heart not yet ready to calm. "Tell me. How's it happening? And how'd you get past your shadow?" Kaysar should be all over her, demanding information about this.

"Oh, Kaysar was easy. I accessed a vision sure to keep him busy for hours." The oracle stunned in a white Grecian gown, as graceful as a ballerina. "Micah and Hador are working with a seer of their own. One of the most powerful I've ever encountered. She's sending me mental collages, preventing me from focusing on where the royals are hiding."

"Now that you know, can you block her?"

"Mostly."

That was great. It really was. But, the return of her abilities put Kaysar's preoccupation on steroids. Cookie's shoulders drooped as she returned her attention to the spyglass. "I'll find our opposition, don't you worry. No one can hide from me for long." Hopefully.

She aimed the end in different directions. A fluffy bush that resembled cotton candy hurled itself onto a rodent, blood spraying from the leaves. In a pond, a fish zoomed past the water's surface and got snagged by a bird mid-flight. Another fish crawled from the water with a million feet to creep along the shore.

With a huff of irritation, Cookie readjusted the angle of the spyglass and scrutinized the border of the Winter Court, home to King Hador and Prince Jareth. Snow and frost stretched forever, creating a sea of white broken only by a massive rock wall, where an army camped.

Kaysar's army. Or a part of it. How long had the men been in place? Tents and firepits abounded, smoke curling through frigid air. Some soldiers trained. Others crafted weapons or performed chores. A majority worked to breach the wall.

He enjoyed being a constant thorn in Hador's paw. And

honestly, she couldn't blame him. But since finding the doll, his obsession had amplified tenfold. It was hurting him and killing her.

He skulked around and muttered under his breath constantly. When his sanity slipped, he cut his arms to make his maps. He'd made a lot of maps. Sometimes he stared at the crimson lines, as if he plotted a path to Viori, wherever she happened to be. *If* she happened to be. Had she survived?

"You can absolutely find specific individuals with the spyglass," Amber said. "If you have their blood."

Seriously? "How much?"

"A single drop here." She tapped the mysterious cylinder beneath the eyepiece. "There's nowhere the person can hide. No power strong enough to shield them."

No wonder Cookie had fallen hardcore for the spyglass. It rocked. "Since I can't thieve blood until I find the people, you're up to bat. Have you seen Micah and Hador yet? One or the other? Hundreds of angry soldiers, perhaps?"

"I've seen a future event. Which is one of the reasons I sought you out." Amber hesitated a moment. "There's something I feel you should see."

Oh, crap. "No, thank you." No need to ponder. She got being prepared. But when did a psychic vision become a self-fulfilling prophecy? "If I know what's coming, I might change my behavior, might make wrong decisions, based on a supposition."

"Kaysar would disagree." Amber flattened a palm on the rounded body of the spyglass, pushing it from Cookie's range. "But I don't want to show you what's coming. I want to reveal something from his past."

"That would be a *big* no thanks, too. I'm not peeping into his business. Not without permission." But she wanted to. Temptation had her number. What she wouldn't give to see a slice of Kaysar's life.

No. She shouldn't. Their relationship was strained enough already. Why add a potential bomb to the mix?

"Do you wish for Pearl Jean and Sugars to live here?" Amber asked.

The oracle planned to talk her around, didn't she? "You know I do," Cookie grumbled.

"Do you want a future with Kaysar? Do you want to win him?"

She flashed a scowl. "I do. But he doesn't desire to be won." When would he fight for *her*? Everything was so one-sided. He either showed her the world's most seductive, attentive Prince Charming or the world's coldest assassin, but never anything in between. "I'm a pretty amazing person," she said, hating her whininess. "I protect those under my care, I'm world-changing in bed, and I'm sure I have other winning attributes, too."

"Do you want to win him?" Amber repeated.

Temper rising, ready for a change of scenery and topics, Cookie clasped the oracle's hand and flittered to the garden she'd cultivated outside her bedroom.

Warm, dusty air became dry and smoky in an instant. Servants worked out here, smiling and laughing as they pulled weeds from a garden. Pride filled Cookie. She had created so many different kinds of plants and herbs for her prototype garden. She'd even begun experimenting and splicing. The bushes and foliage grew from the earth, thriving in the soil.

The revitalization of the land brought her a sense of fulfillment as nothing else ever had.

Grins widened as the servants spotted her.

"They aren't being nice to you because Kaysar demanded it. Though he did," Amber told her, urging her forward. They walked along a dirt path, bushes of every kind flourishing all around. Connected to Cookie but not, exactly as Jareth had predicted. "They know you're the one responsible for the thriving plant life. They are grateful."

"Oh. Well." She cleared her throat. Because of the smoke, *not* embarrassment. Or need. "What am I going to do about Kaysar, Amber? Nothing is working." So much for changing topics. "Before you answer, turn off your foresight and live in this moment, okay? So yes, I'm asking you to pretend you're as dumb as the rest of us."

"Very well. Here's something even a fool should know. To get what you want, you'll have to fight and fall and stand and fight—and accept help when it's offered."

Marched right into that one. See? Hadn't taken long for the oracle to talk her around. "Fine. I'll peer into Kaysar's past. But if he protests about it, you're getting full blame." She fluttered a hand over her throat, pretending to be scandalized. "Kaysar, darling, Amber *forced* me to watch."

The oracle rolled her eyes. "As if you can do any wrong in his mind."

True. A definite mark for the pro column. "Why do you need to show me this, anyway?" Amber might be a gifted talk-arounder, but Cookie was an excellent staller.

"Did I forget to tell you? King Hador and King Micah are on their way to the palace. They'll arrive later this evening with thousands of trolls. That's the bit of news that is currently occupying Kaysar."

"What?" She spun into the other woman with her skirt, then gripped her shoulders and shook. A habit she'd picked up from Kaysar. "Why didn't you start with the headline, you exquisite nut? Tell me everything."

"I'll give you the highlights of the future, so we can

return to the business of the past. The two kings will arrive and seek an audience. They'll offer a truce Kaysar will refuse."

"Shocker."

"This will mark a crucial moment in your relationship with him, and I want you prepared."

Crucial moment? Gulp. "Are you gearing up to tell me I…lose?"

The seer gave her a pitying look. "That depends on you. And no pressure, but your actions with Hador and Micah this day will have eternity-long consequences."

No pressure. Right. "I swear you have five seconds to explain what—" Cookie went silent, her spine bowing, throwing back her head. A scream ripped from her.

"Oh, yes," Amber said with a sweet smile. "I probably should have warned you. Accepting an image or two is easy. Receiving an entire memory is not."

"You're the meanest of us all, aren't you?" she asked between wheezing breaths.

The oracle's smile widened, her eyes twinkling. "Probably."

A response lived and died within the same heartbeat, Cookie's mind consumed with a virtual reality she couldn't switch off. She watched a young boy lead a younger girl through the forest. They were the most beautiful children she'd ever beheld, with wavy jet-black hair and light brown eyes framed by ultra-long lashes.

She didn't have to ponder who they were. The knowledge came with the memory. This was Kaysar and his sister, Viori. The realization punched Cookie, and she flattened her hands on her stomach to ward off an oncoming ache. The siblings were so thin, so dirty, wearing rags and boots barely held together by string.

Kaysar carried a large satchel on his back, stooped from its weight.

"This," Amber said, "is the day Kaysar lost her. Watch it. Watch his capture. And his escape."

Her heart squeezed painfully. This was going to tear her up inside, wasn't it?

CHAPTER THIRTY

MICAH AND HADOR. Here. Soon. Not soon enough.

Kaysar poised at the edge of Chantel's throne, vibrating with readiness, Drendall in his lap. A group of farmers had come to request his aid regarding some kind of swamp monster and offer bribes. He half listened, his mind too active.

Did Micah know Viori? Had the usurper ever interacted with her? Had one of his people? Had someone simply found the doll? But why store it in a treasury? The lack of answers left him ragged.

Failing Viori.

Losing Chantel.

More and more, his woman stared out windows, pensive. Anytime he inquired about her thoughts, she smiled the most heartbreakingly sad smile and changed the subject.

They lived in the same castle, with her glorious plants budding around every doorway and window, yet he missed her as if they were separated by oceans. She kept a part of herself separate from him now. He *felt* the distance.

They hadn't made love again.

Chantel had said she wouldn't ask him to choose her over his sister, and she'd kept true to her word. Why did that disappoint him?

She still hadn't donned the claws, their team uniform. Her mouth often smiled at him, but the affection no longer sparkled so brightly in those big, beautiful eyes. Though he'd held her lush curves in his arms every night, they'd stopped whispering secrets to each other. She'd kissed him once, forever ago, but his guilt had prevented him from enjoying it, and she'd never tried again.

The strain was starting to wear on him, his patience nonexistent with everyone but her—with effort. But he'd never been a calm individual, and he feared the inevitable snap. Would he only drive her away faster?

But how could he enjoy his woman while his sister suffered a fate unknown? Did Viori need him? He didn't know. Had she forged a life for herself? One filled with regrets? Horrors? Was she happy? Dead?

Kaysar pulled at hanks of his hair, the uncertainty increasing the likelihood of that emotional snap. He'd already used up the drops of satisfaction and contentment he'd gained during those too few times they'd made love. Nothing remained of them, and he desperately, fiercely yearned for more.

Why couldn't she accept the life he offered, as is? Why did she have to want more, too? He'd given her everything. New gifts. Weapons. Jewelry. Weapons made to look like jewelry. A framed map of the Dusklands, her kingdom. But she wanted what he *couldn't* give. Unless he could.

Part of him screamed to let go of his vengeance. To end the Frostlines at last. To say goodbye to Viori. But how could he? How, how, how?

You know I'll always protect you, yes?

To break his promise to the little girl who owned his heart...to *lie* to the one who deserved his every truth...

Until he knew what became of Viori, he could not, should not rest.

"In case you were wondering, your most recent strike against me is truly diabolical," Jareth said from his post on the dais. He popped a small croquette into his mouth. Croquettes were *not* on Kaysar's approved menu for the captured prince. Obviously, someone was dying today. Or tomorrow, after he'd dealt with the upcoming visitation. "Letting me watch you self-destruct? I'm positively *teeming* with misery."

"When your opinion is wanted," he grated, "I'll rip it from your throat." Where was Chantel? Still redecorating bedchambers?

He scanned the "new and improved" throne room, loving the erotic statues positioned around the walls, like soldiers having sex in front of every occupant. The most sedate florals accompanied them, framed in gold at their sides. The whimsy of her eclectic tastes charmed him.

"—majesty?" a farmer said. "I-is this gift satisfactory?"

The fearful, hopeful question pulled him from his musings. He realized he'd been petting Chantel's lock of hair over his forearm.

He swept his gaze over the group who'd brought two chests of elven spices, cured in the marshes. "Perhaps *you* should tell me if this gift is satisfactory. You are the ones who selected it, after all. So, do it. Tell me. Did you choose an unsatisfactory gift for the queen you wish to act as your champion?"

"I... You..." The farmer looked at his companions for support, who merely peered at the floor. "Your majesty—"

"The gift is more than satisfactory," Jareth announced. "The finest from your fields, I'm guessing."

"Yes, yes. The finest from our fields," the man rushed to agree.

Kaysar flicked his tongue over an incisor. Jareth kept doing this, kept interrupting and making a nuisance of himself. "You truly believe this?" he asked the prince. He didn't wait for a response. "You will agree to receive their punishment or reward, whichever I decide is deserved."

"Agreed," Jareth said with a nod. "I will take their punishment or reward."

The farmers shuddered with relief before filing out of the room as fast as their feet would carry them.

Kaysar forced himself to relax. Stroking his chin, he told the prince, "How magnanimous of you. Once, you wouldn't even speak up to save a servant girl you desired. Now you risk your life for strangers."

The royal flinched. "You want to discuss this here? Very well. I was as much a prisoner as you were. Do you think you were the only one abused? Do you think I hadn't tried to escape and failed? Do you think, even for a moment, that I wasn't saying and doing exactly what was expected of me as I worked to strengthen, hoping to break out? That day in the field, I hoped to save the girl from a fate worse than death. I knew my family would kill her regardless of what I did or said. I picked a more merciful path for her but—" He pressed his lips together and bowed his head, as if his shame weighed heavy on him.

"Well. I didn't know your intentions were so *pure*," Kaysar sneered. Perhaps Jareth spoke true, perhaps he lied. Either way, it was done, and he deserved to suffer. "You despise Hador so much, yet you associate with him before your citizens. You laugh together."

"I *never* laugh with him. Not anymore."

He narrowed his eyes. "Shall I pardon you for being a weak coward?"

Another flinch. Then the prince met his gaze, exuding defiance. "Perhaps you should pardon *yourself* for it first?"

Kaysar, a weak coward? How *dare* the prince? "I will have your tongue before the day's end."

Jareth remained unfazed. "If my forced stay has taught me anything, it's the truth of your nature. The big, bad Unhinged One fears losing everything he loves yet again. You wear an invisible collar, binding you to a prison of your own making, where time has no meaning and nothing ever changes. Then a beautiful princess comes along, offering you a key, and you pretend you can't see it. You treat yourself worse than you've ever treated me. I think you like your misery—I know you deserve it."

I will gut him where he sits. Kaysar gripped the arms of the throne, barely able to hold himself back. "I told you to *never* speak of her."

"Would you welcome a revelation about her? Because I'm willing to admit she's yours. That much is clear. Your insanity complements hers, and I wish you both the best. I have no desire to take her from you. I'd prefer to…help you. To make amends for what I failed to do as a child."

Help Kaysar? Fury churned deep, soon to erupt. "I need *nothing* from you. You cannot make amends."

The front doors swung open without warning. Eye rushed inside the room, calling, "Sorry to interrupt, my king, but Hador and Micah have arrived, and they are mere seconds behind me."

Finally. Every inhalation dagger-sharp, Kaysar lifted his chin and squared his shoulders. The prince was forgotten.

As soon as Kaysar had received word from Eye, he'd called off his guards. Nothing would hinder this meeting.

The oracle halted at the side of the throne, a fine glaze of perspiration glistening on her dark skin. "I would have gotten here sooner, but Cookie wished to change her clothes." She winced. "My sincerest apologies for her latest choice, majesty."

What aspect of her magnificent personality had she chosen to emphasize for the coming battle?

For the second time, the doors swung open. Excitement spun through him as King Hador Frostline and Micah marched in, their heads high. They'd forgone armor for the meeting, selecting tunics and leathers instead, as if they had no fear of Kaysar's claws. Eight guards trailed them. Four fae, four trolls. The paltry number irritated him. Had he lost his edge? Were people getting *comfortable* around him?

Only Chantel had the right!

Hatred sharpened Kaysar's focus as he met Hador's ugly gaze. The urge to kill frothed inside him, reviled memories surging and crashing.

Wandering, grasping hands. Ragged pants. Hot breath on his flesh.

Growls brewed. *Hurt him. Make him suffer.* Yes. Kaysar would coat his skin in his enemy's blood and dance to screams of his agony.

"What a wonderful non-surprise." Pasting on an indulgent smile, Kaysar motioned to Eye. "Shall I send my oracle for refreshments now or after you've screamed in pain for a bit?"

"We won't be staying long," Micah replied. Either he read lips at this close range, or he'd taken the drug to deafen himself again. He dropped his gaze to the doll and blinked.

A tell of recognition? Confusion? Which, which? Kaysar struggled to mask his anxiety.

Hador pointed to Jareth. "I won't leave without my son."

To his credit, the prince remained seated, appearing furious about his father's arrival. "I am where you should be. Unless you'd like to switch places, I won't be going anywhere."

The king narrowed his eyes but said nothing else.

Though the byplay bothered Kaysar, he maintained his indulgent expression. Where was Chantel?

"Leave the Dusklands of your own volition, King Kaysar." Micah's command boomed through the room. "I have no wish to destroy my kingdom and rebuild from the foundation up yet again. But I can and will do so if you force my hand. I won't allow you to rule over innocent, hardworking people."

How to explain this in a way the male would understand? "If you strike at me or mine, even once, the kingdom *will* be destroyed. I'll make sure of it."

Micah's cheeks lost all color.

"Now that pleasantries are over." *Careful. No hint of urgency.* "Do you recognize little Drendall, Micah?" He set the doll on the throne's arm, allowing her big eyes to stare at the intruders.

The usurper's gaze returned to Viori's former companion, his brows drawing together. "Should I?"

Genuine perplexity? Kaysar barely stopped himself from ripping at hanks of his hair. He'd known the possibility was minute. He'd desperately hoped otherwise. "The doll belonged to my sister, long ago. One way or another, I will ferret out the truth of her time in the Dusklands." Best to be clear. "Any who harmed her will soon seek the sweet release of death. Those who lie about an association with her will never find it."

"Harm a child? A female?" Micah scoffed. "Never. The rules of my kingdom are simple."

Kaysar…believed him. But the unsatisfactory exchange stripped another layer of civility from him. "Your choice of teammate confuses me."

"Enough war," Hador shouted. "I'm tired of fighting you, Kaysar, but I will help Micah oversee your defeat if I must."

"You're tired of fighting?" The words left him as little more than a whisper. "Well, let's give the child rapist what he wants."

Micah lurched with horror. "The *what*?"

The king averted his gaze, his cheeks reddening. "You are more destructive than I ever was."

"Tsk-tsk," Kaysar replied in a singsong voice, earning moans of pain. "You cannot make the monster, then complain when it bites you."

Hador scrubbed a hand over his face. "I'm sorry for what occurred between us, Kaysar. So incredibly sorry. You must know that."

Do not close the distance. Do not rip out his heart. He deserved only suffering heaped upon suffering.

Kaysar schooled his features. "Ah. We've reached the excuses portion of our interactions. My least favorite, I must admit, but please. Do continue. This always precedes your harm by my hand."

A lone tear slid down the king's cheek, quickly followed by another. "I assure you, I've paid for my crimes a thousand times over."

"Do tell. Fill my ears with your miseries."

A muscle jumped in Hador's jaw. He offered no response, just heaved his breaths.

Because he was a liar, and he had not paid enough.

"I've changed," the king insisted. "I've learned the value of life."

"You've learned the value of nothing."

Once again, the doors burst open. Everyone turned to face the newest intruder. Kaysar went still as a stern-faced Chantel marched into the room. She'd anchored her mass of sable hair into a severe knot at her nape. Not a single strand of pink. A voluminous black robe draped her.

He shot to his feet, aware of a hammering pulse migrating through his body. *Such power. Such passion and beauty.* She was a fae queen without equal. A velvet-covered blade. A woman beyond compare, and every sexual fantasy he'd ever had come to life.

Why hadn't he savored her these past nights?

Why hadn't she savored him?

The fierce glaze in her mercury eyes struck him as slightly demented, and he nearly dropped to his knees to worship at her feet.

She climbed the dais steps and crossed over, stopping at the throne. She held his gaze, telling him with a firm voice, "Please, excuse me." The request fit her actions but not the added weight in her tone, as if she asked for multiple pardons at once.

He moved aside, waving toward her throne and bowing his head. "Your majesty."

She sat with quiet authority, magnificent with her back ramrod straight. "Shall we proceed?"

Vines shot from the floor, marble slabs flying. The stalks snagged the two men and their guards in punishing vise-grips. Poisonvine thorns injected venom directly into their veins, preventing them from flittering. Or moving. Wet crimson dripped upon emerald leaves.

"Micah," she said, using that same uncompromising tone, "I'll start with you."

As the thorns retracted, the frozen man eked out, "What gives you the right—"

"The Dusklands are mine," she interrupted sharply. "I can do what you never could. Revitalize the land. Perhaps you heard the laughter outside on your way in? Or noticed the garden? It's the first of many."

The pounding cadence in his head that screamed for

retribution…weakened as she spoke. Kaysar was unsure what was happening. Or how. Whatever it was…soothed his battered mind.

Micah scowled, saying nothing.

Chantel banged a fist on the arm of the throne. "With that settled, the First District Court of the Dusklands is now in session. The perfect Judge Cookie presiding. Micah the Former King, how do you plead?"

A CAULDRON OF rage boiled inside Cookie. What Hador and his brother had done to young Kaysar sickened her. The Winter king would be dealt with. Soon.

After her visions of Kaysar's past, she understood him so much better. He stood beside her, a strong tower. And yet he'd never needed her more. Today, he settled his case. Tomorrow, she settled hers.

Had the peek into the past steered their future, as she'd feared? Oh, yes. *Everything* changed today.

Cookie frowned as the silence stretched on, everyone looking at everyone else for answers. She waved an imperious hand. "This is the part where you enter your plea, Micah."

"Plea for what?" he demanded. "I plead for nothing."

"You are charged with the crime of attacking the future and current king and queen of the Dusklands upon their arrival. Fair warning. I'm also the witness of the crime, so I'm going to be difficult to sway."

Micah bellowed, "You are not the king and queen of—"

"So you plead guilty?" She scanned the room and nodded. "Everyone else heard guilty, yes?"

"We attacked the maddened king who randomly appears in the Dusklands to ravage our fields and destroy our beasts," he spat. "The help and the hindrance we will hide from no longer."

"Well. We didn't learn the main lesson, I see. Do not screw with the evil king—his girlfriend might be worse." She dropped her chin, pinning him with her stare. "Are you willing to war for these lands, Micah?"

"Yes," he offered simply, making it clear he meant it. "I've only begun to fight, princess."

"Your Honor," she corrected him.

He frowned, his eyes narrowing. "I have resources I have yet to tap."

"That's good. Because so do I. I won't back down, and I'll never surrender. I will always protect what's mine. No," she added when he opened his mouth to respond. "Let me finish. You are hereby pardoned of your crime."

When his brow furrowed, she explained, "You strike me as an honorable guy. Granted, I'm not an amazing judge of character, only an amazing judge. You fought for your land to the best of your ability, but you lost. Twice. You cannot give my people what they want and deserve, so I won't return them to your care. Take the pass and be grateful I've cleared your slate. One day, we might be allies. But come at me and mine again, and the real battle begins."

Thanks to her connection to the vines, she had no trouble flittering Micah to the swamplands. He could deal with the swamp monster she'd been hearing about.

With the first docket cleared…the time had come for the second and last. Kaysar's choice, whatever it was, decided their relationship.

Her vines squeezed Hador so tightly his face mottled. "No need for a trial. The verdict has come in. Guilty as charged." She cast her gaze to Kaysar. "You decide his sentence, baby. We kill him here, together, or I let him go today, so you can continue your vengeance tomorrow."

Did he understand what she asked? The choice came with consequences, whatever he decided. Be with Cookie, or without her. They'd run out of side options.

If he needed the connection to his sister, so be it. His life, his choice. She would clear the path of debris, and offer him a future. But she wouldn't be second or third place any longer.

Cookie judged herself worthy of more, too.

She purposely kept her features blank of any emotion, unwilling to sway his response.

Sweat dotted his upper lip. His gaze darted between Hador and Cookie. He aimed fury as his past abuser, and desperation at her. Anxiety rippled from him in waves.

Elation swelled in her heart as he stepped closer to her. Then he heaved a tired breath, and she feared the worst. He wasn't ready to give up his quest for retaliation, was he? Not for her. Not even for himself.

Profound disappointment gave way to gut-wrenching hurt, but she revealed none of it. Smiling softly, she told him, "It's okay. There is no wrong answer, Claw Man. What you want, you get. That is *my* gift to you."

"Vengeance," he croaked, his expression savaged. "To-morrow."

Sliced to ribbons, hemorrhaging inside, she held the smile and flittered Hador into the swamplands, next to a fuming Micah. *Enjoy with my compliments.*

Kaysar had made his choice.

Now, they would both live with it.

"What did you do with him?" he asked as his breathing evened out.

"Don't worry. He's alive." It took some effort, but Cookie

bottled up her hurt and placed it on a shelf in the back of her mind. Audience forgotten, she stood and molded herself against the man she loved beyond any doubt or reason, her palm flattened over his racing heart.

His breath hitched, and he tentatively wound his arms around her, as if he feared her reaction.

One last night. Desire surging, she rasped, "Take me to bed, Kaysar."

CHAPTER THIRTY-ONE

KAYSAR FLITTERED CHANTEL to their bedroom, materializing at the foot of the bed, but he didn't kiss her. Not yet. His instincts were pinging again, telling him trouble brewed. But she peered at him with such fervent desire as candlelight bathed her delicate features, he told himself he was mistaken. Only pleasure waited in his future, his dreams coming true right before his eyes.

He had his mate, and he would continue to have his vengeance, the two no longer at odds. Kaysar could hurt Hador Frostline during the day and enjoy Chantel at night. What male in all of Astaria would lead a better life?

His joy knew no bounds. Except for that damningly persistent ping. And a small kernel of unease…set within a larger pod also filled with kernels of disappointment and despair. And he didn't know why.

Now wasn't the time to dissect every thought and emotion. He'd missed Chantel too much to lose himself to fear.

Gently smoothing a lock of hair behind her ear, he told her, "You were magnificent today. A fierce protector of your land, and your male."

"I know." With a sensual maneuver he would forever replay in his fantasies, she shimmied out of the robe. The dark cloth puddled on the floor as Chantel stood proud before him, wearing azure lace over her breasts and between her legs. Miles and miles of creamy skin, flushed with arousal—and marked with a crimson map.

He looked her over, amazed. Humbled. Awed. When he returned his gaze to hers, her irises were set aflame, blazing with wildfire. "You drew this yourself?" he asked, voice breaking at the edges.

"I used dye the servants made with my roses. It's the reason I was late to tonight's festivities. Well, one of the reasons. The map details the palace. The mystical doorway. The treasure troves. I wanted to be perfect for you, no matter what you decided." A pause. Then, "Do you like it?"

His gaze shot back to hers, the fire in his irises brighter. "I will *never* part from you. Woe to anyone who tries to take you from me."

Something shuttered over her eyes, and his heart skipped a beat. Then she purred, "Do you want me naked, Kaysar?"

He forgot every thought but one. "I *need* you naked, sweet."

He watched, mesmerized, as she freed her hair from confinement, the dark tresses tumbling into place. The mind-boggling things he felt in that moment… He nearly staggered at the extraordinary weight of them.

"Let me tell you what *I* need," she breathed, her eyes hooding. "Your kiss. Your touch on every inch of me. Love my body in a thousand different ways and help me forget the hours we spent apart before and the hours we'll spend apart next. Give me everything you promised. Hold nothing back."

Next? The honeyed scent of her desire frayed his control, and he pushed aside his foreboding. "Everything. Nothing," he croaked. She'd utterly consumed his thoughts. "Show me more."

She trembled a little as she unhooked the upper garment,

bearing her beautiful breasts and their tight ruby nipples. A groan lodged in his throat.

"The rest. Let me see the rest." *Missed her so much. Missed this.* The sweet exchange. The sense of communion. The utter peace of passion, every other facet of him shut off.

She dragged her panties down with a waggle of her hips. The cutest kick flung the material away. Then she stood before him, bare.

And he'd thought her proud before. Head high, shoulders back and those lush breasts thrust up for his view, awaiting his caress. "I will play with your body until you scream for me," he boasted. To seal his vow with a kiss, he dipped his head and sucked on one straining crest, then the other.

Her moan of surrender echoed as she shoved her fingers into his hair. He kissed his way up her sternum. The length of her throat. Straightening, he met her gaze. Dilated pupils, glassy irises. He loved how quickly and intently she desired him.

"I'll brand your body until you never forget me," she boasted back.

Awareness crackled in the space between them, the pull stronger than ever before. But even then, he felt as if she were slipping from his fingers. No. He wouldn't let her. With a snarl, he cupped her backside and her nape in unison, forcing her closer.

COOKIE OPENED UP, eagerly greeting Kaysar's tongue with her own. She moaned her pleasure, overcome.

He eased the tempo of his kiss, as if her reaction soothed some ferocious beast inside him. Fast and uninhibited became slow and deliberate, every stroke of his tongue a sensual onslaught.

Possessive. Primal. Ruthlessly...gentle? To gentle her?

He wasn't kissing her anymore. He was making love to her mouth. Seducing her until she had no air in her lungs. Until she couldn't survive without him and didn't want to try.

With an expertly executed movement, he kicked her feet apart and inserted his knee between her thighs. Leather razed her aching clitoris, and she cried out at the exquisite bite of bliss.

Panting a little, he lifted his head and pressed his fevered brow to hers. "You are precious to me. Tell me you know that. Tell me you know I will freely die for you."

"I do know." She truly did. But she would rather he *lived* for her. "You are precious to me, too. I love you. One hundred percent."

Whiskey eyes soft but fierce, he rasped, "You love me?"

"So much." Her legs teetered, almost too weak to hold her body upright. She settled more of her weight onto Kaysar's thigh. *So good, but need more.* Cookie…moved. Yes! She undulated against him, riding his thigh. The friction built. "Feels so good, baby."

His eyelids hooded at the endearment. "You want more of me?"

"I want *all* of you." The tattoos on his chest snagged her gaze. Mmm. *Going to lick him there. There. Everywhere.*

"The way you look at me." His calloused palms rocked her against him, wringing a gasp from her.

Groaning, he pressed his mouth to hers. The first foray of his tongue nearly undid her. He took bold swipes, dismantling her control, and oh, he tasted better and better, every note sweeter. She trembled and ached and fought for breath she couldn't catch. How she burned.

Cookie tore at his clothes. When he stood naked before her, she wrapped her fingers around the base of his shaft.

He picked her up and eased her onto the mattress. The kiss deepened as he braced his fists at her temples. Then, he raised his head, revealing wild eyes and puffy lips.

"I love you, too," he rasped.

The words jump-started her heart, throwing the organ into an erratic rhythm. He loved her, and she rejoiced. She also fought the urge to sob. He loved her, she knew he did, but he didn't love her enough.

Her mind shied away from thoughts of tomorrow. They had tonight, and she would savor every second.

"Kaysar," she breathed as he settled his delicious weight over her. He kneaded her breasts and pinched her nipples the way she loved, pleasure and pressure crashing again and again.

For minutes and hours and days and weeks and only a split second, he worshipped her body, kissing and licking and kneading and branding each part of her. His touch was tender and rough and brutal and gentle, and she adored it. She craved all of him, each side of him equally. And yet, in a matter of hours, she would tell him goodbye.

A strangled sound erupted from them both when he plunged a finger inside her. Helpless against the bombardment of sensations, she arched and clutched at him, clinging. Desperate. "Kaysar. Love. Give me more."

"The things you make me feel," he breathed, working her. His features were agonized, his drive to come as ferocious as hers. Tendons strained and protruded.

The head of his shaft grazed her leg, leaving a trail of wet fire, and she shivered. Shameless, she writhed beneath him. "More." A command. A plea.

"Is this enough for my sweetling?" He fed her a second finger, and she groaned.

"More." She thrashed as the pad of his thumb circled her clit. "I'm so close." There. Right there. There, there, there.

"My insincerest apologies for what's about to happen, your majesty." The diabolical king took his thumb away from her. And his fingers. Argh! As she beat her fists into his shoulders, he grinned with savage, devilish delight. "You don't get your pleasure until I get my screams."

Frenzied mindlessness teased her. "Make me come, Kaysar. I need it. Just one? A small one? I promise I'll scream so loud."

He cupped the sides of her face, tracing his wet thumb over her bottom lip. "You could not be more precious." Though he used a coaxing tone, he looked far from relaxed, sweat slickening his brow and trickling from his temples.

"Perhaps you'll scream only when you come," Kaysar pondered. He licked away the desire he'd deposited on her mouth and rocked his hips, grinding his rigid length against her core. "Perhaps I'll continue your torment all night long."

She gasp-groaned. "Want you in me now. Please, love. Please. I need you. I ache so bad."

"All right, sweet. Let's ease your hurt." Holding her gaze, he finally, finally, finally pressed his thumb against her clit again and slid one—two—fingers inside her. "But sweetling? I'm afraid it's not going to be enough."

Relief parted her lips. Filled again.

He plunged his fingers in and pulled out. In. Out. Scissoring. Stretching. Cookie bowed her back and moaned as a powerful orgasm rolled through her, her sheath squeezing him. An avalanche of heat and pleasure crashed into her, gaining speed. But he was right; it wasn't enough. Her need was simply too great.

"I want more." Did she sound drugged to him? "I know

I didn't scream, but let me show you how much I love you. Won't that be nice?"

"I'll show *you how much I love you*." He flipped her onto her hands and knees. Rising up behind her, he urged her face toward a pillow, forcing her backside higher. With one hand, he clutched her hip. With the other, he massaged the head of his shaft against her swollen clit. "I will go so deep you'll feel me in every part of your body."

"Yes!" Her heart thundered as her chest clenched. "Go deep."

"You'll take me, won't you?" Strain turned his words into glass shards. Massaging… "My beauty is soaked."

And almost levitating! "Kaysar!"

Allowing no reprieve, he set his erection at her entrance and slammed home, filling her with a powerful shove.

Ecstasy…broke. Another orgasm consumed her, wrenching another groan from her. The pleasure! The bliss and the rapture. Rolling on and on and on and on. But still she craved more.

Leaning forward, he planted a fist in the mattress and settled his weight there, pumping into her. "I'm going to be in you every day. Every night for the rest of our lives."

His words drove her crazy. With his free arm, he reached around her to spear her clit between two fingers. As he pumped into her, he rubbed that little bundle of nerves, ratcheting her need higher.

She thrust an arm forward, slapping her palm against the headboard, desperate to hang on to something before the tidal wave pulled her under. Too much pleasure or not enough? Far too much. And, and, and…so good, so good, so good.

"More, Kaysar."

As her inner walls spasmed around his length, he

rolled her hair in one hand, fisting it. With his other hand, he gripped her waist and wrenched her backward as he pounded forward. The entire bed shook. The entire palace might be quaking.

He had her pinned to the mattress, her body under his complete control. The force of every slam vibrated through her entire being, sensitizing already sensitized nerve endings until everything acted as a stimulant. Cool sheets, hot touch. The sweet fog of satisfaction, lust and love. The music of their groans and husky breaths blending.

He pressed a hand into the center of her back, pushing until her distended nipples brushed the sheets with every thrust. Gasping and moaning, she turned her head and caught sight of his reflection in a full-length mirror across the room.

The tatted, screwed-up killer king possessed her without reservation. Bulging muscles flexed. Veins swelled. Sweat glistened as he snapped his hips again and again. Had she ever beheld a more sensual sight?

He turned his head, and their reflections locked gazes. Just like that, her peak reached a new crescendo, and a scream barreled from her.

Kaysar threw back his head, roaring as he came.

CHAPTER THIRTY-TWO

KAYSAR LOVED CHANTEL for hours. His female made him insatiable.

In between ferocious bouts of sexual fever and leisurely exploring, they whispered in the dark about everything and nothing. He soaked up knowledge about her, unable to learn fast enough.

He'd called her "my precious" and she'd laughed with delight, saying, "I'm your precious? Well, I guess that makes you Gollum and me a powerful ring, so yes, I am your precious. Never call me anything else."

A rainstorm raged outside, blustering through the open balcony doors. Sheer white curtains billowed as dew caressed his skin.

For the first time in his entire existence, he experienced complete contentment. A sensation as valuable as it had been elusive. Satisfaction had collected the burdens he'd carried for so long and removed them from his shoulders. He felt lighter than he'd ever expected or dreamed possible.

He and his queen lay side by side, curled together. Fatigue clawed at him, but he refused to sleep. He never wanted this moment to end. Why would he? He had his mate, and they were going to be a family. The people she loved would adore him—he would make sure of it, forever pampering and protecting them.

All really was well. But the word *family* continued

to echo inside his head. A problem nipped at him. For a moment, he imagined little versions of Chantel running around, doing whatever they desired. An unexpected smile bloomed, incredible longing nearly rending him in two. He could sing the darlings lullabies each night.

Except, her children belonged to the Frostlines. Unless he traded Viori's vengeance for a family he didn't deserve. He shook his head. He couldn't, he couldn't, he couldn't.

"Kaysar?" Chantel asked in the candlelit darkness, no doubt sensing his change in mood.

Unwilling to sacrifice the perfection of this time with her, he hurried to distract himself. "Has your glamara recharged?" Was she able to open doorways yet?

"Not yet. I think…well, I think it's tied to my emotions. When I'm happy, I power up fast. When I'm furious, I get temporary bursts of power. When I'm…not happy or furious, I regress."

Guilt singed him. Her powers had weakened before the trial. Because of Kaysar. How unhappy had he made her lately? He needed to learn more about Chantel, so he could make her happy no matter what the situation warranted.

"Tell me about your parents." He smoothed a lock of hair from her cheek. "You once told me you had no desire to relive your childhood in your adulthood. Will you tell me what your childhood was like?"

"My parents divorced—er, split up, which is what I plan to do with Jareth FYI. I mean, for your information. Anyway, Mom and Dad married other people when I was young. They started new families and seemed to forget about me. I got passed between them for a while, but never really fit with either."

Her sad smile made his chest hurt. "I won't leave you again," he vowed. "From now on, we'll render each strike against the Frostlines together." How dare *anyone* not focus their every waking and sleeping moment on this female? "I should have known you raised yourself."

"I—yes. I suppose I did." She snuggled closer. "But why should you have known?"

"Because you do everything well."

Her smile returned, but it still held a tinge of sadness. "What about your parents?"

"They were pixiepetal farmers in the Summerlands. Hard workers who survived rather than thrived, and yet they were happy."

"So the most feared king in the land has humble beginnings, hmm, making him even more impressive than I previously believed." She gave a husky chuckle at the prideful expression he couldn't wipe from his face. "What are pixiepetals?"

"Special flowers that bloom where pixies roost, used as medicine for the fae." Kaysar tracked a smeared line of map along her upper arm. "My parents died of a plague when I was twelve. Viori was such a joyful child before that. But she blamed herself for their deaths. Her voice... It was like mine. Powerful. Compelling. She hoped to save our mother and father from the sickness, but she used the wrong tone and they deteriorated fast."

"Tone truly matters that much?"

"Tone is everything. The vessel responsible for carrying the compulsion."

"I wish I could have known Viori. But. Um. Speaking of." Chantel worried her bottom lip. "I have to confess something."

He went still, not daring to breathe. "You remembered more about Jareth?"

"No, nothing like that."

"Tell me. Whatever it is." The suspense was more than he could bear.

"Earlier, Amber showed me something," she said. "Two somethings, actually. The day you lost Viori, and the day you killed Prince Lark."

Oh. "I'm glad." Kaysar had no secrets from her. "I killed Prince Lark too soon. His death was too easy. I won't make that same mistake with Hador. He'll suffer for centuries more."

Chantel lightly scraped her nails through his beard stubble. "What if your sister is living an amazing life? What if she's married with a million babies? Someone wonderful could have found her in the forest and protected her, the way you found and protected me."

Oh, how he wished. But… "Why hasn't she approached me? Why can't Eye see her?"

She contemplated for a moment, sighed. "All right. Let's travel down the road of worst-case scenario. Viori could have been discovered by a terrible person. She might have suffered and died in those woods."

He squeezed his eyes closed, a hot tear escaping.

His beautiful Chantel wasn't done. She wiped the droplet with a trembling finger, saying, "You might never know the truth about what happened. For the rest of eternity, you'll have to live with the mystery. It's awful, it isn't fair, but it's your reality and there's nothing you can do to change it. Despite that, your most amazing days can await you, if you'll let them."

His eyelids popped open. He shuddered with his next breath, agonized…but comforted? "If I kill Hador at long last, you mean?"

"Yes."

Familiar panic. The moisture in his mouth drying. He

darted his gaze as he struggled to breathe. "I can't," he croaked. "Don't ask it of me." *Not ready to say goodbye.*

Another sad smile, a light in her eyes dying. "I won't, love. I told you I wouldn't ask for this, and I meant it. I never will. Not now, not ever."

His regret persisted and his foreboding resurged, but Chantel and her soothing won his focus. Bit by bit, his muscles softened.

"Imagine your vengeance is satisfied," she said, stroking his chest. Specifically the tattoo that prevented conception. "What will you do with yourself?"

Longing returned, ravaging him. "I'll have children with you. If you want them. We could be a family then."

Her breath hitched. "Oh, Kaysar." Sobbing, she hurled herself into his body and pushed him to his back. She draped herself over him as tremors rocked her. Warm teardrops quickly soaked his chest.

A riot erupted inside him. His heart thudded, his stomach turning over again and again. "Chantel? What is this?"

"I love you so much, and I'm going to give you the most amazing life." She squeezed him tight before sagging against him. "Just hold me, okay? I'm not ready for this moment to end."

That, he understood. Kaysar enfolded her in the strength of his arms. In the silence, his eyelids grew heavy. He fought to remain awake, but that wondrous contentment was spreading through him again, burrowing deeper.

When he realized her heart beat in sync with his, he lost the battle.

"Tomorrow is the start of a long, joyous life for you," she told him softly. Her voice called to him. "Sleep now."

"For you, anything," he said, the words slurred. As Kaysar fell into the abyss at last, he smiled.

I WILL SET him free.

Cookie stole five minutes for herself. Three hundred seconds to savor Kaysar's strength and warmth. Because she knew. By morning, his love for her would morph into hatred. A fact she'd accepted. Better his hatred than his continued misery.

Kaysar craved a family of his own, but he couldn't have it while Hador lived, and he wouldn't want one with Cookie once she did what she planned. Or maybe he would? She didn't know, but she suspected...not.

Either way, she killed Hador today. For Kaysar.

No longer would he be shackled to the past and his unending quest for vengeance. He could create his family with another woman. He could be happy. Cookie's gift to him. That was how much she loved him.

Tears welled anew, but she blinked them back. She must be strong. He *craved* an end to his torment, and she could give it to him. Easily. The only cost—her own happiness. Her future. He *would* hate her, at least for a while. But even still, he needed her to do this. Deep down, he must hope she would settle the matter. So she would.

Fighting another round of tears, Cookie detangled from Kaysar at last. Naked, she strode into her closet, accompanied by flashes of lighting and the pitter-patter of rain.

Kaysar slept on.

She peered at the gown she'd avoided since its appearance in her closet. The white one with sharp angles. A weapon Kaysar had gifted to her. A way to help with this mission, as a part of him must have known. Not wedding apparel, after all, but a supervillain. The merciless assassin willing to do *anything* to avenge little Kaysar and Viori.

The material cinched to Cookie's body, adhering to every curve as if painted there. The sharp edges around the collar, shoulders and wrists fit her current temperament. Split sleeves provided peeks of her arms as she moved. Multiple slits in the skirt did the same for her legs. The hem pooled around her feet, reminding her of a snowdrift.

A thick frost glazed her insides, leaving her icy cold—deadly—in all the best ways. She plaited her hair into war braids. Satisfied with her appearance, she gathered the elderseed she'd plucked from the potted plant and stashed it in her pocket. After flittering to the throne room, she collected the Winter king's blood, stored inside a thorn.

Jareth slept on the dais, but awoke before she could sneak away. He eased up and looked her over. Comprehension dawned, and he whistled. "You are the female he needs, but after tonight, you might not be the female he wants."

"Tell me something I don't know." She raised her chin. "When I return, I'll free you from your bonds." She wouldn't ask—she would just do.

"I don't know if I wish to go," he admitted.

Ready to find and destroy Hador, she flittered to the hallway of treasures. As she passed the elaborate, full-length mirror, something strange happened to the glass, and she slowed. Stopped. Ripples blurred her reflection, raising her hackles. She readied her claws.

The ripples halted, Micah's image filling the mirror, staring back at her. "Hello, Chantel."

Far from relaxed, she nodded. "Micah." He was more handsome up close, rugged and with hidden depths of intensity she'd missed before. But then, in Kaysar's presence, all men paled in comparison. "How kind of you to stop by."

He tilted his handsome head to the side, studying her from head to toe. His expression revealed a grand total of zero thoughts. "You go to kill King Hador." A flat statement, rather than a shocked question.

Why deny it? "I do." She quirked a brow. "Are you planning to stop me?"

"I am not."

"Why accost me then?"

"The Winter king expects you. He waits at our former campground with a hundred armed fae encircling him, each ready to die to protect him and execute you."

Suspicions rose. "And you're telling me because…?"

"If you succeed and Hador dies, as he deserves, then you become Kaysar's greatest enemy."

Ahhh. Smart man. Micah doubted his ability to win against her *and* Kaysar. The dream team. But once Cookie and Kaysar were pitted against each other, their focus divided, Micah's chances for reclaiming the Dusklands skyrocketed.

"The whole of Astaria knows the person who kills the king of the Winter Court replaces him in Kaysar's mind," he said. "You will become a target for the Unhinged One's wrath."

"I'm willing to risk it." For Kaysar? Anything. "You and I will have our reckoning, Micah." He wouldn't stop, but neither would she. "Be aware. I won't leave the palace outside of a body bag."

"Trust me, *princess*. I will *ensure* you leave the palace in a body bag." He offered the threat with a shrug, and she smiled with chilled delight.

"And he trash-talks, too." She raked her gaze over him. "Are you single and possibly interested in an old crone with a few extra miles on her face and a wonderful sense of humor?" Pearl Jean might forget her plethora of diseases if she had a man of her own. "No, no. Don't answer that. Unless you are, in fact, into old crones?"

Blink, blink. "Are you always like this?"

"You mean a motivated go-getter who does whatever it takes to finish the job? Yes. Thank you for noticing."

He frowned but said, "While you battle Hador, I will not attack you, the fortress or Kaysar. You have my word. Before you tell me the offer isn't necessary, allow me to show you why it is."

His image vanished, replaced by another. In a valley between mountains, thousands upon thousands of trolls stood in formation, as still as the statues she'd placed in the throne room. Awaiting a command from their master, King Micah?

Most of the trolls hit the seven-foot mark, though many were taller. Some had horns, others tusks. All had muscles stacked upon muscles.

Cookie decided then and there to acquire an army of her own. Men and women from any court, of any species, willing to pledge their loyalty to her and fight for her kingdom and causes.

Micah's image reappeared, erasing the trolls. He offered her a smug grin. "The guards surrounding King Hador hold containers of stickysap. They have orders to douse you the moment you're spotted."

Ugh. She remembered stickysap. The blood from the killer tree. The substance supposedly like a melding of quicksand and superglue.

"If drenched in it, your vines will cease to grow, rooting you in place," he explained. "I'd rather not have your focus divided yet." .

She pressed her tongue to the roof of her mouth. The king had tricks. Good to know.

Her mission was a bit more complicated now, but change her mind? No. She'd have to be more careful, that was all.

"Any other tips for me?" she asked, ready to get this show on the road.

To her surprise, he nodded. "Avoid contact with Hador. He's a drainer, and his glamara has strengthened over the centuries. With a brush of his fingertips, he can steal energy you are unwilling to concede."

Another complication, but still not a deal breaker. The thing about Cookie? She no longer feared obstacles. She wasn't afraid to die for her cause. No, she welcomed the opportunity. A worthy sacrifice to punish the one who'd wronged Kaysar. "Thank you for the help, Micah. It's not going to save your life if you attack, but it's much appreciated." In another life, they might have been friends.

He offered a slight incline of his head. "Kill him well, Princess Chantel."

"It's Queen Cookie. And he's as good as dead."

CHAPTER THIRTY-THREE

COOKIE SQUEEZED THE thorn she'd collected from the vine, dripping King Hador's blood into the spyglass's container. When she peered through the peephole, she spotted the monarch near the former campground, exactly as Micah had warned. A hundred soldiers surrounded him, waiting for her arrival. Men who stood in the way of Kaysar's happiness.

Tents littered the area behind them, other guards hiding within them, no doubt.

She smoothed the lines of her dress and inhaled. This was it. The day she severed Kaysar's tie with the past. Without a driving need to punish Hador, his dream of peace and family had a fighting chance.

Kaysar could begin to heal.

As they'd lain together, she'd felt his deep longing to let go. She'd known he simply required help.

With a steady hand, Cookie placed the elderseed on her tongue. Chewed. Swallowed.

Heartbeat...

Heartbeat...

Heart*boom*. Power exploded inside her, as hot as she was cold. Thorn claws readied, she flittered to a spot near the camp. She was on the clock now, and she wouldn't be able to flash directly home. She needed to return to the castle before she passed out.

Dusk prevailed, only thin slivers of moonlight penetrating the gloomy veil. At least the pounding rain had dwindled to a light mist. Freezing but perfect for her frame of mind.

She didn't try to hide herself from the soldiers or skulk through their numbers, killing in the cloak of darkness. Wanting Hador to witness every atrocious act she committed against him and those who willingly followed his orders, she stepped into the brightest sliver of light.

The first line spotted her—the men holding the containers of stickysap. Shouts and commands rang out. "She's here."

"Positions!"

"Attack on my signal." Guards obeyed, shifting to prepare.

"How kind of you to gather together for your own slaughter," she called to one and all. "Saves so much time."

"There's no need for a battle this night," the king shouted from the midst of his mercenaries. "Kaysar told you to let me go."

"And I did. His case is settled. Mine is not." Her voice hardened. "You killed my relationship with the man I love. Now, you die."

Cookie waved her hands, throwing a volley of thorns from her fingertips. The elderseed powered the missiles, producing double the number with twice the speed. A row of men grunted as the thorns tore through their bodies; they dropped weapons and containers as they clutched their wounds and toppled. Stickysap poured out, glugging over the ground to create dangerous pools.

Other soldiers blasted her with arrows and spears, but she summoned vines from the earth, blocking them. The wall of stalks absorbed the hits, the stings barely registering.

Footsteps pounded. A lot of them. Foes raced to surround her.

As she pushed forward, winding through the stalks, she summoned other vines—in the midst of the army as well as the tents. Screams rent the air, and the ground shook, coils of vine snatching and squeezing anyone in their path.

The guards able to avoid capture either dropped from the quakes or hurled other arrows and spears at her vines.

When she climbed to the other side of the tangled wall—past the pools of stickysap—she hurled more thorns. Some of her targets fell. Others hacked at the stalks, her slight stings escalating into sharp pains. Still others sprayed stickysap upon her leaves, stunting their growth.

Movement. She spun—Hador leaped over fallen bodies to reach a vine untainted by the adhesive. The entire vine withered to ash before she released it—weakening Cookie.

Micah's warning echoed. *A drainer.*

She released her hold on the ground vines, as well. No more weakening from the king's touch. Dangling soldiers toppled.

"I will drain you to death, woman," Hador bellowed. "You'll never reach me."

He'd been unable to drain her in the throne room, because she'd paralyzed him with venom. She could do it again.

A whisper of noise. She whirled around. Twenty men rushed from the trees, brandishing containers of stickysap, bows and swords. Thinking fast, she sprayed a volley of thorns—at the containers. The thick syrup oozed out, stopping opponents in their tracks, one after the other.

"Argh!" A sharp pain erupted in her calf, and she glanced down. An arrow protruded from her limb.

Black dots flashed over her vision as she yanked the projectile free. Despite the pain, she jumped and dodged other whooshing arrows. Healing came fast. Fingertips burning, she threw more thorns, stopping the soldiers with bows. But she had to grow new vines to avoid a procession of spears, allowing Hador to weaken her further with a simple grab.

Even with wobbling knees, she straightened and unleashed a fury of thorns upon the king, aided by the elderseed. He ducked, avoiding most of the missiles with shocking grace and speed for someone his size. But even as agile and quick as he was, he missed the last one, its poisoned tip slashing through his torso.

As he fought the momentary paralysis, his people raced to surround and protect him. People she downed with thorns, two…three…five at a time. Around them, soldiers tripped over the injured or dead, falling into the random puddles of stickysap.

"Why do you fight for him?" Hador grated into the darkness. He must have realized his team was losing, his numbers dwindling quick. "Kaysar will not thank you for this."

No, he wouldn't. Not until he'd found his happiness and forgiven her. But Cookie didn't bother answering the king as she finished off what remained of his army.

Finally, Hador was the last man standing.

They faced off, only twenty feet apart, surrounded by the dead and dying, raindrops falling in a soft stream.

The king panted heavily and fisted his hands. "I think killing you will bring me great joy. Kaysar will know hurt, as I have known hurt."

Most of her injuries had already healed, but time wasn't her friend. She smiled coldly. "As far as final words go, yours are pretty stupid."

Snarling, he tossed a dagger. She grew a vine, blocking. He'd expected the action and lunged, reaching out with his free hand to touch another section of her vines before she severed the connection. More weakness for her, more strength for him.

That strength empowered him. Made him brave. *He* smiled coldly and trekked closer. Realization. If he got his hands on her or her vines, she would lose the battle, elderseed or not.

Or maybe not. An idea took root. Dangerous, but worth the risk.

For Kaysar.

Dampened by mist and splattered with droplets of sap, Cookie summoned a vine from the ground, catching the king around an ankle, shackling him as she unleashed more thorns.

He grunted as crimson rivers soaked his tunic. Somehow, he fought the venom and crouched, grabbing hold of the vine to drain another tendril of her strength. Which *she* had expected.

Let him think he had this.

She sprinted...jogged...trudged closer to him. Water and weakness blurred her vision, but Cookie kept moving forward. He didn't attempt to stop her. He *wanted* her closer. Finally, mere inches away, she hit her knees, as if she were completely wiped.

Their gazes clashed, and he brightened. He thought he had her. He assumed the wheezing girl had nothing in reserve. That he had only to reach out and kill her.

Fool. "Kaysar believes your suffering ends when you die." The statement eked out between heaving breaths. "I believe it's just beginning. Be a dear and let us know who's right." Using the last bit of strength she possessed, she swung an arm, raking her thorn claws across his vocal cords.

He released her vine to clutch his gaping neck. But he'd filched so much of her power, he healed in seconds.

The moment he recovered, he reached for her. She struck again, raking the thorns from his sternum to his navel, leaving his entire torso gaping open this time. Then, she clawed him again. And again. And again.

Only when he ceased moving did she pause to catch her breath and take stock. He lay on the ground, bleeding, his eyes wide, blood gurgling from his mouth.

Cookie leaned over to clasp a fallen sword. This man had harmed young Kaysar and probably others.

Her arms trembled as she slowly lifted the blade. With glassy eyes, he pleaded for mercy.

"If I'd planned to spare you, I'd have worn a different dress." A lone blow did the trick, his head separating from his body. And like that, victory belonged to Cookie.

Panting, heart a war drum, every muscle on fire, she fell on her haunches. It was done. For good or for ill, Kaysar's abuser was dead.

"Chantel?"

A stouter whistle of wind masked her surprised intake of air. Lightning flashed as she flipped her gaze up. Kaysar stood upon a pile of corpses, his dark hair blowing around a disbelieving expression. His wild eyes darted here and there, horror pulsing from him.

"What have you done?" he croaked. He shook his head, as if to clear his field of vision. "Tell me you haven't done this terrible thing. *Tell me you haven't done this, Chantel.*"

She remained on her haunches, trembling. Because she knew what was coming. The inevitable confrontation. Cookie had thought she'd prepared for it. But how did you prepare yourself to break your lover's heart? To have your own shattered in return? Still, she couldn't regret her actions. Kaysar deserved the future her actions would provide, even if she doomed herself in the process.

"Answer me." His demand sounded more like the last bray of a wounded animal, turning it into a plea to dispute what his eyes unveiled as truth.

Cookie licked her dry lips and labored to her feet. "I killed the Winter Court king. The final Frostline responsible for your suffering."

He blanched, but said nothing.

She extended her hands to him in a silent plea for understanding. "I gave you a chance to live again. A real beginning. The first you've ever had."

His eyes slitted, his broad shoulders vibrating. He ignored her request for connection, acting as if the arms she stretched toward him were invisible. "You didn't give me anything. You stole. You robbed me of my only lifeline."

The bitterness in his voice summoned beads of sweat across her brow. Her stomach pitched, and for a moment she battled unrelenting doubt. But, she'd done the right thing, yes?

"I did this for you," she told him softly, her hands falling to her sides.

A man possessed, he pointed a claw in her direction. "You did this for *you*. You *betrayed* me, so I would have no reason to leave you again."

"I never betrayed you." She took a step back. "But you had *already* left me, Kaysar, even when you were with me."

She'd expected his anger, not the quiet finality of his tone. And that frightened her more than ghost trolls, or centaurs, or any of the multitude of truly threatening things she'd encountered since walking through the doorway into this land. To him. This king she adored.

The man she was losing.

Her shoulders slumped, her eyes burning. "I loved you the best way I knew how, Kaysar."

He stalked closer at last, a predator through and through. The predator she'd never before faced—the one so many other feared. "You planned this," he hissed. "Even as you pleasured me, you planned this."

"Yes." She jutted her chin, unrepentant as she remembered why she'd followed this path. Unrepentant but broken. The cold raindrops blended with her hot tears. "Your obsession was destroying you from the inside out. Now you can heal."

"I don't want to heal! And I don't want you here, in my land, breathing my air." He lunged. Gripping her by the nape, he dragged her through the camp. She struggled to keep up.

"You will heal, Kaysar," she said, "You will heal, and you will regret this."

"Shut up. Not another word."

When she tripped and fell, he yanked her to her feet and kept going.

"Just listen to me. You had linked the king's misery to your sister. You aren't angry with me." Maybe? "You're mourning the connection you think you've lost." The very reason he might never forgive Cookie, even after he healed. Even though a part of him had longed for this very outcome.

His footsteps stalled, and she stumbled into him, bouncing back. He twisted to glare down at her with pure malice. "I assure you, my anger for you is very real."

Cookie tried again, cupping his cheek, but he flinched from her touch. She dropped her arm at her side. "Now, at least, you won't think of Hador when you think of your sister. You can remember the little girl who followed you around as she clutched her pretty doll. You can smile. Peace is yours, if only you'll grab it."

When he started forward at double the speed, dragging her behind him, Cookie's lower lip wobbled. She'd lost. For the first time since discovering her powers, she felt utterly powerless.

As soon as the mountain appeared in the distance, Kaysar flittered her into their castle. To the room with the permanent doorway. He held her before it. "You will leave this realm, Chantel. You will leave, and you will not return. From this moment on, *you* are my enemy."

The way his voice crackled... She'd expected a one-sided war with him. She hadn't predicted banishment.

"Don't do this, Kaysar." Tears gathered and poured. He didn't know she'd eaten elderseed. That she was soon to pass out, and she was too afraid to tell him. Too afraid he'd do this, anyway, and that, *she* couldn't forgive. "Astaria has become my home. I belong here."

"I. Don't. Care." With that, he pushed her through the doorway.

COOKIE STUMBLED THROUGH the portal and tumbled into a dark, wooded area without pixies or poisonvine. Weakness stole through her, as if she'd lost the power of the elderseed as soon as she'd entered the mortal world. Fueled by a surge of adrenaline, she clambered to her feet.

She spun, hoping to dart through the doorway— "NO!" The gateway was gone.

Bone-deep cold invaded her quivering limbs. Fighting to remain upright, she darted her gaze left, right. Trees and bushes, nothing more.

Her vision blurred, obscured by more tears. What was she going to do?

Self-preservation instincts kicked in. Find shelter while

she still had the chance. Soon the elderseed would steal her consciousness. But what if Kaysar changed his mind? What if he forgave her and came to fetch her? She should be here. Maybe they'd even work things out and live their happy endings *together*, after all.

He would remember he loved her. Any minute, he might come.

Cold wind blustered, turning her soaked gown to ice. Her teeth chattered, and she drew her arms around her middle. Though she tried, she couldn't grow leaves to warm herself.

Any minute…

He was stubborn, so he would need a bit of time to work things out in his head.

But he didn't come. A lump grew in her throat, trapping a sob. Cookie stumbled forward, frantically searching the area. Nothing mattered more than survival. She'd find shelter. Call Pearl Jean. Rest. Cry. From there, things got fuzzy.

Something loomed ahead, and her heart leaped in recognition. A cottage. Even though the quaint Victorian beauty struck her as familiar, she knew she'd never visited. Had Lulundria?

Was anyone home? Common sense bellowed, "Only witches who bake people in tea cakes live in cottages like this." Which meant Cookie had a higher likelihood of finding a friend. Finally. Something might swing in her favor.

Although the cottage's owner might take one look at her and freak. Torn white gown. Blood-smeared. Sapsplattered. Twigs tangled in her pink-and-brown waves.

She accelerated and missed the rock in front of her. The sharp edge sliced her foot, the pain slowing her momentum. When had she lost her shoes? Despite the pain, she didn't pause to catch her breath. When she stopped moving, she stopped for good.

Blood trailed her as she climbed the porch steps and staggered over to bang on the door. "Hello? Someone? Anyone?"

No answer.

She banged harder, using the last of her strength. "Please."

Still no answer. No movement or light, either. She tested the knob, surprised when it twisted easily. Obviously the odds of finding a serial killer inside had just doubled. Did she turn around? No.

Hinges squeaked as she pushed the door open, revealing a shadowed space. "Hello?"

Again, there were no indications of life.

Cookie tripped inside, the door whooshing closed behind her. She blindly patted a wall for a light switch. What surrounded her? Normal furnishings? A torture chamber?

She banged into something, and a sharp pain exploded in her big toe. Nausea curled her stomach. Though she fought to remain upright, she lost in record time and crashed to the floor.

A dark cloud engulfed her, obscuring the thoughts in her head.

She'd lost Kaysar.

If he'd used his glamara, there at the end, she might be unable to return to Astaria.

She still loved him.

She might hate him.

She...

Game over, Cookie.

CHAPTER THIRTY-FOUR

COOKIE AWOKE WITH a groan, her eyelids popping apart. Morning sunlight bathed her, and she blinked rapidly to soothe her burning, watering eyes. As her sight cleared, a wood-paneled wall came into focus, and she frowned.

This isn't the Dusklands.

Memories surfaced. Hador's death. Kaysar's reaction. The doorway and her forced eviction. Her heart shriveled, reminding her of her vines when she severed their connection to her.

Had she spent the night in the cottage she'd discovered? The one filled with shadows?

She tried to scramble upright, but her dress had become stiff and itchy and now stuck to the floor. Great. A lock of her hair had gotten stuck, too.

Gritting her teeth, she struggled to free herself. The gown ripped in places, but the material remained adhered to the wood planks. Stupid stickysap.

She lay still for a moment, her mind whirling with next steps. Free herself, obviously. Search the place. Clean up and rush home to Pearl Jean and Sugars. Cookie's forced slumber—however much time had passed—had restored enough energy to produce leaves. Already they budded beneath the surface of her skin. Could she create a doorway at long last?

Tears stung her eyes as she used her teeth to gnaw

through the glued hair. When she finished with that, she contorted in a thousand different ways, finally slipping free of the dress.

After covering her nakedness with leaves, thankful the ability worked, she studied her surroundings. Beautiful furnishings, all antiques, with feminine decorations. Lace doilies and weird porcelain dolls. A tea party set up on the coffee table, each dish made of pink crystal, only in different shades.

Curious but unsure, she prowled through the rest of the cottage. To her relief, no one hid in the shadows, and she found no evidence of cameras. No computers or TVs, either. If someone had visited the place, they hadn't cleaned. Dust layered every surface. What's more, the cupboards were empty.

Her most astonishing finds were framed photos. One contained an image of Angel Ashtower, the creator of *The Fog A.E.* The others included Lulundria and three unfamiliar women, all in modern mortal clothes. The princess must have come here before *and* after getting hit with those ice daggers. But who were the rest?

Holding one of the frames, she padded upstairs, hoping to find a bedroom.

Her search offered a bountiful reward. A master suite waited beyond the last step, a spacious chamber as spinsterly as the rest of the house.

A ruffled comforter with pink flowers draped the bed. A vast closet provided an array of gowns. The same kind of gowns Cookie had worn in Astaria. Her eyes watered all over again.

A tunic hung closest to her. A tunic she'd seen before. In a vision. When the injured Lulundria had fled Kaysar. The bloodstains were gone, the tears lovingly repaired with pink thread shaped in a rose pattern.

Well. Here was confirmation. Lulundria *had* come here to

die. And she'd met with someone—or several someones—who'd repaired the shirt. The women from the photos?

Cookie removed the garment from a hanger with a trembling hand. Forget the princess. Nothing mattered more than returning to Pearl Jean and Sugars.

What was meant to be a quick shower stretched into half an hour as she scrubbed off the battle grime and cut a hunk of hair. She didn't let herself think of Kaysar. Not how much she loved him or hated him or missed him. Certainly not the way he'd hurt her. She didn't wonder if he loved her or hated her or missed her, either, and she didn't care if he regretted what he'd done yet. Because the answers didn't matter in the slightest. Not anymore.

Throw me out once, lose me forever.

Under the spray of cooling water, lingering aches and pangs faded. When finally she emerged from the stall, she almost felt like a brand-new model fresh off the factory line. Almost. She dried off the old-fashioned way and donned the tunic, the hem reaching her knees. Good enough for a trip home. Now she had to figure out where she was. No, she just needed a phone.

Spotting a landline on the nightstand, she rushed over and dialed. Raw emotion battered her as she waited through the rings. "Come on, come on."

Finally, her best friend answered, her voice nothing but a tired rasp. "Hello?"

A sob escaped. "Pearl Jean? It's me. Cookie. I...I'm back."

SEVEN DAYS AFTER Cookie's return to the mortal world, she rested her head on her friend's shoulder, ready to take the next step for her life. They sat in the backyard, reclining on a swing of her own creation, made of vines and cushioned with leaves and flower petals.

After three days of avoiding her and three days of hissing in her face, Sugars had forgiven her for leaving. About thirty-eight percent, anyway. He currently stalked a bug around a garden of roses that had sprung up overnight, despite the cooler weather.

Turned out, the permanent doorway in the Dusklands' castle led straight to Oklahoma. The cottage was less than ten miles from her farmhouse. Cookie had found a map—a lump grew in her throat, but she swallowed it. She'd been able to provide Pearl Jean with exact directions. Only fifteen minutes later, she'd been enfolded in the woman's arms, sobbing and telling her about every trial, leaving nothing out.

"Your doormaking ability returned, huh?" Pearl Jean asked, her tone cautious.

There was no reason to deny it. "It did." Last night, as Cookie climbed into her own bed, in her own home, she'd sensed the full charge of her glamara. She knew she'd have no trouble opening a doorway again, and she didn't have to wonder why. She'd gained control of her emotions, realizing her happiness didn't depend on Kaysar, but herself.

She could rule her kingdom, help her people, love her friends, and do everything she'd ever dreamed—without him. As soon as she'd barred him from her heart, the pain would fade.

"How'd you know, anyway?" she asked.

"Your attitude is much improved today. And before you get the wrong idea, I'm in no way saying your attitude is good. Because it isn't. You're still pouting over your beau."

Pouting? Pouting! "He's not my beau." Cookie didn't

want him in a romantic way anymore. She'd given him every part of her heart, and he'd thrown it—her—away.

"Whatever he is or isn't, you're going back to Astaria, aren't you? Despite cannibal centaurs, ghost goblins and vengeful kings?"

"I am." Though Cookie had been gone from this mortal world only a few weeks, everything had changed. For her, at least. Nothing felt right here. Mortal clothing didn't fit properly. The scents lacked the sweetness she'd grown accustomed to. Her cold mattress reminded her of rocks, sleep impossible. "I want you and Sugars with me. I'll protect you from the monsters, I promise. And I've already picked a boy toy for you. You'll get to live in a castle, of course." She would be winning hers back, whoever she had to fight. "You'll have servants, magical medicine for every disease you're soon to contract, and—"

"I don't need the hard sell, hon. Hot fae men? Of course I'm going with you. That isn't even a question."

She snorted. "You won't be sorry."

"Of course I won't. I'll be with you." Pearl Jean patted her hand. "What about Kaysar?"

"What about him? We're done. I'm in the process of kicking him out of my heart and hanging a vacancy sign. There's nothing he can say or do to make this better. So good riddance. Better now than later. I like being single, anyway. His loss, right? There's plenty of trash in the sea. And I'm not protesting too much, so stop thinking I am."

"Whatever you say, hon."

"I'm moving on," she insisted with a firm nod. Through her example, Kaysar would witness what letting go of a turbulent past and grabbing hold of a bright future looked like. If he chose to war with her, fine. They'd war. She wouldn't kill him; she didn't hate him. But she refused to let him hurt her anymore. If she arrived and he suggested they get back together, well, he could go screw himself.

She'd expected his hate, but not his cruelty. He'd banished her from his life—from her home. A crime that came with a lifetime sentence.

"Are you sure you're moving on? Because you look like you're going to kill someone. And really, what if the man merely suffers from Redirectile Dysfunction? Think about it. You bombed his lifelong plans, forcing him to navigate a new path. He might just need time to acclimate."

"I don't care." She'd given Kaysar *everything*, as she'd said she would, risking her own happiness to purchase his. If he couldn't see that, he wasn't a man worth knowing, much less missing. "And I'm done discussing him."

"Fine. Don't squeeze my head off like you did to those soldiers. Just tell me when we leave, and I'll be ready."

She regretted, slightly, telling Pearl Jean every detail about the battle. "Tonight. Eight," she said with a firm nod. Enough time to do whatever needed doing. She'd been away from home long enough. "I'm not exactly sure what we'll find on the other side of my door, so we'll pack only the essentials. Things we can't live without."

"Deal."

They gathered Sugars and headed inside. The rest of the day passed with a flurry of activity. Cookie decided the essentials included snack packs with arrays of donuts, bottles of wine, a pair of yoga pants and Daisy Dukes, cowboy boots and costumes she'd had overnighted. Also food and litter for Sugars, as well as a special backpack with mesh walls for ventilation and a clear panel for his hobby. Spying.

If she required anything else for him, she'd return to the mortal world for it. The farmhouse had just gotten a demotion, from forever home to vacation retreat.

Pearl Jean selected medications for every ailment known to man and probably some that weren't. A guide for identifying your diseases before they became critical. Yarn and knitting needles. Muumuus for every occasion. A six-pack of beer. And a collection of romance novels they would be sharing.

At 8:07 sharp, they met in the living room. Sugars rested in his pack, secured on her shoulders, and furious to be trapped. The strap of a black duffel bag crossed her chest, the bag itself threatening to topple her with its weight. *Worth it.*

A new game was starting, her excitement reviving. The (currently) displaced Queen of the Dusklands and her scrappy team had leveled up. The prize? A life of adventure.

"You ready?" she asked Pearl Jean…who sat upon her scooter.

Dark blue eyes lively, she honked the scooter's horn. "I've been ready for years."

Deep breath in. Cookie anchored a rope around her waist and gave the dangly end to Pearl Jean. She pictured the spot she wished to land and stretched out her arms. As her audience of one oohed and ahhed, she grew vines from both hands, the stalks linking together in the center of the room, several feet from the coffee table. This time she wasn't pulled through it. She'd gained too much control for that. If Kaysar had compelled her to stay away? Big deal.

"Do not let go of the rope until we've arrived," she instructed.

As soon as her friend offered assurances, Cookie inhaled…and walked through with Pearl Jean remaining close behind. Suddenly, the castle filled her vision. The room with the permanent doorway, aged stone walls and—

"Amber?"

"About time," the oracle cried, rushing over.

The rope fell from Cookie as they embraced, clinging to each other.

Being welcomed by a friend who'd missed her... Nothing had ever felt as amazing as this. Well, except being with— no one of importance. Anyway. Moving on.

"I'm so happy to see you," Cookie said, a catch in her voice. "I missed you terribly."

"Trust me, I missed you, too. *Everyone* missed you. Kaysar has never been more...Kaysar."

Even his name caused her pulse to flutter. "Spill the tea and make it hot. Tell me everything that's happened."

"I will. But first things first." Amber straightened and smiled at Pearl Jean. "So lovely to see you again, Pearl Jean."

Duh! Introductions.

"Again?" her friend asked, confused. "Either I have Alzheimer's or you're the seer Cookie mentioned. I think the little brat referred to you as her first non-geriatric confidant."

"That's me." The oracle returned her attention to Cookie and motioned to a teapot she'd placed on a rock. "Now, your tea."

"That's not what I meant. Oh, never mind. Tell me about Kaysar."

"Well, upon your departure, he summoned his army, stopping an invasion of Micah's trolls. Kaysar has held off those forces from the front line ever since. No one has been able to bypass him to breach the fortress. You can watch the battle from any balcony, and I highly recommend you do." A dreamy smile spread. "Trolls are surprisingly... handsome. So many muscles await your viewing pleasure."

Pearl Jean snagged a beer from her bag, saying, "Don't

mind me. I'm absorbing the conversation. But if you want to repeat that part about the trolls, I wouldn't mind a second listen."

"Why is Kaysar protecting the fortress? For me?" Cookie asked Amber. To give it back to her? Had he realized... *I don't care, I don't care, I don't care.* The answer wouldn't make a difference.

The seer folded her lips between her teeth and shook her head. "No. Sorry. He issued orders that you aren't to be harmed, because you are his enemy. He's protecting the fortress for himself."

The opposite of what she'd hoped—er, expected to hear. Cookie cleared her throat, swallowing a barbed lump. Seemed she hadn't destroyed Kaysar's vengeance, after all. She'd simply given him a new target, exactly as Micah had predicted.

"You were right to ditch him, hon." Pearl Jean belched in her hand. "Let's find you a new beau. I think I recall the seer mentioning something about muscles?"

Cookie pasted an unconcerned grin on her face. "Before I get my friends settled and kick off my takeover, I gotta know. Who are you siding with? Kaysar? Or your beloved queen?"

"Both." Amber gave a weary sigh. "I told him how badly he'd handled things with you, and he banished me from his presence forever. Or until he needs me again. Whichever comes first. With your return, he'll definitely need me. I've seen the twisty road ahead. For once, he's without a map."

Well. "Like I said, I've got a lot to do today. If I'm going to watch the battle, I should change." She had the perfect outfit in mind...

CHAPTER THIRTY-FIVE

KAYSAR RAKED HIS claws over troll after troll. The female who'd taken everything from him had returned, just as Eye had predicted. Thanks to his oracle, Chantel's image was imprinted on his mind. She'd come through the permanent doorway, wearing clothing similar to what she'd worn the day they met.

He dispatched his next opponent. He didn't care about the princess's arrival. She'd stolen his future. The one he'd begun to envision. She'd killed his vengeance, ensuring there was no one to punish for his sister's loss...other than himself. The pain—never—went—away.

He hated his pink-haired queen. But he loved her, too.

He slew another troll, and another. Still another. He'd gone too long without seeing Chantel. Too long without scenting or touching her. Without anticipating the gown she'd donned, or witnessing her brilliance in action as she dealt with her foes. Without cuddling her, or speaking secrets with her, or plunging inside her, or kissing every inch of her, or yelling at her, or challenging her, or begging for her forgiveness, or demanding she explain herself to his satisfaction, or luxuriating in her adoring gaze, and he was breaking inside. One day he feared he might shatter into too many pieces to ever fit back together.

How was he supposed to live this way for an eternity? How could Chantel have done what she did? He'd finally gained the life he'd never known he needed, and with a single act, she'd ruined everything.

She must pay.

Slash. Jab, jab. Duck and spin. Slash. Two trolls dropped. Had Chantel paid already? Had she paid *enough*? She'd been so weak when he'd pushed her through the doorway. Where had she ended up? If someone had harmed her...

He shook his head, pretending he hadn't considered following her through the doorway countless times. No. Eye had also assured him Chantel's safety was never at risk—only her heart.

With a roar, he massacred another dozen trolls. He could have sung, but he had no desire to end the fight too soon. Grunts, groans and cries of agony rang out, creating the perfect melody. The stench of death saturated the air, as heavy and as cloying as a thick morning mist.

"You know she is returned, yes?" The question came from Jareth, who fought at his side.

He'd freed the prince from his shackles the day Chantel had left Astaria, but the annoying male had followed him around like a bad habit ever since. Although, he supposed Jareth wasn't a prince anymore, now that his father was dead. The male was to be crowned the sovereign ruler of the Winter Court.

"Leave before I give you the troll treatment," Kaysar snapped. Two other bodies toppled.

The fool stabbed a troll of his own. "You should apologize to her."

"She betrayed me." So why didn't he long to kill her? Why did he sometimes long to gather her close and cling, as if his life depended on it?

Hack. Rip. Stab. Stab. Stab. More trolls fell.

"She set you free," Jareth pointed out.

"*This* isn't freedom." He hacked through a line of combatants. This was misery.

"With one hand on your vengeance and one hand on your mate, the tug-of-war was ripping you in two. You could go nowhere, except in pieces. Maybe that's why you needed her to wield the strength you couldn't, hmm? You sought healing the only way you know how—through the misery of another."

"No." Healing? When he'd never felt more vulnerable? Hack, hack, hack. He had absolutely nothing left. He would never have sought this position. Except…

When Kaysar had filled her closet with gowns, he'd purposely given the white dress a place of honor. One easily noticed. Even though he hadn't known why. He'd only known he'd thought, *She will save us both in this*, the first moment he'd beheld it.

His motions slowed.

Now, at least, you won't think of Hador when you think of your sister. You can remember the little girl who followed you around as she clutched her pretty doll. You can smile. Peace is yours, if only you'll grab it.

Her words echoed inside his head. *Had* she saved Viori, by saving him? She had removed the only obstacle in the way of their future together. Had ended a chore he'd no longer enjoyed.

His motions slowed further. Even in the middle of his storm of hurt and fury, Kaysar thought he sensed a sliver of…peace. For the first time in memory, he could imagine Viori happy, wherever she was. Just as Chantel had promised he would.

Neither of his abusers walked the land, lying to their subjects in public, hurting innocents in private. The con-

stant pull to cause pain and suffering to his foes—as well
as himself—had eased. Current circumstances excluded.

Was he healing?

A confused Jareth battled around him, acting as a guard
when Kaysar came to a complete stop. Had he yearned to
let go of the past and lied to himself about it? Him, the unrepentant truth teller? Had he longed to move forward?
Had he hoped for more? For better? Had he then passed
the blade to Chantel, unable to make the cut himself, and
blamed her for the outcome?

Surely he didn't.

But what if he did?

The moment—the very second—he entertained the possibility, he had no defenses against it. The truth suddenly
shined so clear. He *had* yearned and longed and hoped. To
protect himself from the pain of letting go of his past—his
sister—he'd let himself believe Chantel had betrayed him.

He'd betrayed himself. What was worse, he'd betrayed
her.

An agonized groan burst from Kaysar, regret and shame
slicing his calm to ribbons. He'd hurt the only person who'd
loved him.

*You protect, honor and respect what you value—or you
lose it.*

He'd owed Chantel everything, yet he'd treated her like
garbage. Would she forgive him? He wasn't sure he could
forgive himself.

He…he… Why were the trolls forgetting about his presence? The troll army had ceased fighting; the soldiers faced
the fortress where poisonvine slithered down, down, down
the walls, sweeping over the battlefield, catching trolls
without squeezing the life from them.

Heart in his throat, he cast his gaze higher… A woman

stood upon the throne room balcony, sipping from a wine-glass. Pink and sable hair danced in the breeze. A half top squeezed her breasts together and bared her perfect mid-riff. A pair of tiny blue shorts possessed so little material, the inside pockets stretched beneath the hem. The strang-est boots rode to the center of her calves.

Kaysar clutched his chest and stumbled. Had any female ever exuded such magnificent beauty?

Desperate to win back the greatest gift he'd ever re-ceived, he flittered to the balcony.

"Hello, Kaysar." Chantel's voice was a light in a dark, barren wasteland. A beacon.

He had to plead his case. Had to get past her hurt and fury. Could he? "Chantel—" When he stepped toward her, she halted him with a vine. The thorns pierced his torso.

"My foes aren't allowed near me...unless I'm about to kill them. Also, you can call me Cookie."

He held up his hands, palms out, while bellowing curses internally. "Chantel. Cookie. I will call you anything you wish, but I will never be your enemy."

"I'm confused. Are you or aren't you the man who tossed me out of my home? Didn't you issue an edict that I wasn't to be harmed by others so *you* could harm me?"

He flinched. "A thousand times, I almost went through the doorway to find you." Only three things had stopped him: his wrongly directed rage, his utter stupidity and Eye's assurance. "I should have done it, despite Eye's assurances about your safety. The regret I feel now..." It had begun to claw at him.

She'd tried to warn him, hadn't she?

With a slow, easy drawl, she told him, "Maybe we're not enemies, but we're definitely not friends, either. So don't give the past another thought. It's over and done. Now we move on."

Over and done? If only. Move on? Never. He scrubbed a hand over his face. How could he reach her? "I long to make amends. I'm so sorry, sweetling. I—"

"Sorry?" She chuckled. The awful thing? She actually sounded amused. "You don't need to be sorry, Kaysar. I actually understand your anger and your actions. I'd even expected them. And honestly, looking back, I can see I missed a crucial fact. You'd already had your free will taken from you once before, yet I callously did it again. For that, *I'm* sorry. But you took away the only things that matter to me. My home and my family. I can't trust you not to do it again."

The words were a blow, but he persisted, trying to explain. "When I saw Hador's body, I felt as if I lost my sister all over again, as if I failed her in every way imaginable. I lashed out. Admitting that you'd done what a secret part of me hoped you'd do meant I had to admit that I *allowed* her to be lost to me a second time. That I wanted to let go." The guilt ate at him even now, but its razor-sharp teeth had dulled. "I am so sorry," he repeated.

"It's fine, Kaysar. Really," Chantel said after sipping her wine. "I've remembered more of my time with Jareth. Who knows? Maybe there's something there."

Panic and jealousy frothed. He tried again to step forward, to touch and hold her, but the vine pushed him back. "I love you. With every part of my being, I love you. If you wish to be with Jareth, I...I won't stop you. But please, sweetling, give me a chance to prove I can be the better male for you."

Another sip. With a determined pivot and sad glance over her shoulder, she told him, "There's no need. You can't. And there's no need to prolong this, either. No reason to fight an unwinnable battle and waste everyone's time. I truly hope you have a nice life, Kaysar. I certainly plan to. Maybe we'll see each other around."

THE MEET AND GREET with Cookie's subjects arrived two weeks after her confrontation with Kaysar. Who she refused to miss. Or even consider. He'd maintained his distance, as she'd asked. And that was great. Everything was great. Wonderful. But...

He'd also negotiated a temporary truce with Micah. The other king would be setting up camp on the other side of the Dusklands, where he would stay for a year. Anyone who wished to serve him, could. Any who opted to remain with Cookie, would. Once the year was up, all bets were off.

Kaysar was working tirelessly to ensure she had a secure home, and she didn't know how to feel about it.

Anyway. Cookie had chosen a skintight, strapless scarlet gown with a heart-shaped neckline and pooling hem for the occasion. A high-collared cape draped her shoulders. Ruby jewels glittered from her ears, neck and wrists. On her head, a crown of her own thorns and roses. She'd almost picked the crystal one Kaysar had given her, but she hadn't wanted to think about him every second of the event...like she was doing now.

She drummed her thorn nails against the arm of her throne. The man didn't deserve her consideration. He'd claimed he'd wanted her; when she'd shot him down, he'd ditched her. Again. *Anyway.* Enough of that.

She'd decided to be a queen of hearts. She would win her people with her fair judgments and an amazing revitalization plan. Anyone who harmed innocents would face

Judge Cookie. Everyone else would just have to learn to live with her ever-changing personality quirks.

Speaking of personality quirks, Pearl Jean and Sugars had settled in nicely. Pearl Jean had moved into the room next to Cookie's, and Sugars had claimed the entire castle as his toy box. Servants doted on the oldest-looking person in all the land and treated the hissing little panther with the adoration he deserved.

The two had thrones of their own, Sugars to her left and Pearl Jean to her right.

Only Amber and Jareth had visited Cookie. She'd told the prince everything she'd learned about Lulundria and given him the photo she'd pilfered from the cottage, and he'd unashamedly shed a tear. Cookie had hugged him, affection for him growing. Affection, but nothing more. She actually counted the guy as a friend.

He stood between the biggest thrones, acting as guard as joyous citizens of the Dusklands brought her gifts of welcome, thanks and praises. Plant life thrived once again, and the people celebrated.

"What's the holdup?" Pearl Jean demanded. She took to her role as second-in-command *quite* seriously. "Where's the next well-wisher? Let's get this done." Rubbing her lower back, she shifted to get more comfortable. "My sciatica is flaring."

Sugars yawned.

Fae, minotaurs, centaurs and an assortment of other species had traipsed about the throne room for hours. But Cookie had seen the line before convening with her first subject. The procession should continue for hours more. So why wasn't anyone movi—

Never mind. The answer strutted inside with a determined expression. Kaysar. Her heart jumped at the sight of him. He looked good. Shirtless. Leathers. Combat boots. Eyes and hair wild. Amber strode behind him.

"Is that who I think it is?" Pearl Jean asked softly. "Because me-wow."

He stopped before the dais and bowed. "Your majesty."

"Kaysar," she said with a nod. "I have nothing left to say to you." And yet, she longed to hurl herself into his arms. But she'd made that mistake before.

"I know you don't, sweetling. So, if you don't mind, I'll do all the talking." He offered a small but affectionate smile, and her chest constricted. "I have tasted of what life is like without you, and there is no worse future for me. My lesson has been learned. That is why I've come to welcome you to the Dusklands, as so many others have, and pledge my fealty. From this moment on, your enemies are my enemies. Those who wrong you, wrong me. Those who harm you will suffer my wrath in ways that would make my treatment of the Frostlines seem like a child's game. My present and future belong to you. I humbly beg you to accept them, but I understand if you refuse. Either way, you are my only family, and my loyalty remains unwavering."

"Kaysar—"

"There's more," he interjected. As she watched, slack-jawed, he sank his claws into his shoulder and with a little digging, ripped off the birth control tattoo. He tossed the section of flesh at her feet. An offering. "My vengeance against the Frostlines is over. Done. When you are ready for children, I am ready to give them to you."

"Now, that's a grand gesture," Pearl Jean said, sharing a grin with Amber.

Her mouth floundered open and closed. "You once told me any children I bear will belong to the Frostlines."

"Jareth will permanently disavow his marriage to you,

or Jareth will die," Kaysar said with a glare at the other man. "Any children we bear will be known by one and all as ours. They will rule *our* kingdoms. The Midnight Court and the Dusklands."

Don't give in. Not again. "I just can't—"

"There's more." He snapped his fingers, and two soldiers raced into the throne room. The first carried a small birdcage with…not a bird inside. What *was* that? The second hefted a medium-size box. "For the queen's handmaiden, Pearl Jean, I gift the heart of a royal fae." The guards placed the gifts at the edge of the dais. "I assure you, the recipient was most deserving of its loss. The organ is mystically preserved. If ever she decides to live forever, she has only to eat it. For the royal feline, I bring a box made of enchanted wood. Inside it, he will heal from any injury. Among other things."

"She says yes," Pearl Jean called, already rushing over to claim the birdcage with grabby hands. "Do I eat the whole thing or just a bite? Never mind. I'll eat the whole thing to be safe."

Cookie did not even want to know which royal had parted with their life. "I… No." She shook her head, refusing to get her hopes up again. Kaysar had given her the most amazing gifts. But this was what he did. Grand gestures. Disappointment always followed on their heels. "I meant what I said. I can't trust you anymore."

He closed his eyes for a moment, as if overcome by pain. When he faced her again, he raised his chin and rolled his shoulders. "I know that, too. But I'm willing to go to great lengths to ensure I have the time to earn back your trust."

Oh, really? "And how do you plan to do that?"

He flittered to the dais, a length of chain in hand and hooked one end of the chain to her throne. Then he moved several feet away, out of her reach. With his hot gaze on her, he slapped a metal collar around his neck—a link of chain kept him tethered.

Oh, no he didn't. "Remove the collar, Kaysar. Now." She hated to see him in it, knowing the cost.

"I will. After my mission is complete, my team back together."

"Kaysar." She white-knuckled the arms of her throne. "You can't just—"

"I have two other gifts for you," he interjected once again. He moved directly in front of her, with his hands braced on the chair. "I give you the three little words you have deserved for so long—you were right."

Her breath caught. Okay, yeah, the pronouncement got to her. Maybe she could give him another chance, after all?

"Last," he said, "I give you *my* heart. In every incarnation." He dropped to his knees before her and sank his claws into his chest, where the skin had already begun to heal. "I will show you how it beats for you."

Cookie grabbed his wrist, stilling his hand. "Don't," she commanded. Chained was bad enough. But injured, too? "Let me think for a second."

With a soft, hopeful expression, he told her, "Please, do. I'll be here no matter how long it takes. You are stunning, by the way. You captured my heart all over again at first sight."

Astonishing. He understood her choice of outfit. But then, he'd always understood her moods, hadn't he?

As Cookie's heart thudded, her mind whirled. The man whose freedom had been stolen as a child was willing to give up his freedom as an adult, simply to be near her, proving his claims with action.

Now he watched her so earnestly, as if nothing mattered more than her response.

Did she believe he'd forgiven her for the terrible act she'd committed for a greater good? Yes. So how could she not do the same and forgive him for something he'd done in the midst of a centuries-long culmination of grief? Why was she holding on to her hurt, letting fear rule her life?

Yes, he'd messed up and lashed out. But he'd owned it, and he was fighting to get her back. Fighting. For her. He was doing everything in his power to make amends, as promised. And she did love him. So much. The complicated king with a thirst for revenge had brought her to life in ways her two hearts never had.

Without hurt there to color her thoughts and perceptions, she had to admit the truth. Her desire for him had never faded. If anything, she craved him more than ever. Nights without him sucked. Days without him sucked worse. Even with Pearl Jean and Sugars here, she'd felt so alone.

For Cookie, Kaysar was connection and connection was Kaysar.

She met his gaze once again, and he smiled so brightly her eyes watered.

"You've forgiven me one hundred percent?" he asked, winding his arms around her to slide her butt to the edge of the seat. "You'll wear the team uniform again?"

"I have, and I will." Leaning toward him, she cupped his cherished face. "We can start a new game. So remove the collar and take me to—"

Blink. The collar was gone, and Cookie and Kaysar were inside her bedroom, flat on the bed. He peppered soft, lingering kisses all over her face, giving each of her features a personal welcome home.

"I love you today," he said between those kisses. "I'll

love you tomorrow. And the next day. And the next. And the next. There won't be a single moment you aren't certain of my adoration for my precious."

Smiling, she cupped his jaw and met his gaze. "Your enemies are mine, Kaysar. Those who wrong you, wrong me. Those who harm you will suffer *my* wrath. My present and future belong to you."

How he loved his mate. "I will give you the world, Chantel."

She winked at him. "Not if I give it to you first."

EPILOGUE

KAYSAR HELD A naked Chantel in his arms. After a two-week marathon of lovemaking she'd referred to as "make-up sex," they lay intertwined on their bed, talking as they loved to do.

"Jareth's coronation as king is tomorrow," she said with a grin. "I'd like to attend."

"Then we shall attend," he replied. Though he hated to admit it, and he would never admit it again, he kind of liked the pup.

"He's asked that we not kill anyone."

"And you told him…?"

"That I can't make any promises. What if someone deserves it?"

"That's my darling girl." Always thinking fifty slaughters ahead.

She traced a fingertip around his nipple. "Is it bad that I hope someone deserves it?"

He smoothed a strand of hair from her cheek, hooking it behind her ear and smiled. "It's perfect, love. You are perfect." Strong enough to do what he couldn't. Brave enough to free the wounded bear from its cage. "Before we leave, you should fill the palace with poisonvine, so that Micah can't enter it without suffering. Lest he decide to renege on our bargain or sneak in and steal something."

"Of course," she said with a nod. "You know, you should take me to see the Midnight Court first. I should tour the place, so I can explain to Jareth all the reasons your kingdom is better than his."

Kaysar shot rock hard. She knew how to arouse him in seconds.

He kissed her brow, the tip of her nose, her lips. "It's not my kingdom, love. It's ours. What's mine is yours, and what's yours is mine. And stopping by the Midnight Court is wise." He thought for a moment. "I suppose I must command a portion of our armies to cease warring with Hador's—Jareth's soldiers at some point."

"Speaking of our armies, do you think…maybe… possibly…any of our men have a thing for horny old ladies?"

"Pearl Jean seeks a suitor? Very well. Only the best for our friend."

The bedroom door opened. Though no one peeked into the room, Pearl Jean called, "Sorry, but this is happening. He's been a little monster, and I'm too busy coming down with a fae-cold."

The door closed after Sugars strode inside, the master of all he surveyed. He jumped on the bed, claiming a spot on the pillows.

The cat had taken an instant liking to him. In fact, the little darling preferred him to anyone else, including Chantel. A fact she found highly amusing.

Contentment cocooned Kaysar, as surely as Chantel's vines often did. Life had never been better.

Perhaps he and Chantel would spend some time searching for Viori. He kept Drendall on lock and key at the Midnight Court, awaiting his sister's return. Until he found her or her body, he would not give up. Not again.

All would be well.

For the first time in his life, he believed it with every fiber of his being.

* * * * *

Read on for a sneak peek at New York Times
*bestselling author Gena Showalter's thrilling
and sexy novel,*

The Warlord

the first book in her Rise of the Warlords series.

PROLOGUE

Excerpted from The Book of Stars
Author unknown

THEY ARE ANCIENT WARRIORS, *evil to the core and loyal only to one another. Known as the Astra Planeta, Wandering Stars, the Warlords of the Skies—the beginning of the end—they travel from world to world, wiping out enemy armies in a single battle. Drawn to war, they finish even the smallest skirmish with pain and bloodshed.*

To see these warriors is to know you'll soon greet your death.

With no moral compass, they kill without mercy, steal without qualm and destroy without guilt, all to receive a mystical blessing: five hundred years of victories without ever suffering a loss.

If they fail to obtain this blessing, they automatically receive the curse: five hundred years of utter defeat.

The time has come for the next bestowing, each Astra Planeta forced to complete a different task. To start, their leader, Commander Alaroc "Roc" Phaethon, Emperor of the Expanse, Rock of the Ages, Giant of the Deep, the Blazing One, must wed an immortal female of his choosing. Thirty days after the vows are spoken, he is to sacrifice this bride on an altar of his own making. If she dies a vir-

gin, even better. He and his men receive a second blessing. If not...his greatest enemy receives it.

The Commander has never wavered in his duty. He cannot. If one Astra fails to complete his task, all fail.

Little wonder Roc will cross any line to succeed.

There has never been a woman alluring enough to tempt him from his path. No warrioress powerful enough to overcome his incredible strength. No enchantress desirable enough to make him burn beyond reason.

Until her.

CHAPTER ONE

Harpina, realm of the harpies
2248 AG (After General)

THE NIGHT OF her ninth birthday, Taliyah Skyhawk stalked through the royal Harpinian gardens amid a chorus of buzzing locusts and chirping birds. She approached a blazing firepit where multicolored flames crackled. Three moons painted surrounding thickets with an eerie, cerulean glow, the scent of skullflowers and smoke hanging heavy in the air, saturating her every inhalation.

Her mother, Tabitha the Vicious, stood shoulder to shoulder with her aunt Tamera the Widow-maker and her fifteen-year-old cousin Blythe the Undoing—Taliyah's idol. The armed trio created a wall of strength.

"A death squad? Just what I wanted," she quipped, but no one smiled.

Rather, her mother readjusted her pose to better show off a sword made of fireiron. A material used to battle fae and other elemental species. "Kneel," she ordered, her small fangs bright in the firelight.

Excuse me? Taliyah's gaze darted from one family member to the other. What was going on? Earlier, when Blythe requested a midnight meeting, Taliyah had expected a surprise party. Maybe a few games. Pin the dagger inside the enemy had always been a favorite.

"Kneel," Aunt Tamera echoed. She wielded a demon-glass dagger, the best tool against angels and Sent Ones. Those who came from the heavens.

Blythe gave a firm nod of encouragement. "Kneel." She clutched a stake carved from cursedwood, the best defense against demons, witches, vampires and even harpies.

Screw this. Taliyah narrowed her eyes. "I'll kneel for my General because I respect the position, but only my General."

"Good answer." Her mother smiled…and promptly swept Taliyah off her feet with a brutal kick.

She crashed into a too-cold ground that never lost its chill, no matter the season, air abandoning her lungs. Without pause, she scrambled up.

Her aunt's gut punch sent her tumbling down once again. Stars winked through her vision, but still Taliyah scrambled up. No time to gloat. Blythe darted behind her and dipped low, slicing the tendons in her ankles.

Pain flared as she hit her knees, breathing more difficult. *Still* she attempted to clamber up.

Never accept a picture of defeat.

She had to pick her poison. The pain of persevering or the agony of regretting. She chose perseverance, every time.

Striving, struggling. Her lower body refused to cooperate, keeping her in a subservient position. Taliyah remained determined. You only lost when you quit.

Panting, fighting harder, she glared up at women who should rejoice that she loved and trusted them. "Someone better tell me what's going on before I rage."

Her mother's eyes glittered in the darkness. "The time has come, daughter. In twelve months, you will leave your family to begin your combat training, just like the harpies before you. Unlike the others, you must train as you are meant to be, not as you are."

Wait. "This is some kind of ritual for status or something? Well, why didn't you say so?" The tension drained from her. Until she replayed some of her mother's words. "How am I meant to be?" Because she liked herself just fine, thanks.

Ignoring her questions, her mother asked, "What do you want most in life, daughter?"

"You already know the answer." They'd had this conversation many times already.

"Tell me anyway," her mother commanded, her expression every bit as vicious as her moniker warned.

With black hair, amber eyes and bronzed skin, the Vicious looked as fragile as an elf and as innocent as a Sent One. Even dressed in leather and chain mail, she appeared incapable of cursing, much less killing everyone around her.

The white-haired, blue-eyed, pale Taliyah shared her mother's delicate bone structure, but nothing more. Well, and her fiery temperament. "I fight to become harpy General."

These women had drilled the words into her head. At some point, the desire had become her own. For harpies, a General was the equivalent of a queen. The ruler who led her people to greatness. Who wouldn't want to rule?

Aunt Tamera lifted her chin, just as cold, beautiful and deadly as her younger sister. "What are you willing to do to achieve this goal?"

"Anything."

"List them," she insisted.

Any harpy vying to become General must accomplish ten specific tasks. "I will serve in our army for a century and win the Harpy Games." A series of contests meant to reveal strength, speed and agility. "I will convince the reigning General to do something she doesn't want to do, and also present her with the head of her fiercest opponent. I'll oversee a victorious military campaign, negotiate a major truce, steal a royal's most prized possession, win a battle with my wits alone and sacrifice something I dearly love."

"You listed nine tasks. What of the tenth?" Her mother arched a brow. "When the time comes, you must challenge the reigning General to battle, no matter who she is or what she means to you. Do you have the courage for this?"

"I do." As mandated, Taliyah would do it all while remaining a virgin, her body given to her people. Which wasn't really a hardship, because gross. Boys were big babies. Break their faces, and they cried for days. "Nothing will stop me."

"Why will you do these things?" Tabitha asked.

"Because I'm Taliyah Skyhawk, and *nothing* will rob me of my birthright." Other words her mother had drilled into her head.

As soon as she'd learned to walk, she'd begun to prepare for the privilege of becoming General. Something many harpies attempted, but few accomplished. But, from the very beginning, Taliyah had proved more determined than most.

While others searched for ways around a problem, she grabbed the problem by the balls and squeezed. Others complained when a door of opportunity shut, then waited for another to open; she beat her way through whatever door she pleased with frightening focus.

Everything happened for a reason? Yes. That reason often involved her fists.

"You aren't just Taliyah Skyhawk." Her mother offered

the barest hint of a grin, as if proud of her. "You will go by many names throughout your lifetimes, daughter. To others, you are the Cold-Hearted. To us, you are forever Taliyah the Terror of All Lands."

Terror of All Lands. Tal. A grin of her own spread. "I am the Terror of All Lands."

Her mother dipped her head in affirmation. "You are stronger, faster and far more powerful than other harpies. I made sure of that by handpicking the male I wished to father my first child."

Procreating by design was a common practice among harpies. A must when you were related to demons and vampires, and everyone referred to your species as "beautiful vultures." Many armies hunted harpies for sport. Or worse!

Nowadays, the harpies who decided to squirt out a couple of kids selected powerful males who produced more powerful children.

"You speak of the snakeshifter," Taliyah said, trying to hide her eagerness. Over the years, her mother had only ever shared the man's species. For so long, she'd wondered...

"He isn't a snakeshifter. Not entirely. He is the *creator* of snakeshifters...and he's only one of your fathers."

"What?" Um... "*What?* How many fathers do I have?"

"There are two, and they are brothers, one able to possess the other, something you will never mention to others. Even your sisters cannot know."

Her gaze dropped to her mother's rounded belly, where twins named Kaia and Bianka grew. She gulped.

"Do you understand, Taliyah? We must take this secret to our graves. If ever *anyone* discovers the truth about your origins, you are to kill them without delay."

"But *I* don't even know what I am now!" *Reeling.*

"I'll explain," her aunt piped up. "Before your birth, the brothers appeared in Harpina every fifty years. One terrorized our villages, and we couldn't stop him. The other mended the survivors. Sixteen years ago, the two appeared to me in secret and offered to spare us for a time...if I spent the night with them." Her tone thinned. "Though I fought to become General, I agreed to their bargain. Nine months later, I gave birth to a healthy baby girl."

Tamera had given birth only once. Which meant... Blythe had two fathers, too? Wait. Blythe was Taliyah's sister? *Reeling faster.*

"Five years later," her mother said, her tone just as tight, "the brothers reappeared. This time, they came to me, offering the same bargain. I agreed, despite my own bid to become General. Nine months later, I birthed you."

Taliyah licked her lips. *So much to digest. Too much at once.* She centered on the most difficult to accept, trying to make sense of it. Her fathers. In history class, she'd learned about twin brothers who'd done exactly as described. Warriors so powerful, they evinced terror in everyone they faced. *Not just warriors. The sons of a god.*

"I'm a daughter of Asclepius Serpentes and Erebus Phantom, sons of Chaos." The words tasted odd on her tongue.

Asclepius was known as the Bringer of Life, a god of medicine able to raise certain immortals from the dead. He was also the creator of snakeshifters and gorgons.

Erebus was his opposite. Known as the Bringer of Death, he destroyed whatever he touched. His contribution to immortal species? The creation of phantoms. Mindless soldiers able to take both spirit and bodily form. To survive, these phantoms consumed the souls—the very life—of the living. A grotesque act to harpies. To all immortals, really.

The two were gods in their own right, yes, but they came

from a greater god known as the Abyss. That meant... *I came from the Abyss.*

Well, of course I did! Frankly, she was amazing. A defender of all harpykind.

"Where are the brothers now?" Oops. Did she sound too eager? Harpies weren't supposed to care about such matters.

Her mother hiked a shoulder, the answer clearly of no importance to her. "Rumors suggest the two picked a fight with the wrong warlords, men who once served as Chaos's personal guards. They killed the brothers, but Erebus came back...wrong."

So, one father was dead and gone. The other lived, but not well. Her stomach churned. "Does Erebus know about me? Does Chaos?" Would they visit her? A flicker of hope sparked. Maybe they'd want to get to know her or something.

"If they know of you, daughter, they care not. You are nothing to them, and they are nothing to you."

"Right." Her shoulders rolled in the slightest bit. "Good riddance, I say. Who needs them?" She did just fine on her own. Better than fine! The best! The pang in her chest bore no significance to the situation.

"You're right. You don't need them. Soon, you'll wield abilities beyond your wildest imagination."

She perked up at the thought of new power. "What abilities?" And how soon?

"You won't know until you've shed your first skin for your second," Blythe told her. The black-haired, blue-eyed beauty smiled and—Taliyah gasped. Her irises! Specks of black shimmered in their depths. "If you're like me, you'll push your spirit from your body, possess others, communicate with the dead, walk in the spirit world to spy on your enemies and recover from any death...even your first."

Her *first*? She zoomed her gaze to the weapons. Realization punched Taliyah, leaving her winded. Her family planned to kill her and raise her as a phantom.

Warring impulses surged, one after the other. Flee. Protest. Cheer. Die? In the end, she bit her tongue and remained silent. What mattered more than her dream? To walk in the spirit realm and spy on her enemies, to recover from death...

She would do *anything*. There'd be no greater General.

"I, too, fight for the right to rule," her cou—sister said. "When the time comes, the two of us will be forced to battle for the honor. But it will be a fair fight. Fair and right."

"Fair and right," Taliyah repeated with a nod. "But I'm still going to win." Facts, and all.

Blythe gifted her with another grin, there and gone. "We shall see."

"Like your half sister, you will only ever use your new powers in secret." Her mother's harsh statement cut through the night, the slightest tremor shaking her. "Erebus and Chaos have enemies who will stop at nothing to apprehend and use you, if ever your identity is discovered. Do you understand? For all we know, the gods themselves will want you dead."

Though she feared nothing, Taliyah offered a clipped assertion. When had the Vicious ever trembled? "I understand."

Satisfied, her mother lifted the fireiron sword. The dark metal glinted in the moonlight. "Are you prepared to die to become the phantom you were meant to be, my daughter?"

No! "I...am?" Though she hadn't yet lived a decade, Taliyah had already participated in two major battles. The first with Sent Ones—winged assassins of the skies—and the other with wolfshifters. She'd watched friends enter the hereafter in the most painful ways, helpless to save them.

If dying today meant better protecting harpykind tomorrow, so be it.

Harpies today. Harpies forever.

"I am," she offered with more confidence, jutting her chin.

"So be it." Her mother repositioned into a battle stance, and Tamera and Blythe followed suit. "May your end serve as your beginning."

That said, Tabitha shoved the fireiron straight into Taliyah's heart.

Searing pain exploded through her. Blood rushed up her throat and out her mouth, choking her. All thoughts of dying for a cause vanished, survival instincts kicking in. Taliyah fit shaky hands around the hilt and pushed outward. *Can't breathe. Need to breathe.*

"May your loss serve as our gain." Without a shred of mercy, Aunt Tamera thrust the demonglass next to the fireiron.

More searing pain. More blood gurgled from the corners of her mouth. Weakness invaded her limbs, and tears welled.

"May your return serve as an eternal reminder. Death has lost its sting, the grave has lost its power." Blythe slammed the wooden stake beneath the other two weapons.

The agony! Excruciating and unending. A loud ring erupted in Taliyah's ears. *So cold. Dizzy.* What little remained of her strength abandoned her in a rush. Already hobbled, she fell.

Impact rattled her brain against her skull—a skull quickly wetted by an outpour of her blood. All she could do was peer up at a spinning night sky. Dazzling stars beckoned her closer…

She fought. She fought *hard*, because she couldn't not fight. Warped by the blades, her destroyed heart raced. Slowed. Until…

It stopped.

Taliyah wheezed a final exhalation, every muscle in her body going lax. Maybe she died, maybe she didn't. A part of her remained aware, but without time. She floated in a sea of darkness, the barest pinpricks of light blinking here and there, reminding her of the stars. All pain faded.

As the sea carried her farther and farther away, panic set in. She wished to return to her family. She *would* return. Taliyah renewed her struggles, kicking and clawing.

Blink. Blink. *Fighting harder.* Lights flared faster and faster, whizzing together. Harder still. Finally—

Taliyah gasped, her eyelids popping open.

Her mother hovered over her, a calculated smile blooming. "Congratulations, daughter. You are officially the second royal harpy-phantom in existence. You'll do great things or you'll die again trying."

Don't miss The Warlord *by* New York Times
bestselling author Gena Showalter!

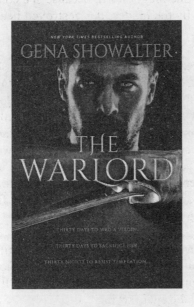

Get 4 FREE REWARDS!

We'll send you 2 FREE Books plus 2 FREE Mystery Gifts.

FREE
Value Over
$20

Both the **Romance** and **Suspense** collections feature compelling novels written by many of today's bestselling authors.